I0691564

The Python of Caspia
Tales from the Netherscape - Book One

By Michael Green

Cover art by Alexey Rudikov

1st Edition

ISBN: 978-1-950593-02-6

For William, Tina, and William

A second family who brought me into another world: a world of boundless imagination and frightening possibility.

Table of Contents

Chapter 1: Field Trip

Andy was the last off the bus. At least he would have been, but something kept him from taking that final step down to the curb. He looked out to the plaza which lay before the museum. Cars and taxis rumbled nearby, their humming motors punctuated by the sharp laughs and jeers of his classmates. The diesel exhaust blended with a riot of perfume and pungent body sprays popular among his peers.

Perched on that step, none among the huddled groups noticed him. They churned, a sea of human mist, smiling and jeering, moaning and complaining, comparing and contrasting, as he stood alone.

Morning frost had slipped between the tall buildings while he slept. His city was cloaked in a blanket of glittering crystal; encrusting windows, coating stairs, glazing asphalt, and thickening blades of grass. At the top step, between bus and world, the chill threatened to envelop him, it struggled to draw him out. It bit at his body and face as he stood, reminding him that he would have to step down and join his peers.

While his teacher, Mr. Holt, was occupied with the roster, Andy idled, adjusting his backpack and running his fingers through his brownish-blond hair. Inspecting himself in the bus's sideview mirror, Andy noticed his hair was blonder this morning. His eyes, an equally indecisive blue-green, stung as a frosty gust poured through the street.

Andy smirked at his awkward face, halfway

between boy and man. He squirmed in his navy overcoat until the hood rolled up his neck. He considered hiding under his hood, but reconsidered; that would only attract attention.

Staring at his peers, Andy spotted Lysette and Emma, cloistered with their fashionable friends. Their noses and cheeks were tinged pink and, occasionally, he spotted a hand brushing away tears, shed before the chilly gusts. The girls wore bright and heavy winter coats. Several carried folded umbrellas and expensive handbags.

Lysette and her sycophants had bullied him during his first few months at school; these days, they largely ignored him, though it hadn't been without some effort on his part.

Andy gulped as Mr. Holt corralled the students into groups, pressing the girls closer to the bus, and closer to him. Andy had no one to huddle with, to retreat to. He was about to step down and blend with the mob, but Emma caught sight of him.

"Look, Letty, the new boy is posing on the steps."

Andy's arms had been planted confidently on his hips; only now did he realize how silly he looked. Cringing, he lowered his arms.

Lysette and Emma rounded on him, their friends filling in on the sides. Their hungry eyes flashed his way, and behind them he sensed something—was it jeering bloodlust, or only curiosity?

Despite their numbers, Andy focused on Lysette. Her clear, light eyes fixed on him with a look he didn't understand. Her gaze, cold and aloof, may have been cruel. Or maybe she was just tired. Her face, half hidden beneath a fall of black hair, bore a subtle beauty that hadn't yet become self-aware.

"What are you staring at?" Emma demanded. Emma, in contrast, wore a sharper face, not unpleasant in its lines, but so often stretched beneath drastic expressions that Andy couldn't say what she really looked like.

Andy stepped down onto the sidewalk, searching for an escape route through the girls, who refused to part for him. Not sure where to turn, Andy stood still; he felt his cheeks flushing.

Lysette glanced his way and almost yawned. "He likes the attention," she said.

"If he likes attention so much, why not give him a new name?" Emma implored.

Andy tensed at the mention of names.

Lysette rolled her eyes. "If you insist," she muttered. The other girls smirked, clearly amused by this morsel. "What's he called?"

"Andy," Emma said, "but his real name is Ly-san-der." She struggled through the three syllables.

Lysette looked him over, "Lysander—rice-ander, lies-ander, belt-sander," she said tiredly and paused, narrowing her eyes, "but call him, 'lice,' for short."

They smirked cruelly, their silence inviting reply, though Andy had none.

"Lice! Because he won't leave," Emma insisted.

He wanted to say something, to produce a witty retort, but he was mute.

Mr. Holt pushed past the girls.

"Lysander, check," he said, minding his roster.

Andy's blush deepened as the girls tittered, presumably at his name.

"Mr. Holt, not my real name, please—"

"Oh, it's a fine name, Lysander. Historical and— Greek, I think." He looked up from his roster. "Who are you paired with?" Mr. Holt asked.

Andy sighed and caught sight of Emma, who mouthed the words, "You have no friends."

Mr. Holt realized that Andy had no partner and turned his gaze on the large group of girls, who, sensing his intention, shrank away.

But as Mr. Holt was poised to shatter their forthcoming bliss on this field trip—several hours of ignoring the tour, gossiping, and bathing in the collective glow of their popularity—a commotion rose up among the students, and Mr. Holt's focus shifted.

A grown woman, clutching the arm of an unfamiliar child, was pushing her way through the mass of students. The woman was wrapped in a purple shawl and the boy was oddly over-dressed, wearing a collared shirt, with a tie sticking out of his pocket—likely removed when the boy saw the casual state of this mob. The boy's eyes darted here and there, fearful of the curious faces. His cheeks were bright red, though that might have been the wind. He was rail-thin, a sharp contrast to his mother's expansive carriage, which was highly effective at ploughing through the students.

"Are you Mr. Holt?" the woman asked, not waiting for a response. "Yes, Mr. Holt, so nice to meet you, sorry for being late—it's so hard to get across town—you know—oh! This is Dean. Yes, Dean Loggia—check him on your roster there, so it's official. Of course I couldn't have him miss his first day of class, even if it is an inconvenience for me. We just moved to the city, you see—"

The curious students stood apart from the newcomers, unsure what to make of the woman and her son.

Mr. Holt smiled politely as she rambled and finally found a moment to speak, "We're very happy to have Dean with us—"

"We missed you at the school this morning, but the museum is on my commute. The tunnel was terrible—and forget the bridge—oh you must know all about it! What with working in this part of town—" Then turning to her son, "Don't excite yourself—you have your inhaler, Dean—use it if you need to, baby—but call me if you do—and send me a text message when you get back to school! Make some friends now, and *behave!*"

Dean's mother straightened his glasses, collar, and hair before turning and, like an ice-breaker through an arctic sheet, cut an exit through the crowd. She turned to wave, and cried out an agonizing goodbye at least twice.

Andy cringed at the display and then noticed Emma, her face slack and gawking, as if the new fare on offer was too good to be true.

Mr. Holt, recovering from the daze produced by Dean's mother, pivoted and placed a hand on Dean's shoulder. "Well, his arrival was unique—"

Andy realized Mr. Holt was about to introduce Dean to the class. *Don't do it now!* he thought. *Not after his mother said all that—give it a few hours, so they'll forget.*

"Class, say hello to Dean."

Silence.

Dean raised a hand and gave a stilted wave. Andy watched as the gawking faces split even wider at the sad, spindly arm and the limp wave.

Mr. Holt cleared his throat forcefully.

"It's cold," a student insisted.

"The sooner we all act politely, the sooner we get to the art museum."

"Art museum?" a few voices groaned.

Mr. Holt crossed his arms and muttered. Andy, being nearby, caught what he said.

"Be grateful it isn't the Modern Art museum."

Andy knew that many of his classmates had been expecting the zoo, but this was very clearly not the zoo. Logic aside, several clearly held out hope that a few African Elephants might be hiding away, somewhere inside this dignified building, whose columns and triangular pediment reminded Andy of a super-sized bank.

Dean's introduction forgotten, Mr. Holt shepherded the class across the plaza and towards the wide stone stairs beneath the museum. As they approached, the girls slipped through the crowd, closer and closer to Dean.

"You didn't forget your inhaler, did you?" Emma asked, her voice as flat as she could make it.

Dean was baffled by the question. "I have it right

here," he said, producing the device from a pocket.

A few chuckles rose from the group. Their eyes glittered, and their cheeks burned under the strain of smiles stretched so wide. What a gift they had been given on this, already bountiful field trip day.

"Are you going to behave?" another girl asked Dean, causing Emma to guffaw.

Finally understanding that he was being mocked, Dean reddened and quickened his pace, hoping to find safety nearer the teacher.

"Dean, baby, you're so red—you need your inhaler!" Despite her intermittent cackle, Emma did a fair rendition of Dean's mother.

Several students broke out into laughter.

Mr. Holt turned to investigate. He saw Dean, beet-red and on the verge of tears. Mr. Holt's eyes flashed across a collection of quickly slackening faces, before settling on Emma.

Something about her reaction caused his brow to tighten.

"What?" She replied guiltily.

Mr. Holt tilted his head.

"What?" Emma repeated.

"How many days?"

Emma scoffed and rolled her eyes.

"I can do all week," Mr. Holt said.

Emma was silent.

"One day's lunch detention," Mr. Holt said, his eagle's glower scanning the mob of students for only a moment longer.

Andy considered Dean and the girls. He knew that they would only dig deeper into Dean, especially now that Emma had been punished. Part of Andy, a small, petty part, felt grateful for Dean's arrival. Today, he was no longer the new kid. Andy balked at his smallness, recalling that his arrival had been nowhere near as embarrassing, and he had received his first nickname just minutes earlier. *They'll probably forget all about my name, now that Dean's here. If I'm careful, I can go unnoticed for the rest of the year. Maybe I'll pick up some friends, and I'll be in good shape for high school.* Andy rolled his eyes and quickly dismissed this as too hopeful.

The class poured in through the heavy, glass doors. A rush of warm air hit their faces, and the recently-donned winter clothes were soon shrugged off and tied about waists or placed over forearms.

"Alright, class, we're very lucky today; we'll be touring in smaller groups, allowing you all time to ask plenty of questions and pick which parts of the gallery you would like to see. But each group will be responsible for its members," Mr. Holt said. His brow raised, as he noticed several students had drifted off from their assigned groups, only to glom onto their usual friends.

Mr. Holt's glower deepened to a state that Andy and his peers recognized as quite serious, and he cut a swathe through the students, rearranging them. Andy stifled a laugh as Lysette and Emma were separated from the rest of their friends. When Mr. Holt turned his attention to a museum attendant, Andy realized that he was still standing alone. He felt nervous and wondered if Mr. Holt had forgotten him on purpose.

Andy raised his hand, and when Mr. Holt noticed he said, "Don't worry, Lysander. Just wait a minute."

Alarmed at the second mention of his name, Andy's gaze drift towards Lysette. She wasn't paying any attention to him, and was busily rearranging her purse and coat. Andy's eyes cautiously rested on her. She was wearing a black sweater under her coat. She craned her neck back to take in the floral mosaics and sparkling chandeliers far above. Her lipgloss glittered, and her mouth bent in a mischievous pout as Emma whispered to her. Their eyes flashed backed to him, and he looked away.

Mr. Holt addressed the students. "They are getting the tour guides ready for us." As he finished, Mr. Holt noticed Andy and Dean. He approached and motioned the two to come closer.

"Andy?"

"Yes, sir?"

"This is Dean Loggia. It's his first day with us."

"I know."

"Then you'll remember how hard it was for you on your first day. I'd like you to look out for him. Show him the ropes."

Andy glanced at Dean. His eyes were glued to the floor.

Mr. Holt continued. "Any questions?"

Andy silently searched for an escape, an excuse not to be with Dean, but nothing came to mind. Mr. Holt attached Andy and Dean to another group of huddled students, none of whom bothered to look up at the newcomers.

A docent arrived and called them into the main hall. "This way, please."

They circumvented the long lines of people waiting for tickets. Andy's hand brushed across the red velvet rope and burnished bronze of the barriers. The hum of visitors echoed through the old hall. Andy started to feel hot. He peeled off his blue coat, revealing a plaid shirt. He tied the coat about his waist.

Dean finally spoke as they jostled past the other groups, "I didn't catch your name. Is it Andrew?"

Talking about his name was always irritating. "Andy. Call me Andy. I saw all that trouble with your mom. What are you, twelve?"

Dean cringed. "I'm thirteen, and yeah, Mom can be a hurricane. At least that's how my dad puts it."

"Do what I do: I let my mom know she has to stay at least thirty feet from the bus. That way, no one can hear anything."

Dean laughed nervously. "I'll have to try that."

Mr. Holt stood by, recording on his roster as the students were assigned their guides.

Andy and Dean's group were paired with an older woman named Adelaide, who smiled widely at the sight of so many young, wind-bitten faces.

"This way," she said, gesturing down a grand, central hall. "The museum is divided into sections by era and location. Down the first hall is our collection of classical Greek pottery and statuary— on the right, we have a visiting exhibit from Egypt—"

Watching Lysette and Emma, a few groups

ahead of him, Andy realized that they were scheming. A few whispers passed between the girls and some agreement was reached. The two broke off from their group, while Mr. Holt was looking away.

"Did you see that?" Dean asked.

Andy nodded.

"Do you want to—let the teacher know?" Dean asked, turning to Mr. Holt, not far behind.

Andy had thought the same thing and, as much as he would like to see the girls suffer a week's lunch detention, part of him knew it would be wrong to tell on them.

Andy shook his head and Dean understood.

"I've never had that happen before," Dean whispered. "I knew it was coming—the bullying, I mean—"

Dean's hands were clenched and his face downcast. Andy took a breath, not sure how to explain that Dean's future was practically set in stone.

"Do you have any advice?" Dean whispered.

Andy felt suddenly guilty and, when no answer came, Dean seemed to deflate, realizing exactly how isolated he was. Too ashamed to meet Dean's gaze, Andy stared down a hall and spotted Lysette and Emma, laughing and enjoying themselves.

He turned to Dean, his brow furrowed. Andy felt anger stirring within. He imagined Dean, every inch of him a victim, being teased and belittled daily, for months that stretched on into years.

Adelaide spoke, "Down this hall are a few featured pieces from the early Renaissance, most are religious—"Andy barely heard her.

His face hardening, Andy grabbed Dean by the arm and gestured down the side hall. Dean's face widened.

"Do you want every day, from here on out, to be the same as this morning?" Andy whispered.

Dean shook his head.

"Then come on."

Dean gulped. Andy released his arm and slipped away as Adelaide gestured to a fine Deco mosaic that adorned the ceiling.

Andy found himself in a hall filled with paintings of sailing ships. Advancing, he expected silence, but, moments later, he heard footsteps.

Expecting a docent, or even Mr. Holt, he turned, and saw Dean, abashed, but apparently brave enough to follow.

"Come on," Andy whispered, "I've got a plan."

They walked silently down side halls, avoiding guards and keeping an eye out for Lysette.

"So, do you know those girls?" Dean asked.

"They've teased me since I was the new guy."

Dean looked confused. "Well, they've got me to bully now. Wait, I don't understand why you're doing this, Andy. We don't even know each other and— what, uh, what are we doing exactly?"

"Just keep up," Andy said, catching sight of Emma's hair, bouncing around a few rooms ahead.

Andy sped up, Dean on his heels.

"How did I get myself into this situation?" Dean whispered. "First day—I've already been laughed at by everyone, and now I'm falling in with the wrong crowd. Mom was right!"

Andy nearly burst out laughing at this assessment. He glanced at Dean, to see if he was being serious. Distracted, Andy turned the corner and failed to notice something large sat squarely in his path. He skidded to a halt, just shy of a bronze statue. His feet slid on the smooth floor and his hand rose, barely grazing the bronze. He felt a burst of fear, but no one had seen.

Andy slowed to a stop and took a breath. He blinked and felt suddenly lightheaded.

"Are you alright?" Dean asked.

Andy rubbed his eyes, which were oddly sore. "I'm fine; I think I've got something in my eyes."

"Just be careful—you nearly ran into that statue. I don't want to get in trouble, especially on my fist day," Dean said, his voice rising.

"We're fine," Andy replied, looking around for guards. "I barely touched it."

"You touched it?" Dean whispered, incensed. "There are cameras all over the place! We'll get thrown out, or put in detention, or suspended—" he fell silent as Andy glared.

Dismissing Dean, Andy regarded the statue. He walked around to the other side and had to back away to get a full view of the piece.

A heroic warrior struggled against a massive python, resisting the snake with his bare hands. The python coiled around his legs, attempting to overpower him, but the man gripped his foe by the throat, keeping its fangs at bay. Andy stood transfixed, watching the primal struggle, frozen in

13

bronze.

"Andy?" Dean was tugging his sleeve and craning his neck. "It's a nice statue, but we should go back and find that lady—Addy? Adel?" He suddenly panicked. "What was her name, Andy? I can't remember!"

A rickety old guard on a stool lowered his newspaper and hushed Dean.

Captivated, Andy barely noticed.

"Andy—" Dean whispered, his eyes on the guard, who had returned to his paper.

"I've never seen anything like this."

Dean glanced at the sculpture, unimpressed. He read the placard: "An athlete wrestling with a python. Bronze. By Lord Leighton."

"Why'd you read the description? That ruins it."

"Ruins it?" Dean sounded confused.

Andy crossed his arms. "Yeah, well—a little. Before I knew it was an athlete, I thought it was—humankind."

Dean looked again and spoke skeptically, "Humankind—wrestling a snake?"

Andy suddenly felt annoyed. "No. It's more like all of us wrestling with a—" he fell silent, his face pinched in thought, "—It's like we're all struggling. Life is dangerous."

Dean was quiet for a moment. He had forgotten that they were skipping out on the tour. "I get it. So, it's like we're all him. We're all dealing with problems in our lives." Dean reached into his pocket to find his phone. He was about to take a picture, but paused. "Smile, or do something," Dean said.

"I've got it." Andy positioned his legs and copied the statue's pose. The phone flashed as Dean pressed a button.

"Posing with a statue?"

Emma appeared from around a corner, a humiliating grin stretched across her face. Lysette wasn't far behind.

When they were cruel to him, Andy had felt like he almost deserved it. Now he felt something entirely different. This time, as he looked at Dean's cowering posture, the way his shoulders stooped and how his hands fidgeted, he felt himself becoming angry.

The girls approached.

Lysette scowled. "It's almost like you're actually enjoying this place."

"Posing with a statue?" Emma repeated. "That's sad, even for you."

Dean shuffled backwards, trying to escape.

"I'm sorry, Lysette; I didn't realize it was a crime to be interested in things." Andy said, surprising himself.

She went rigid and turned, a bemused look on her usually haughty face.

"You can't talk to her," Emma scoffed, "go away, Lice."

"No," Andy retorted. "We were here first."

Dean grabbed Andy's arm. "Let's just go— they'll get their friends to beat us up. They're the popular girls, right?"

Andy spoke quietly, "Yeah, but I don't care anymore." Then loudly, to Emma, "I'll talk to whoever I like, and we were here first, and the statue is like—ten times more interesting than you."

A brief laugh escaped from Lysette, cut short by a wounded look from Emma.

Andy wasn't finished. "I don't want to take a picture with either of you, and neither does Dean." he glanced toward Dean. "Right?"

Dean was silent, and very interested in his shoelaces.

"Ew," Emma said, "that means the baby has a crush on one of us. God, I hope it's you, Letty."

Lysette cringed and grabbed Emma's arm. "Don't make me sick. Let's go."

Then, to Andy's astonishment, they walked away.

Somewhere between amusement and disbelief, Andy stared at their retreating forms.

Dean gazed somberly into the distance. "Enjoy it while you can. They'll have the football team on us before the week is out, and you can take that to the bank. Just don't drag me into it when it's time for revenge."

Andy gave him a doubtful look.

"What? I've got a bad back. My doctor says I can't be doing any strenuous physical activity—"

Andy ignored him and pointed at the statue. "It was the statue, Dean; the statue did it."

"The statue?" Dean repeated.

"It made me brave. I can't explain it. I wouldn't have done any of that this morning."

"That doesn't make any sense. I think your age is getting to you. My doctor told me about hormones.

They make you crazy, and they can strike at any time."

"Yeah, but this morning I was afraid, and now— It's the only thing that changed—well, you showed up too—but I'm sure it was the statue."

"Okay, okay. But I think you should see someone if you think statues are affecting your behavior—" Dean continued babbling, "—my dad might know someone downtown who would be great for you."

"It changes today," Andy said, looking down the hall after the girls, "If we're going to take a beating, let's earn it. We'll take the fight to them."

"I need your number," Dean said, fumbling with his phone. "Andy, how do you spell your name— wait, what? You want to—take the fight to who?"

"Hurry," Andy said, heading after the girls.

Dean followed along, complaining all the way.

Chapter 2: A Mouse

"Look, we had one good argument with the girls. Let's just call it a day, retire as champs—" Dean gave his new friend a pleading look, "—come on!"

"Quiet down," Andy hissed, "they'll hear you." Andy peeked around a corner, glimpsing the girls in a room ahead. They were huddled together, whispering.

"Let's go," Andy said.

They turned the corner, Dean dragging his feet all the while, and found themselves at the mouth of a long room filled with rough drawings, studies, and sketches for larger paintings.

"Get your phone ready," Andy whispered. "We'll snap a photo of them without their group. It's proof they were breaking the rules."

"Are we really going to tell on them?"

"No—that wouldn't be right. We'll just—uhm, if they try to bully us, we'll threaten to tell on them." Andy sounded uncertain.

"I see, classic blackmail."

"Not really; we're not robbing them, just trying to—to keep the peace."

After a moment of uncomfortable shuffling, Dean worked up the courage to disagree. "Look, Andy, this is moving a little too fast. I don't even know you that well, and it's my first day—maybe I should settle in a little bit before we get all 'mafia.'"

"I'm not forcing you to do anything. Why don't you go find Adelaide and take the tour? Leave your new buddy alone—I'm only trying to stop them from picking on you for the rest of the year."

"I'm already feeling the pressure—you don't have to rub it in—Wait! You knew the old lady's name this whole time?" Despite Andy trying to hush him, Dean's voice reverberated through the halls.

Hearing this, the girls turned and noticed their pursuers.

"Stalkers!" Emma blurted out, disgusted at the sight of them.

"Dean—the picture." Andy said quietly.

Dean fumbled for his cell phone, readied it, and snapped a picture of the girls.

"Oh—they *are* stalking us." Lysette said, her bored expression slipping away.

"No," Dean said, "this picture proves you're not with your tour guide. We'll show this to Mr. Holt if you trash-talk us anymore. It's called *insurance*." But he whispered to Andy, "Right, Andy? This was the plan?"

Emma stammered, but Lysette quickly produced her own phone, and took a picture of the boys.

"Aw—" Dean said.

Andy felt irked for a moment, though he was more impressed than annoyed.

I should have known she'd do that.

Lysette showed them her phone's screen. "Now what, Lice?" she looked from Andy to Dean, and paused thoughtfully, "Loogey? You can't tell on us, or we'll tell on you."

"No—don't call me that," Dean moaned under his breath.

"Hey look," Andy interrupted, "do you see that? Something's there." Andy's eyes were fixed on the ground nearby; a blur of movement and color had distracted him from Lysette's taunting. He pointed.

Everyone fell silent and looked, though they saw nothing.

"Beneath that sketch," Andy insisted, "it looked like a little mouse in the corner."

He was met with three dubious stares.

"Hugs, not drugs, Lice," Lysette said dismissively and turned to leave, but then she gave a sudden start. "What did that mouse look like?" she asked, staring at another corner.

"It was white, with a red face," Andy said, scanning the room.

"I knew my first day would be bad, but I wasn't expecting this," Dean said, backing away toward the entrance.

"There it goes!" Andy exclaimed, rushing down the hall.

Lysette charged after Andy. Dean and Emma shared an awkward moment before they followed.

"I see it," Lysette called out.

Andy slid to a halt across the floor and then turned. He was now behind Lysette.

They shrank under the glower of a guard and slowed their pace. Andy tried not to laugh as the man's suspicious eyes followed them through the hall. The next room was tightly packed with a large tour group.

"I lost it," Andy said.

"Me too," Lysette replied, peeking under a

bench.

"Andy, what—exactly—did you see?" Dean asked, reaching into his pocket for his inhaler.

"A little white mouse," he answered.

"With a red face," Lysette finished.

"Yeah, all right, red mouse, white face. I'm not deaf."

Lysette and Andy both scowled.

"What? I didn't see it! Blame my prescription," Dean concluded sarcastically, pointing at his glasses.

"I didn't see it either," Emma said, keeping away from the boys, and looking desperately like she wanted to be anywhere else.

"See?" Dean gestured at Emma, "I'm not crazy. I may be with the mean girl on this, but I'm not crazy."

Andy laughed. Emma's eyes flicked back and forth between them, impotent outrage blooming across her face.

"There it goes! It's leaping from painting to painting," Lysette said, now leading the chase. "How did it get up there?"

They pursued the mouse into the main hall and found themselves pushing through a few tour groups, all circled about a painting featuring waterlilies.

"—industrial revolution was a major contributor to several modes of escapism," the tour guide explained.

Andy spotted Mr. Holt in the crowd, trying to supervise his students, though he seemed more interested in the lecture. Mr. Holt spotted Andy and recognition filled his face.

Andy gulped, and looked over his shoulder to see Dean and Emma, just behind.

Mr. Holt nodded approvingly.

"Renaissance and Medieval revivals filled canvases and a new wave of novels, culminating in many you now know—though a far simpler response to belching smokestacks and poverty was later found by the Impressionists. They went to the park and painted what they saw—though columns of soot and the outlines of mills sneak into several of these pieces, lending them a tragic aspect."

After a moment, Andy realized they weren't in trouble and relaxed. Lysette tugged on his sleeve. Her eyes were wide, and a smile threatened to break across her face.

"He saw us," she whispered to Andy, referring to Mr. Holt.

"Yeah, but I think he was checking to see if Dean was still with me."

"Well, at least he's good for something," she whispered looking back at Dean, who visibly wilted beneath her glance.

"But why is it bad?" a student asked the tour guide, indicating the painting.

Andy felt a collective gulp resound through his peers, and barely a chuckle followed the question, though the tour guide, surprisingly, laughed at this.

"What makes the painting bad?" she asked the offending student.

Andy smirked at the question but, as he studied the painting, he realized that he too questioned its merit. At first glance, it resembled a thousand seemingly random splotches. Of course, all paintings are just streaks of color or splotches, but this one seemed too obvious about it.

"It's bad because the water looks wrong, and so do the flowers, and the bridge too. Other painters make them look right," the student reasoned. Several classmates nodded in agreement, though many turned to Mr. Holt, who seemed untroubled by the likely disrespectful comment.

"Well," the tour guide started, "students often have this response. Impressionism is also a response to modernity. Imagine being an artist around 1870, times are tough, yet paintings still sell. But then, along comes the camera, and with it, the photograph." She paused for emphasis. "Suddenly, pictures represented a perfect recreation of the world."

Lysette raised her hand and the tour guide nodded her way.

"So, artists could be replaced. Something that takes them days or weeks to create can be done in moments."

"And for considerably cheaper," Dean added.

"Absolutely correct, both of you. Leaving behind strict realism, artists searched for something more ethereal. Their aim was to grasp at the feeling of a moment, at its *impression*."

Murmurs of comprehension filled the air, though most of the students still seemed unsatisfied by this answer.

The painting hung on a wall near a flight of wide stone stairs which led to the second floor.

Lysette nudged Andy. She gestured with her eyes to the stairwell. Andy looked, but saw nothing.

She leaned in, her hair brushing against his cheek. "The mouse, he's on the stairs."

Andy felt his stomach flutter at the nearness, the fresh smell of something that might have been perfume, lotion, or something for her hair. But, most alarming, was her uncharacteristic lack of disdain. He stared a moment longer and spotted the mouse, tucked away at the base of the railing. The mouse, apparently aware that it had been sighted, turned and resumed its skittery climb up the stairs.

The tour guide continued, "Let's go back in time, and turn towards Romanticism—down this hall behind us, we'll find works that might better suit your tastes."

Mr. Holt chuckled as he directed the students.

"Should we stay with the group?" Andy asked.

"Yes," Emma and Dean said, their voices overlapping.

"No," Lysette scoffed, turning toward the stairs. Andy made to follow her.

"Some new friend you are," Dean complained.

Andy smirked. "Feel free to stay with Emma. You two could learn a lot from each other."

Andy hurried to catch up to Lysette, while Dean and Emma shared another painful moment together. They immediately followed.

The mismatched pairs bounded up the stairs to the second floor. Emma and Lysette looked one way down the hall, while Andy and Dean turned the other.

"If I had known you were infatuated with—"
Dean started, and was instantly silenced by a glare
from Andy. "All I'm saying is that she's supposed
to be queen of the bullies—and you were stuck on
moral principles a minute ago."

Andy knew Dean was right, that he was acting
strangely but, why not make friends with these
girls? It seemed better than blackmailing them into
decency, and, even if he couldn't admit it to himself,
he had been curious about Lysette since his first day,
several months before.

Dean stared, waiting for a reply but, gratefully,
Andy spotted a blur of red down the hall. "Down
that way," Andy said, ignoring Dean.

The girls followed, and Dean choked back his
complaints. They found themselves at the mouth of
a dim wing of the gallery. The paintings here, largely
somber landscapes or dark ocean scenes, were
moodily lit from above.

"I lost it," Andy and Lysette whispered in
unison.

They walked slowly down the hall, their eyes
moving carefully from painting to painting.

"So, this isn't just an excuse to run around
and feel rebellious? You guys are *definitely* seeing
something in the paintings, or is it jumping from
painting to painting?" Dean asked in a whisper.
"Because I'm thinking optometry might be a good
idea."

"No, it's on top of them, climbing along the
frames," Andy said.

Emma's face twitched with disgust every time

Dean spoke. She pulled on Lysette's wrist with a sense of desperate futility. "Letty, let's go. I can't stand them."

"In a minute; I'm having fun."

Emma reached into her considerable arsenal of exasperated expressions. Rolling her eyes dangerously, waving her hands widely, and hissing in anguish, Emma couldn't have been clearer. All this went unnoticed by Lysette, who gasped at the sight of red and darted down the hall. Exhausted, Emma followed along as they approached the end of the hall.

Several quiet museum goers occupied the nearby benches. Many were sketching a painting that featured a windmill perched on a crag above a dark lake.

"That's a popular one," Andy said, noticing all the sketch pads.

They stood still, taking it in. The ruddy hues of the foliage bending in the wind made Andy feel uneasy.

Lysette was the first to speak, her eyes shifting from the sketch pads to the painting. "But look at their sketches," she said, a note of mystery in her voice.

Andy winced, his eyes straining as he inspected the canvas. "They're not right—" He glanced at one notepad, then up at the painting again. "It's not the same."

Dean followed their glances. "Guys, it was funny before, but—"

"This isn't funny at all, Letty," Emma muttered,

as she turned and stomped her way back down the hall.

Lysette's eyes lingered on the painting as she spoke, "Bye Em—see you at lunch," she murmured, and then said to Andy, "Do you see the letters on the cliff?"

"Kind of," Andy whispered, squinting. "I think they're words."

"Yeah," Lysette said, "They're definitely words, but they aren't in any of the sketches."

Emma groaned and returned to the group, more afraid of being alone than being near the boys. Lysette inched toward the painting, reading the placard. Andy was about to join her when he felt a slight tickle at his ankle.

The mouse with the red face was tugging at his pant leg. Andy sensed that the mouse was trying to keep him away from something.

Andy heard Lysette gasp. Looking up, he thought she was recoiling from the painting. He tried to get past Dean, who was busily shooing the mouse away.

"Hey, don't shove—Andy, you've got that mouse on your—"

Not believing his eyes, Andy saw smoky tendrils, purple and inky, reaching down from the frame of the painting and swirling towards Lysette.

One of the tendrils struck her, and Lysette stumbled. Andy reached out, but was too far, and she fell on her backside.

Rushing forward, the boys helped Lysette to her feet.

"My head," she complained, standing.

"Why did you fall over?" Dean asked, just shy of chuckling at her.

"Didn't you see those things?" she asked, looking back at the painting. "...they're gone now."

Dean, opened his mouth with clear intent to complain, but Andy rolled right over him. "I saw them. It looked like one hit you—there, on the arm."

Lysette lifted her arm for them to see. There was no trace of the tendril.

Emma pushed the boys aside and inspected the arm. "Nothing's there," she whispered, clearly concerned for her friend's sanity.

Again prepared to complain, Dean was cut short as almost every person with a sketch pad stood at once. Without a word, the artists shuffled from the room.

"We're just that annoying," Andy said, sounding more nervous than he intended.

Andy remembered the mouse but, looking down, found him missing again. "You frightened him, Dean. That was the mouse we were after. You saw him too, don't deny it."

Dean gawked. "Oh, *that* mouse! I didn't realize that was the mouse—"

"Look," Lysette said, cutting a potential diatribe short.

An artist was still sitting on a nearby bench. When she noticed them staring, she put down her pencil sharply. "Will you kids quiet down, please? We're in a gallery."

"Sorry," Andy said, approaching. "Why did

everyone get up and leave?"

The artist rolled her eyes and raised her pencil. "Art appreciation zombies—they spend five minutes sketching and move on. I haven't seen anyone taking a selfie with a painting, but I'm sure it's imminent." The woman cringed at her own observation and twirled her pencil before continuing, "And then, middle-school field trip—" she surveyed them disdainfully, "—starts falling over and arguing about a mouse."

Lysette and Andy smiled as the artist aired her grievances, which only encouraged her.

"Right—" Andy finally said, wanting to continue the conversation, but not sure how.

"Or maybe they just went back to their bus," Emma snapped.

"Speaking of buses, we should get back. Someone's going to notice that we're gone," Dean implored. Andy ignored him and glanced at the woman's sketch.

"Or worse, no one will notice, and they'll leave us here! Andy—" Andy raised a hand, motioning for silence.

He saw the strange words on the cliff-face almost present in her sketch; they resembled vague wisps of the letters he saw in the painting. "You can see it too?" He pointed to the cliff.

"Yeah," she said tiredly, "Maybe it's a reused canvas, or it might be a mistake, but the painter is an Old Master; I don't see how this got by. It's almost like something's written there."

Almost?

"Maybe a vandal came along. It's very faint, like it's been mostly cleaned away." Her pencil skated across the paper, sketching in more of the anomalous spots. "Step off, kid. You're in my light."

"Sorry," Andy said, backing away.

"You two are having vision problems. There's no writing on that painting," Dean said, and Emma nodded in agreement.

"There you are!" Mr. Holt barged into the hall. "Over here, at once!" It was the angriest whisper Andy had ever heard.

"Oh, thank goodness!" Dean raised his hands to the sky. "Wait—what am I saying? This means detention for sure."

Andy approached Mr. Holt with the others, but felt a sudden urge, and looked back at the painting.

This is important.

He focused his eyes on the cliff. The letters were suddenly clear, but the words were in another language. His eyes hurt as he stared, but he refused to look away.

He forced himself to memorize the message as quickly as he could. He repeated the words over and over in his head, when suddenly, someone had him by the shoulder.

"Don't ignore me, Mister." Mr. Holt's heavy hand rattled Andy's concentration. "What's gotten into you? I ask you to take care of Dean, and this is what I get? Mr. Vanavarre, are you listening to me?"

Andy was still focused on the words in his mind.

As they were marched from the gallery, Andy fumbled for his cell phone to record the message.

30

"You'll get *this*—" Mr. Holt yanked the phone away, "—back from your parents."

Sighing, Andy looked back into the hall as they turned the corner and saw a heavyset, bald man in a suit, flanked by two guards, entering from the far end. The man watched as Mr. Holt dragged them away.

They suffered the fearful stares and whispers of their classmates as they left the gallery. Mr. Holt walked them out to the bus, and then ordered them to stand and wait.

Andy sighed, shielding his eyes from the sun. He tried to avoid looking at Lysette and Dean.

Eventually, the other groups of students returned. Looking bored and hungry, they clustered on the wide stairs of the gallery to eat lunch, served by the museum cafeteria and delivered to them in boxes. Mr. Holt handed them their boxed lunches, but then separated Emma from the rest; she stood alone beside a flagpole, serving her detention for bullying Dean earlier. Andy preferred the lunch his mother packed and found himself with extra food squirreled away in his pack.

When Mr. Holt was out of sight, Andy glanced at Lysette and Dean. Dean was still exasperated, likely imagining some inevitable punishment, but Lysette looked pleased with herself as she leaned against the bus.

"Hey, uh—I'm sorry for getting us in trouble back there," Andy said.

"On my first day, too—" Dean muttered.

"Shut up about getting us in trouble! I'm just as

responsible." Lysette pushed her hair from her eyes. "It was interesting, anyway."

Mr. Holt appeared from the other side of the bus. He eyed them harshly.

Andy spent the rest of his lunchtime thinking about Lysette. She seemed to enjoy herself, running around after the mouse. She had always been cruel and joyless. Andy was too flustered to make sense of her. An uncomfortable memory surfaced: when the lights changed, and she stumbled, but did something else happen? Andy found a piece of paper in his pack and jotted down the words he had seen in the painting.

Mr. Holt called the class to their feet and directed them to the bus, leaving Andy, Lysette, Emma, and Dean to stand still and suffer stares as their classmates filed aboard.

Finally, Mr. Holt rounded on them and simply shook his head. They climbed the stairs onto the bus and took their seats in silence.

Andy had the distinct impression that he had never been in more trouble. He wasn't concerned for himself, but felt guilty that Dean and Lysette might be punished for his urge to chase a mouse. Then it struck him: He felt bad for Lysette.

In that moment, his stomach turned. To think that he felt bad for Lysette, who had always ignored, or treated him with contempt, made him uncomfortable in a way he had never experienced. All at once, he was certain that his life had changed.

Chapter 3: Consequences

After coming home, Andy's father had ushered him into his bedroom and slammed the door. He stood rooted to the spot where his father had left him, his heart pounding, unable to imagine the forthcoming punishment.

He was in trouble so rarely, and it hardly seemed like a major infraction. They hadn't left the museum; at worst, it was a case of ignoring instructions. He remembered the mouse, the flashing lights, and the artists all leaving at once. He wanted to mention all this, if only to dampen his wrongdoing, but he knew his parents wouldn't believe any of it.

Andy strained to hear the conversation between his parents and Mr. Holt, but could only make out a few words. Someone mentioned Dean. Of course Dean was fine. Nothing bad happened. Andy took a breath and sank into his chair. He felt almost safe, because they were too busy talking to punish him. But the feeling was short-lived. A moment later, the front door closed with a snap.

Here it comes.

He felt his father's footsteps through the floor.

There's nothing I can do.

Startled by a darting shape, Andy fell backwards, his chair crashing with him.

"What's going on in here?" his father asked as the door swung open. His eyes scanned the room, before landing on his son. "Why are you on the floor?"

Andy opened his mouth to respond, but noticed a white and red shape hiding behind his bed post.

That little jerk!

It was the mouse, the same mouse with the red face.

But how?

Andy's father grabbed him from under the shoulders and pulled him to his feet.

"That scared, huh?" His father's vivid, lively eyes locked onto his. There was no anger there. Instead, Andy saw concern and suddenly felt ashamed.

"I—we—nothing happened. We just walked around the museum."

His father righted the toppled seat and motioned for Andy to sit. "Yeah, I got that impression."

"I—" Andy tried to speak, but no explanations came to him. He sat down and stared at his hands.

"I don't like to disagree with your teacher. Mr. Holt was right to be concerned. But I think he got a little too upset. Just keep him happy for the rest of the year." He paused for a moment. "What's the old rule? I think it was: Follow the teacher's directions, even when they don't make sense." He nodded to underscore the point. "When you're old enough, you can tell them all where to get off. Not yet, though." His father's expression, always a step from wry sarcasm, implied that all of this should be obvious.

"Yeah, I know. I couldn't help it. I had Dean there, and he's new."

"Dean? Did he put you up to it?"

Andy laughed, which surprised his father. "No—no, not Dean. The girls were giving us a hard time, and we saw them walk away from their group—"

His father interrupted, "Ah, now it makes sense."

Andy tried to interrupt, to explain how it really happened, but he couldn't get a word in as his father related a similar story from his youth. "—but back in those days it was a quick whipping for stepping out of line. Just think about that next time. How much easier you kids have it makes me sick. If Mr. Holt is the worst you ever see, call Heaven, thank God, and ask for seconds."

Andy shook his head, grinning at his father and yet another odd saying he had never heard before.

"Now, don't give me that look. I went through it all, young man—" he paused for a moment, "—but if Mr. Holt asks, you're grounded for the next week."

"Aw! But you said—"

"I know what I said. All right, it's only fair. You're semi-grounded. Nothing fun outside the apartment, but you can do what you want here."

Andy considered this. "Can I have Dean over?"

"If—and only if—I see proof that you've finished any and all studying and homework for every one of your classes."

"No legal talk, please, and okay, fair enough. Thanks for not throwing the book at me."

His father turned to leave, but something on the desk caught his eye. "What's that?"

He was looking at the scrap of notebook

paper that held the painting's message. Andy had agonized over the message during the bus trip and felt confident that he recalled it correctly. "It's just some notes from today."

"What do you have written here?" Andy's father lifted the paper and examined it. "Do they have you taking German?"

"No. I saw it today at the museum," he said, feeling nervous.

Andy's father scratched his chin and sounded out the words, "Om personen dat deze kan lezen: Vermijd artsen van het oog," he paused at the end, "vermijd? Oog? I think you're looking at Dutch here, not German."

"Oh. Thanks for letting me know. I'll run it through the translator," Andy said gratefully.

"Sure—say," his father paused, about to leave, "you were all over the museum. There were hundreds of paintings and artworks from all over the world—why did you write that bit down?"

Andy paused for a moment before answering; his father noticed his hesitation.

He won't believe me...and if he did, that'd be worse.

"It stood out to me," he finally said, reassured that he hadn't lied.

"Getting an artistic eye?" His father nodded with a surprised, yet knowing look on his face, "That, or you were trying to impress a girl. Mr. Holt mentioned you had also run off with Lysette."

"Dad! Come on!"

His father laughed, raising his hands in mock surrender as he retreated from Andy's room.

36

The instant his father left, Andy leaped to his feet and hunted around his room for the mouse.

I know I saw you. You're in here somewhere. He dropped to the floor and looked under his bed. *Nothing!* He picked up piles of clothes and threw them on his bed. *Not here either!* After a few minutes he was staring at a bare floor. *The jerk made me clean my room. And my dad thinks I'm involved with Lysette, and who knows what else—where is that mouse?*

But all was silent. Nothing moved. Surrendering, Andy sighed and sat heavily in his computer chair. Confident that he could at least get this right, he picked up his note with the words from the painting.

He found an application online that would translate the message. He struggled, typing in the strange language. Finally satisfied that the message was correct, he paused, his cursor hovering over the "translate" button. Andy wondered if he should be encouraging this. He began to doubt that any of it actually happened.

Dean saw the mouse. So did Lysette. Lysette also saw the letters, and so did that artist.

That made sense to him.

If I'm crazy, they are too.

He clicked the translate button and saw the words, "To those who can read this: Avoid all physicians of the eye."

Filled with pained exasperation, Andy rose from his chair and fell into the pile of clothes lying on his bed. That was enough for one day.

As he lay there, the day's excitement withdrew,

leaving fatigue to wash over him. He shifted around in the piles of clothes, until he had worn himself a small nest between jackets and jeans. He was vaguely aware of a white mouse with a red face scurrying nearby.

I said no more today, brain. I'll deal with it tomorrow. And with that, he fell asleep, and slept soundly.

The next day, he awoke refreshed and eager for school. He convinced his parents to let him walk to the bus stop alone, after relating the tragic story of Dean's first day. He had earned their sympathy; they exchanged stark looks and relented. He was thirteen, after all.

He helped Dean find which classes he was taking and where his locker was. Andy led him through the halls, hunting down all the right classrooms—they shared a few—until Dean was satisfied that he wouldn't get lost. They had the same homeroom, with Mr. Holt. Andy approached his teacher and apologized before homeroom started.

"I understand, Lysander." Mr. Holt didn't look angry. "I was your age once. Just don't drag people down in an effort to look cool. It isn't worth it."

Andy wanted to disagree, to argue about his motive for not following directions, but he couldn't, mostly because he didn't know why he did it. Mr. Holt patted him on the shoulder as they entered the classroom.

Maybe I was trying to impress Dean.

Andy took his seat, close to Dean, and not far from Emma and Lysette. The girls had seen him talking with Mr. Holt outside. Dean was texting on his phone, and Andy felt his pocket buzz.

I should've told him not to text in class; Mr. Holt confiscates phones.

He heard Emma speaking in a deliberately loud whisper, "I guess you have to be a teacher's pet when you have no friends."

There were a few stifled chuckles.

Andy's cheeks threatened to brighten in shame, and then he felt angry at himself for being ashamed at all. He felt his pocket buzz again, and cautiously checked his phone while Mr. Holt's back was turned.

The message had a picture attached, and the picture made him uncomfortable. It was the photo from yesterday. He was standing next to that bronze statue, imitating its pose. His face bore a stern, determined look. He felt embarrassed, not about the photo, but about himself.

He hid his phone and sat up in his desk. Troublesome thoughts became troublesome impulse and he turned to Dean, who, despite their new friendship, immediately recognized the look in Andy's eyes.

"Whatever you're going to do—don't do it— just ignore them," Dean whispered as the morning announcements concluded.

Andy turned around in his seat to get a good look at Emma. Part of him wondered what he was doing.

"What is it, teacher's pet?" Emma asked sarcastically.

Dean's eyes darted between Andy and the girls, his face taught in anticipation.

Andy's brow furrowed as he stared. Then, without warning, he delivered a crisp rejoinder, "Woof woof."

Emma blinked, dumbfounded, with her mouth half-open.

Dean's eyes went wide, and he coughed loudly, choking back a laugh. Andy's gaze never left the girls, daring them to reply. Dean's cheeks puffed up, and he finally burst out in laughter.

The whole class froze and stared.

Dean was oblivious. "Oh, God! Hahaha. Their stupid faces! Hahahaha!" With tears in his eyes, he slipped off his chair. Worse still, other students started laughing. Even Mr. Holt, who in Andy's experience should have taken charge, simply leaned against the board, a look of wonder on his face.

"I wish I could still laugh like that," Mr. Holt muttered, as Dean finally pulled himself back into his seat.

With Emma's face red, Andy turned around in his seat, but before he did, he noticed that Lysette was also red-faced, from laughing rather than embarrassment. As her smile faded, Andy saw that she looked tired and almost disheveled.

"Well now. Let's not hear whatever the punchline was; it will never live up to our expectations. Come on everyone, attention back up here. It's good to get it out, but—" Mr. Holt went to his desk. He produced a yellow slip, quickly filled it out, and approached Dean, "—there you are, Mr. Loggia, a nice ticket to lunch detention."

"Mr. Holt. I thought you understood," Dean

complained.

"I do, and that's why it's only one day. Don't worry, all the best people are in lunch detention. Right, Andy? Lysette?" Both students shifted uncomfortably in their seats. Andy had lunch detention for the whole week, but he was grateful that Dean only received a light punishment for his outburst.

Wait—what did I just do?

Andy tried to settle himself as Mr. Holt gave his closing announcements. He looked over at Dean, who was wiping a tear away from his red eyes.

Right—I barked at the girls.

Andy retrieved his cell phone and inspected the image again. It didn't make any sense, but he felt certain that the statue had somehow caused his outburst.

The museum should put up a warning, Andy thought, half-serious.

They shuffled out of homeroom and on to their classes.

At lunchtime, Andy found Dean in the hall outside the cafeteria.

Dean was grinning like an idiot, and jabbering. "You're a madman. Stay away from me. I've got lunch detention and I don't even care! I think something is rubbing off—like maybe your craziness—I'm afraid it's contagious."

"I wouldn't worry too much. Let's get our trays before Mr. Holt loses it. And what was that laughing fit about? Are the hormones getting you?" Andy asked.

"Maybe they are, Andy. Don't doubt it. We're getting worse by the day, and we won't level out for years."

They waited in line in the cafeteria and overheard people discussing the new kid's in-class hysteria. Dean was embarrassed and lowered his head.

"Embrace it. Hormones or not, if they think you're crazy, they won't bother you," Andy reasoned.

"That might work for you, but I've got a future with these people. You know we'll all end up at the same high school, then the same colleges. We'll have to network with them at some point. Oh God, I didn't ruin it already, did I?"

"It'll be forgotten by tomorrow." Andy interrupted.

At least it should be.

Dean was about to resume complaining when Mr. Holt walked into the busy cafeteria. "You two! And you, Lysette. My room."

"Yes, sir." Dean shrunk as he picked up his tray.

Andy didn't appreciate being snapped at so loudly, and in front of everyone. For a moment, he felt irritated. He took a breath and remembered all he had done to earn this, though the looks on Dean and Lysette's faces made it hard to stifle his anger.

Andy looked over his shoulder and saw Lysette and her group following. He couldn't help but think that Lysette looked somehow worn.

Having friends like them would tire me out too.

As they exited the cafeteria with their food, Andy slowed his pace to let the girls catch up. Dean saw what he was doing and scowled. "I'd try to stop you, but I'm a quick learner."

The girls were now alongside. Andy flashed Dean a grin before speaking. "Lysette, how hav—"

Emma interrupted him, "Don't talk to her, freak."

Andy gave her a wry look, "Freak now, not teacher's pet?"

Before Emma could answer, Mr. Holt called out to them from further down the hall.

"Only Dean, Andy, and Lysette please. The rest of you, go back to the cafeteria."

"Mr Ho-o-lt—" Emma drew out his name in a whine. "You can't leave her with them! I mean, them! Of all people!"

"Do you want detention again, Emma?" Mr. Holt's face bent with frustration. "Of course you do, what am I saying?" Then more loudly, "—get back to the cafeteria. Your friend will survive."

Andy wanted to ask Lysette about the mouse and the message on the painting, but Mr. Holt was looking volatile and he wouldn't risk it.

Dean, however, chanced a whisper, "Andy, what the heck is wrong with you? You can't talk to her. We went over the beatings, didn't we? You even agreed."

"Did I?" Andy whispered, "Well, we talked to her yesterday and nobody beat us up. Where did you even get that idea?"

"Okay, but when the football team comes for vengeance—"

"Yeah, yeah, I shouldn't expect to see you hanging around. Listen, we don't even have a football team. This is a middle school, and she isn't a cheerleader. We don't have those either."

Dean scratched the side of his face in consternation. "Oh—well, it's basically still my first day." he said quietly, as if this justified his persistent anxiety.

"Yeah, but you did come from another middle school—I don't think any of them have football teams, or cheerleaders—do they?"

"Andy—I—don't spread it around, but," Dean lowered his voice further, "I was home-schooled."

Andy's eyebrows almost disappeared into his hairline. Suddenly it all made sense.

They walked into the classroom, took their seats, and ate quietly. After a few minutes, Mr. Holt stepped out. He gave them a significant look before he left, but didn't bother telling them not to talk.

Andy immediately turned to Lysette, full of questions, but she silenced him with an angry glare.

"Don't talk to me."

Andy was shocked.

She was fine yesterday—even friendly.

"Told you," Dean whispered.

But Andy was undeterred. "Lysette, no one else saw what we did yesterday. And that mouse was at my place last night; the same one with the red face— you remember—we chased it."

"Again with the mouse thing, Andy. She was just humoring you," Dean butted in.

"I can speak for myself, thank you," Lysette snapped, before rounding on Andy. "It didn't happen, okay? So don't bring it up again," she looked away for a moment, but quickly turned back, "and if you have to talk to me, call me Letty. I hate my name."

Andy understood the sentiment, but noticed what appeared to be a cloud of dark steam rising off her shoulders. He didn't know what to say. He glanced at Dean, who shrugged. When he looked back to her, the dark cloud was almost gone.

My imagination?

A sudden movement caught his eye, and he saw another mouse. This one was eyeing Letty, and it was solid burgundy. It was hiding beneath the teacher's desk. Andy gawked and pointed, but when he did, the mouse bounded away in a flash.

Mr. Holt opened the door. He looked at them suspiciously, but the room was silent and nothing appeared out of place. He even checked the trashcan—though Andy had no idea what he expected to find—before finally taking his seat.

The final minutes of lunch detention were uneventful. Their last two classes of the day were similarly ordinary, though Andy was distracted through both. He kept quiet in Math, and only offered up vague answers in English. After the final bell rang, he met up with Dean.

"Come on, let's go to your place. I've got my copy of Wall Street Privateers. I even paid extra for the Bail-Out Edition. You've got a 720 game-system at home, right?"

"It's my dad's." Andy felt a strange sadness as he looked to the street and saw Letty climbing into her mother's car. "I'm not into it right now, Dean."

Dean leaned in close to show off the case. "Not into it! They barely ever make business sims for a console! Come on, our fortunes await—" Dean paused and stared at Andy.

Andy leaned away as Dean's stare deepened. "What is it?" Andy finally asked, rubbing his face as if something might be there.

Dean reached into his backpack and pulled out a worksheet from earlier in the day. Andy recognized it from biology class.

"Hey, what color are your eyes, Andy?"

"Blue-green," Andy scoffed, annoyed at the attention.

"What?" Dean asked, surprised by his reaction, "It's just a question. Remember today in biology, all that about heredity?" Dean asked, waving the worksheet.

Andy nodded, still not understanding why Dean was staring.

"Well, you'll have to change your answer on the worksheet, because you're wrong. Your eyes are like purplish. No, what's the color—" Dean trailed off, lost in thought.

"No they aren't. They're blue-green, like my mom's."

"Purplish? Periwinkle? Peridot? No, that's wrong—"

Andy looked away, just as Letty's mother was driving off. Something felt wrong, and all he could think about was the mist he had seen hanging above her.

"Violet! That's what they are, violet eyes."

46

Andy glowered. "There are actual problems out there. Enough about my eyes—" he looked dumbstruck for a moment, and pointed to the paper, which listed the various eye color combinations, before continuing, "violet isn't even an eye color people can have! Violet? Come on Dean, no wonder you didn't see the mouse."

Dean put the worksheet away and picked up the videogame case. "All right; I thought we were cool. Here I am, thinking we're cool, then you give me all this—and the mouse stuff again—" Wincing, he glanced at Andy to see how he was taking the criticism.

Andy regretted snapping at Dean. "I'm sorry, it's just this day. No one believes me; she's the only one, and she won't even talk to me."

Dean sighed, staring at his game.

Andy relented, "Yeah sure, we'll play, but no starting as a mega-corporation; that takes the fun out of it."

Dean embraced the change of subject. "Andy, the game is meant to be played from a conglomerate point of view. They just put the mom-and-pop option in for suicidal people. Come on, who do you hate—business wise? We'll take 'em out. And your eyes were violet, but only for a moment. Now they're back to being greenish. It was probably just the light."

"Dean—"

"All right, fine. But we're playing service sector—maybe food—we can expand vertically in the production chain, imagine the profits."

"I think shooting games can get boring too, but this is just going overboard."

Dean laughed. "Shooters are for plebeians; we're management, upper management even. This is an investment in our future, Andy."

"Dean, why did you stop homeschooling? You clearly aren't cut out for this place."

Dean examined the strap on his backpack before answering. "Keep it between you and me. I already passed the high school equivalency test, but my parents think I need to learn to socialize, if I'm going to succeed. So here I am, at least for a few years."

"Wow." Andy was astonished. "You've graduated high school already? Why come to middle-school though? Couldn't you socialize at college or something?"

"Yeah, that's what I said, but my developmental psych convinced my parents that I need primal exposure. I need to be thrown in the jungle—as they say—with people my own age."

Andy's eyes went wide, "Who says that? Wait, never mind—why is this place the jungle?"

Dean cast his view across the school walkway, at the mass of other students, and then glared at Andy, "Are you serious?"

Andy shook his head, trying to see his school through Dean's eyes. He saw clumps of students, all belonging to different groups and cliques. A few insults flew back and forth between two groups. After a moment, someone was put into a trashcan, but they were helped out fairly quickly.

"It's not that bad," Andy offered.

"I was called Loogey on my first day and laughed at by a bus full of kids. I'd say 'jungle' describes this place perfectly."

Andy laughed, "Fair enough."

A car beeped its horn.

"That's us," Andy said.

"Alright, we're still playing Wall Street Privateers?" Dean asked, climbing in beside Andy.

Andy sighed. "Sure, why not?"

"Not too much time on the video game, boys," his father said.

After Andy introduced Dean to his father, he was shocked to find that the two were fast friends. Luckily, the drive home was quick.

Between rounds of Privateers, Andy left the room and rushed to his computer. He searched for the artist who had painted the windmill; he was Dutch. Andy considered the name and tried to sound it out. At least the first part was comprehensible. "Rembrandt," he whispered, staring at the man's self-portrait.

"Andy! We're being fined by the B.B.B., but I think I can bribe the judge to reverse the order."

"Go for it!" Andy yelled, before continuing his search.

He looked up a few of Rembrandt's paintings. "There it is," he whispered, as he saw the windmill again. It didn't look right. The words were gone, though a bare trace of them remained in outlines on the rocks. Andy wondered if he had seen anything at all.

He stared closely, but it was just a cliff, albeit a suspicious one. Andy recalled the artist they spoke to. She had seen something as well; she thought the letters were mistakes.

"Andy! We need to bribe judge Conscientious. What do we offer?"

Andy wondered where he could see more of these paintings. He searched for Rembrandt's work, and was shocked at the prices these paintings sold for, before finding a nearby gallery that featured more of his work.

"Andy! What do we do?"

"What are the options?"

"Cruise in the Bahamas, 100,000 cash, a tearful plea, or a new hospital wing in his name."

"Better go with the hospital wing," Andy replied absently, as he printed out directions to the museum.

"But that's the most expensive one!"

"Just do it—hey, do you know how to get to the Masters Gallery?"

"Okay, okay. And no, I don't know it."

"It's by the arena." Andy looked up the train schedule. "We'll have to take the subway."

"What? Do I have to go?"

"I just played two hours of Privateers, so yes, you have to go."

"Isn't it that museum next to the Card Emperor's Emporium?"

Andy glanced at the computer screen and saw that, indeed, a few doors down from the Masters, was the Card Emperor's Emporium.

"Yeah, it's just down the street."

"Well in that case, I offer no objections."

Andy heard the door creak open. It was his father.

"Going to the Masters?"

"Uh—yeah? And Dean wants to go to the card shop next door," Andy replied.

"Meeting that girl there?"

"Dad! No! I'm interested in the paintings."

"So—what you mean to say is—*she's* interested in the paintings."

Andy gave his father a pained glare.

"Hey, that's good with me; we'll go Saturday. I'll drive."

Andy exhaled heavily as his dad left the room.

Can't take that guy anywhere. He's a living nightmare.

"Andy! Your dad'll drive us," Dean said from the other room, "and get in here, we're being sued for copyright infringement!"

Him too.

Chapter 4: The Night Watch

Letty walked into her first class of the day: history. A few glances held on her longer than she liked. She refused to meet their eyes, wondering how much they knew.

She had only missed two days of class while she was in the Netherscape. Emma waved, while Becky, Brook, and Quinn gave her six raised eyebrows.

Hurray.

Letty took her seat, and she tried to keep from sneering.

"Where have you been?" Becky and Brook asked in the same instant.

"That boy people saw you with, the Lice boy—some people think—well, people are talking, Letty," Quinn said, displeased. "This looks bad, and we couldn't even reach you."

"I told you, she was grounded after the museum field trip. She has strict parents; obviously they took her phone," Emma retorted, before Letty had a chance.

"Right—" Letty said, ready to let it go, but she continued dryly, "I donated my collection of last winter's clothes and they found out."

"What's wrong with that? I do—"

"I do that too! Oh, we're so alike, you know," Becky preened, interrupting Brook.

Quinn wasn't convinced.

"I'm basically off limits for the rest of the week," Letty said.

"Yeah, okay, so you're grounded for the week,

but where were you for two days?" Quinn asked.

"My parents know how much I love you guys. Going to school wasn't enough of a punishment," Letty said, hiding her face in her backpack. She found her cell and saw a dozen missed calls and ten times as many text messages. Letty rolled her eyes and dropped the phone back into her pack before retrieving her binder.

"That's not fair!" Brook complained.

"We need to talk; everything went crazy when you were gone," Becky rambled.

Finally, Ms. Aldridge walked in.

"Ah, Lysette is back. I'd like your report on— what was it? Valley Forge, I believe. Now please, you already had extra time."

Oh God. I didn't do it.

"I'm sorry, Ms. Aldridge. Due to private circumstances, I didn't actually have a chance to—"

"See me after class," she interrupted calmly, before writing the day's lesson on the white board.

Letty's face flushed red, and she clenched her fists.

Damn! I was on a roll in this class! This will sink my grade. Hell, everyone is staring again.

Dean walked into class quietly and tried to dodge the teacher's line of sight. He made it to the desks before nudging one, attracting Ms. Aldridge's attention.

"Lunch detention," she said.

Wow, she must have a hearing aid or something—that was ridiculous.

Dean stopped as he saw Letty. He looked to

Andy's empty desk and then back to her.

"Take your seat, Mr. Loggia!" Ms. Aldridge was beginning to fray.

Dean rushed to his seat, but Letty felt him staring her way for the rest of the hour.

The bell rang, and she rushed to leave, but Ms. Aldridge stopped her cold with a glance. She stood by her teacher's desk as everyone left. Dean, Emma, and Quinn all tarried on their way out, clearly trying to listen in. A glare from Ms. Aldridge sent them running.

"So, where were you, and why didn't you do that report?" Ms. Aldridge asked.

"Call my parents, please. I don't want to talk about it," Letty said, looking at the ground.

Ms. Aldridge leaned back in her chair. "Well, I will call your parents. I hope nothing happened. I can always refer you to the school psychiatrist if you want to talk to someone more privately."

She isn't mad at me.

The woman was concerned.

I wish she was mad at me. I feel even worse for lying.

Letty turned down the offer and thanked her before trying to leave.

"We just found out that Lysander—Andy, is missing. His parents have been calling. He's been gone since Sunday. You don't know anything about that, do you?"

"No, ma'am," Letty said, biting her cheeks.

"Okay. I wish you could tell me what happened, because, as it stands, you'll have lunch detention today for not handing in your report. I'll give you more time, but don't let this—whatever it is—sink your grades, young lady. It isn't as important as your future."

Letty nodded and walked out.

She felt herself start to tear up.

In homeroom, Mr. Holt made an announcement about Andy's disappearance. He asked if anyone knew anything. He gave Letty a plaintive look which drew more attention her way. When he asked to talk to her after homeroom, she ran out, sick of the scrutiny.

Her next few classes went by with no issue, and she even felt herself calming down.

Finally, lunch came, and she went to the cafeteria to grab a tray. Her friends followed.

"Can't you skip detention? Like, do it tomorrow—we need to talk," Brook said. Letty thought Brook might explode with questions and pointless insinuation.

"I don't think it works that way," Becky said.

Letty gave them a sad look before heading back to the hallway.

At least I get to eat lunch in peace—provided Mr. Holt leaves me alone.

Dean bumped into her, and she scrambled to keep from dropping her tray. "Watch out!" she snapped at him.

"I'm so sorry, Lysette—I wasn't paying attention," he stammered, picking up his milk carton and brown-bagged lunch.

Damn, he has lunch detention too. I was hoping for peace.

Letty rolled her eyes and rushed down the hall with Dean a few steps behind.

In Mr. Holt's classroom, she suffered a stern glare for walking out earlier.

Mr. Holt closed the door, but as he did so Emma appeared out of nowhere with a tray of food and slammed into him. He was doused in milk and rectangular strips of pizza.

"Emma, why?" Mr. Holt exclaimed.

"Sorry! Oh my god! I'm so sorry," She said. Letty spied the slightest smirk at the corner of her mouth.

Mr. Holt looked at Letty as if she was responsible.

"You want lunch detention that badly, fine, you can have it for the rest of the week. And I'm sending a note home to your parents," Mr. Holt said as he headed towards the washroom, dripping with milk.

"Fine—thanks, Mr. Holt," Emma said, walking into the classroom.

She gave Dean a cruel look before sitting down next to Letty.

"Where were you?" Emma's tone was almost desperate. "I went to your place and your parents—they were crazy—it was like they didn't even know me or remember you! What's going on? I thought you were dead, and they were in denial!" Emma rambled, her face going flush.

"You don't want to know, and you wouldn't believe me if I told you."

Emma wasn't satisfied and stared with entreaty.

"Look, I'm grateful that you cared enough to check on me, but you don't want to get involved."

"The weird thing is, Andy's parents still remember me. And now you show up, and he's still gone," Dean said, butting into their conversation.

"Don't talk to us!" Emma retorted.

"Wait, you said Andy's parents still remember him?" Letty asked.

"Yes, they do, and I'm sure your parents remembered you too. Not to call you a liar, Emma," Dean said rationally.

"No," Letty said, shaking her head, "the people Emma saw at my apartment weren't my parents."

Dean grimaced.

"There's no point in even talking about it; you won't believe me," she said softly.

Silence.

"Dean, look, I need you to tell me what Andy was up to before he went missing," she said firmly.

I need to find out how he got into the Netherscape.

"Why? Are you looking for him?" Dean asked.

"Yes. I'm going to find him."

Dean shook his head. "I barely know the guy. I almost wish I didn't. The last thing we did together was go to the Masters Gallery with his dad."

The Masters? I should check it out.

"We talked about him getting glasses at the museum. He was shaken up about it. You don't think he ran off because he didn't want to get glasses, do you?"

Letty shook her head. "I saw him at the optometrist's. That's all I remember, until..."

The images of Caspia and Andy being captured flashed before her.

"I managed to escape, but he didn't make it," Letty said, looking down at her uneaten food.

Emma and Dean shared a concerned look. That made Letty angry.

I don't need them; I've got Quill and Staza. They're fearless and they know the truth, unlike these two.

Letty sighed and tried to eat.

At least I know what Andy was doing before that day at the optometrist, but I don't know what happened to him after.

Eventually, Mr. Holt returned. He still looked too damp to have only suffered a polite mishap. He sat down and glowered at them for what felt like ages. Letty could barely stomach half of her pizza before the bell rang.

She rushed her tray to the cafeteria before getting to her next class. The rest of the day went by slowly, but she finally had a plan.

When school was out, she went to the park and found Staza and Quill being spoken to by a police officer. Startled, she rushed over.

"Look, you can't be fighting in the park. I don't care if it was only with sticks, you could hurt someone or yourselves. If you have to busk, maybe try juggling or playing an instrument. I don't want to see this again, all right?" the officer finished. Gratefully, it was well-intentioned chastisement.

They agreed, and the officer continued down the path.

Letty tried not to grin.

He was on them about play fighting with sticks and not truancy.

However, after another look at her friends, she could see why he made that mistake. Something about their bearing made them seem older than just their looks implied.

"Letty!" Staza said, pleased to see her.

"The surface is a strange place. Apparently, sparring in an open space is in breach of your code of conduct," Quill said judgmentally.

"I thought those people were watching us though. They even dropped their money on our jackets."

"You made money again?" Letty asked, surprised.

Staza held out a handful of small bills and coins for Letty, who laughed in astonishment.

"Making money isn't usually this easy, but, come on—we should get something to eat. I'm starving. Also, I've learned a few new details, and we need a plan."

Letty took them to a diner famous for its hamburgers. Of secondary appeal was its large, open patio.

Only a few people sitting outside. This is good, we'll have some privacy.

After confusion at the counter, Letty ordered for all of them. They stepped outside with a tray of hamburgers and a second of French fries.

"It smells—interesting," Staza remarked as they sat at a shaded table.

Letty ran back in to grab the drinks.

Better just get tea; they probably won't like anything too sugary.

Returning, she noticed nervous expressions on the Caspians. She hoped they wouldn't hate the food.

"Extraordinary," Quill said, daintily eating a fistful of fries.

"One at a time," Letty said, trying not to grin.

Quill leaned back from the table as he considered a fry. He watched as a business man walked away from the restaurant, unwrapped a burger, and took a bite.

He grimaced. "Walking while eating? Can't you see the ingrained haste of your civilization? Look at this hamburger for instance," he lifted his burger, "The elements of food bundled into a self-contained package. What is this?" He picked up a bun and flopped it back and forth.

"That's the bun," Letty said, a wry look on her face.

"You see! That's exactly my point." He nibbled on the bun before continuing, "This tasteless hunk of baked dough was designed only to make the mobility of the hamburger possible; it detracts from its flavor."

"Eat the damn thing, Quill," Staza said, after a bite of her own.

Quill did so, and his face lit up.

"Well—contrivance of haste or not, it has appeal."

Staza took a sip of her drink. "What is this?" she asked.

"Iced tea," Letty said.

"Mhh, we have tea as well. Though I've never

had it served over ice before. It's refreshing," she said, pleasantly surprised.

It's like they prepared for disappointment. Letty smiled, trying not to rush through her food.

They enjoyed a few quiet minutes. Quill spoiled it by claiming the noise of the street was an adulteration of the sound of flowing water. A car horn blared, only triggering a wave of honking from aggravated drivers. The Caspians both shot from their seats, but, after Letty explained, they enjoyed the rest of their meal in relative calm.

"The way I see it, we have two problems," Letty said, pushing her tray away. "First, we need to figure out how Andy got into the Netherscape, or failing that we need to find a different entrance. Afterwards, we need to learn where he is in the Netherscape."

Quill and Staza both agreed.

"I've learned from Andy's friend that they visited a certain art gallery, before I saw him at the optometrist."

"Andy has allies here?" Quill asked. "We should work together."

"No, that's not a good idea," Letty said, thinking about how Dean responded to her. "He would slow us down."

"This is good news! We have a lead now," Staza said.

Letty nodded and continued, "I will do everything I can to find out how we can get back. Just remember, that once we're there, I'll go back to being useless. You two will have to figure out where they have Andy, assuming he's still…"

There was silence.

"Look, Andy is valuable to them. He's still alive; I'm sure of it. And you aren't useless," Quill laughed. "With the Argument, you're a better fighter than the pair of us."

That made Letty feel better.

"We talked about it," Staza said, looking at Quill, "and we should try to find the exact portal Andy used. A different portal will likely lead to other parts of the Netherscape."

"What do you mean, other parts?" Letty asked. "You mentioned it last night, but I didn't have time to ask."

"Well, the Netherscape doesn't work like the surface. There are dozens of Netherscape domains, but you can't just walk from one to the next. There are a few paths that allow travel by sailing or airship, but the fastest way to travel is to take a portal, and preferably a safe one," Quill explained.

"Last night we took a potentially unsafe portal," Staza added.

Quill nodded before continuing, "We come from Pansubprimus, but there are many other domains, some of which we know next to nothing about."

Letty wasn't happy to hear this.

"Well, why do you call it the Netherscape then, if all these pieces aren't even connected?" Letty asked, a little annoyed.

"At one time they were connected. The Axiomatic wars took their toll on the Netherscape, far more than the surface. Despite where it stands today, the Argument was the stronger side for centuries," Quill said.

"Andy could be in any of the other Netherscape domains," Letty said, coming to grips with the new facts. "Do the ryle control all of them?"

Quill scowled. "No. Some of the domains are inhospitable to all living things, even the ryle."

"Well, even if we find the right portal, that doesn't mean Andy will be in Pan—what? Pan-prime?"

"Right, he's with Ziesqe, who I imagine can go anywhere he likes." Quill said.

"How the hell are we going to figure out where he is? We can't just walk up to a ryle and ask, 'Hey do you know Ziesqe?'"

"We might learn something if we go back. Maybe we can ask our Mistress," Staza said.

"We can't risk going back to Caspia right away. Maybe in a week or so," Quill said.

"But we need to do something now! We're wasting time, and who knows what they're doing to him!" Letty said.

Staza and Quill shared a sad look.

They think it's impossible.

Letty sighed and let her head fall into her hands. Her hair tumbled over her face.

"Letty," Staza stood and put a hand on her shoulder, "anything could have happened. But no matter what, we're going to search with you. Right?" she asked Quill.

"Of course. We owe him that much at least."

Letty stood and went to throw the trash away.

She put the trays on top of the bin, before turning to her friends with a small smile. "I appreciate it. Let's go to the gallery."

Letty texted her parents and let them know that she would be home late, before finding the route to the museum on her phone.

"We'll take the subway, and remember, it's nothing to be afraid of."

At the station, Letty bought tickets for the Caspians, and had her own subway pass ready. Quill and Staza followed close behind, and she navigated the crowds and serpentine tunnels with the skill of a native. They arrived at their platform with a minute to spare.

Letty noticed that Staza and Quill were on edge, clearly nervous, and likely claustrophobic. The crush of people was oppressive. Their eyes shifted from person to person, and she noticed their hands resting above what she expected were hidden daggers.

It's not even that busy, but they're freaking out. I should do something.

"It's okay, just hold my hand," Letty said, reaching out and taking both of their hands.

Quill and Staza seemed offended, but patronizing them had the desired effect. The shame of it calmed them.

The train arrived, and they jostled onto a car. Quill and Staza both took the opportunity to free their hands. They stood near the door.

"Grab hold," Letty said hurriedly, as the train accelerated.

Quill and Staza were both quick on their feet. They stood firm, though their nervous expressions returned.

"We are in an underworld, but it's the surface's underworld. And you can just come and go? No, there was a machine gatekeeper," Quill wondered loudly enough to attract attention.

"The subway is for transportation. Think of it as a huge car on tracks. But because there are so many people in the city, it's always crowded," Letty whispered.

"A crowded underground road," Quill muttered to himself, his eyes still darting from face to face. "Fantastic."

After a few stops, a busker came on board with a saxophone. Staza and Quill couldn't help but stare.

Great. Don't make eye contact, or he'll come over here.

Letty nudged them, but it was too late; the fellow was on his way over.

He played to Quill and Staza's fascination. Staza opened her bag, and to Letty's surprise pulled out a sketch pad. She started a quick drawing of the man in pencil. He was wearing a heavily patched sports coat over a green button up shirt, as well as jeans also covered in patches and various logos.

He played the theme songs from a few television shows she knew.

He's not bad.

Letty held out a few dollars, and the man accepted them.

"God bless you," he said, pleased that they were entertained.

"Hold on," Staza said, ripping the page out and handing it to him.

The man was taken aback when he saw the drawing. He rustled around in a pocket and found a safety pin. He pinned the page to the front of his coat.

"I'm wearing this today, but tonight it goes up on the fridge. Thank you, young lady." He walked off and readied his instrument for another song.

A moment later, they heard him playing in the next car.

"So, this is how your society works. People trade performances," Quill said, fascinated.

"Well," Letty wanted to disagree, but, after some pondering, she couldn't disagree. "Maybe it is. Sometimes the performance, or service, is making food, or teaching a class, or playing music for just three people on the subway."

The train stopped, and Letty realized this was their station just before the doors closed.

"Come on!" she said, grabbing the Caspians and rushing.

They made it off, though a conductor on the platform blew his whistle and pointed disapprovingly their way.

"Sorry, I haven't been to this stop before," Letty said.

They took the stairs outside and walked the few blocks to the museum.

"Andy came here with Dean, not too long ago. I think he had his sight at the time, and we need to keep an eye out for anything that he might have seen. Titus told me that a few paintings contain messages only people like us can see."

"We're Sensates, Letty, or Seers, depending on who you ask," Staza said.

"Seers, right," Letty said, with a strange feeling. "Titus told me that places like this are trapped and patrolled by ryle, or their servants. This time around we can't depend on Titus to keep us out of trouble."

"Keep us out of trouble?" Quill repeated.

"Yes. The mice also patrolled museums to keep an eye out for young Seers, like us, and to help us avoid the traps. Sadly, it's hard to do that as a talking mouse. Titus did his best, but I still got snagged. That's how all this started."

"Of course," Quill said, annoyed at his forgetfulness, "that was their purpose in the first place."

"Wait," Staza interjected, rooting through her bag. "We spent some of that money today."

"I noticed. That bag is new, and your sketch pad too. I didn't know that you drew," Letty said.

"I don't really, ah—here they are," Staza produced three pairs of dark sunglasses. "These should hide our eyes."

Letty was impressed.

Such an obvious solution.

They put their sunglasses on and walked into the Masters.

"I hope it works, because we look ridiculous," Letty muttered, as they were waved past the line by a guard, after he had seen Letty's student ID.

A kindly old lady gave them a map as they

passed her stool.

In the first hall they visited, Letty spotted distracting and bright colors on a painting.

"There's one," she whispered.

They slowed and looked.

The canvas featured people dancing. One dancer, a man in a pinstripe suit and trilby hat, stood out. The stripes on his suit shone in the bright colors that Letty associated with the Infiniteye.

"Are you seeing that? His clothes are like nothing else," Letty said, nudging Staza.

"Yes, but look at the frame," Staza replied.

Letty felt her skin crawl at the sight of grasping tendrils, which she hadn't noticed until Staza's warning.

The frame undulated with dark purple trim. Tendrils lined up with the carved motifs of the actual frame underneath. She realized the tendrils were moving, and they were moving slowly towards her, stopping about a few feet from where they were rooted.

Letty felt her stomach sink. She was suddenly paranoid. Staza nudged her away, and they moved on. Though Letty couldn't shake the feeling that someone had seen them stare for too long at the painting of the dancers.

As they walked through the hall, she looked back and noticed that the tendrils moved to stay pointing at them.

That's how the first painting got me; I was too close.

Letty sighed and then said, "That painting was trapped, but I didn't see a message for us."

"Not every artist set out to put secret words in their work," Quill whispered as they moved through a crowded room.

A picture of water lilies also shone with a brilliance that made it feel like the pond was trembling beneath a wind.

"Like that," Quill continued. "The painter has used pigment that only we can see, but he may never have realized that other people couldn't experience it the way he intended."

The idea astonished Letty. *How could a painter not know that he was a Seer? She looked at the painting in wonder. Well, I didn't know until recently. What if nobody told me? Maybe I would just think that I was a little different.*

They walked into the next hall and found it full of statuary. None of it stood out to Letty, but she began to doubt herself. *What if I see something and I don't realize it's different?*

"You aren't seeing anything?" she asked.

"There are some marvelous pieces, but nothing for us," Staza said.

Quill considered a statue of a man chained to a rock. A large bird of prey stooped over him, and a fallen torch burned nearby.

"Prometheus, punished for that most egregious sin," he said, looking up for an answer.

Letty drew a blank.

"He defied the gods and gave mankind forbidden knowledge," Staza finished, her expression chagrined.

"You have mythology too?" Letty asked,

remembering the story of Prometheus.

Quill gave her a speculative look. "Of course. We share most of the same history, though a fair portion of it is suppressed up here."

"It's suppressed down there too, Quill," Staza rebutted.

As they left the statuary, Staza grabbed Quill and Letty.

"Careful, turn around," she said quietly.

Letty did so, but looked over her shoulder, and saw purple tendrils lining the doorway. A thin screen of mist also filled the doorway. She hadn't seen it when they were approaching, and even now she could barely distinguish it.

"Good catch," Quill said, trying to slow his breath.

"Nobody saw us turning around," Staza said, motioning them down another hall.

Letty's paranoia and nervousness returned. She looked around and noticed the little black domes that hid security cameras.

Maybe someone saw us. I shouldn't alarm them, or should I?

"Do you see those little black domes?"

They both looked and nodded.

"Guards can see us through those, on television screens, but there is no guarantee that someone is watching on the other end."

Quill and Staza stiffened, realizing the domes were everywhere.

"I'm starting to think that we should get out of—" Letty paused as she saw something familiar.

"I see it too," Staza said, looking at a painting.
Letty sat on a nearby bench.

"There's something there," Quill said.

"The sign of the Argument," Staza whispered. "There on the drum."

Letty opened her backpack and found Andy's notepad. The Caspian's joined her on the bench as she flipped through the pages and found a rough sketch of this painting, followed by several abortive attempts to draw the Infiniteye. There were also a few words he had written, but they were from another language.

"Andy was here! He saw this." Letty showed them the sketches. "What did you call this?" she asked, pointing at the symbol.

"It's the sign of the Argument—essentially a religious symbol. Its creation is punishable by execution in some places. The ryle spent extra effort hunting down those who could make it," Quill said.

"I don't think there's a person alive now who knows how to paint it anymore," Staza added.

"Is there a trick to it?" Letty asked, inspecting Andy's awkward attempts on the notepad.

Quill nodded.

"Why don't they destroy it?" Letty asked, staring carefully at the militiamen.

"Our Mistress says the ryle have a fascination with Seer artistry, even though they can't see what makes it special: those pigments that give off the brilliant shine," Quill whispered, looking over his shoulder.

"In Caspia, Titus told me that Andy discovered

the truth about optometrists from another painting. This one here is by the same artist," she read the placard next to the painting. "Rembrandt. We know that Andy saw the Infiniteye here. So, moving forward, Andy would associate the eye with Rembrandt's good information. Do you think that changes anything?" she asked.

"I don't know, but it's a start," Staza said.

Letty stared at the painting and saw the Seer script. She had the urge to lean in, but, even though she saw no tendrils on this painting, she was afraid.

"Can either of you read these letters?" Letty tapped a copy of the painting in Andy's notebook. "I don't know the language."

They both shook their heads.

Wait. Hold on.

She found her phone and pulled up a translation application. She typed in the text.

"Dutch," she said. She read the translation, "The symbol guides our steps."

"If Andy translated the message, he would have been keeping an eye out for the symbol," Quill said.

"I'm sure he did," Letty responded, feeling hopeful, and then nervous as if the hope was premature.

"She's right," Quill responded. "All we need to do is recreate the day everything started. We need to discover where he was. I'm certain that somewhere on his path he came across the symbol, and after reading that," he pointed to the translation, "he would have followed it and found a portal or the mice."

72

"Titus said he just walked into their city," Letty said.

Quill's face lit up.

"This is good news," Letty added, "but I don't know where he was. I can hardly remember where I was that day. Who knows what he did after the optometrist? He could have gone anywhere."

"Well, it wasn't going to be easy. Do we continue tomorrow?" Staza asked.

Letty checked the time on her cell and the angry messages from her parents. "Yes. We need to get back," she said, standing and stretching.

They were careful on their way out of the museum and had to avoid two inky screens of tendrils before finally exiting.

As they returned to the subway, Staza stiffened beside Letty and bent to whisper in her ear, "Someone's following us. They have been since the museum—I'm sure of it."

Letty grasped the Argument.

"Stay with me," Staza said, stepping ahead of the group and leading the way.

When they rounded a corner, Staza broke out into a run. Letty and Quill followed. They turned down the nearest alley, and Staza drew a dagger from beneath her borrowed jacket.

"What are we doing?" Letty asked, a glow coming from her hand.

"Put that out!" Staza whispered.

Letty loosened her grip. She hadn't realized that she was clenching her fist.

Footsteps came closer.

In a flash, Staza reached out and pulled their pursuer into the alley with them. Their bodies tumbled to the floor, but Staza came out on top, and had her dagger at the man's throat.

Letty felt her eyes focusing, and after a few seconds she realized the man was a ryle. The ryle wore a tailored suit, and Letty suppressed the urge to laugh at the curious sight.

"Do you see it?" Letty asked.

Quill and Staza nodded.

The ryle made a sudden move, but Quill struck with his right leg and knocked a pistol from the ryle's grip.

"Do it again! I'd love to learn the color of ryle blood!" Staza leaned forward as she whispered.

The ryle's fleshy face contorted in surprise.

"What do you want from me?" he asked.

"Why were you following us?" Letty replied.

The ryle's face twisted into an expression akin to annoyance. "Look at you," he hissed, "why do you think I was following you? No wonder your side lost."

Staza gave the ryle a few gentle slaps with the flat end of her dagger. "Careful now, don't forget that you're an inch from bleeding to death."

"Just kill me," the ryle said, pushing himself closer to the dagger.

"No—you don't get away that easily." Letty said, pulling Staza back.

"They'll do worse when they find out three mature Seer children just avoided all of my snares, and then...overpowered me in the street."

Letty huffed. "Where are your brutox?"

The ryle huffed right back. "Brutox? At my age? I'm alone in this garbage ward, pulling museum duty. I've spent years looking for you little rats. Here are the first ones I find and look what happens. I'm useless spawn at this point."

The Seers shared a surprised look. Letty almost felt bad, but Staza had a grin on her face, and Quill could only shake his head in astonishment.

"Tell us, do you know a ryle named Ziesqe?" Letty finally asked.

"I know five!" The ryle hissed.

"Zyzqe Ziesqe," Quill said.

"Ah, that tart. He calls himself Ropt up here. Yes, he's come into some serious trouble recently," the ryle paused, his beady eyes going as wide as they could. "Of course. It makes complete sense. You are the thorns in his side, eh? And now you're on a rampage through the city? Tell me, is this a full-scale rebellion, or just an isolated incident?"

They gawked at how quickly the ryle figured them out.

"I just would like to know if I'll be remembered as a casualty of a treacherous coup, or a fool who couldn't do his job," the ryle rambled, resigned to whatever came.

"Hey," Staza gave him another slap, "pay attention. No editorializing. Where does Ziesqe reside in the Netherscape?"

"I'm not his mother!" the ryle complained gratingly.

Quill laughed, and gave the ryle a soft kick in

the ribs. "I'm starting to like him."

"And why would I tell you anything?" The ryle countered.

"Fair enough," Letty said, considering. "How about, you tell us everything we ask, and we let you go."

"Yeah," Staza interjected, "and if we find out that you lied to us, we'll come back. Don't forget, we know where you work," she concluded, a conciliatory expression on her face.

The ryle coughed up a nervous laugh, as if it were a joke. His eyes shot back and forth between them. "Fine," he finally agreed.

"So, back to Ziesqe," Staza said.

"He's one of the richest and most powerful in the city. I don't know what to tell you. He has interests all over the surface, Pansubprimus, and Euboia. His famous palace is in the Nightmare. It's called Zentule. They made a big performance about him building the first settlement in the Nightmare for centuries."

Letty took the pistol and pocketed it. "That wasn't so difficult," she said.

Staza and Quill released the ryle, and stepped back, their daggers at the ready.

The ryle stood and brushed itself off. It turned to leave, but then spun towards them, a weak purple blade shot from its hand.

It swung at Staza, and she parried with her dagger. The two blades locked. Staza's blade quickly gave way as the purple sword burned through. Letty felt a sudden pain behind her eyes flare at the sight

76

of the ryle's blade.

She grasped the Argument and drew her own blade. The pain in her head evaporated in an instant.

The ryle stumbled backwards in shock. Its face contorted in agony.

She swung her blade, and the ryle pulled away, as if he wanted to keep the blades from meeting. He was too slow, and a loud crack echoed in the alley. The pea sized purple orb shot from the ryle's hand. Letty's blade also fizzled and the orb flew from her hand as well. Recovering from her stumble, she turned and recovered the Argument while Staza and Quill held the ryle at bay with their weapons, though Staza's dagger was cut almost to the hilt.

"It's a piece of Counter-Argument," Quill said, unimpressed.

Letty, her orb in hand, walked towards her foe's weapon and felt the urge to strike out at it. She summoned her blade.

The ryle yelled, "Don't!"

She struck, and the Counter-Argument burst apart in a small explosion. A stain of what looked like smoky, black and purple glass stretched for many feet, even climbing walls and a metal trash can.

"No! You can't imagine how expensive that was!" The ryle whined, before promptly receiving an elbow to the face.

Staza waved her destroyed dagger inches from his face. "I made this myself, it was one of a kind!"

Quill restrained her.

"We should kill it," Staza complained. "It's

traitorous!"

Letty blinked, realizing that Staza was serious.

"Hey!" A voice yelled. They saw a burly man in an undershirt standing at one end of the alley. "What's going on here?"

Letty gritted her teeth at being found. "Listen!" she said to the ryle. "We know where to find you."

A few more people appeared next to the burly man.

"Run!" Letty whispered, leading the way.

They ran out of the alley and slowed to a fast walk when they turned the next corner, but they didn't relax until they descended into the subway station and hopped on a full train.

"We should be fine now," Letty said. "Hopefully no one called the police; there are cameras everywhere."

Those people will think we were mugging that ryle, and he'll probably tell them the same, but will they call the police?

Letty felt anxious and scanned the length of the car for any activity. She gave Staza a questioning glance.

"I don't think anyone followed us," Staza said.

A station later, some seats opened up. Letty sat and felt the shape of the gun in her pocket. She remembered it was a revolver.

What am I going to do with it? I don't want to throw it away; we might need it.

She remembered Andy being disarmed by Ziesqe, and something similar just happened to her.

If Andy had a second weapon, he might have escaped. I

shouldn't toss the gun.

Letty looked at the others.

Quill behaved like I expected, but Staza... I need to remember that they come from a violent place. If I'm not careful, she'll kill someone before I can stop her.

Staza sighed and Quill noticed.

"You still have your sword," he said.

"I can't carry it openly," she complained. Letty sensed that Staza wanted to insult the sad state of surface civilization.

"Well, we did learn where Ziesqe lives," Quill said.

"He said Ziesqe could be in many places," Staza retorted.

"What was that name he mentioned? The Nightmare. Do you know it?" Letty asked.

Quill shook his head, and Staza slumped in her seat.

Letty leaned back and looked out the window as a station rolled by. Bright lights flashed between pillars as they slowed to a halt. The doors opened and closed with barely a handful of people moving on and off.

The rest of the ride was quiet, and as they left the station Letty received a call from her father.

"I told you, we went to the gallery. It was fun. No—we're on our way back now. We'll be home in a few minutes."

Letty listened for a long time.

"No, we'll be back in a minute. I swear. We're just down the street," Letty's voice was suddenly nervous, and the Caspians could tell. "Yes, that's fine."

Letty put her phone away, but her face had gone pale.

"What's wrong?" Staza asked.

"The police came by while we were gone. They have questions for me," Letty said.

Chapter 5: Doctor Ropt

Andy woke with a shock. He recalled the mice and the one with the red face in particular. He'd conversed with this mouse, but there was something else.

He leaped from his bed and inspected his arms and legs. He looked all over for signs that something had happened to him. Again, he found nothing.

More than that, he felt great. The dizziness was gone. Everything looked normal, but that dream.

Andy tore apart his room. He looked under everything. He pulled his bed away from the wall and flipped over the mattress and box-spring. Nothing.

Next, he tore into his closet, pausing only to grab a few plastic bags to finally get rid of the piles of old and ragged toys he had lying around.

The mice are making me clean again.

For a moment he wondered if it was all a trick to get him to sort out his room. It seemed too involved for his parents.

As he pulled his computer desk away from the wall, he cringed at the noise it made. A moment later, his parents poked their heads into his room.

"What's going on in here?" his mother asked.

They came in and looked around. He could only stare. Worse yet, he felt a guilty look growing across his face.

His father sensed the issue. "Finally cleaning your room? That's great. But you're still going to the optometrist."

His mother stared at the bags and piles of clothes as well as the moved furniture, clearly concerned. "You are cleaning your room, right?"

Andy nodded. "Yup, it needed it. I'd swear we have mice in here too."

His father looked behind the desk. "It's probably just mouse-sized tumbleweeds of dust rolling around."

Andy was silent. He didn't want to go to the optometrist, but he couldn't come up with an excuse. Then he remembered the dream and what the mouse had said. It was something about the symbol.

"You've got a few minutes to sort this out before we leave for the optometrist."

His parents closed his door. He heard them muttering between themselves moments later.

Distracted, Andy couldn't recall what the mouse told him the night before. He knew it was important, and that it had to do with seeing the optometrist, but he couldn't remember the exact words.

He rushed to rearrange his room. When the last piece of furniture was back in place, he breathed an exhausted sigh and lay on his bed.

"No way!" He exclaimed, seeing the symbol from the painting glowing on the ceiling above his bed.

"Don't try and argue your way out of this, mister. You're going to the optometrist," his mother called to him from the front room.

"Yes, mom!" he said, leaping to his feet for the second time that morning.

How?

He stood on his bed and gently touched the symbol. It pulsed ever so softly, and it felt slightly raised, like it had been painted on.

Maybe if I—

He poked at it with his fingernail and found it would peel away easily if he tried. He was about to tear it off before the image of The Night Watch shot into his head. He remembered the drum and the symbol.

There were other words too! More Dutch writing next to the symbol! How could I forget?

He left the symbol and hopped off his bed, looking for his sketch pad.

"Where is it?" he whispered angrily.

He tore through his things and found his backpack. He turned his computer on before opening the sketch pad.

"Come on—come on!" He flipped through the pages and finally found his first attempt at copying the symbol.

As the computer booted up, he glanced at the ceiling and back to his sketch pad.

They look nothing alike.

But he knew the symbol on his ceiling was a match for the one in the painting. Staring at the intruding mark, his head started to hurt.

I don't want to repeat that—better stop staring, it seems to make it worse.

"Lysander? Come on!" His father called.

He pulled up the translation page and typed in the words letter by letter. "Can't we reschedule for next weekend?" He tried to sound helpless and sincere, but came off sounding determined.

"No, we are going today."

"Let's reschedule. The room's really coming along—I don't want to stop now." He finished typing the sentence, but the translation didn't make sense. He nearly panicked, but looked back and forth before realizing that he had misspelled a word halfway through.

His parents were quiet for a moment, he could sense their concern through the door.

Come on!

He clicked the translate button as they walked into his room.

"Wow, it looks great in here," his mother said.

His father looked around and agreed, "Yes, it does. Therefore, no reason to delay."

"But—"

"I won't have you falling over during P.E. and cracking your skull because you're afraid of how you'll look. You are getting glasses today," his father concluded.

His mother glanced between them nervously.

Andy relented. He stood up to go but read the translation before stepping away. It said: 'Guides our steps.'

He wondered if the translation was off again, but as he put his seatbelt on, the meaning struck.

The symbol guides our steps.

He wanted to write it off as an inside joke between artists, but he had seen the same symbol above his bed. He had to take it seriously.

It guides our steps? But why is it above my bed?

How did it get there? Should I tell my parents that I need to see a psychiatrist before the optometrist?

For a moment, he considered breaking down and admitting everything he had seen.

They might call off the trip—but it wouldn't be forever. What did the mouse tell me? Something about the eye exam, or a test. He mentioned seeing—or was it, not seeing, the symbol?

He considered his parents. They were both tense but his mother more so.

Maybe they know I've gone off the deep end. This might be a trip to the asylum after all.

His grim hopes were dashed when they pulled into a parking lot and he saw the sign for one Dr. Ropt - Optometrist. They left the car and approached the building.

Andy stared at the sign and saw different letters appearing above the doctor's name, like they had been painted over. They glowed and shimmered in a way almost reminiscent of the paintings at the gallery and the symbol above his bed, though the color of this script was chaotic and greasy to look at. These new letters were incomprehensible and from another language, but one unlike any he had ever seen. As he focused, he felt pain and was oddly certain that the letters were pushing his vision away, as if he was not supposed to see them.

Beneath the alien script were similarly shining letters. These were English, and it took a serious effort to work through them.

187th Ward—Lord Ziesqe, The Just and Master of Zentule, presiding.

Andy gawked, and felt certain that he was losing his mind. His head strained with the effort of reading the script, and he had to lean against a car for balance.

"It's okay," his father said, rushing to help him, "just take a second; we've got time."

He nearly stumbled, but with his father's help, he kept his feet.

"What's wrong?" his mother asked.

Andy was as truthful as he could be, "My head starts to spin and hurt when I read some things. I can't stand up, I need to sit down when it happens."

"Oh, let him sit," she said, pulling a water bottle from her purse.

Andy took a moment and tried not to think about what he had just seen on that sign.

I just need to stop seeing these things. If I try, it'll go away eventually. I just need to stop caring, stop feeding it.

He took a drink and steadied himself. His parents hovered close by, as they walked to the door. Andy sat while they filled out medical forms.

"Do you have his insurance card?"

"Yes, it's here in my wallet."

He tried to ignore his parents, and the spinning in his head, by looking around. There was a familiar face in the waiting area. Letty's mother was sitting across from them.

"Excuse me," Andy said.

The woman looked up.

"Are you Letty's mother?"

The lady gave a slight smile, "So, she has

everyone calling her by that name."

"Lysette, I mean," Andy corrected himself. "She just asked me to call her Letty."

"Hmm." The woman grumbled, looking away.

"My son isn't fond of his given name either," his father interjected.

An odd look bent the woman's face. She seemed between concern and annoyance. "What is he called?" she asked in a plain voice.

"We called him Lysander, after a Greek hero."

Andy tried not to frown at the adults talking like he wasn't there.

"Lysander?" The woman asked, casting an appraising look at Andy. "No wonder he doesn't like it."

Andy wasn't sure how to respond, the words were insulting, but her voice wasn't.

Andy's father scowled before addressing his family, "Look everyone, it's a rude person in their natural habitat. They remain calm and neutral after striking, as if that should confuse us and excuse her."

Again, the woman had that look of annoyed concern, "Oh no, I didn't mean to be rude. It's just that young people are so set on either fitting in or standing out. We both hoped for stand outs; it's clear with names like theirs, but they simply haven't grown into them yet."

Andy's parents weren't sure what to say, neither was he. But the woman continued anyway.

"What name have you chosen for yourself?" she asked.

"I go by Andy."

She laughed. "See parents, there's still a trace of your name in that. Andy—Andy, wait, are you the boy who got Lysette in trouble?"

"I—uhm—" He looked for help from his parents.

His father gave him a knowing grin and a wide-eyed shrug.

"Yeah, that was me," he admitted.

The woman looked ready to launch into a rant, but the doctor's assistant came in and called for Andy.

He gratefully followed the man back into the darker rooms. Computer screens lit the way, and strange instruments covered tables. The man asked him to take a seat.

After a minute, he heard a creak. He looked over his shoulder and saw another figure sitting in the dark, at a table.

"Don't stare, Lice, it's bad for your eyes."

It was Letty. Her voice was drained and heavy.

"You too?"

She didn't respond.

"It started that day at the museum, right? Dizziness, seeing odd colors? Annoying parents?"

She let out a small laugh. "Yes, to all three."

Andy wanted to be frank with her about everything he'd seen, but he remembered the last time he tried.

She's in a better mood; maybe I can risk it.

She continued, "They don't know what's wrong with my eyes. I've been here all morning. They sent for my father, but he was all the way across town."

"Why did they send for your father? You're here for an eye exam. That doesn't make any sense."

She dismissed him with a wave of her hand. "I'm defective; they need to cosign the demolition papers."

She stared at the ceiling, upset and impudent all at once.

How can I lighten her up?

"I met your mother out there," Andy said, a bit of hesitation in his voice.

"Oh, God." Lysette sighed, "What did she do?"

"Eh—she," Andy wasn't sure if he should lie or not.

Letty straightened out and leaned forward at the delay.

He knew he had to be honest. "She kind of made fun of my name."

Letty thought little of that and leaned away from him. "I kind of make fun of your name."

There was silence.

"I see where you get it," he said in a sideways tone.

"Get what?" She asked, disengaged and annoyed again.

"The attitude," He said plainly. She gave him a sharp look, but he continued anyway. "That's the problem with being too smart for your age or group. Your friends put you to work as their queen, making up petty names to bully people with. It's pretty obvious that you don't enjoy it."

He expected an attack, or possibly a denial, or complete silence. Instead, she asked a question.

"Have you been seeing those mice? You mentioned one the other day."

Yeah, and you chewed my head off for it.

Now Andy sulked. "I don't know what's been going on the past few days. We saw something back at the museum, and I'm still seeing things. But I think we need to get over it. It's—"

"So, you have been seeing them. The mice, I mean."

Andy wanted to deny everything, but he couldn't. He had spoken to one last night.

"Did they come to you last night?" he asked.

"Yes," She replied earnestly. "But I failed. They told me not to see it, but never explained what it was."

Andy considered that odd. The mice told him not to see the symbol.

Maybe not seeing it is difficult. But nothing bad happened to her. At least she seems fine.

Letty shook her head. "I saw something strange on the paper he held up, I think that was what the mice wanted me to ignore. I could barely see it, but I did, and he noticed."

"You saw what? The symbol?"

"Yeah. The Infiniteye."

"Infiniteye?" Andy thought about the symbol, and the name made sense.

"I'm scared. I'm scared of what's going to happen to me. But I'm thinking that I'm not completely crazy because you're seeing everything too. Now I don't know if something bad is coming, or if the whole mouse episode was just—a shared insanity."

Andy still felt an urge to deny it, but he knew that it wouldn't help if he did.

She continued, half rambling to herself. "How can I know that my crazy head didn't invent you too?" She reached out and put a finger on his shoulder. "Seems real," she said before pushing him out of his seat.

He fell to the floor and nearly pulled the table, and its expensive equipment, down with him.

"Yeah, at least you're real," she spoke through a few breaths of sad laughter.

"You!" An attendant came back and spotted Andy getting back into his chair. "What are you doing? Never mind—you're wanted in room two, Mr. Vanavarre. And you," he spoke to Letty, "you still need to wait for your father. Please stay out of trouble."

Andy stood and endured the glare from the assistant as he headed for room two. He heard Letty repeating his last name over and over, trying to get a feel for it.

Great, now she'll make fun of my last name too—and why the hell did she knock me out of the chair?

"This way, please." The assistant glowered at him as they passed an office door that was slightly ajar.

"Marvin?" a cold voice called out as they passed.

"Yes sir."

"Would you come in here for a moment?"

Marvin sat Andy down in a chair some distance

from the door and walked into the office.

"Is the girl's father here?"

"No sir, and you have another waiting. Symptoms sound like tetrachromacy—I think the two know each other. What should we do?"

"First of all, close the door."

Marvin shut the door.

What did I just hear? Tet—something—omacy?

Andy stood and inched towards the door. He put his ear against it but could barely make out what they were saying.

"There's nothing to do about the boy. I'll test him. If it's drastic we'll have them make two trips, if not—"

"But Master, if the girl disappears—they know each other; I even saw the parents speaking. It won't work."

There was a pause. Andy felt like backing away from the door. He forced himself to keep from shrinking away.

"How long have I been doing this? Is this your first year? Are you forgetting your place?" the speaker left long pauses between each question.

"Master, I—"

"Who created you?"

Andy only heard a dull mumble in reply.

"What is your purpose?" The doctor continued.

"To serve."

Silence.

There was a quaver of desperation in Marvin's voice, "My concern is only for you. Two of them so intertwined—please, this situation calls for immediate response, we need to remove them from the population."

Remove them from the population! Andy strained over the words, certain he must have misheard, but they echoed, in blank certainty, through his mind.

Andy stumbled backwards in fear, and nearly crashed into the wall.

Are they going to kill us? This is just an optometrist's office—

He heard a loud crackle coming from the doctor's office and a purple light flashed under the door.

Andy rushed back to his seat and tried to get his breathing under control.

The door opened and out came an unfamiliar face.

The doctor.

He looked around and saw Andy sitting quietly.

"Hello there, young man," he said, approaching. "I hear you've been experiencing a little dizziness and head pain."

Andy wanted to scream and run, but he could only stare at the doctor's face. He saw lines there that didn't belong. There was a glow burning in the pits of his eyes. His teeth shone in the dull light as he smiled through his introduction.

"I'm Doctor Ropt, and you are Andy, correct?" The doctor held out his hand.

"Yes, sir." Andy forced himself to shake the doctor's hand. It felt cold and oddly smooth, like it was hairless.

"I hear you know another one of my patients."
Andy nodded.

"Are you friends?"

Andy paused. "Not really, sir."

The doctor chuckled heartily. "No need for that, young man; doctor is fine. Come on then, let's get a look at your eyes."

The doctor shone a light at his face and looked closely.

"What color eyes would you say you have?"

"Greenish blue, sir."

"Mhh—has anyone ever said you have violet eyes?"

Andy stuttered, "N-no, sir."

The doctor tilted his head in thought. "There is a rare condition—easily treated—that your symptoms match. Curiously, the sufferers of this condition can experience a fluctuation or gradual change in eye color at about your age. Certain pharmaceuticals and foods can help treat this condition—carrots, for instance," the doctor paused, expectantly.

Andy shook his head.

The doctor smiled. "We'll get you figured out in no time." He led Andy back to the room where he last saw Letty. She was gone.

"Take a seat, please—yes, there behind that machine." Andy did as he was told.

"Look here." Andy obeyed and felt a sudden blast of air hit his eyes. He reeled back in shock and felt the doctor's hand holding him in place. He felt the muscles around his eyes tense like they did at the museum.

Andy felt his chest clench at what he saw. Sheets of bright light shed off the doctor's body. The outline of his form had changed, his face looked bottom heavy and his skull and nose were smoother, but the light kept Andy from seeing more than a silhouette.

"Okay, it'll just be a few minutes wait," the doctor said, as if nothing was wrong.

He was about to walk away when something caught his attention and he leaned forward with his instrument to look into Andy's eyes again. Andy saw more than he wanted.

What is he?

The doctor had purple flesh.

Andy bit down on his cheeks to keep himself from screaming.

"How does the world look?" The doctor asked in his cool voice.

Andy felt his head start to spin and throb. He took a deep breath and focused his eyes on the floor. "I'm a little dizzy sir, but everything looks fine."

"Hmm. You don't see anything strange?"

Andy stared into the two burning pits that were the doctor's eyes. "No sir."

He nodded. "It'll just be a minute. Wait here, please."

Andy suffered through the next few agonizing minutes by keeping his eyes closed. He wanted to find Letty. Holding onto the table barely helped him to stand. He knew that a step in any direction would be disaster. He sat back down and waited for the spinning to stop.

"Andy, my boy. How are those eyes?" The doctor put a hand on his shoulder and had him look up. "You're ready to come back and have a look at a few slides for me." The doctor paused for a moment, "No one has ever told you that you have violet eyes?"

Andy shook his head, and followed the doctor, grabbing at furniture or the walls for support.

"Right." The doctor carried a clipboard and was marking a page before he noticed Andy's behavior. "Dizzy—hmm, take your time now, don't rush. How long have you been unbalanced like this?"

"It's not all the time, sir, and it's only been a few days."

They entered into a room crowded with an assemblage of curious machines, most featuring metallic view scopes and slides. Andy took his seat.

"Did anything trigger the first dizzying event? Any strange colors or bright lights?"

"No sir. I'm not sure what set it off, I just woke up dizzy one morning—it comes and goes."

The doctor paused and gave him an appraising look.

Please believe me.

"Have you been seeing things that aren't there? Anything strange at all? Small creatures that shouldn't be there, perhaps?"

"I saw my dad pull me away from cleaning my room this morning. You might want to get him back here."

The doctor scowled and leaned in closely. His voice crisp and constant. "None of that now. These are serious questions; I will not have my time wasted." Andy felt a heavy hint of disapproval in the last few words, "Answer the question, son."

Andy met the doctor's gaze.

Andy wanted to tell the doctor everything, if it meant that he could leave. He wanted to tell about the mice, the paintings, the symbols, and the dark mist. Most of all, he wanted to tell the doctor what he saw inside those flaming eyes. He wanted to ask him what they planned on doing to Letty. But Andy knew, with a strange certainty, that it would mean the end for him and likely for his family too.

He was afraid, but he shook his head no.

"Look into that scope, please."

Grateful to look away, he stared into the scope and saw numbers and letters to the left and right.

"Now we'll go through a few of these," he flipped one side to a different lens. "Which looks clearer?"

Andy went through the tests, slide by slide pointing out which was clearer. He could tell that the doctor wasn't pleased, but he didn't know what else to do.

"Enough—enough, young man." The doctor switched the light in the machine off. "Look up here."

Andy stared as the doctor pointed to a chart of letters on the wall.

"Read off the letters, top to bottom."

Andy sounded out the letters, one by one, all the way to the bottom line.

"Your vision is perfect. What's more, I think you know that your vision is perfect. Why have you put your parents through all of this?"

The doctor stood up and found a metal tube, he pulled the end off and slid out what looked like a scroll.

Andy barely registered this as he was surprised by the question. "What do you mean? I'm dizzy, you saw—"

The doctor stopped Andy dead in his tracks by unfurling the scroll. "What do you see here?"

Andy's eyes shot to the center of the scroll and saw the symbol. The doctor stared hungrily as Andy's face bent with horror.

Before Andy could claim that nothing was there, the doctor spoke, "Don't lie!"

Andy's head throbbed at the sight of the Infiniteye, he felt his eyes flexing, and then he saw the doctor clearly.

His flesh was purple, and the light from his burning eyes shone across the room and washed everything in a violet red that pulsed like flames. Cords of muscled flesh, each tipped with a barbed claw, hung from the sides of his face. He stood there, inhumanly rigid, holding out the scroll, his muscles tense, and all of his focus directed at Andy's eyes, at what they saw.

There was a bang on the door and Andy felt himself blacking out. His vision lost focus and the last thing he recalled were the voices of his parents. They were screaming.

Chapter 6: Sentinel's Watch

Andy's eyes shot open and he took in a violent gasp of air. His hands reached out, grasping in every direction. They found purchase and he pulled himself up.

"It's okay, sweetie." It was his mother.

He let out a pained sigh. "Thank God it's you." Andy realized he was in the backseat of his family's car.

"Does your head hurt? You fell over in the office."

"Where's dad?" he gasped.

"Inside, getting your prescription."

"What!" Andy reached for the car door. His mother held him back.

"It's okay—he'll be right back."

"No! Let me go!"

Andy saw his father coming to the car, and he stopped struggling.

Taking the driver's seat, his father seemed furious. "What the hell are carotenoids, and how are they supposed to help you see?" His father asked, slamming the door and then holding up a bottle of pills.

Andy looked out the window and tried to focus. "We aren't at the optometrist's anymore?"

His mother answered, "No. We had to drive to the pharmacy. You were in and out for a while there. The doctor said you would be fine, and you're back to normal now." Her last few words sounded more like a question.

Oblivious, his father was fuming, "Tetrachromacy. What a joke!"

"What do you mean, dad?"

"There's something wrong and they don't know what it is. You're falling over in the exam room—we're lucky you didn't get a concussion. Oh, but we can check back in two weeks! What are we supposed to do?"

Andy was frightened by the desperation in his father's voice. His hands were clutching the steering wheel; his nails pressed into the leather.

They were silent.

Finally, his mother spoke, "The pills might help. Maybe he doesn't need glasses after all. It might be a new medication; we should be grateful there's an option." She took the bottle from his father and inspected it. Smiling she said, "Oh, I've been taking these for years—see, it's no big deal. You just need to be good about taking them every day."

His father visibly relaxed. "Do you have this tetrachroma—thing? You said they were for your brain."

"Well, things go a bit weird if I don't take them, and I don't know the name of the condition. I was prescribed the pills in my teens. I've taken them ever since and had no problems," she said, hoping to encourage Andy.

Andy, however, heard none of this. He shivered, thinking about what he saw back in the optometrist's office. He was certain that he'd never take those pills, and then he remembered Letty.

Looking out the window, Andy realized they

would be passing the office again, on their way home. His heart twisted and leaped at once.

"Did either of you see Letty?" he asked, masking the desperation in his voice.

"Who?" His parents both asked at once, one annoyed, the other frantic for something to break the silence.

"Letty! We spoke with her mother—"

"Lysander! You will not raise your voice to us." His father's shoulders tensed as he spoke.

"No, Andy, we didn't see her," his mother answered calmly, "but her father arrived right before—well."

Her father showed up. They were waiting to do something to her—waiting for him to arrive.

Andy looked out the window and saw that the car Letty's mother drove was still parked outside the office.

Oh God, they're going to murder me. But I have to— this is my fault. She walked through the ink because of me, they took her because of me. Even if she acts like a bully, she isn't really, and either way, she doesn't deserve this.

He wasn't sure what he could do, but he knew that he had to help Letty.

Taking a few deep breaths as they drove past the office, he slowly unlocked the back door and released his seatbelt. Neither parent noticed. He pressed his fingers firmly against the door handle. He waited for a red light and then bolted from the car.

Racing down the street, he shook with fear. He nearly tumbled over a passing family before catching a torrent of complaints from the parents.

"Andy!" He heard his own parents yelling after him. Car horns were blaring and he knew they had stopped in the middle of the road. He wanted to yell at them, to reassure them that he'd be fine, but he refused to look back. He knew he might surrender if he looked back. He might forget all about what he saw and give in to common sense if he looked back.

I was willing to deny it all this morning, but now another person's life is at stake—because of me—I have to do something. What if I am crazy? What if Letty's fine? Well, I am crazy—but I can't take the chance, I have to know. I have to see her cruel face before I'll quit.

He ran up to the office and found the front door locked. The lights were out, and the sign read: "Closed," though it was barely past noon.

Back door?

Andy skirted around the side of the building and spotted a door, but his eyes also sensed the painful bright and morphing colors on the periphery. He didn't want to look at whatever it was.

It might be important.

He sighed and chanced a look. Across the alley and behind the optometrist's office, there was a large metal gate that closed off a concrete underpass. Waves of inky steam rose from between the metal links and from under the corrugated siding interlaced with the fence. Jagged markings glowed across the metal surface. They were the unfamiliar language he had seen on the sign out front.

He heard a rumbling as he stepped closer to the

gate. Guttural voices reverberated on the other side, but they sounded far away. He noticed the lock was hanging open on the latch; the gate would swing open if he gave it a nudge. He grabbed the latch.

Stay calm.

As he opened the gate, he felt a cold wind across his forehead. He saw a streamer of inky mist reaching down from the arch to swing at him.

Andy recoiled, stumbling back until he slammed into the optometrist's office. A wave of the mist arced down and swung gently in front of the gate, as if waiting for him.

Andy suffered with the feeling that he was surrendering. He was afraid to approach the gate, and instead focused on the back door to the office. He found it open, and hoped Letty was still inside.

He quietly slipped in and let the door slowly creak shut behind.

He allowed himself a moment to breathe, but in those few seconds he felt a flood of common sense, personified in the voices of everyone he knew. Everybody would be screaming about this; they would be calling him crazy.

Only the mouse might understand, if he's even real.

Andy looked around the back room and saw two handbags and a few jackets lying on a table.

No. Please. Don't be—

He stepped forward and opened one of the handbags. He pulled out the wallet and found an ID inside. He read the name, Lysette Van Arndt.

"No—" he felt tears stinging his eyes. He wiped them away viciously.

Ink or no Ink, I'm going in there.

He gritted his teeth, walked back out the door, and was shocked to see a man locking the gate.

"No! I've got to get in there!"

Surprising himself, Andy rushed the man and grabbed for the keys.

"Get lost, you little thief!" The man struggled with Andy for the keys before he finally lashed out with his fist.

The impact sent Andy flying into the fence. His head buzzed with pain, making it difficult to open his eyes, but he kept his footing.

"Back off now; you don't want to know what I can do to you."

Andy lunged and shoved the man, who slipped on the slick alley floor and stumbled backwards.

"Give me the keys!" Andy demanded.

The man got to his feet and produced a switchblade from his pants pocket. The blade snapped open.

Andy felt his eyes flex, and for a moment he was certain that the man was as purple fleshed and red eyed as Ropt had been.

Andy bolted.

He slammed headfirst into a pedestrian. He tumbled back onto his feet and kept going, wiping the tears away as he ran. He raced across busy streets and was nearly struck by a car before he stopped, exhausted. His legs refused to move any further. He looked back with a sense of dread, but there was no one in pursuit, only a few people walking on the sidewalk. One stopped to look at him, but Andy ignored her.

I left them back there. But he was going to kill me. I can't help them if—

More people were staring. He felt a tickle at his nose. Rubbing it, he saw blood on his fingers. Looking around, Andy realized that he had run to the border of a city park. He walked down a shaded path and found a water fountain. He drank and cleaned his face as well as he could. Unsure where to turn, he continued further into the park.

I can't go back; they'll have people guarding the gate, and it's locked—and I might get stabbed. Maybe, if I get bolt cutters and come back tonight.

He walked up and down the paths, wanting to cry out at the faces that passed. His nose had stopped bleeding, though it throbbed, but he refused to notice the pain.

I can bleed tomorrow and I can sleep tomorrow.

He saw a mouse hiding beneath a park bench.

Sure.

He ignored it and walked on.

If I had money I could buy bolt cutters, but I can't go back to my parents. I haven't done anything to fix this! I've just—

Andy saw a pulsing glow at the edge of his vision. He looked closer and saw the Infiniteye painted on a brick wall, supporting a rail overpass.

Ha! There it is again!

He kept walking until he saw a bush rustling. He looked inside and saw a score of mice piled together, tussling. A few were familiar. The white mouse with the red face was clawing at the burgundy mouse.

Several others had formed up on both sides and looked ready to pile on. All at once, they noticed him peeking in on their shrub and stopped.

"Don't let me interrupt. It's only my brain melting." The mice stared, shock clear on their small, pointed faces. "Well, get back to it!"

Disgusted, he walked away from the bush. A dozen paces later, Andy stopped and sighed. As absurd as it was, the mice were his only option.

He sighed and turned back to the bush.

Looking in at the mice, he said, "So what about the symbol on that wall back there? I'm pretty sure it means something."

The mice clamored again. The red face ran towards him and pulled on his pant leg, pointing to the rail bridge, while others tried to stop him.

"Andy—" The red-faced mouse called his name, but was immediately silenced by a dozen paws clamping his mouth shut.

"Hey, play nice."

They ignored him, and a mass of mice grabbed the one with the red face and swarmed deeper into the shrubbery.

"Sure thing, guys. I've already heard you talk before, so there's no use in pretending you can't."

Andy continued down the path towards a round, cobbled plaza ringed with benches. He saw a familiar bald head and large round face, which appraised him with a wary look. It was the man he had bumped into in the gallery, sitting on a bench, glaring in his direction.

Andy felt uncomfortable. Then, as if

unprompted, he remembered the painting. He saw the painting moments after bumping into this man.

The Night Watch. Rembrandt was right the first time in the Windmill: Avoid eye physicians. The second painting—the second message said: The symbol guides our steps.

Andy turned on his heel and headed back towards the bridge with the Infiniteye.

Rembrandt hasn't led me astray yet. I should have listened to him in the first place.

He found the symbol and followed the path beneath the bridge. Moments later, he spotted another symbol scrawled next to a heavy metal door.

Andy grabbed the handle, turned it, and pushed. He almost fell off balance when the door opened smooth and silently. Incredulous, he saw the hinges had been well greased, and, though large amounts of garbage littered the path ahead, the space just behind the door was clear.

Andy closed the door behind him and headed down the brickwork service tunnel.

I'm under the rails.

The passage was dark and damp but he spotted the symbol again. It faintly lit the way with its quicksilver sheen.

Andy paused at a slight sound. He heard angry voices somewhere up ahead.

As he inched forward, the voices became clearer. He had the urge to turn back. The echo of their words was so grating, he felt goosebumps rise up his spine and arms, but he kept pushing forward.

This is it, Andy. It doesn't get any crazier.

"The boy isn't ready! He's too young!"

"It doesn't matter how old he is. He sees! We know he sees!"

"So he has a marginal gift, it doesn't mean his mind is capable of tolerating the full breadth of—"

"It's too late to argue, he's in their sights now. We might have already lost one to your over-cautious stance. If we don't educate him now, he'll be at great risk every day of his life!"

"If it's not the purple, the Usurper will have his way!"

Andy kept inching forward, careful of the empty cans and bottles.

Are they talking about me?

The voices were suddenly gone. Andy wondered if they had heard him. He froze and held his breath.

While waiting, he realized how dark it was. He knew that he shouldn't be able to see, but tufts of lichen growing on the brick gave off a faint blue-green glow. The broken bottles and piles of old leaves looked as if they had been blown by gusts of wind into erratic waves like dunes of swirled sand. He sidestepped the debris, and pushed the leaves out of his way, with his feet, instead of crunching them.

He had come to a turn in the path and was sure that the voices were just beyond. He peeked around the corner and saw his own eyes staring back. He nearly jumped.

A mirror? Oh—look at me.

About twenty feet up the hall, something reflective stood in his path. Even in the dim light he saw the bruise across the left side of his face. The mirror was a flat plane and, as he stared, it gave the impression of fluid glass, but he felt that what he was seeing must be impossible. His eyes tensed and he saw a sheer surface of brick, much like the rest of the wall.

He blinked and tried to focus.

My eyes are broken; they can't decide what's there.

The wall seemed to meld between brickwork and waves of glass. He saw no sign of the mice.

He advanced, alert for the slightest sound. He reached out and laid his palm against the wall. It felt vaguely warm, and responded like liquid smoke, swirling around his fingers.

Sooner or later I'll wake up, and I'll forget all about this, but until then—crazy impossible liquid wall, make way. I'm coming in.

Andy took a deep breath, as if before a dive, and stepped through.

On the other side, he was stunned by the immediate impression that he had grown into a giant.

The hall that had been there a moment ago was replaced by fortified mountainsides, and the ceiling above was ribbed like the roof of a cathedral. Turrets and crenellations looked carved from the mountain walls. Ballistae and catapults pointed squarely at him. But everything was miniature. The weapons and walkways and stairs were all made for people about half a foot tall. To his sides stood other doorways, though only the one he had just come through looked fluid. The others were blank.

It's a miniature fortress, but it's still huge. Did the mice do this? Everything is their size. They must guard these doors.

He leaned in to examine the weaponry and noticed the Infiniteye and several other symbols carved into the archways and facades of the fortifications. He heard scurrying, but saw nothing. He wondered if they had noticed him yet, and if they would try to kill him for intruding.

A glow came from up ahead, and he heard the faint echoes of conversation. The mountain fortress surrounded a nicely paved valley floor wide enough for Andy to pass through.

The floor was slick beneath his feet; he looked down and noticed that it was made of miniature cobblestones. A canal ran down the center, barely a few inches deep.

He moved forward, his hands outstretched for balance, and brushed against the carved fortress and delicate weapons running up the valley. He heard their conversation more clearly. It sounded like someone giving a speech.

"And this is why we must not take a new Seer into our protection!"

"No!" Yelled an adamant voice. "Times may be difficult, the Vychy may have won many to their side, but what would be better proof of our worth than arming a new Seer?"

He heard voices cheering in assent, others booing disagreement.

"Arm him? To what end? You want to see the Usurper lead another child to his death!"

The conversation was baffling.

Andy continued, but the mountain pass ended in a right turn. As he approached the curve, he saw the cavern roof reaching higher. There were arcing vines, reminiscent of ivy, racing upwards with the curve of the ceiling. Pulses of light glowed in waves up one strand of vines, then the next. The vines shimmered with many colors, but silver was predominant.

It's like the holidays, if people put lights on the sky.

Turning the corner, he saw chains stretching across the way at odd angles, blocking his progress. He felt the chains were intended to impede large things, like him, from penetrating any further. He reached out and grasped the first set of chains.

Maybe I can fit—

He lifted a leg and got half of himself through before he heard a shrill cry. It sounded like a tiny horn.

Did they spot me?

He finished pulling himself through and saw an absolute swarm of mice mount the battlements all around. They formed up in ranks on the ground before him, halberds arrayed like the spines of a hedgehog. They wore small suits of plate armor over simple robes.

Yeah—they spotted me.

"I'm not an enemy!" Andy insisted, as teams of mice readied the ballistae.

He felt the urge to do a little smashing if they became violent, but after a few seconds he realized how surrounded he was. There were thousands, and they would have him riddled in seconds.

Andy put up his hands.

The white mouse with the red face called out for order in the crowd. "This is our boy! Our new Seer! He's found us already! It is proof that the blood is strong! Lower your weapons this instant!"

The burgundy mouse disagreed. "No! No! He has invaded our colony! Fire! You on the parapets, fire!"

The mouse with the red face drew a heavy broadsword. The burgundy drew his own, and the crowd was on the verge of violence.

"Peace! Peace in the halls!" A powerful, if mouse sized, voice echoed through the pass and stilled the heated crowd.

They all lowered their weapons and gazed upward. Standing on a balcony at the tallest level was a venerable silver mouse. He raised his paw in a call for order.

"The praetor!" Andy heard them mutter back and forth.

The silver mouse continued, "We will treat the boy with the rights due his kind. If he is found capable, he will be shown the path, no more. Put up your arms and uphold your vows! Break the chains and part the towers! We have company!"

Chapter 7: Runaway Cygnus

Andy balked before the small, encircling army, as a team of mice crawled out onto the chains and unlocked them. The chain mice turned keys in locks and swung with the chains as they fell away from the path. The hedgehog of spikes gently poked him forward.

So much trouble just to open the door. They probably don't get too many guests down here. The burgundy mouse was leering his way. *Especially if that one has any say. It looks like he and my friend with the red face give orders, but they are both junior to the silver mouse.*

As they led him deeper, Andy gawked at miniature mountains, turned upside down and floating above the floor. They were different sizes, but most looked to be ten feet tall. Each mountain was carved through with arches, stairs, and halls. He could see right through the galleries of one, out onto the face of the next. These mountains hung in the air, a couple feet from the ground, and each was tied in place with half a dozen chains of its own. He saw one rigged with a series of propellers and rudders casting a hook down to a large ring on the ground. It was coming in to land.

Mice pedaled the propellers into reverse and slowed the mountain's descent.

Still more were being fitted with their own propellers, while one, in a docking area, was having its removed.

Chains stretched between cleats recessed in the

cobbled floor, while others linked the mountains in a network. Andy watched the mice work to move these aside. There were so many parked that they hemmed him in.

The mice unhitched their mountains from the floor in large teams of dozens to a chain. As they moved their mountain cities, a path slowly opened for him. He counted over twenty such mountain blocks moved for his sake.

He wanted to ask questions and thank them for being polite, though he couldn't help feeling like he was in some trouble. When the silver mouse called out orders and names he didn't recognize, mice rushed from the mob to obey.

The burgundy mouse gestured with hostility, while speaking to his cadre. Andy couldn't make out what he was saying, but he noticed a distinct group forming around the burgundy mouse. None of these looked pleased about his presence. Many bright colors speckled the mice, but teal clothing prevailed on or around the faces that looked at him coldly.

"I said, Gula cohort! Detach Cygnus!" The silver mouse commanded for the second time. Andy sensed a collective nervous twitch. The Gulas had missed an order from the silver mouse.

"Aye praetor!" Called the burgundy mouse, evidently their leader. "Gulas! Double quick, to the Cygnus!"

With that, his mice spilled out of the mob, their teal robes fluttering, and raced to a mountain block, quickly unchaining it. Their weapons and armor clanked as they moved. They had stacked their halberds into standing pyramids, interlocking their heads so they remained upright. A few mice guarded the weapons, while others, more agile than most, climbed the chains. The rest, led by the biggest and strongest, arrayed themselves on the released chains to pull the floating mountain.

It looks like the pressure on those chains is pulling skyward. Those mountains want to float away.

Andy was charmed by the sight, but it was all beyond reason. He wondered what else didn't make sense down here.

He wanted to ask about the floating mountains, or why the burgundy mouse considered him such a threat. More than that, he wanted to ask what would happen to him, but he wouldn't risk upsetting them. The field of points following at his heels underscored that doubt. Not helping matters was the torrent of shrill cries and the general ruckus produced by thousands of industrious mice.

The silver mouse appeared from the fortifications with his armored bodyguards. Both praetor and his guard were clad in gleaming plated armor, and where the praetor wore a purple cape, the guard wore purple sashes and plumes in their helms.

Andy noticed that Cygnus, the nearest mountain block, didn't move out of his way at the same speed the others had. He had to slow and stop as he was now face to face with the floating mountain.

A child mouse in a window wailed at seeing

Andy, a giant, peeking into his window.

"Gulas! Report!" A mouse in purple fringe called out.

There were cries of alarm and a sudden rush as the mountain slammed into Andy. He stumbled backwards and saw the field of halberds ready to catch him if he fell.

"Nope!" Andy declared. He reached out and grabbed Cygnus.

His fingers ripped through walls and furniture before grasping tight.

"Sorry! I'm sorry!" He said to the chorus of screams that echoed through the mountain block.

With a gasp, Andy realized that Cygnus was pulling him off the ground.

"I'm going up!" he said, his toes scraping the floor.

"Dextra! To the boy!" The mouse with the red face led his brigade in a lightning-fast climb up Andy's legs and arms, into Cygnus.

The mouse with the red face was on his shoulder in a flash and desperate for his attention. "Lysander!"

"What do we do?" Andy cried.

"Hold! We're moving the civilians to the upper levels, so you can get a better grip."

"Okay, then what?"

"One step at a time! Just don't slip off!" The mouse left his shoulder to direct the others.

Teams were coming with heavier chains. They climbed up his legs. Andy felt like he had the strength to pull Cygnus down, but he couldn't get purchase with his feet. Worse still, his feet kicked off against another mountain in their flailing, and he suddenly felt Cygnus moving faster.

"The bottom is clear!" The lead mouse called out to him from inside.

Andy moved his hands to a better position, and let his body hang against the floating mountain. His feet were now a few inches off the ground. Though teams of mice were pulling at the new chains, it didn't slow Cygnus.

Andy looked in every direction he could. "Can I get a grip on one of the other mountains?" he called out to anyone who would listen.

"It would be too much pressure on their chains! We're moving too fast." Andy looked into Cygnus and saw the mouse with the red face staring squarely at him. "Now isn't the best time, but I'm Titus, and I know who you are. We can't use the other blocks as ballast, and we can't allow ourselves to fly up into the cavern. If we do, Cygnus will be blasted by the storms, and we'll fall to our deaths."

Andy stared at Titus. "What do you want me to do?"

"The wall! The wall!" A cry went up, and the mice were pointing off to the distance.

Andy and Titus saw marble statues ringing the city. They were coming closer.

"The shield wall!" Titus called out, "Use your legs to get hold!"

Andy tried to comply but slammed into a statue. He felt his grip on Cygnus slip, but he tightened his left leg over the statue's shoulder and tried to wrap the other around the statue's neck. He had the sudden impression it was bright out, though he was staring at the gray mountainside of Cygnus. The marble of the statuary was glowing.

"What are all these statues doing here?" Andy asked, still struggling.

"They are our city wall," Titus replied.

One of Andy's fingers lost its grip.

"I'm slipping!"

A team of mice wrapped a chain around a marble arm.

"Grab hold!" Titus yelled.

Andy reached and got a firm grip with both of his hands but his legs slipped free of the statue. The chain snapped and a stream of dust and marble chips rained down. Frightened, Andy reached with his legs, but only kicked them further away from the city.

They were headed toward rocky and rooted ground.

"Titus? Will those roots hold?" Andy asked.

"They might—" Titus cupped his hands to his mouth and called out, "Chain teams, lead us to the badlands! We will tie down to the roots!"

Two more teams had tied their chains around the thick columns of Cygnus, and jumped out to the ground, pulling in the right direction.

After a moment they drifted closer to the roots. Andy felt his arms getting sore. He knew they wouldn't be able to hold for much longer.

I can't let go yet.

"A little bit more, Andy, there are hundreds of

us in here! We need you to hold!"

Andy held.

The chain teams howled out in victory as they hopped over the jutting roots, wrapping their chains around as they went. Andy felt some of the lateral movement in Cygnus slow as the chains tightened. His feet scraped a root.

"No! Watch out!" A voice cried as a chain ripped free.

Another snapped and tore chunks of the mountain away. The chain whipped out through the air and struck Andy across the side.

He grunted with the sudden sting.

"Cygnus is so brittle from being carved through; its structure can barely stand the pressure!" Titus yelled.

The mice flew off the chains as they ripped away, landing in piles on the badlands.

I've got to do something—maybe if I—

Andy tried to get his foot under one of the jutting roots, but it slipped. He felt himself rise again.

"Again! Wrap another chain around a root!" Andy called out to the mice.

There was only one chain team left, but they obeyed. Andy felt Cygnus lower right before the last chain burst free. His foot grazed a root.

There!

He kicked and jammed his shoe beneath the root.

"I've got it!" Andy called out.

Andy felt Cygnus pull against his body. The

root slowly lifted away from the ground. He felt his muscles and limbs stretching past their limits. He pulled and felt the root slip.

No!

Andy let go of Cygnus with his left hand and reached down to another root. He grabbed a hold and, with one hand grasping a root, and the other on Cygnus, he pulled with all his strength, forcing them as close together as he could.

Cygnus cracked and shuddered. Hundreds of mice screamed, the sound echoing through Cygnus as a fracture ran up the side of the mountain.

Andy found a foothold for his other foot, jammed it in place, and grabbed the mountain with both hands before pulling with every limb.

"Stay with it!" Titus yelled into his ear. The mouse was hanging from his shirt collar and lending his own weight to the effort.

Finally, Andy felt the momentum die. The mountain stopped trying to tear him in two.

He twisted his body around and put both arms over his head to hold onto Cygnus. He pulled forward until the mountain finally rested on his shoulders.

That's as close as it gets.

Cygnus was at rest.

A cheer went up from the mice.

"Well done, Lysander!" Titus said for everyone to hear.

"Andy, please."

Not daring to move, he held his position as more chains were brought and attached to Cygnus.

He listened as the mice discussed what had happened. No one knew why the mountain had lunged so strongly.

Andy felt Titus grab his collar and lean into his ear. "The Gulas, Lysander. It was blatant; I am certain that they are responsible."

"How do you know?" Andy asked as quietly as he could, but scores of suspicious glances came his way.

Titus's voice quavered as he spoke out of the side of his mouth, "Don't bother whispering, Lysander; anyone with ears can hear you."

Andy smiled awkwardly to the crowd as more chains arrived to relieve him.

The praetor came and oversaw the work. "That was a breath away from disaster, newcomer. This will work in your favor during the tests to come."

"Thank him!" Titus whispered in Andy's ear.

"Thank you, sir—"

"Don't call him 'sir,' call him praetor!" Titus interrupted.

"Uhm—thank you, praetor—I didn't even know what I was doing until it was over."

The praetor's face bent with a slight smile. "Of course. Virtue is spontaneous—particularly in the young."

Andy didn't know what to say.

After a moment they asked him to let go. He slowly loosened his grip on Cygnus. Chunks of the mountain slid away as he freed his hands from its mass. Andy cringed as he dusted his hands and eyed the deep fissures running up the mountain. The chain mice had a strong grip, and they towed it back into the city.

"What caused Cygnus to jar so strongly?" The praetor asked.

Nobody had an answer.

"What are we going to do about the damage? That split runs all the way to the core," others were complaining.

"The masons will see to the repairs, and they will investigate the source of the catastrophe." The praetor answered the crowd as Cygnus finally stood in its place, securely chained to the ground.

Andy stretched his arms. A dull ache filled his limbs as he finally let himself recognize the pain. He stretched and let out a slight groan, but Titus called up to him.

"Lysander! Don't lose focus."

"Andy, please," he said to Titus, who was busy calling for water and food.

Andy sat down, taking up an indecent amount of space in a mouse plaza, and tried to ignore the aching.

"We should have a moment to feed you before the test begins." Titus said looking over his shoulder.

"No prompting the invad—newcomer," said the burgundy mouse, approaching them.

"Be gone, Coriolus! I expect you have evidence to hide." Titus put his paw to his sword and motioned for his brigade to form a wall between them and the Gulas.

The soldiers faced off, but they were all wary of the mice wearing purple, who approached and scoffed. Shamed, both sides broke off.

"That was Coriolus, my unfortunate peer in the Departmentum Expeditia—but we have no time for introductions or formalities. The test!" Titus said.

Titus had gone very serious at the sight of Coriolus and his mice.

"What's this test? I haven't studied," Andy said, suddenly anxious.

"No, not like your schoolhouse tests. The praetor will test your character, test your loyalty, and test your eyes. The first and the last you have already proven. But the second—"

"Look, Titus, I don't have time for this. I need to find Letty. She and her family have been taken. You mice are everywhere, especially when something weird is happening. Let's put off the test and find her. Together we might—"

Titus shook his head sadly. "That isn't how things work here, Lysander. If you run from the test they'll—" He took a heavy breath and ran a finger across his throat.

Andy grimaced and looked to the praetor. "But I just helped—"

"Of course you did. The failed attempt to sabotage your introduction by the Gulas might be just what saves your life—" Andy tried to interrupt, but Titus spoke over him, "The praetor's guard is coming to escort you to the Amphitheater. Do as they say! Answer honestly. Coriolus will try to derail us, but I have a plan to deal with him. I'm sorry I can't feed you yet, they're eager to start."

"Titus! I have to find Letty; I don't have time for

this!"

"You have to save yourself first."

Despite the mouse face, Andy saw concern in his expression.

"Newcomer! You will accompany us to the Amphitheater. We are ready to receive you." The guards were cordial, but Andy could tell by their stances that they were ready to fight at the slightest hint of disobedience.

Andy followed the escort deeper into town, but they marched quickly, and he could only glance at the floating structures and the mice among them.

"What is your city called?"

"Sentinel's Watch," a bodyguard said.

The cobblestone lanes and plazas terminated against a wall of sculptures and artifacts that ringed the outer portion of the city. The inner portion butted against a mountain that reached up to the cavern ceiling and the lights there.

The portal into the park is back where the city meets the mountain, near the mouse-sized fortresses.

The statuary that ringed the city shone with a silver glow that was dwarfed by the riotous colors pulsing so far above. Despite the contrast, Andy felt himself drawn to the warm light.

"What's with the wall of statues?" Andy asked.

The bodyguard seemed confused by the question, "They are all Grecian. Many are Athenian, though the western flank is largely Corinthian. Most date to 400 BC."

Andy found this surprising. What he wanted to

know was why they were there, but at hearing this, his line of thought changed. "How long have they been here?" He asked, still not convinced.

The bodyguard didn't answer. His question had prompted a pained look that Andy could just see, thanks to the guard's raised visor.

"Why do they shine like that?"

"Positive etherium pigment keeps away most trouble. It coats many of our weapons too."

Etherium?

Andy walked with them over the path prepared between the mountain blocks. He saw Cygnus floating near the fortified cavern wall. Engineers were busy at work repairing the cracks. He caught sight of mouse children running from mountain to mountain across rope and plank bridges. They were watching him attentively and whispering.

When they approached the Amphitheater, Andy noticed that Titus was already present. The mice could walk under their floating mountains, where his human sized path zig-zagged across town.

The Amphitheater was carved out of the cavern wall. The great ring of rising seats reached to about twice his height. Every seat was taken.

He remembered standing in center of a stadium once as a child. It was an empty stadium his father got them into, and he learned that it seated 50,000 people. Despite his new size, this amphitheater looked the same.

Is this 50,000, mice? Is it more?

Andy started to feel nervous. He saw the praetor, Titus, Coriolus, and a few other, older mice, in what reminded him of graduation robes, complete with mortarboards and colored cords. The group was in heated discussion.

"He must stand before each trial now. None may be delayed!" Coriolus was reading from a scroll, "It is spelled out plainly, look here—" he gestured angrily, trying to get Titus and the praetor to pay attention.

"Listen here, you sad coward, the boy has saved lives, lives your poorly led cohort put in danger! You should be hanging your tail in shame and skulking back to the shadows after that blatant sabotage!"

Andy was grateful to have Titus on his side.

"Would you accuse the Gulas of your own treachery?" Coriolus feigned a look of disgust and shock all at once.

The praetor raised a brow at the saber-rattling, ending their argument. He gestured to the audience. "Will the boy face the challenges immediately? Vote now!"

The mice crowding the stage rushed to their seats. Andy watched as each mouse cast a token into one of two, almost imperceptible holes at the base of each seat. Two tanks received the tokens, one marked Yea, and the other Nay.

Andy was surprised at how swiftly the tanks filled with tokens. Though both were filling at the same pace, many were still discussing the issue before casting their vote. But then Andy noticed the Gulas, by the green brocade and plumage they wore, jostling through the seated mass of mice, nudging here and whispering there. He saw coins change paws.

They're giving out bribes!

Andy looked at the praetor, who could clearly see what was happening.

"Praetor, sir?"

"Silence!" A guard called up to him.

Titus looked his way and motioned for him to remain quiet.

The vote was in. Yea had won.

"The trials will begin immediately," the praetor announced.

Coriolus cast a smug glance their way.

"Retrieve!" The praetor called. The mice rushed the stage in waves. Dozens of dispensers on the sides of the tanks returned the tokens.

Andy expected it to take forever, but again, they were swift. A few mice tried to take more than one token. These were apprehended by the guards, lashed, and thrown out.

"Very well," the praetor announced. "So we begin. Scribes?"

"Present and able!" the robed mice said, scrolls and quills at the ready.

"State your name for the Misenmot!"

"And—hm—" Andy cleared his throat. "Lysander Vanavarre."

"Proof and a voucher?"

Andy could only stare.

"I and the whole Dextra vouch for Vanavarre!" Titus called out.

Coriolus jumped to his feet and shouted, "I— and the Gula counter-vouch against this invader!"

The praetor was tired of the bickering. "There is no such stance, Coriolus. Scribes, count the boy vouched—but proof?"

Andy found his wallet in a back pocket and produced his school ID. He held it out for them to see.

"Down here, boy." The praetor waved him down.

Andy slowly took a knee, careful not to crush anyone, and held out the card. Thousands of mice leaned forward to look.

"Can we trust a document from the tainted halls of men?" Coriolus bellowed.

"Indeed!" Titus retorted, "What other proof can a human offer? And further, what proof would a hateful traito—erm—What proof could ever satisfy you?" Titus struggled to hold back another wave of furious insults.

The praetor motioned him to take the ID away. "Identity proven!"

A quick cheer went up from the crowd, though the guards motioned for silence. Andy saw that many were on his side.

"How did you come to this place, Vanavarre?" The praetor asked.

The audience quieted, listening for his reply. "I followed the sign, the Infiniteye."

There was a curious mumbling.

"The boy has clearly seen the sign; he has found this place, but let us hold to tradition." The praetor paused and held up a scroll. "What do you see here?"

Andy leaned in.

There's nothing there.

He suddenly felt nervous.

What do they expect me to say?

He remembered Titus urging him to be honest.

"I see nothing."

The audience heaved a sigh of relief.

"And here." Another scroll unfurled.

The Infiniteye glowed across the page.

"This is the symbol I followed."

A cheer went up, far louder than the first.

"The blood is strong," Titus insisted.

The guards struggled to silence the crowd. Coriolus and his men struck a menacing contrast with their grim faces.

"The proof stands, you have the violet eyes, you see, but are not yet a Seer in the eyes of our order."

Andy took a deep breath.

One last test.

"Loyalty—the most difficult to prove," the Praetor said.

Titus approached the stage, Coriolus close behind.

"The boy saved Cygnus! His muscles tore, and his body crashed against our walls to preserve our own from destruction! Countless lives spared a gruesome death. The boy's heart is pure!" Titus concluded, glaring at Coriolus and daring him to disagree.

The praetor gestured for Coriolus to say his part. "Yes, the boy helped to save Cygnus from a potential catastrophe—I won't dwell on the fact that the catastrophe was suspicious in the first place." He cast a doubtful glance towards Titus and Andy.

"But the praetor said it best a moment ago. Some virtue acts in an instant, without thought. Yet, it is a different being altogether who has a moment to think. This boy must be tested in a way that proves his loyalty over the long term. Give his thoughts the chance to be self-serving, and you will likely find that the boy abandons us to his baser desires."

He's right, I can't sit around for a long test. I need to find Letty.

Andy glanced at Titus, who pointed back to the audience with a forceful look.

"There! See there how the boy looks to his handler, who most assuredly coached him through this test—and dare I venture to lay blame for the late catastrophe at their scheming feet as well!"

There was a grumble at this.

"I—only—" Andy stumbled over his words. He felt himself getting angry, "You unchained Cygnus and lost control of it!"

"Or perhaps when you sunk your titan's claws into our homes, you wrested control and created a false emergency—a false emergency! For the purposes of ingratiating yourself upon fine, unsuspecting mice such as these," Coriolus gestured out to the crowd.

The praetor raised a palm to calm the grumbling. "We will hear no accusations. This assemblage must decide the boy's fate. An investigation will be the forerunner to any decision on the Cygnus incident."

That soothed the crowd. The praetor scratched his chin and wondered for a moment.

"I propose the young Vanavarre escort our foragers from Cair Fromage back to Sentinel's Watch. His presence will intimidate the bandits and the Vychy alike, and prove his patience and loyalty to our purpose. He will also have the chance to learn more about us and our traditions."

The crowd approved of the proposal. The Gulas did not. Coriolus tried to interrupt, but the praetor continued before he had a chance, "Vote!"

The mob voted as the Gulas rushed in with bribes, but it was too late. Andy watched as the tube marked Yea filled almost to the top.

"So, it is decided!" The praetor called. "Young Vanavarre, I attach you as a specialist to the Dextra cohort under the command of Expeditious Extraordinary Titus. You will set out at once for Cair Fromage."

The crowd cheered and Titus climbed up to his shoulder in an instant, "Don't be brash! I know what you're thinking."

Andy was thinking that he had no time for escort duty.

"Listen to me! Turn around and walk! And for God's sake don't step on anyone!"

Andy sighed and did as he was told, taking extra care of his feet around the hordes of mice.

Titus called out to the crowd, "Dextra!"

A few hundred voices went up from their places in the crowd, "Aye!"

"Armaments and supplies for two day's travel. Form up outside the Twins!"

"Aye, sir!"

Andy saw the blue sashes and plumage of the Dextra move with purpose through the crowds.

"Titus—" Andy whispered when they were free from the masses.

"No, do not complain!" Titus interrupted loudly into his ear. "We are lucky to get what we did; I think the praetor approves of you, but Coriolus almost had us."

Andy sighed. "If I leave to find Letty, what will happen to me?"

Titus paused before whispering, "He's sent us in the likeliest direction to find her."

"What?" Andy gasped, "Really?"

Titus grabbed him by the collar, "Keep it down, boy! Your voice will shatter windows, and rouse suspicion."

"Sorry," Andy whispered, "but, what's the plan? When do we leave?"

Titus laughed and tugged on Andy's shirt collar to turn him right. "That way first."

They approached a few tall silos. "You need to eat and drink, so do my mice." Titus climbed down and found a few of his Dextra stocking their packs with supplies. "Head out past the twins—the two sisters armed for war—and turn right after about one hundred of your giant steps. There is a spring and a well laden apple tree. Eat and drink your fill, but be quick about it, and meet us back by the twins."

Chapter 8: The Netherscape

Andy followed the canal of Sentinel's Watch to the wall of glowing statuary that ringed the settlement. He found the gateway chained and saw the statues on both sides were twin women bearing round shields and short swords.

Andy bent and stuck a leg through the chains. Halfway through, he noticed a pair of guards staring at him from the ground. Embarrassed, Andy explained, "I've got to help out at Cair—something."

They nodded. "Cair Fromage, and you could have waited a moment; we would've taken the chains down."

Still hunched, Andy blinked. "Sorry about that, I'll remember next time."

One guard rolled his eyes, while the other shrugged.

I didn't see them and now they think I'm being rude. I need to pay attention.

With the embarrassment behind him, Andy followed the canal and saw the grove of apple trees. He took in the sight of a wide pool nestled between the trees. He heard the stream trickling in from the cavern wall and saw the colors, high above, reflecting in the still water.

The apples look great, or maybe I'm just starving.

Andy walked the distance and ran a hand over a trunk. The tree seemed normal, but something bothered him. Was it too dark for trees to grow?

He looked at the cavern ceiling and saw the

endless expanse of glowing vines.

"Hmm."

Andy noticed that the leaves weren't quite green, though he had a hard time saying what color they were. He thought purple, or a deep red.

Hunger reasserting itself, he ignored the leaves and plucked a few apples. He bit into the first and found it refreshing. He quickly ate three and then knelt down by the spring.

This water flows into the town, it must be good to drink.

Andy felt a slight nervousness about drinking, but he cupped his hands in the stream and drank. Everything grew brighter as the cool water ran down his throat. It was perfect.

Andy drank more and more. He felt his vision clearing. He took a deep breath and felt calmness come over him. He sat still, above the water and let the moment stretch, until he sensed something was wrong.

He felt eyes, watching.

Andy had the urge to bolt back to town, but kept still.

He took a breath and let his gaze drift towards a slight motion. There was a staring face. It poked through an embankment of reeds a few feet away. The face was expressionless and smooth, like carved glass.

He heard a snap and the thing shot from the reeds and was on him in seconds.

"Stay back!" Andy tumbled as he rolled to his feet, his hands and knees suddenly muddy from the rush.

"Back, back, back, ever back." A hollow voice resounded through the grove. It was right behind him and distant all at once.

The lithe frame with the glass face circled, turning its body by degrees as it weaved between trees, though its eyes locked on him for every moment of their circuitous chase.

Andy slammed against a tree. The thing lurched sideways, leaping one moment, then shuffling and lunging the next. It stopped, inches from his face.

"Back to before you."

"What?" Caught by its blank, dead eyes, Andy thought he was in a nightmare. "What do you want?"

It stared at him, face to face. After its excited dance, Andy noticed that, in contrast to his heaving for breath, the thing was now motionless.

"Permit, will." Its hand shot up to Andy's forehead, and paused an inch away, as if waiting for consent.

Andy slipped between the thing and the tree. "Don't touch me!" He backed away, tripped over a root and tumbled to the ground.

"Permit!" The sound had a tinnier, almost insistent edge as it coursed through the trees.

Andy backed away on his hands. He was shaking and couldn't stand. He looked up and saw there was something more to its face.

It danced a step forward. Its torso spun independently of its legs and a second face locked onto his.

At first, the faces might look identical, but there were fine differences. One bore the vaguest trace of a grimace, where the other had its brows just turned up in an expression of grief.

"Who are you?" Andy asked.

"Two things, neither of them now." The words came to him through the reeds. "I see her."

That was the last thing he expected it to say.

Does it mean Letty?

"Letty," the voice echoed his thought.

Its hand twisted all the way around, the fingers gesturing for calmness.

"Fine." He braced himself for it to lay a hand on his forehead.

When it did, Andy felt like he had been hit by a wave. A rush of sound and sight tore across his senses and shocked the breath from him. He felt like screaming. His mouth was shut but a sharp cry tore through his mind.

The sensory rush halted. He was standing in the museum. Dean was there. Andy could see that Dean was talking, but couldn't hear his voice. It was like listening to someone underwater.

Why am I seeing this? Andy wondered.

"Here, here! Lysandy boy! Here!" It was inside his head, talking alongside his own inner voice.

He turned and saw the bronze statue. Instead of burnished bronze, the statue was aflame. White and silver arcs of light raced off its body. The serpent however, dripped with very different colors, deep purple, crimson red, and sea green all twisted in a flux.

"Look, boy!"

The images moved backwards. Andy watched his conversation with Dean rewind. The movements paused at the moment he had brushed against the statue.

He saw Dean fall out of his chair laughing.

The moment faded away and the rushing tide of images and noise swept back over him until he was gaping at the thing's face.

The head twisted around slowly, the sad face gave way to the grimace, and the other hand came up. Andy didn't resist, but he noticed something.

The grimace was wider.

When the hand reached his forehead, he felt a buffeting wind from behind. The force of it pushed him violently forward. The flashes and noise were different; they were disjointed and broken, half-formed and discolored.

"Andylys Navarre! Ensconced, ensorcelled, enveloped, entombed. No word quite catches the way you are caught. Destined for freedom, yet unfree from destiny. Where most sparks are mere punctuation—commas and colons at worst, periods and indentations at best—You! You will be spoken like an Argument. Hahaha! That was a joke that you do not yet know to hate, just as I was once companion to a person you will not know how to hate."

"What are you talking about?"

"What are you being about, Dylysand? Every hand will grasp for you, yet one has already won." The voice cracked with laughter like lightning across the sky, as a moment in time froze before his eyes. In this moment, he was looking up at a giant silver orb.

The moment passed and the voice cried, "Thus solvent!"

Andy blinked, and instead of the orb, saw Letty bound and laying on a stone table.

"She lays, tied, trussed, an offering! Seer's blood for knowledge is their accord."

"Where is she?"

"See! Eyes thee see!"

Like a pair of blades, two massive yellow eyes floated in the air above Letty's body.

"Ahh—ahah!" The voice cracked wildly, as if in pain.

Letty disappeared, and her agonized face burned like fire across his mind. He felt a pop, reminiscent of pressure change, and his eyes opened.

"Flense the wretch!" Titus's voice rang out, followed by a roar of loosed crossbow bolts.

"No!" Andy shot up and yelled.

The thing was peppered with glowing bolts. It tumbled backwards and deftly leaped into the pool.

Titus was on his shoulder in a flash and speaking into his ear, "Calm down lad, we're here!"

"He was showing me! Letty's in trouble!"

Titus ignored him and called out orders. "First maniple, ring the pool! Shoot at anything that moves. Second, to the boy! Apply the minoe." Titus was looking down into his eyes, "My boy! I'm so sorry, I shouldn't have let you go—it was just beyond the twins—I was certain you would come to no harm."

"It's okay, Titus; it wasn't that bad." Andy rubbed at the back of his head. The mice were applying a salve. He brushed their paws away, and looked at his fingers. There was blood coming from the back of his head. His throat hurt, like he had been screaming.

"The Twister is a murderer. We shall burn a million aphids in thanks for your survival."

Andy didn't follow. "Burn—what? Titus, don't burn anything. And don't take this—" Andy grunted with the effort of standing, "—as an excuse to treat me like a child."

Titus laughed; a few of his mice tried to join in, but Andy felt their sense of dread would not abate. He groaned and sat back down, letting them go to work on his wounds.

Minutes later, Titus said, "Brave lad, independent to the last. Is there any pain?"

Andy put his hand to the back of his head and found it dry. "No, I feel fine. The pain is gone."

"That's the minoe, you might remember it from the night we first spoke."

Andy did recall waking to find them brushing his limbs. It was the night after he ran into the mist at the gallery.

"This minoe was what they used to cleanse the mist," Titus said, watching as the mice arrayed themselves in marching columns.

"We can't sit around and hunt all day, but the Twister can sit at the bottom forever, so we're back on directive. Second maniple, send a squad of runners back to refill our stock of minoe, it may be needful ahead. The squad will regroup with us on the road."

The order was relayed by the Second manipular commander, a centurion, and then a more specific order was given by the centurion. Andy watched as Titus pointed out the details of the maniple reforming. Titus had taken to commanding from atop Andy's shoulders.

They made their way to the road as the runners headed back into town. "Are you going to stay on my shoulders, Titus?"

The mouse wrinkled his brow as he held a paw out to Andy's collar for balance. "Well—it is a damn good view up here—and," he trailed off.

"And what?" Andy asked seriously.

"A human mount is a rare badge of honor."

Andy bent his neck to glare at him.

"No, no—don't think of it that way—think of a knight on a warhorse!"

"That's not much better, but since you saved me from the—you called him the Twister?"

"Yes." Titus said with an edge of concern. "You are feeling normal—nothing strange at all?"

"Besides the blood, which your minoe took care of, I'm fine."

"Good," Titus said.

"Can I ask you something?"

"Certainly, we have some time on the road."

"How is it that trees and grass can grow down here?"

Titus laughed. "We don't have biologists and the like, which you have grown used to on the surface, but it is said that vinlight from above acts much like sunlight in your world."

"Vinlight? You must mean the light coming from the glowing plants."

Titus nodded.

"Are there few like me? It sounded like you haven't had a Seer around for some time."

Titus tugged at a whisker. "The ryle are effective. We try, but as you experienced, most fall prey to their examinations."

"When was the last Seer here?"

"Well, there are others living in the Netherscape—"

"Netherscape," Andy repeated glancing up at the cavern ceiling.

"Of course, where'd you think you were?"

Andy scowled.

"Not all of it is reachable via traditional methods, but yes, this realm is part of the Netherscape—the details of which I will let others bore you with, but to return to the question of Seers. Consider the Elazene, for instance. Their cowardice aside, they share blood with you. Seers from the surface are hard to find, and harder to keep. The Usurper is worse than anything else—but you won't need to worry about that for some time."

"What?" Andy asked. "Who is the Usurper?"

"Just another monster who will try to enslave you," Titus spat.

Several mice shared nervous glances.

"Fine, but what is a Seer then?"

Titus took a long moment. "To be a Seer has meant many things. The past few thousand years were tumultuous. At one time it meant being a warlord, at another, it made you a philosopher, and in more modern times, it makes you a fugitive. Our order is old enough to encompass this all. Despite a certain rigid timelessness and certainty, we may not serve you best in these late days, Lysander. For in every age, being a Seer has meant being a hunter, a killer, and the most valuable commodity to your ancient enemy, the ryle."

"The ryle," Andy repeated, the word almost familiar.

"Keep your thoughts and let them branch. Questions and fears should fight within. When one defeats the other, then you might know what path is right. Until then, you are going along with us on a simple mission. I will make certain you have a chance to go back to the surface, if you reject this life."

"What if I want to find Letty?"

"That may be beyond you, Lysander. There are beings down here even the champion Seers of old would flee."

Andy remembered the yellow, viper eyes.

"The Twister showed me something."

Titus shook his head and his ears flattened, as if nervous.

"What? Does it lie?"

"No one has ever survived an encounter."

Andy was silent. They walked on quietly.

If no one has survived, that means no one knows if it shows you the truth.

That was disappointing, though Andy felt the visions were real. Her face was real.

"You said it showed you something," Titus said. Andy noticed the Dextra were listening. He knew that no whisper could hide what he said.

He was ashamed to answer but felt he owed it to Titus and his mice to be honest. "I saw my past, a moment from a few days ago. It was when I bumped into the statue, the same day I saw you for the first time."

Titus nodded, his ears high and attentive.

"Then it—I'm not sure. It showed me what I wanted to know, in exchange for what it wanted to know. I think that was the deal. I asked it where Letty was. It showed me. I saw her bound on a stone table. But there was something else there."

Titus remained silent.

"Something with giant yellow eyes. They were the kind with bladed slits for pupils."

Titus huffed in surprise.

Andy expected that Titus wouldn't know, but he had to ask, "Did it show me the truth?"

"Like I said, no one we know of has ever lived. You are the first. The archivists will want to interview you. Sadly, no one can say if what you saw was true."

Andy sighed. "Maybe it's better that way."

A call went up from a returning scout, "Alert at Cyburn! The yellow banner flies!"

"Hmm," Titus murmured before giving orders,

"We are obliged to investigate. Pacward at the fork!"

The cohort turned left at a fork in the trail.

"What is Cyburn?" Andy asked.

Titus pointed. Andy saw another floating mountain not too far off, at the peak of a natural hill in the caverns. There were low walls and fields zig-zagging the landscape nearby.

"The holds are named for the first family to tame a cyclostone and make it livable. The Cyburns were always independents. They have refused to join with the O.O., the Occidentus Obscurus. Yet they also resist the Vychy, our enemies. In a way, the Cyburns benefit from their neutrality; they can trade goods or knowledge to either side. As long as they preserve a standard of neutrality, either faction will protect them from the other."

As they approached, conversation on both sides of the wall ceased.

"You mentioned something called the O.O.?" Andy whispered.

"That's us; try to keep up."

"Right, but who are the Vychy then? I've heard that name a few times."

"They are the traitor mice who have chosen the wrong path. They radically discourage loyal mice from the righteous life. They would let young people like you fall prey. I suspect our friend Coriolus to be a Vychy collaborator."

That the mice weren't unified was distressing to Andy.

"Wait, I saw Coriolus looking after Letty."

Titus cringed. "Yes, I expect he and his Gulas

deliberately failed to protect her."

Andy nearly screamed in outrage.

"Careful! Careful, now!" Titus said.

I'll make him pay.

Before Andy could ask another question, a bell rang.

"Hail Expeditious!" A voice called to them from a watchtower.

"Hail! Mice of Cyburn!"

Hundreds of the Cyburn approached and scaled the walls for a look. They were mottled in color. He saw browns and reds, greys, and even some cold blues among them.

"A mighty mount you've tamed, Expeditious! You must let us have a look at him!"

Andy ruffled, upset at being seen as an elephant.

"Not today, I'm afraid. He's on the path to being a Seer! Or close enough now, he's on the third trial!"

The Cyburn sentinel was hounded by questions from his people, but he pushed them away. "A Seer?"

"Look at his eyes!" Voices called out from the wall.

Titus leaned in and whispered to Andy, "Stare at the pediment above the gateway into Cyburn hold."

Andy did, and saw a new symbol etched there, he felt his eyes work to focus on it.

The crowd gasped.

"Violet eyes. History walks among us," The sentinel muttered, loud enough to be heard.

Andy thought he sensed shame in the words.

"What is the alert, Cyburn? We are on directive, but we have time for old friends."

"No great concern, Expeditious. We sighted the Twister, mere hours ago. The monster was headed sur."

"Don't say a thing," Titus whispered into Andy's ear. And then loudly to the sentinel, "Yes, we ran him off not long ago, it cost us a few bolts in the process. Say—Cyburn? Is there any other news?"

"There might be." The sentinel seemed cautious, and eyed Andy nervously.

They are afraid of me.

Titus motioned towards his men. Andy felt tension rising again.

A dozen Dextra moved towards the gates and left a few heavy bags. Mice from inside came out and retrieved them. A chorus of whispers rose on both sides. Titus quieted his mice with a gesture.

"Very good, Titus! Blue hops are always appreciated."

"I'd have brought barrels of our blue, but I know how specific you are about beer in Cyburn. Brew it in good health, friend!" Titus answered patiently.

"As to the other news. There is word on the aphid wing that another Seer was retrieved recently. Female, dark hair, about the age of this one here. She's with a trio of brutox who command at least a cohort's worth of slithers. They were headed nor by nor-lanticward. The sighting is not three hours old."

Titus nodded gravely. "The blood is strong," he said in an almost reverent voice.

Andy noticed the sentinel wince and look to the floor. Many of the other Cyburns were bothered as well.

146

"We must hurry! Dextra, about face! Double quick to the road!" Titus commanded.

The mice bounded forward on all fours down the path, their weapons slung over their backs. Andy had to pick up his pace. They moved at a speed between a fast walk and a slow run.

"Was that—did they mean?"

"Calm yourself. It may be nothing, but from the looks of their faces—I don't know."

"Are we going nor by nor-lanticward, whatever that means?" Andy asked.

"It's almost the same way to Cair Fromage. But it was hours ago they were spotted, Andy. They are far gone by now."

Andy kept silent as they jogged across the endless cavern. It was huge beyond description. He was amazed by the farms and cities he had seen, even if they were mouse-sized. Though Letty could have been mere miles away, he knew that he had to stay with the mice, at least for the moment.

Andy looked over his shoulder and noticed the hill sinking behind thorny shrubs, reminiscent of ragged, hedge-sized trees.

A scout called to Titus, "Blessed stone or Marcus's switchbacks, Expeditious?"

"We can't pass the stone," Titus mumbled sourly. "We don't have the time for honors, but the switchbacks will delay and tire us as well."

Andy saw that the path split up ahead.

"Hell—the switchbacks!" Titus called to the cohort, and then spoke to himself, "The stone could take hours, especially when they sense that we are in a rush. We aren't carrying a satisfactory tribute, not after Cyburn."

They turned left at the fork and jogged for a few more minutes before Andy saw tiny switchbacks leading up a rocky slope. The slope was about three times his height. Andy scowled and counted the switchbacks. There were at least thirty. It would take Titus and his cohort some time, even at mouse speed, to climb up.

"Wait!" Andy called out.

Titus called the cohort to a halt. "What is it?"

"I've got a plan—everyone, climb on my back—just don't stab me please."

Titus was impressed. "Fair enough, if you think you can handle it. That is five hundred fully equipped soldiers."

Andy nodded and Titus waved them up. A surge of prickly paws grasped at Andy's pant-legs. In a moment, they had reached his arms, and before a minute had passed the entire cohort was hanging onto him.

Five hundred mice, ha! My backpack weighs more!

"All right—" Andy huffed and bent forward to get a grip onto the stone slope.

Okay, maybe this is a bit heavier.

He pulled himself up, using the pathways cut into the slope as hand and footholds. He felt the small bodies sway and grasp tighter with each step.

"Well done!" Titus called. "You're almost there! This would have taken an hour!" Scores of mouse voices rang with support as Andy paused for a heavy breath.

"Watch out!" One called from his left arm.

Andy felt the pathway tearing apart under his grip. "Hold on!" He grunted as he lunged upward for the next handhold. A few mice fell from him in the rush.

He grasped a rock firmly. "Climb back on!"

Titus climbed over his mice to see. "They're back on, Andy! Keep moving! By the by—you would make a brilliant siege engine!"

"Yes—sir!" Andy climbed, and huffed the words as he went.

He reached for the ledge and felt like his strength would give out. "Thirtieth floor!"

"Off! Off you go!" Titus helped the Dextra bustle off and onto the cliffside.

With the mice streaming away, Andy felt them tickling his arms. He gritted his teeth against the urge to laugh.

They raced off him, but he felt his grip slipping. When he felt like he couldn't hold still for any longer he heard Titus shout, "We're free, pull yourself up!"

Unencumbered, Andy had little trouble hoisting himself onto the cliff, though his clothes were now both muddied and torn in places from the rocks.

Titus looked down over the cliff side. "We'll have to get the pioneers out here to rebuild the switchbacks. You did a number on them."

Andy wanted to argue, but looked down and saw it was the truth.

"Nothing for it. Now let's get moving!"

"With that attitude, Titus, you can walk the rest of the way," Andy said, trying to brush the gunk off his clothes.

Titus belted out a hearty scoff as he organized his mice into thinner columns, to better navigate the tighter path. "The foliage is overgrown in some places. It might slow us down, but thanks to the lift we're well ahead of schedule."

"I'll lead," Andy said.

Andy had to push the shrubs aside as he went. Titus didn't argue as he headed to the front of the column. Andy listened as they followed, their tiny arms clinking softly as they marched. He snapped away the dead branches that choked out the path and tossed them further into the foliage.

"How far, Titus?"

Titus grabbed his pant-leg and tugged. "May I?" The mouse pointed to his shoulder.

Andy sighed. "Sure."

Titus leaped up in a few bounds but hid behind Andy's neck to avoid the branches. "Not far now. The road curves lanticward—eh, to the right. Could I ask you to hunch a bit, please? You might give us away." Andy hunched and continued advancing. "There's the tenth acre marker on the road ahead. See it?"

Andy saw the stone with the painted X poking out from a shrub. "Yes. Does that mean we're almost there?" Andy whispered. The mice behind him also bent low and held their weapons carefully, to keep quiet.

Why would they hunch? I'm still twenty times larger.

"Yes, Cair Fromage is near. Stop and listen."

Andy slowed to a stop, the mice halted behind him. They were silent.

He heard a sound like ringing, or chains being rattled.

"Hear that, Titus?"

Titus nodded as he listened with one ear raised towards the curve in the road. "It's up ahead. I've heard the sound before—move, swiftly but silently—don't break any branches."

Andy nodded, squinting as the branches slapped him across the face. The stretch of thick shrubs suddenly gave way to worked fields, many filled with countless plump, green insects that milled about in their enclosures. Andy didn't have time to give them much attention, because in the distance sat the city.

"They're under attack!" Titus moaned.

Andy saw the floating mountains the mice carved from cyclostones. A dozen were floating fifty feet from the ground. They were chained and lashed to each other. A central, far more solid mountain was held to the ground by three heavy chains.

Lithe and bony shapes darted here and there across the spaces inside the city walls. They were waving their rickety weapons wildly and looked to be celebrating as a muscled beast chopped away at the chains with a heavy blackened axe. The beast looked colossal next to the mouse structures in the city. Andy realized that it was likely his size.

"I think it's trying to cut them loose," Andy whispered.

"And with no propellers they will float helplessly to their deaths," Titus said, his eyes flashing to the figures in the city.

Andy got down onto his hands and knees to crawl up the roadway as Titus called his second in command up to the nape of Andy's neck.

"We will split the cohort. Take the Third and Fourth centuries with you to the far side of the city; attack when you hear the gates are breached."

"Yes sir!" The mouse leaped from Andy and led his centuries away and to the far side of the city.

"Lysander, I have to ask you to do something dangerous. I need you to use your giant's strength to kick down the gate facing us, that will allow my mice a way in. You must then run through the enemy, yell and scream to shock them, and then kick down the gate on the far side of the city to let in my second and his centuries. We will surround them."

Andy nodded, poking his head up to see the gates, but his eyes stuck to the hulking frame of the beast, trying to split the anchoring chains. He noticed too that something lit the center of the city. A tall pillar of white flame burned so brightly that the beast and the smaller fiends were avoiding it.

"The slithers are nothing to you, not one on one at least. Whatever you do, don't get cornered by that brutox! The beast is your size, but dense, and a born killer. Its axehead is forged from rare nightsteel, they need it to cut our chains, but a wound from that weapon will be impossible to heal, even with minoe."

Andy's breath quickened and his muscles tensed. He lifted his body into a running stance.

"Hold on my boy, let me down. I need to lead."

Andy paused for Titus to leap to the ground. He saw an adjutant run up with a helmet and sword for

Titus.

"Whenever you're ready, Lysander."

It was up to him. Andy felt the earth under his hands. He was shaking. The beast made him want to turn and run home.

Brutox? Nightsteel? Don't get hit, Andy. Let the mice take care of business; they have weapons and training.

He felt his mind reaching for reasons to turn around. His heart trembled at the flexing muscle running down the beast's trunk as it struck the chains.

A chain snapped and a ripple went up through the floating mountains. A few mice fell the distance to the ground. The slithers, their lithe forms poised for violence, pushed and tore at each other to get at the mice.

A squeal of pain reached his ears.

I can't let them be killed!

His mind went blank as he kicked off the ground. The earth blurred past as he raced. He kicked open the gate and vaulted over the wall, which came up to his waist. He hardly noticed the siege engines parked against the wall, and the signs of battle.

Andy screamed. "Here! Come here!"

Every moving shape in the city stopped to look up at him.

The flames from the towering pillar shot higher into the cavern.

The brutox, momentarily startled by the surprise attack, raised a heavy arm and pointed at him. Reluctantly at first, but then with more speed, the slithers broke away from their victims and ran toward Andy from every direction.

He felt a slight stab in his leg. Andy reached down and grabbed the small beast before hurling it like a discus out of the city.

"Break the rear gate!" Andy heard Titus yelling at him as the mice charged in from behind.

Right, the other gate!

Andy kicked his way through the mass of slithers, ignoring the stabbing as he went. The brutox clicked at him curiously as it leveled its axe and made to approach.

Andy grabbed a slither that had climbed up to his waist and hefted it at the brutox, who cleaved it from the air without pause.

Titus and his troops formed up and advanced towards the city center. Crossbow volleys and leveled halberds cut an inky path through the mass of confused slithers.

Andy weaved left, but the brutox followed. He ducked to the right and narrowly avoided a felling stroke from the heavy axe. Andy heard it ring through the air, just inches from his face.

He felt the skin on his back tingle, as if the axe was still flying toward him. He raced to the rear gate.

"Clear the gate!" he yelled, barreling into it and tearing the gatehouse clear off the wall as he plowed through. Andy kicked the debris aside so the centuries could enter the city unhindered.

The fighting mice wasted no time pouring around Andy and through the wreckage of the gatehouse.

He stood back as the mice formed up and loosed a volley of bolts into the wavering mass of slithers. He watched as the bolts struck one of the rickety creatures. It fell to the ground and melted away into a tarry puddle.

The mice were gaining the upper hand. The slithers were almost routed. The few that remained swung wildly at the lines of halberds before getting tangled in the blades and melting into viscous purple liquid.

The brutox wasn't impressed. Andy finally had a good look at the thing in the light of the pillar. It was something like a beetle crossed with the frame of a tall chimp. The mandibles and face were insect-like, but the body was plated and thick. It looked built for hard work, or violence.

Andy stepped forward.

"Stay back, boy! Leave him to us!" Titus's second ordered forcefully.

The brutox cackled a clicking laugh as the bolts bounced off its plated flesh. It buried the axe into one of the smaller freestanding buildings, tearing the bottom floor loose from its foundation, it chopped again, and split the building free from the ground. Dropping the axe, it lifted the severed structure over its head.

"Scatter!" Titus roared.

The building went sailing through the air, straight for Titus's line of mice, who ran as quickly as they could, but many were caught under the falling wreckage.

Andy bolted forward and reached out for the axe. The brutox turned and saw him coming, but did nothing.

For a moment, Andy thought that strange, but he grasped the axe. His hand grazed the dull end of the axehead as he raised the weapon.

He cried out and fell to the ground. The axe seemed frozen, and stuck in his grip. It felt like electricity was shooting through his body.

A cold, hard hand grasped his throat. He felt himself lifting off the ground. The brutox took the axe from him, and the jolting ceased.

Multifaceted white eyes mirrored Andy's bloodied reflection. The brutox choked the breath out of him as it looked on, calm and uncaring.

Suddenly, the world was shrinking, everything felt like it was getting further away and he struggled to breathe.

The world blurred as his vision darkened. The planes of the brutox's carapace seemed to bend and twist into a nightmare of starless nights. That night was suddenly pierced by falling bolts of light, like a burst from a firework.

This is it.

Another shower of silver sparks came flying down from the floating mountains above. Andy's mind was at the point of giving in, but something about the image forced him to hold for a moment longer.

He felt the air rushing through his hair from behind.

I think I'm falling.

The feeling dragged out longer and longer. It stopped suddenly and he felt the warm ground.

A tower of silver flames shot out of his chest and filled his eyes. He had landed on the pillar of flame, and considered it one more piece of poor luck.

He knew he had to roll over.

Andy reached out with his arm and pushed, forcing his body to roll. With difficulty he looked over and saw he had indeed been lying on the pillar of flame. The brutox had dropped him onto it, but he was neither impaled nor burned.

He focused on the source of the flame. Looking closer, his eyes tensed. Deep in the column was a single floating orb, about the size of a large marble. He reached out and grasped it.

A pulse of light shot out into the cavern. Andy felt the ringing in his ears clear. The world refocused, and his breath came back.

Andy rolled to his feet, suddenly furious. He felt freshly fed and just wakened from a full night's sleep.

What's happening to me?

The mice were shielding their eyes. The brutox too bowed his head and stepped back.

Andy was compelled by something within. He walked towards the brutox and clenched his fist around the marble. The brutox raised his axe and swung. Andy tightened his fist to the point of pain and a flaming, silver blade exploded outward from his clenched palm. The blade blocked the axe, and the brutox leaped away in surprise.

"God damn! Where did that come from?"

The pillar of flame had been erupting from the marble, but now, with the marble tight in his grasp, the pillar changed into a flaming silver blade that ignited outward from his clenched fist. As he raised his hand, it felt like lifting nothing.

"Kill him, boy!" Titus cheered from behind.

But Andy didn't hear. Instead, he turned the weapon over in his hand, feeling it respond like a pencil or paint brush.

The brutox saw that Andy was distracted and lunged to strike again.

Andy countered the blow, almost without effort.

On a whim he swung at the brutox, who parried. The nightsteel axehead deflected the blow, but when Andy attacked again his blade struck the axe's haft, which split apart at the touch, leaving the brutox standing with a chunk of rounded wood in his hands.

Andy swiped with the blade.

Despite its fleshy armor, the brutox split into halves. The pieces crumbled into smaller and smaller chunks that grayed as they eroded. After a moment Andy would have sworn that he only saw a small pile of sand, noteworthy only because of its slight tinge of purple.

"There's a lad!" Titus led a cheer. "Pull them in!"

Andy opened his palm; the blade vanished. He saw the marble resting there.

No one will ever believe the first thing about any of this.

Andy looked up and saw the mountains lowering, there were teams of cowled and cloaked mice with longbows holding onto the chains.

"They were the ones—the shower of silver sparks I saw. They saved me."

"That's right!" Titus called.

The mountains were decoupled from one another and led back to their places. The cheering drowned everything out. Andy was applauded, but he could only stare in disbelief at the marble in his palm. The cavern felt far darker now that the blade had extinguished, but the multi-colored vinlight from above maintained a constant, pulsing glow.

"You can wield the Argument," Titus said.

"Is that what this is called?" Andy asked, hefting the marble.

"You raised the blade almost out of instinct! And you fought brilliantly—well, you'll want practice. Your form isn't right, and you need to learn how to hone the blade. I can't remember the last time I've seen it done. You would need to train with the Praetor himself to learn a fuller use of the Argument," Titus rambled excitedly. "But this guarantees it! They must accept you!"

In all the commotion, Andy didn't notice a cowled mouse trying to get his attention. The mouse yelled, tugged at his pant-leg, and finally climbed up and onto his shoulder before grabbing his ear and calling out, "Seer!"

Andy jumped. "Yes—yes, what is it?"

"I've heard you're hunting a twin. I've found this!" The mouse held up a rolled piece of paper.

"That's a scroll—wait, twin? What do you mean?"

Titus also climbed up and stood beside the cloaked mouse, who had his bow slung over his shoulder. "Andy, this is Taptalles, veteransus of the Wisps."

Taptalles nodded at the introduction, but rushed to speak. "Enemy correspondence; we found it by a fallen slither." He opened the small scroll and read, "Confirmed, limited strike from Norbrok - target: mouse outpost, CF, on schedule. The mice will be distracted, and the girl will be spent at P without interference. Do not question the Master again." It was signed, "Zava, campaign schedule intermediary."

"The girl will be spent at P?" Andy repeated.

Titus leaned in. "The strike at CF, that's Cair Fromage—the siege we just broke, but the rest."

Andy stared at Titus desperately. "You have to know, what does it mean by P? It has to stand for something. That's Letty! They're talking about Letty!"

The cowled mouse pulled back his hood to reveal solid black fur and three furless red scars running across his face. "I think I know where she is."

"What? Where? Speak up!" Titus said, distraught at the downcast look on the black mouse's face.

"We saw brutox near the Python's Howe."

Titus took a sharp breath. "The other two! The Cyburns mentioned three brutox with the girl, we only slew one."

But Andy was stuck on the word, Python. His

mind jumped back to the Twister and what it had showed him.

Those giant yellow eyes.

Chapter 9: To Python's Howe

Oblivious to the cheers and noise of Cair Fromage coming back to life, Andy considered running. He had already fled once today. Titus and Taptalles glared at him, as if perfectly aware of what he was thinking. Titus was the sterner of the two, while Taptalles wore a sarcastic smirk.

"We can't go off directive, Andy. Under any other circumstances, I'd be on your shoulder—charging out to do the right thing, but this is your future. Coriolus is waiting for you to run off; he'll use it as evidence that you are not loyal, and the praetor will have to exile you, or worse! You must realize that Coriolus will use his influence to insist on the most severe punishment!"

"Most severe punishment?" Andy repeated.

"My friend is trying to say that they will be forced to execute you. Those mice in purple cloaks, they will have to—by writ of law—end your life, because you have seen too much, and are demonstratively disloyal."

It changes nothing, Andy thought. *I can march around with the mice, after I find Letty.* He took a heavy breath. *And I'd like to see them try to execute me—now that I have this.* He gripped the small marble and a glowing silver light appeared around his hand.

Andy thought back to the maniples in marching order, with their crossbow-mice protected by a wall of halberdiers. *Hmmm.* He remembered watching Titus lead the Dextra against the enemy a few minutes ago. *Even if I fight with the marble, they're probably too much for me, but I can't go back now.*

Andy sighed.

"My loyalty wasn't for sale, Titus. I owe it to someone else first. If I can free her, I will return to your praetor and his punishment." Andy balked at his own words. He wondered when he had become so brave.

The mice considered each other for a moment. Titus had a grim set to his jaw, but his eyes showed understanding. Taptalles grasped his cloak and looked away before speaking, "Fair is fair, lad. You fell into our world and had no say. If the worst should happen, you will be remembered with honors—by the Wisps at least; you saved our city."

"This is a mistake," Titus insisted.

"I don't suppose a guide or an escort can show me the way."

Titus shook his head. "Once you leave, I'll have broken the law. And as much as I would like to escort you personally, if I lose my position, there will be precious few mice capable of opposing Coriolus. I have a duty to my people. It shames me that I have failed you so."

Andy felt his face redden.

They stood, wordlessly; the cheers from the victorious mice faded as it became clear what was happening.

Andy turned to go.

"Wait!" Taptalles stopped him. "Look at the cavern above. Go on, look up."

Andy was suddenly suspicious, but he did as he was told. The cavern ceiling, so far above, glittered

163

with the brilliance of an ocean sunset. Waves of color crashed into each other, shimmering as they collided.

"There!" Taptalles climbed up to Andy's shoulder and pointed. "See the amber vein flowing there?"

Andy spotted the barest trace of amber hues lost amid the others, but he could see it. "Yes, but it's hard to make out."

"It doesn't matter, as long as you can follow it. The pulses of color will get stronger the closer you are to the Howe."

I can follow the colors? Andy watched the ceiling for a moment, wondering what the other colors meant.

"What is the Howe?" He finally asked.

"The ancient home of the Python." Taptalles answered, apprehension in his voice.

Titus shook his head at the conversation and crossed his arms.

Taptalles couldn't hide the desperation he felt. "Don't speak to the monster if you can help it—it will try to entrance you."

"The beast is vicious, but it has its own ethics. It won't break a compact." Titus countered.

"Ethics?" Taptalles blustered, but Titus held up a paw to calm his friend.

"Beast?" Andy remembered the eyes he saw in the vision sent from the Twister. "It's a giant snake," Andy said, shivering.

"You don't have to go!" Titus called as Andy turned to the amber. "Follow the silver back to

Sentinel's Watch! Undo this mistake!" Titus called out.

Andy looked back for a moment. "I'm sorry to disappoint you."

With his goodbye said, Andy left Cair Fromage. He kept his eyes on the path and avoided the hundreds of hurt faces watching him leave.

His anxiety waned as his legs worked. He felt better moving towards something, even if he wasn't sure what to expect.

A shiver climbed up his spine as a warm wind blew through a stand of bare, gnarled shrubs, which grew wild on the far side of the fields surrounding Cair Fromage. He found a road cut through the growth that went in generally the same direction as the amber vein.

Andy realized the path was cut for creatures far smaller than himself. Cruel barbs on the branches caught his attention.

He looked back over his shoulder to Cair Fromage and the mice. He wondered how long the shame would linger. He looked away.

Here goes.

Arms shielding his face, he plunged down the path.

"Ow!" Andy batted away the spiky, whip-like branches. He wanted to keep an eye on the cavern above, but every time he glanced up he suffered another cut. He paused to wince at a cut on his arm. He felt suddenly alone, and his stomach sank.

This is what I wanted. This is what I get. Andy refused to let himself wallow and tore away another branch.

He pushed himself as quickly as he could, taking care to avoid the worst branches. He stopped for a moment, looking up at the cavern roof.

No sun here—I can't tell the time.

Andy wasn't sure how he felt about that, but then he laughed. No sun, no way to tell time. *This place must be great for procrastinators.*

He struggled forward and found himself staring at a fork in the path. He checked the ceiling again. The amber vein traveled between the two paths; neither offered a better route.

Looking left and right, his eyes hunted for a clue. His legs started to shake.

Andy grimaced and picked at random.

He took a grateful breath and trudged down the right-hand path.

A few minutes later, he felt vindicated. The path opened, and the shrubs gave way to full-size trees. He strained his eyes to follow the amber and could barely make it out through the foliage, though he was grateful to be free of the thorny branches.

Andy tripped. A thick root had caught his foot. He stood and saw a shiver ripple through the trees.

He crouched, ready to spring away, but couldn't see what shook the leaves.

He suddenly thought the Twister had found him again. He bounded forward, running through the trees. The branches were quaking and shivering all around. Without thinking, Andy ran.

Andy looked in every direction for a sign, for anything to explain what he was seeing.

He kept his eyes on the ground and dodged the thick roots and rocks as he went. It looked like the roots were moving, but he knew it was impossible. He ran until the quivering finally died down. The trees were still thick in every direction. Had he made any errant turns while he was running? He looked up through the branches and caught a glance of the amber.

I need to get out of these trees.

Andy took a slight step backwards and his foot slipped into a hole.

"Not again!" he growled, stumbling backwards and slamming into a tree.

Andy checked his ankle for a sprain. It didn't hurt to bend. Grateful, he looked around suspiciously, thinking his luck couldn't get worse.

The trunk of the tree he was leaning against began to shift beneath him.

Andy dashed away and spun about. The tree looked like it was twisting around. A patch of bark, six feet up the trunk, split apart and a single, ocher eye stared at him.

Andy put his hands up apologetically. "Sorry, I didn't know—"

The tree started shaking.

No thanks!

Andy bolted, his heart pounding. He had no idea what they were, but they weren't trees. Somewhere, deep within, Andy realized that running from these trees was foolish. He nearly skidded to a halt as he approached another shaking tree, before edging around it.

Andy passed a few more motionless trees and burst out into a field of orange grass. Not caring to stop, he kept running towards a gentle hill, not far off. He slowed as the elevation sharpened, but once he hit the crest of the long, narrow hill Andy was confronted by a horizon filled with a black sea. Far out in the distance, past the sea, the tops of great spires loomed like jagged streaks across the colorful horizon. Forked bolts of lightning played occasionally back and forth between the spires; his eyes strained to make them out at this distance.

What a nightmare—it's something worse in every direction.

He gazed up, hoping to find the amber, but the sky swirled with clouds, and he couldn't see through them to the ceiling above.

Andy heard what sounded like a sudden burst of falling hail. He turned back to the forest, and saw it was shaking as far as he could see. He raised a brow, annoyed, and had the vague impression that the not-quite-trees were laughing at him. He felt slightly embarrassed.

Andy turned and walked down the spine of the hill, away from the forest. He felt suspicious of the orange grass, but, after walking for miles over the hills, he realized the grass wasn't likely to surprise him with a burst of aggressive waving, though the foxtails did have an affinity for his socks, which had picked up several of the sharp, orange stragglers. Andy considered picking the foxtails from his socks, but looked out on the rolling orange hills, and sighed.

Further ahead he spied a curiosity on the gray stained shore. For several moments, he doubted his eyes. Yet, minute after minute of walking refused to change what he was seeing.

Are they ships, or folded pages?

Andy's eyes played over what might have been the wreckage of several ships. But instead of cracked beams and tattered sails, he saw the pages of books, torn and somehow folded or inflated into the many forms of these broken ships. It reminded him of origami.

He rubbed his eyes and looked away for a few moments, hoping that as he got closer things would make more sense.

A bellowing voice echoed to him on the wind.

Andy saw a bear of a man darting between the huge sections of torn pages.

A giant mantis, sectioned in colors of darkest green and glossy black, swiped its serrated claw through the air and tore through a piece of hull. The folded words tore with the sound of ripping cloth and burning letters burst out into the air from the wound. The beast reminded him of the brutox, but taller and lithe.

Andy gaped as the warrior leaped backwards into the air to avoid a strike.

He has no weapon—it'll kill him!

Andy fished the marble out of his pocket and grasped it in his palm. The burning silver blade burst from his closed fist, just as it had before. He ran towards the fight.

The warrior had taken hold of a fallen section

of page and raised it up like a shield. A serrated claw rent through the page, getting stuck halfway through.

The man let out a towering laugh as he twisted the page. The mantis squealed as its limb wrenched the wrong way.

"Ha!" Andy leaped another step forward. The fight was still more than a hundred paces away. The mantis only had to strike out with its other serrated blade and rake the warrior, but the sudden reversal and the pain of the wrenched arm were too much for the mantis.

With a quick twist, the warrior tore the limb clean off and, in an instant, he tore it free of the page and flipped the arm around, bearing it as his own weapon.

Andy paused, his eyes wide.

Stylishly armed, the warrior made quick work of the mantis, and in two strikes had decapitated the beast.

The warrior lifted the serrated limb to the sky, and bellowed. His resonant cry sounded more like a crazed laugh the longer it went on.

Looks like he has it well—in hand.

Andy grimaced at the pun, and wished Dean, or his father, was here to endure it. The warrior disappeared back into the wreckage of the ships, and Andy thought back to his time with Dean.

What's wrong with me? If Dean was here, he'd be clawing his eyes out.

Light from above caught Andy's attention. He saw the clouds had parted. A large vein of amber coursed through green and blue. He was getting closer.

Andy wanted to stay and talk to the warrior. He wanted to look at the wreckage and try to figure out what was going on with the pages.

With a disappointed face he turned and jogged back up the crest of the hill. He looked over his shoulder and spotted the large man working to join the pages.

Jogging felt good and he kept it up. The sea breeze was refreshing, and the fields of orange grass waved gently. He reached out and felt the foxtails brush against his palms. He tried to avoid looking out across the sea, but even that ominous horizon held an otherworldly beauty. Whether minutes or hours had passed, he couldn't guess, but the next time he looked up, the cavern ceiling was mostly amber.

Wait—

He dug into his back pocket and found his cell.

This whole time? I've had this—

He sighed, shaking his head.

He was about to unlock it, but paused, not wanting to see the dozens of inevitable messages and missed calls from his parents.

He felt the sudden urge to throw his phone into the sea.

I don't need to know what time it is, and I'm in more trouble than—

He couldn't possibly quantify how much trouble he was in.

To hell with it.

He put his cell back in his pocket and continued. *Let's keep dreaming; it's too good to wake up.* He laughed at himself as he went. *I'll probably scream and wake up when the next giant bug swipes my head off.*

Further ahead he saw a vineyard. He was suddenly hungry and eyed the bundles of unwatched grapes. Andy sneaked up to the rickety stands. He plucked two bunches of red grapes and felt guilty.

He stood tall and looked around for someone to pay, but there was no one in sight. He took out his wallet and found a five-dollar bill. He rolled it up and stuck it firmly in the wooden stand before heading closer to the coast.

He knew that no one here could probably use the money, but the owner might find the bill and consider it a curiosity. That alone made Andy feel better.

He gorged himself on the grapes and leaned back in the grass. He felt his eyelids dropping, but was too tired to do anything about it.

Andy rolled over and realized that his back hurt.

How long have I been lying down? Did I sleep?

He got up and stretched. Looking around, nothing seemed different, and that made him uncomfortable. He rushed back to the path on the hillcrest and continued on.

Minutes or hours later, he came on a circular hollow dug into a grassy embankment above the shore. A ramshackle wooden tower stood in the center of the circle. A black banner covered in stars and featuring an open palm containing a purple orb hung loosely from a pole. Nearby was another banner. This second banner was covered in amber scales and featured a viper's eye. Andy shuddered, knowing he was getting closer to Letty, and whatever had her.

The perimeter of the circle was lined with doorways. A few shimmered, each with its own color, but most were blank or covered in wooden planks. A jagged script was etched on the planks above each portal. The letters flickered and looked like shining purple quicksilver. He tried to read them, but they weren't English.

I saw letters like these outside Ropt's office. They're different from the messages Rembrandt left in his paintings though, those were silver. These letters hurt to look at, while the others only make me dizzy.

His eyes shied away from the script, and settled on the tower, which was considerable, at least three floors high. Andy was certain that something his size had built the tower, and not the mice.

Staring, Andy realized how oblivious he had been. There was something manning the tower.

He fell to his hands and knees in the wispy grass. His eyes focused on the watchman. It had the familiar plated and segmented limbs of the brutox, but this one bore the face of a spider. Light glinted off its many eyes. It wasn't looking his way; it was staring in the opposite direction, and he was certain it had spotted something.

Lucky for me it was distracted.

The brutox leveled its crossbow.

What's it aiming at?

Andy spotted movement on a hillside past the circle of portals. He bent low to move stealthily in an arc around the circle. He kept his eyes on the brutox, who was still trained on something.

"Hail!" a voice called out.

Andy saw a young man, of an age with him, maybe a few years older. The young man was garbed in a sea green tunic. A cowl of shells covered his head and shoulders, and he carried a barbed trident. It was the second human he had seen, and he looked far more reasonable than the man on the beach.

A growl came from the tower. Andy saw a bolt fly; it barely missed the young man.

"Get down, you idiot!" Andy rushed forward and plowed into him, knocking them both into the grass. "Stay low!" The young man tried to straighten his cowl; he didn't seem nearly alarmed enough.

Andy peeked through the grass and saw the brutox struggling to work the winch on his crossbow.

Andy felt an overwhelming impulse to charge the tower.

That's a foolish idea—isn't it?

Before he had finished the thought, he was on his feet and racing towards the wooden watchtower. The beam of light exploded from his hand into a flaming blade and he cut through one of the tower's legs, then another, and finally a third, all in a matter of seconds.

He heard a cry as the tower collapsed. The spider-like brutox tumbled across the ground, its many legs flailing as it scrambled to its feet.

The blade in Andy's hand sputtered and vanished. He took an exasperated breath and saw his reflection in the brutox's many eyes.

It flinched and was staring at the crossbow on the floor.

Andy dived and grasped for the hardwood stock; the brutox did likewise. They slammed into each other in midair. Andy had a hand on the crossbow, but the spider slapped him heavily across the face.

Andy laughed at the unexpected attack, but sputtered as the slapping turned into choking.

Not stopping to check how many spider hands or feet were trying to strangle him, Andy secured the crossbow and bashed the brutox over the head with the heavy weapon.

The brutox squealed and leaped back. Andy scrambled with the winch and nocked the string. The brutox, bent on its many legs, would have seemed coiled for another strike, if not for the one limb rubbing the sore spot on its brow.

"Come on, come on!" Andy found the quiver in the tower wreckage and pulled out a bolt. He spared a half-second's glance at the young man, who was leaning on his trident. "Feel free to jump in any time now, friend!" Andy growled as he loaded the bolt and raised the crossbow.

The brutox shuffled backwards, looking back and forth between the two humans. In a snap it hopped, with lightning speed, away and into the far grass. Andy watched it leap and bound with immense strength. It spanned the length of a school bus in a single jump.

Startled by the intense acrobatic display, Andy hardly noticed the young man come up and start rooting through the wreckage.

Andy looked down at the loaded crossbow and the winch. *How did I load it?* He had seen the brutox struggle with the winch. *But how did I know what to do? I got it on the first—*

A loud crack caught his attention and he saw the young man pull a banner free from the wreckage.

He planted the amber banner in the ground and then struggled for the other.

"Trophy?" Andy asked.

The young man looked up at him with a pained face. "You have no idea how much trouble you've just made for me." Despite the words, he didn't appear to be angry.

"Sorry—but that beast did try to shoot you—with this," Andy waved the weapon at him, before bending to pick up the quiver and winch.

The young man struck him with an appraising look.

Andy felt annoyed at the lack of appreciation. He aimed the crossbow at the last standing leg of the watchtower and fired. The bolt hit with a heavy thunk. Andy grabbed the young man and dragged him over.

"Look here." The bolt was lodged in, more than a hands length. "You might be dead." Andy tried to free the bolt, but found it firmly stuck.

The young man laughed. "Slyn likes to fire a few

warning shots when he sees me. Our Masters share joint rulership of this site."

Slyn? The brutox have names?

Andy felt his stomach drop. He looked awkwardly at the weapon. "Eh—sorry about that."

"Join me; I'm heading back to Caspia."

Surprised, Andy wasn't sure what to say. "Sorry again. I—I'm Andy." He held out a hand.

The young man stared at his hand for a moment, unsure, but after a second, he reached out and shook it. "Strange." The young man looked thoughtful as he stared at their clasped hands. "I'm Quill."

"Quill?" Andy repeated, not believing.

"Yes?"

Andy almost stammered, but he didn't want to be rude. "What is that you're wearing?"

"Oh, my hauberk?" Quill looked down at the strange, scaled shirt that jangled as he moved. "It's for protection." Andy sensed that Quill was frustrated. "We need to move, Andy. Slyn will be back with more brutox—who may not be so friendly."

Andy agreed with a nod, and they moved on.

"So that thing was a brutox?" Andy asked, "I've seen a few now, and they all look different."

"Oh yes, there are a multitude of types. Luckily, I only know a few. Slyn back there was a pale spider, but I've seen scythed manti, armored beetles, hulking brutons, which are really only pack animals, scouts with the eyes of flies, heavy crabs, ravagers too, though ravagers aren't actually brutox. The trick to them is knowing the coloration as much as the shape," Quill explained this all academically, much to Andy's dismay.

"So, there's a whole world of monsters down here," Andy muttered.

He looked over his shoulder and scanned the horizon. He saw no monsters. Somehow, that wasn't comforting, and he gripped tighter on his new weapon.

"Hey Quill, it won't cause you more trouble if I keep the crossbow?"

"The damage is done, Andy; you might as well keep it. If they find us, it could come to blows."

"How many can we expect?"

Quill laughed and shook his head, as if knowing that Andy was trying to come up with a plan.

That's a bad sign.

"We might expect a squad of a dozen or so; different types, but—" he raised a hand and pointed ahead. "See that?"

Andy saw what looked like the skull of a great whale, and a few dozen huge bones, upright, and planted in the soil. The path ran through its jaw and continued on the other side.

"That marks the lands of my Mistress. We'll be safe after we cross."

Andy grasped the crossbow as they neared the bones, expecting an ambush. Even Quill readied his trident. It was quiet as they passed through the jaws of the once colossal beast.

Andy realized that the bones were ribs at one point. They were covered in writing. Elegantly curving letters fed into each other, and the lines were carved into the bones in spirals that climbed as they turned. It reminded him of the candy-cane poles outside some barber shops. Andy loosened the grip on his weapon and felt the texture of the carving. Quill gave him a knowing grin and let his trident rest against his shoulder as they marched on.

"Stories?" Andy asked, as he looked from one rib to the next.

"Histories, the law," he paused and pointed to the last one in the row, "that one lists the etiquette expected of a visitor to these lands."

Andy paused. "Anything I should know?"

"Do not stare, particularly do not stare into our Mistress's eyes. Remain courteous, quiet, and clean. And lastly, bring a gift."

"A gift?"

Andy cringed, realizing he had nothing that could serve.

The crossbow? He stared at the roughly crafted weapon with a grim look. *Probably not.* His mind centered on the marble in his pocket. *No! That belongs to the mice; I should get it back to them when I'm done.*

"Don't worry about the gift, unless you ask her a question," Quill said plainly.

Andy nodded. "No questions—got it." He wanted to ask why, but realized that it would set a dangerous precedent, and decided to let it rest until he learned more.

They passed the last of the bones and walked along a grassy beach dune. Stressed, Andy listened to the jangling of his companion's armor. He heard the crash of the black sea, and the clinking of his crossbow bolts in the quiver. It was almost serene on the shore, and Andy distrusted this, wondering if he would even be alive in an hour. He suddenly imagined Quill turning on him. He was friendly now, but Andy didn't know more than his name.

He considered his companion and wondered if he could make himself fight this young man.

He sighed and looked out on the waves. Uncertain awe clawed up his throat as he walked along the black coast with the warm wind on his face. He kept up with the steady pace of his oddly familiar companion, every step reminding him that the terrible closeness of violence lurked, coiled and hidden, always near.

Andy wondered if this was the best or worst dream he ever had. He decided it must be both.

He felt a slight rumble in his pocket, and produced the marble to give it a close look. Countless silver speckles swirled across its surface. Perhaps a dozen specks of purple floated among them.

"Hey Quill?"

"Yes?"

Quill stopped and saw the marble in Andy's hand. He took a step back.

"Do you have any idea what this is? I found it in Cair Froma-je, Fromagge?"

"Cair Fromage." Quill leaned in, his brows furrowing.

"A friend called it the Argument," Andy mentioned, remembering Titus.

Quill considered the marble, exaggerated doubt on his face.

"May I?" He asked, reaching for Andy's palm.

Andy felt a jolt of concern, and nearly closed his grip, but Quill was too fast.

"Ahh!" A spark shot from the marble and Quill recoiled, tumbling into the grass.

"Are you all right?" Andy pocketed the marble and helped Quill back up.

"What a jolt! It knocked me off my feet!" he said, surprised and almost laughing.

Besides being a little frazzled, he was fine.

"You don't know anything about it?" Andy felt like it was a rude question, but it had already left his mouth.

Quill smirked. "The shock confirms it: You do possess a piece of Argument. I've never seen it in action before. It really did slice that tower into pieces."

"Why didn't you say anything?" Andy asked.

"Frankly, I thought you might kill me," Quill replied, looking hopelessly at his trident.

Andy rolled his eyes. "Don't worry; I'm not like that."

Quill scoffed. "You did seem violent."

That stung.

Andy took a breath before asking, "Why is it called an Argument?"

Quill scowled at him. "I don't care to discuss religion right now—but it is strange that you can lay hands on it—" He trailed off, before continuing, "You said you found it at Cair Fromage?"

Andy nodded.

"That's a rodent hovel? If I recall correctly."

Andy felt his stomach turn at the scorn in Quill's voice. He couldn't help responding harshly, "They carve cities into floating boulders, not exactly a hovel."

Quill laughed. "Details, friend—ignore me—but in the interest of their wellbeing, you should return that artifact to where you found it."

"Of course, I was going to. But what would happen if I'm delayed?" Andy asked.

Quill shrugged. "Likely nothing happens with it gone. But, there is a chance that, say, the land might spoil, their foes will be emboldened, their luck will turn, and a rodent without luck is a sad thing indeed."

Andy wasn't sure what to make of this. *I might need the marble to free Letty. But I'll get it back to them as soon as I can.*

"You seem to have a fondness for them. If that weren't the case, you could learn a great deal by keeping the artifact. My Mistress might accept it—"

Andy interrupted, "How long could they survive without the artifact?"

Quill's brow bent with concern. He shrugged. "These things don't move very often. You saw what happened when I tried to touch it. I suppose that's why settlements spring up around them. The histories tell tales of Arguments changing axiom, and civilizations crumbling as a result." Quill turned to keep moving.

Andy reached out and grabbed his arm, turning

him around. "Could you go over that last part in more detail please? What's an axiom?"

Quill had a carefree smile. "Come on, Andy! You're going to Caspia! We don't have the problems that others do, no religious strife, no slaver's whips."

Andy stood still on the path. *I'm being manipulated.*

"What were you doing out there by the circle anyway?" Andy asked.

"Patrol," Quill replied. "I like to take the air and stretch my legs; it gets my mind going."

"But why are you so keen on taking me to Caspia?"

Quill sighed. "Look, I'm already in trouble. We have standing orders to bring rogue Seers home by any means necessary. Believe me, it's for your own good. You seem as ignorant as a newborn, so I understand your suspicion. If you aren't satisfied by the end of the day, I will beg my Mistress to hear your questions; I will offer her a gift for you. Just, whatever you say, don't mention the rodents. She can't stand them."

Andy nodded, finally getting somewhere. He looked at the marble. *Axioms and civilizations?* It didn't seem that critical, but he remembered what it could do.

"Caspia, Andy! Just being away for a few hours reminds me of how sweet a life I live. You seem a brave sort, if not reckless. I don't want to get your hopes up, but, if you behave, you might be invited to enroll."

Andy blinked. "Caspia is a school?"

Quill laughed. "Far better than any school you can imagine."

They marched on for a few minutes, before Andy asked, "Are there any new girls at Caspia?"

Quill nodded with a knowing grin. "We are joined by the potential, Solstaci, her birth hour is nearing. There are just a few things that my Mistress needs to take care of before she is enrolled."

"What does—Solstaci—look like?"

Quill gave Andy a devious look. "I haven't seen her myself. Our Mistress tends to keep potentials cloistered before their birth hour. I have heard that she has magnificent raven's hair, but past that—" He shrugged again.

Could be Letty. Sounds like she's caught up in this cult.

Andy didn't know where he got the word 'cult' from, but the longer he thought about what he heard from Quill, the more it fit.

The Twister led me to believe that I would find a snake. That intercepted scroll implied that Letty was taken as a sacrifice here, and now Quill is telling me that his home is like a school, but they sound insane. I followed the amber, but do I even have the right place? I'll have to keep my eyes open.

"Quill?" Andy asked, "When I was back in my world, I saw a creature."

Quill looked his way expectantly.

"It was purplish. I think its face was covered in tentacles, I can't remember everything else—"

"Ryle," Quill interrupted. "The slavers. With those eyes of yours, it's no surprise. They would have found you at some point."

Quill's bluntness was shocking.

Dr. Ropt is one of the slavers, a ryle.

The clarion call of a horn rolled out over the coast.

"We're expected!" Quill broke out into a jog; Andy followed along.

Quill pointed to the top of a jutting coastal cliffside. Someone stood by a banner colored amber with an emblazoned sea shell. The blower lowered their horn and waved.

They jogged to the sentry, who was an armed girl, also about their age. Quill and the girl exchanged greetings, while Andy looked over the cliff, down onto what could only be Caspia. It was not what he expected.

He saw a boneyard that had been gem encrusted, painted, and then re-arranged into a sprawling city-fortress. The structures shone with all the colors of the cavern roof and more. Orange, red, amber, and blue sheets were stretched between the ribs and offered shade for every span of road. The buildings also seemed ribbed, as if made of bones as well. The walls and plazas shone with a speckled hue, like mother-of-pearl. Among the structures sat a massive lobster, covered in stretches of green, as if overgrown. Andy began to doubt his eyes. He tried to take it all in, but it was too much to see at once from so high.

"Is that Python's Howe?" Andy asked, half to himself.

Quill shook his head as the girl grunted and reared with her right hand. Andy almost dodged the blow, but she was too fast and caught him squarely across the face.

"Mind your tongue, unborn, or next time it will be this." She jabbed her spear sharply, pausing just above his ribs.

He wanted to explain his ignorance, but her serious mien silenced him mid-stammer. She crouched slightly, spear ready. Sea green eyes stared defiantly at him through her shock of red hair. Her cloak glittered with blue fish scales, though he thought they were metal, and as they shook against each other, their jangling gave the impression of solidity.

Just like Quill's shirt.

She had a necklace of sea-stars and a jagged scar across her freckled cheek. Her sandals were wrapped in a crisscross pattern all the way up her thigh, disappearing under a deep green skirt that looked to be made of sea weed.

"Excuse me," Andy finally got out. "I'm new here—I didn't mean to offend."

She ignored him and looked at Quill. "A few hours with this idiot would be enough to make anyone go mad."

Andy blushed, and felt suddenly ashamed of his embarrassment. How could he care what this girl thought of him?

"Let me take him to our Mistress. Go, continue your writing, or is it more carving today?" She implored with a friendly face.

"Alas, that I could, Staza. Our Mistress will have to punish me."

She sighed and gestured towards Andy questioningly.

Quill raised his brow in assent. "The watchtower over the circle is down."

"I recognized the spider's crossbow." She said pointing at Andy's weapon.

"Oh well, she is in a good mood with the medial tide. Maybe she'll ignore the crime." Staza said.

Andy looked down at his stolen weapon. His face turned a deeper crimson.

She motioned them towards a stairway that led down the cliff and into Caspia.

Andy nearly tripped on the stairs. His eyes were torn between making sense of the town and trying to catch a glance of Staza.

"The Coelodontus triptych goes well," she said pointing out three images in a courtyard plaza. "You can really see it from up here."

Andy looked down and saw others working on mosaics in the plaza.

They passed two armed guards at the base of the stairs. The guards were enclosed within plated armor, which made them look like giant, axe-wielding lobsters. He paused for a glance and didn't notice when they told him to be on his way.

Quill grabbed him by the arm and pulled. "No time to stand around, Andy."

"Yeah," Andy agreed and continued. "What were they wearing? They looked like shellfish."

"We use everything that crawls out of the sea."

Staza nodded. "We have to kill it first. But then we craft every piece of equipment by hand. Caston and Poll are proud of their suits."

Andy's eyes widened. "Are you telling me those guys fought giant lobsters and made armor from their shells?" There was a tone of frank disbelief in his question.

Both Quill and Staza looked at him strangely.

A girl with a red bird on her shoulder bounded up and plucked a grating rhythm on her lyre, breaking up the conversation.

"Pen the chief! Hail! But what! Have you stolen our peace? Are you now, Pen the thief!" She danced around them as they walked down an avenue, shaded by orange and blue mesh sheets that flapped lazily in the wind.

She looked them up and down, her eyes widening. Andy saw mischief growing across her face. Her large red bird flapped its wings aggressively and cawed at them. Andy didn't recognize the species; it looked like a bloodred crow.

"Hello Somni," Quill answered tersely, as he tried to push past her.

She grinned questioningly, plucking away at her lyre. "Quilly lad, a frilly lad, with a taste for rhymeless verse. He left today for far away and came back broke—But for a slaver's lad, a silly cad, bearing a crossbow! Stolen this—" she tapped Andy's crossbow, nearly knocking it off his shoulder, "and from your Masters too," she wagged her finger in Andy's face before continuing, "bad boy."

Andy swiped at her hand, but she was too quick.

"Thieving boys, with tragic ploys, make for fun

stories, and a breaking Quill will give me thrills—
once our Mistress is through with you!" Finished,
she broke out laughing.

She was far worse than Emma had ever been.

Quill hurried down the plaza. Andy followed
along, but Staza reached out for Somni's lyre. "Step
off, you nuisance! Go and write some more of that
garbage you call poetry!" Somni darted back in time
to keep her lyre. "Don't let me get a hold of that
thing; you won't like what I do to you with it."

Andy sensed that Staza wasn't joking.

Somni stared with wild eyes at Andy. "I'll have
the painters muse a space above your handsome
face, before they give you to the sea—" Somni
grunted as someone pushed past her. Her red
crow cawed in complaint as it flapped its wings for
balance.

"You there!" Andy felt a hand grasp his arm.

"Hey! He's coming with me," Quill interjected.

Andy saw a sprightly face staring into his. This
girl, with auburn hair and ocean blue eyes, grabbed
his chin and stared deeply. "No no, Quill, this is the
face!" She pushed his chin to the left and right to get
a look at his profile.

"Yes, we need him, just a moment."

Andy looked over his shoulder and saw Quill,
Staza, and Somni. Quill ground his teeth, Staza's
brow raised in consternation, and Somni looked
slighted by the assertive girl.

"Guys?" Andy called out to them, before being
pulled off the path.

Andy followed along as well as he could. "Mind

the serpent!" She dragged him around a massive, but unfinished mosaic of a sea serpent.

"Arke! Leave the serpent!" The girl called out to a gangly boy sprawled out on the floor, putting pieces of colored stone and glass into place.

"Why—who?" he stammered.

"It's our Archon, from the first coalition!"

Arke kicked over a bucket of stones as he tried to catch up. "But Musi, the eyes are all wrong!" He caught up and tried to appraise Andy as they charged across a colonnade and then a plaza.

"Damn the eyes! Everything else is right."

Musi and Arke led Andy in a rush through covered avenues, down narrow alleys, and even through a pavilion full of paintings.

"Hey, hey!" Andy yelled, grinding to a halt.

"What?" Musi snapped, stopping and looking back at him. "No time!"

Andy ignored them and felt his jaw drop. Almost every painting was covered in the bright colors he had seen before. He felt an instant twinge of dizziness. Ignoring this, he approached a canvas.

Musi grabbed one of his arms and pulled.

The canvas featured a warrior garbed in glowing armor that shone with bright swirling metallic colors. He bore a sword reminiscent of the blade Andy summoned with the marble, only far more solid and defined in appearance. His eyes were silver.

Andy saw the quicksilver colors weren't being used to leave messages on these paintings. Instead, they were like any other color on the palette.

Andy wanted to stay, but a hard pull from Musi knocked him off balance.

"We can come back later," she insisted.

"It's probably for the best if you just do what she says," Arke said, with resigned embarrassment.

Andy took another look before allowing himself to be dragged through the lengthy pavilion. There were dozens of paintings and sculptures. They all made his head spin and the swirl of shimmering quicksilver was almost blinding.

Beyond the pavilion, they came upon an ornate building that reminded Andy of a museum or a bank. Diverging from their surface cousins, this structure was ribbed with titanic bones from something terrible, likely from the sea.

The columns were heavily carved, spiraled tusks, and the building itself was made of a deep sea-green stone, polished smooth. The surface was veined with ebony and ivory that arced like lightning, playing across the surface. The rib bones bulged through the stone here and there, making the building feel primordial.

A scaffolding was built above the tall entrance way. It allowed the artists access to the giant mosaic they were creating on the wall above and around the doors.

The scene was mostly complete. Andy saw warriors in shining bronze armor with blazing violet eyes standing against beasts of chaotic shape. The monsters had sharp tentacles and purple, reaching limbs. Raking claws filled their side of the scene, and the artists had even torn rents into the structure to simulate the slashes of these claws. The beasts had deep, burning red eyes, but it was a red that was almost purple.

Above the two warring factions, on the lintel space, stood a serene woman with her hands outstretched to both combatants, as if pleading for peace. She was flanked by much smaller, younger characters dressed like the people he had met today.

Musi and Arke positioned Andy on a plinth and did a few quick sketches of his face. He looked up to the human side of the battle and saw that the most prominent figure was still unfinished.

"Stand there and don't move!" Musi called to him from up on the scaffold.

"Sure." Andy answered sarcastically, looking over his shoulder and hoping to see the others.

"Hey!"

Andy's head popped back into position.

"Stay that way."

He took a deep breath and tried to accept that this was happening. He knew it could be worse.

"The eyes won't be wrong, they just need to be solid silver, then you'll see," Musi commented.

Andy watched them work. Cracking larger stones to get just the right shape, they placed a few at a time, before looking back at him, then at their sketches. They pulled a few stones out, disagreeing on color tone or angle.

Andy tried to gauge how large the whole work was. At least forty feet across. He shook his head, trying to imagine these two arguing back and forth for the whole forty feet. It must have taken months.

Between bouts of bickering, Musi stepped aside to grab another bucket. Andy took the chance to look at their progress. It was impressive for so short a time.

He recognized the outline of his face.

It looks like me, only—older, more rugged—facial hair—

Andy's eyebrow raised.

It doesn't look a thing like me—well, maybe in a decade.

"Hello, handsome."

Andy was certain that someone was whispering into his ear from less than a step away.

He turned and leaned away in fright but remembered that he was standing on a plinth a moment too late. He tripped backwards and tumbled to the ground.

That has to be the third time today.

He heard female laughter, at least two or three voices. He felt his face flush instantly, and his heart wanted to jump out of his chest. It had been too long a day.

I don't need to look up. They can wallow in my embarrassment, and I can take a nap.

He took a moment to enjoy being on the floor. *Let them wait for me, the laughing hens.* He counted slowly to ten before looking up.

There was the woman from the mosaic. Tall and trim, sheathed in a dress colored like sunset over a dark lake, deep orange flowing into somber navy. Her hair was ordered like falling waves over her shoulders, and it was held in place with ivory pins. She scowled at him, though her eyes seemed to smile. It made him think that she was either entertained, or considering a punishment for him. The sharp angles of her face focused even the smallest movement into an intense expression. To Andy, she was magnificent and terrifying.

After a long moment Andy realized that he was staring stupidly. He tried to stand but stopped halfway up.

"Letty?"

Standing next to the magnificent woman was a familiar girl.

"Is it you?"

The familiar girl was cloaked in a gown of dark sea shells. Blue sprays of mesh covered her arms and throat, and her hair was adorned with hundreds of shining gemstones, which made her look like the night sky over a dark sea. She wore a vague look of reminiscence, but mostly seemed uncertain. He saw her eyes scrunch up at his prolonged appraisal; a very specific and familiar look of disdain played on her brow.

"It is you! Letty, I can't believe I found you!" He moved towards her, but two spear toting guards, more hulking armored lobsters, stepped forward to keep him back. He tried to push past them, but one elbowed him sharply.

"Now, now!" The woman said, her voice flowing through the air, at once near, but then as if through the wind. "Hands to yourself, please."

Andy wrenched free from their grip, reached into his pocket, and found the marble.

Chapter 10: The Sun and the Moon

Stepping away from the armored guards, Andy freed the marble from his pocket. He wanted to fight. The lobster guards would be slow in their armor, and they certainly wouldn't expect violence. At least, not from him.

His eyes moved through the crowd. Sensing how outnumbered he was, Andy wondered if he could possibly defeat them.

His glance caught on the woman. She had an expectant look on her face, as if she knew what he was thinking, but waited, simply to see what he would do.

Finally, he looked at Letty. She didn't know him. And worse, she didn't look like herself. She'd even recoiled when he approached a moment ago.

If she doesn't know me, how can I get her out of here?

He considered trying to carry her, though he knew it wouldn't work.

But why? Why does she look at me like a stranger? Is she ashamed of me around these people? Is it something else?

Andy's eyes began to water. Forgetting the lobster guards, he couldn't force her to join him against her will. If she didn't want to leave, there was nothing to do.

He felt a pang of depression, and indecent questions formed in his mind.

Does this absolve me? Am I free to return to Titus and Taptalles? Can I go home?

The guards edged closer, suspicious, and with

their weapons ready. The woman held out a hand, "Stay back. Let him make up his mind."

They obeyed.

Andy felt his conscience sting as he looked with embarrassment at Letty. *This isn't what I expected. The Twister showed me something else—she was tied up and she—* he stared at the magnificent woman *—she was a snake.*

He shook his head and let out a sad breath before asking, "Am I free to go?"

There were a few chuckles.

The woman stepped past her guards; they put up their spears as she went. "What a question to ring through my courtyard. It hurts me to hear these words." She was still ten feet away, but it sounded like she was right beside him.

"I didn't mean to offend—" Andy stammered.

She laughed, "All ideas and all thoughts are permitted here. This is, in fact, the most liberated corner of existence."

She wasn't answering him. He wondered if this is what Quill meant when he said not to ask questions.

Andy didn't want to upset her, and took care as he spoke, "When I turn to leave—to take the stairs out of here—"

"My pupils will put up their arms and lament your early exit." She stood at ease and looked away, "And I will find it quite rude."

Andy felt another sting. *This isn't going anything like I expected—it should have been blood and fighting, not this.* Ashamed, he felt his mouth go slack.

He loosened his grip on the marble and came out of his fighter's stance. "I apologize for being rude. I expected—"

"Never mind expectations, boy." She interrupted, a few laughs rang out. "Will you stay for dinner? It'll be ready in an hour. Musi and Arke still need you here," she gestured at the almost forgotten mosaic. "It's quite the likeness." She gazed at him questioningly.

Andy realized that she had asked him a question. "Uh—yes, I should stay for dinner. May I—" she had turned to leave, but stopped, the slightest irritation in her brow. Andy hurried through his question, "May I speak with Letty?"

A few puzzled glances passed between those assembled.

"No need to be confused, pupils. Our newest once had a slaver's name. Her independent streak ran strong even then, and she reforged her old name into, 'Letty.'" Her answer met with sounds of realization and a few conspiratorial whispers.

She didn't answer me—again, and how did she know that about Letty's name?

He opened his mouth to restate the question, but she turned on her heel and walked through the large doorways, her entourage jingled and clanged as they kept close behind.

Musi and Arke spoke quietly with each other. Andy felt his head spin as he watched Letty leave with the rest, the extravagant gown and the glittering stones in her hair seeming at once alien, and yet, somehow fitting.

Dinner in the snake-pit. Maybe I can catch Letty alone. She might be playing dumb for the crowd. She'll know more than I do, and what was all that about slaver's names?

"Look this way, please!" Musi called down to him.

He obeyed.

"Say, Musi," Andy called to their scaffold, "what did she mean by a slaver's name?"

Musi kept working, but answered all the same, "That's what we were called above—no, no, the clear quartz—yes that one—Andy, pay attention." Andy scowled. "When we are reborn as pupils in Caspia, we are gifted new names. Your friend from above will be called, Solstaci, though no one can guess her talent, it's too soon."

Arke interrupted, "Solstaci seems a brooding sort, don't you think?"

Musi agreed, "Yes, she looks like the younger self of our Mistress. Like the minutes before the dawn, where our Mistress is blazing noon."

"Hmm," Arke disagreed, "They are more like Moon and Sun."

Musi paused, almost dropping her handful of small stones.

Andy wasn't the least bit surprised to see her leap away from the mosaic, climb down the scaffold, and run for paper and pen.

"Inspiration, inspiration!" She mumbled as the pen worked on the page.

Arke hardly noticed when she abandoned her post beside him.

"Yes!" She called out, finishing a quick sketch.

She walked over to Andy, "want to see?"

Andy nodded.

She flashed the paper at him but then pulled it away, "Not until it's finished!" She quickly folded the sketch and pocketed it, before climbing back up the scaffold.

I'm in a strange place.

That realization stayed with Andy as the minutes burned away. It felt like an hour must have passed before a gale of chiming filled the courtyard. He crouched, alarmed by the sound and grabbing for the marble. He looked back and forth trying to find the source. It felt like being in a forest full of cicadas, buzzing all at once, but instead of thousands of insects, this sounded like thousands of wind-chimes. Andy counted six distinct bursts, or waves of chiming, before it stopped.

Musi and Arke climbed off their scaffold. Their progress was extraordinary, considering they were only two working across so much surface.

"What the hell was that?" Andy asked them.

The two shared a puzzled look.

"No staring at each other like I'm an idiot, please. I know you heard it too." Andy was sick of everyone treating him like a fool.

Arke's face lit up. "Ah, the chime!"

"Yes! The chime!"

Arke and Musi disagreed about taking Andy somewhere. "It'll just take a moment," Arke insisted.

"Fine! But you'll suffer the displeasure if we're late for dinner."

"This way and quick." Arke jogged down one

of the covered walkways. "A rib is open for upkeep somewhere down here. I know it—Caston is working on them."

Musi laughed. "That fool—working on anything—what a joke."

"Yes, yes," Arke agreed with a chuckle, before skidding to a halt, "here it is."

Andy stopped and saw that one of the supporting ribs that held the canopy was open. He looked inside and saw a network of small metal chimes, all shaped like wishbones.

"Is this what made all that noise?"

Arke nodded.

Each chime was connected to the next by a fine filament. Arke reached into the rib and plucked a string. Hundreds of the metal chimes sounded at once.

"Wow." Andy paused and looked around at all the other ribs. "Are they all like this?"

Arke looked away from the mechanisms, "No. What's the ratio, Musi? I think one in every fifty is rigged like this. The rest of the ribs are hollow, to allow the sound to echo across Caspia. More are still going up, too."

"It's a fool's project," Musi said, looking over her shoulder, and fretting about being late.

Arke looked at Andy. "She's just jealous that an oaf like Caston thought this up."

Musi snapped at him, "It's more than that—this stupid toy is favored, more than—" she took a deep breath and tried to hold back sudden tears.

Arke stood to comfort her. "It's just the flavor of

the week, Musi. The mosaic will be forever."

They left the opened rib and headed back down the path.

Andy was baffled, but he tried to get his thoughts together before dinner.

The young people here are called pupils. Do they each have a project? And what's the point of the chimes? Is it just to call people to meals? Why is Musi so upset by them?

He felt a burning need to figure it all out. *Haven't I already done enough damage? A sideways question might still be acceptable. I just need to know more before sitting down to eat with that woman.* His skin crawled at the thought of her dissecting stare.

"Your Mistress, what do we call her?"

"She is called Pythia, though not to her face, at least not by anyone still living. We call her, Mistress." Arke hesitated as he considered his next words, "I have to warn you, since you seem full of questions, be careful about asking anything. It is best to state what one is considering and hope for a pointed response."

Andy nodded. "Does Solstaci have a project yet?" He braced for an angry response.

"You see—like that, don't ask her a question like that." Arke answered by not answering.

Musi looked back at him, her face red from crying. "No, she doesn't have a project. She isn't even born yet!"

Andy cringed and wanted to improve the situation, "But you're almost finished with yours, Musi?"

She scoffed, "I've finished hundreds—I've

lost count!" She pointed at a glittering sea serpent climbing up a tower in a spiral, "I nearly died working on that one, well before Caston was born."

Arke nodded. "A masterful work. One of your best."

"And the tower itself was one of yours," she replied.

Andy's eyes went wide at that. "You built that tower, Arke?"

Arke gave him an angry look and shook his head.

Oh—he doesn't want me complimenting his work around Musi right now.

"Yes he did! He designed and built almost every building you see. But where is his favor?" Musi had worked herself up again. "When simpletons like Caston, Somni, and even Quill win favor for mere musings, whims and trash—it just makes me—" Arke quieted her. "She didn't even notice the new scene. Arke, we have been working so hard."

Andy was still reeling from what he heard about Arke. *Almost every building?* Andy remembered coming down the stairs into Caspia. There were hundreds, all different shapes, some towering, others sprawling across great spaces. *He designed and built them all? Certainly not alone.*

Andy tried to ask but saw that Arke was annoyed with him. "You'll have to make your own way to the dining hall, Andy. She can't attend in this condition."

"I'm sorry for—" he stopped, not wanting to make it worse, and looked around. "Which way?"

Arke gave him quick directions, and Andy went off, feeling guilty again.

Several other pupils were rushing the same way. He followed and found the dining hall. The building was round and one of the few not baring traces of giant, ribbed supports. Cracked abalone shells coated the surface. Andy felt along the curved walls, which were far smoother than he expected. The cracks between shells barely registered under his fingertips. These cracks had been filled with mortar, which was black and as slick as the shells. The building appeared scorched by lightning, with black rivulets streaking through the shell's glossy surface, adding to the impression.

"Dinner's in here." Staza was staring at him from the doorway. "Mind your tongue; our Mistress has just heard about Quill's trouble at the watchtower. You are not her favorite topic at the moment."

"Thanks, I'll behave," Andy said, as he entered with her.

Inside, the hall was the color negative of the outside. Every surface was a glossy night-black, run through by forking bands of mother-of-pearl. The bands looked like they were pulsing as the light from the sconces washed over them.

"Amazing—did Arke do this one?" Andy asked, passing into the main hall.

"No, this was our Mistress's first creation." Staza pointed out Andy's seat, "You will find your name on the setting."

"Thank you," Andy gasped as he looked down

into the hall. "Wow."

The hall was made up of concentric circles. The outermost, also the largest, had tables and chairs set for hundreds. There was a descent of a few steps to the next circle, and so on, each circle holding fewer and fewer seats. The quality of the furnishings and silverware improved the further down one went. The very last circle sported a single large throne made from what looked to be driftwood.

"Andy!" A voice called from the far side of the hall, at the second lowest circle. It was Quill, waving him over.

As Andy navigated the pathways between circles, he realized that each circle was spinning, if slowly. He nearly tripped, stepping from one to the next.

Each time I think this place can't get crazier, this happens.

He descended to the second lowest circle and found Quill.

"You're sitting next to me tonight. Guests receive elect privilege, and you owe me. She isn't happy with us, and she's having the crossbow you seized, returned."

Andy curled his lip in annoyance, but Quill rolled right over him, "Don't you dare make a face, Andy. I barely had you exonerated. She might still punish you if she senses ungratefulness—don't mention—well, you'd better not say anything— unless she specifically asks."

Even that laundry-list of demands didn't satisfy Quill, who still stared anxiously.

"Don't worry. I feel bad enough as it is." Andy found his seat. There was a little card with the words: "Honored Guest: Lysander Vanavarre - Sensate."

"How did she get my full—" Andy saw Quill's face and cut his question short.

He wanted to know how they found his full name and what a Sensate was. He wondered what punishment they awarded for rude questions and found himself hoping that it was exile.

"Somni isn't happy with you either," Quill muttered with a grin. "Serves her right."

"What did I do this time?" Andy looked over his shoulder and saw Somni, sitting at a seat one row back. She was staring daggers his way.

"Nothing you did really. There are only ten chairs in the elect circle, this means that she took the tenth spot, and was booted back to the peer's circle when you got a spot down here."

"So, she was in tenth place?" Andy asked.

Quill shifted in his seat, considering an answer. "Well, we aren't in competition with each other—certainly not in such a brutish way, but, I suppose you could look at it like that."

Andy was about to argue, but a flamboyant female voice rang through the hall, "Dinner is called!"

Everyone answered, "Aye!"

The speaker was a girl he hadn't met. She sat in the elect circle and was reading from a large, open ledger. Andy noticed a hefty staff lying on the table nearby. "We are joined by one, Lysander Vanavarre:

rogue Sensate from above. Welcome him!" she said, writing something on one of the ledger's huge pages.

"Welcome, Lysander Vanavarre!" Andy cringed at hearing his name, but most people were smiling. A few, Somni in particular, were not.

"Simple business?" the speaker asked.

"Fifteen more single-story structural ribs are ready for use," a voice called from farther back.

The girl who did the announcing began to scribble away. A few more voices answered; one mentioned a large haul of fish, another described a trail that had been cut outside the settlement.

"Anything else?" She asked.

The room was silent.

"Very well. Arise!"

Everyone shot out of their chairs; Andy nearly stumbled to join them.

The speaker took her staff from the table and tapped it on the floor three times. Then, all at once, every voice rang out, "Will the Mistress of Caspia please join us?" They all held out their goblets to toast.

Andy rushed to grab his goblet and splashed water onto the table.

They were silent, each Caspian holding out their right arm. After a minute, Andy began to feel his shoulder weakening. His hand started to shake. He glanced at Quill and saw his arm was rod-straight, and probably far from tiring. Andy wondered if this was a punishment.

"Of course I will!" A happy voice echoed

through the hall.

I didn't hear her steps, or the door open. Andy wanted to look, but everyone was so rigid that he didn't take the chance.

"Drink!"

Goblets lifted and then tipped back.

Andy did likewise, but coughed and nearly choked at a sudden burning in the back of his throat. It wasn't water.

He tried not to dribble as dozens of shocked eyes landed on him. Pythia had stopped in her tracks and stared with a raised brow and crooked smile.

"Drink, but be careful not to choke!" she intoned, continuing her descent.

Everyone had a long chuckle at Andy's expense. He swallowed and fought through the burning. He hadn't planned on consuming his first alcoholic beverage, but there was no going back.

Who would drink this stuff willingly?

Pythia didn't stand by the singular wooden throne. She walked towards the last empty seat in the elect circle. Though still flapped by the burning in his throat, Andy noticed something strange.

I expected someone like her to sit in the center. Why—ow!

Quill had kicked him to get his attention. Quill had his pen in hand and had written a note on his napkin, which he passed over.

Andy read the note, which said, "She might ask you to go down to the—"

"Lysander!" The girl who made the

announcements called out his name.

"Yes?"

He felt another kick. Quill reached over and pointed at the napkin. Andy read quickly, "—go down to the throne and pour a drink."

"Will you pour?" She asked.

Andy wasn't sure what to say. "I—I will."

There were a few mutterings, but he stepped out from behind the table and walked down to the lowest level. He saw an empty silver goblet sitting on the throne's left arm. He looked around for a pitcher.

What do I fill it with?

He spotted a jug on a table one circle up. He reached over and took it.

Everyone stood silently as he poured.

"Inspiration, dine with us tonight," Pythia said, in a voice so calm it almost made Andy drop the jug. All her force and power were replaced with a sentiment that felt out of place. "Lay your head in these halls. Bless our dreams with wonders to astonish, and fill our spirits with the will to achieve."

Three taps from the announcer's staff rung slowly, and at the third, "Inspiration!" From the back of the room to the front, rank by rank, the pupils at each circle called out, "Inspiration," and drank.

After the toasts were concluded Pythia addressed Andy, "Thank you for honoring Caspia. I hope you poured some of your ferocity into our glass. Please join us."

Andy felt himself flush at the praise. He put the jug down and returned to his circle, sure that nerves were making him shake. Luckily, Pythia motioned everyone to sit. A chorus of scraping chairs and people shuffling broke the tension.

Don't trip, don't trip! Andy reached his seat without incident. As he fumbled with the napkin, he spotted Letty. She was two circles up and staring straight at him.

He wanted to leap over the tables and talk to her but felt Quill tugging on his sleeve.

"Don't do it," he said in a low, nervous voice.

Andy sat still, but an unsatisfied frown bent his cheeks.

At least I found her—and she isn't going to be sacrificed or anything like that. She just has to live here, at least until I get a chance to talk to her.

Andy looked across the high, round hall and listened to the conversations that picked up while food was served by younger pupils. He spent a few minutes trying to count how many were attending, but kept losing track because the rotating circles all moved in opposite directions and at different rates. It seemed like a few hundred, possibly more. Andy wondered if this wasn't the worst place for Letty, particularly if she wanted to stay.

The pupils seem well treated—Musi and Arke are not in the best mood, Somni was annoying, and Staza was threatening, but it's not far removed from people at school. Even the teacher pretends to be the same as the students, but it's clear who's in charge here.

Andy couldn't help noticing that, though she sat at the circle with the elect, Pythia's table and chair were the finest present. He glanced at Pythia, who was already staring his way. She didn't look pleased.

Andy tried to look away politely, but she shook her head and leaned forward with an expression that reminded him of someone reeling in a fish.

"Lysander!" Her voice felt softer than it should have been at that volume. It echoed around the hall, and everyone silenced their conversations.

Why did I have to look?

All eyes were on him. He wasn't sure if he should speak or wait for her. Just as he was about to awkwardly open his mouth, her voice seemed to sneak through the hall. "Lysander Vanavarre, rogue Sensate from above." Shivers racked her body as she repeated the last two words, "From above." She shook her head and looked around the hall.

"It's not all that bad above," Andy said.

Pythia rolled her neck and stared. "You cannot perceive even the first truth of your world, Lysander. A mute toy would be more expert on the matter, because it couldn't speak."

That stung.

"Do you see him, pupils? Bold and bright. His eyes may look open, but what they haven't seen is all of creation. Be not proud though, we were all once like this."

Andy bent his fork between thumb and forefinger. *Why is she so insulting? She invited me here!*

Quill spoke up in Andy's defense. "Yes, but he's brave—maybe the bravest here. He disarmed a brutox with only his hands."

"Hah!" Pythia laughed delightfully and lolled

her head back and around as she did so. Many others laughed with her. "Brave indeed. And see where bravery gets us; we can expect an envoy from a particular ryle any minute now. What concessions will he want for this little mishap? Brave indeed—is it brave to pull people into wars? That is on the table now, young man. That is what you bring to dinner."

Andy tried to answer, but Quill beat him to it. "He only meant to help. Slyn was aiming his weapon at me. I've gotten used to it, though it is disrespectful. Andy did the reasonable thing."

"Hmm." Pythia pointed at Somni and then at Quill.

Quill was shocked. His face betrayed disgust, but only for a second. Somni leaped up from her chair and bounded down to the elect circle. Quill took a heavy breath and stood, his chair squeaking loudly across the floor.

"What?" Andy blustered at this unfair punishment.

Quill patted him on the shoulder as he passed. "Keep your mouth shut, if you want to walk away," he whispered in passing.

Somni spilled herself into Quill's seat and leered at Andy until he looked back. "Silly lad," she said, sipping from Quill's goblet. She leaned in and whispered, "You will lay your head upon a pillow—upon a bed, but keep your eyes open wide, for if you drift to sleep—Solstaci shall forget and weep—weep away her surface name." When she finished, Somni stared off into the distance, swirling her goblet and rocking her head back and forth, as if in time with some unheard music.

Fed up, Andy slammed his goblet on the table.

Pythia looked away from the girl with the record ledger, who had been going over something with her.

"Yes Andy?" She asked unsurprised.

"I need to ask a question—" he stammered, "I was told not to ask questions, but I need to."

Chairs scrapped, and throats cleared.

Pythia raised a brow and looked around the room questioningly. Her glance settled on Quill and she shook her head.

"There is a cost. The price, you cannot afford. But—if you were to tell your tale, someone might take pity and offer a fair word."

Andy didn't think he had much of a story, certainly not compared to what they were used to.

Andy told about the trip to the museum. He told about Letty and Emma, Dean, and his teacher Mr. Holt. When he mentioned Titus for the first time, Pythia recoiled.

"Nothing about the rats, please!" There was an uncomfortable shuffling around the room.

"I believe they are mice," Andy responded.

"They are vermin and you followed them into the Netherscape. Skip any parts featuring these creatures, please."

Andy looked amazed. *What the hell? Any parts? The whole story has them, up till now anyway.*

"There was a battle, I helped. My obligation paid, I came in search of Letty. I followed the amber veins. I traveled through a forest of trees that attacked me—they shook and twisted as I ran through them—it felt like they were laughing as I went."

Somni scoffed. "You walked through the restless wood—and came free—and whole—on the other side? And fought in a battle?"

"Yes," Andy said, annoyed at the interruption.

"Boastful Beowulf," Somni huffed and was silent.

"After the trees, I came out onto a beach, and I saw a black sea with crystal white shores."

Andy paused and heard the word, "Lantic," mumbled.

"On the shore, I saw something like boats made from paper. They had been torn apart. They burned, but instead of flames I saw letters rise and float in the air."

Andy paused. He saw recognition on the faces, but no answer came. *They know what I saw.* He saw glances rest on Pythia questioningly.

"Continue, please," she said.

"By the ruined ships, I saw a man. Huge and terrible. He fought with a creature like the one you call Slyn, a brutox, but the one he fought was larger and like a mantis. He killed the thing with its own arm. Then he held the arm to the sky and roared."

"Thrag—he saw Thrag!" The mumbling voices were louder this time.

The name Thrag seemed fitting.

"I found a circle of portals and a wooden watchtower. I thought that I saved Quill from being killed; the watchtower may have collapsed in the process."

"And how was this accomplished?" Pythia asked.

Andy opened his mouth, but then paused. *She asked me a question!*

He leaned back in his chair.

"Quill!" Pythia snapped. "How was this accomplished?"

Andy looked over to Quill whose face was white with shock. "Mistress—I—I'm not certain how he did it."

Andy's eyes went wide. *He's lying. He's lying for me? I showed him the marble; he even knew what it was.*

Andy continued as if Pythia wasn't furious. "Quill and I marched past the border and met up with Staza, who confiscated my captured crossbow and quiver."

Somni chimed in, "A begging braggart belies believability."

"I then stood in as a model for Arke and Musi—who, you'll notice, aren't here right now." Andy knew that he shouldn't continue, but was so irritated that he launched forward with his diatribe. "I learned that Musi has completed hundreds of outstanding works, which cover almost every surface and structure in this place, yet she feels unappreciated."

Pythia leaped from her chair. "Don't you dare!"

Andy grimaced. *That's the limit.*

The room was silent. Andy leaned back, feeling that Pythia was inches from his face, though she was on the other side of his circle.

Everyone sat still, until a fork dropped. A few

people jumped in fright as it jangled on the floor.

"Mistress?" A voice from the doorway called out.

Pythia kept her viper's gaze locked onto Andy, heedless of the voice.

The voice, coming from an armored guard who rushed into the hall, called out again. "Mistress!"

"What is it, Poll?" She answered demurely.

"Ryle on the border! Brutox in the dozens!"

She shrieked and exploded into a shooting column of smoke that burst out of the hall.

Andy gulped, wishing someone had told him what kind of power Pythia had. Had he known, he might have kept silent.

After a few moments of confused silence, the hall burst into panic.

"Andy!" It was Letty, she was calling to him. He jumped from his seat and took the steps two at a time to get to her.

"Stay back!" Someone tried to tackle him. Andy didn't get a look at who it was, but he pushed them aside and down the stairs. He heard the crash of tables and chairs as they tumbled and sent silverware flying.

"Letty! Do you recognize me?"

She half stood and half sat at the table, unsure of what to do. "I do—I didn't earlier, but when you told the story, I started to remember, and now I do! How do I wake up?"

Andy stared at her desperate face, shocked by the question. He had stared too long, and was surprised by a sudden rush. A guard tackled him and knocked him sideways.

"Tie him up! Now!" A pair of guards approached from each direction. Andy pulled the marble from his pocket and felt the blade flash into existence. He breathed heavily, furious, and the blade seemed to flutter and grow stronger, like a flame fed by a bellows, pumping in time with his heaving chest.

The guards slammed him with the blunt ends of their weapons. But he sliced their spear hafts in two with a single stroke and, on the back-swing, punched one in the face with his free hand, causing the guard to stumble down the stairs.

"Come on!" Andy pulled Letty out of her seat.

He wanted to rake his blade across the last standing guard, but knew it would kill the man and relented.

Instead he yelled, "Back away, or I'll cut you in two!"

The guard considered his spear haft and stepped carefully away.

Andy and Letty raced for the hall doors, shouts from the others resounding chaotically. Letty had to hike her dress up to run.

When they reached the outdoors, Letty stopped.

"Come on!" Andy tugged at her.

"Shut up for a second." She ripped the train off her dress, using a dinner knife she had tucked up her sleeve, and made her dress into a jagged skirt. "Okay! Keep running!"

Once they turned the corner Andy realized that he had no idea where they were in Caspia. The chiming bells in the ribs sounded violently from all around, making it hard to focus.

"We came down a giant set of stairs!" Andy yelled. He spun, looking for the right way, but the tall, sprawling buildings confused his sense of direction.

Glancing up, he saw the colors on the cavern ceiling. *Wait!* He thought back to Titus. *The silver! Follow the silver back!*

Andy spotted the thinnest strand of silver thread pulsing away from the city.

"That way!"

"How do you know?" Letty asked.

"Long story—involves mice!"

A few minutes later, Andy slowed as they came to an intersection. He leaned around the corner of a tower and scanned for guards. There were none.

He noticed an enclosed stairwell on the building they were leaning against. He was tired and expected that Letty was too.

"Let's take a minute to catch our breath," he said, gesturing to the stairwell.

Letty nodded and went ahead.

They sat on the stairs, but Andy kept leaning forward to look onto the lane.

Wiping sweat off her brow, she asked, "What was that you used on those guards? It was amazing!"

Distracted, Andy was slow to answer, "I don't know; I think something happened to me."

"Hey, pay attention," she insisted. "What was that thing you were fighting with?"

"I'm not really sure. It saved my life twice now. It's called an Argument." Andy held the marble out to Letty. "Be careful, it jolted Quill when he tried to touch it."

Letty reached out and took it.

Nothing happened.

She peered closely at its surface. "It swirls, as if it's liquid inside."

"Try holding it out, and grasping it tightly," Andy said.

She did so.

"But point it away from me," he joked, pushing her arm aside.

She tightened her fist and a glow appeared. After tightening it further, the blade flashed into existence.

"All right!" she said with a smile on her face. "I'd like to see them mess with us now."

"Yeah. I'd let you keep it, but I need to give it back."

"Huh?" Letty loosened her grip and the blade vanished. "Don't be stupid, of course I'm not going to take it from you. If you find a spare, hold onto it for me."

Andy remembered Quill mentioning how rare they were. "I'll keep an eye out."

They were quiet for a moment as footsteps rushed past on the lane below.

Letty handed Andy the marble.

The sound of the runner faded.

"Why didn't you say anything to me back there? When I found you, it was like you didn't know me,"

Andy asked.

"They did something; I barely remember anything. Seeing you act like an idiot in the hall knocked some sense into me."

Andy tried to scowl, but it was half-hearted.

"I was pretty stupid back there. Their Mistress is not happy with me."

Letty shuddered. "Good. I do not like her."

Andy nodded, and they were silent again.

"Say, Andy. Why did you come all this way to find me?" Letty asked, too casually.

Andy blinked. He knew why, but he couldn't find the words. He looked at the ground and said, "Let's go."

They peeked back onto the street and waited for another runner to pass before barreling out. Andy nearly tripped on a flagstone, as his attention was stuck to the skyline.

"Pay attention!" Letty snapped, "I can't carry you if you break your leg."

Andy finally saw the stairway up to the cliff. It was steeper than he recalled. He pointed. "That's the way."

"You're kidding!"

"I wish I was."

"We can't run up that!"

Andy turned a corner and stopped short. There stood Pythia, her guards, a handful of armed brutox, and the purple-skinned ryle that called itself Dr. Ropt.

"There they are!" Pythia said with a delighted voice. "And what a couple they make too—did you ruin your dress?"

Chapter 11: Drinks on the Wall

Andy held out the crossbow and quiver. Slyn, the spider, stepped forward with a jittery gait and reached for his weapon.

Andy grimaced, his fingers clenching. An armored lobster had given him the crossbow, quiver, and winch a few minutes ago, specifically for the ceremony. Andy recalled the guards hesitating at the order to arm him.

Slyn leered with eight burning, faceted eyes.

"How's that bump on your head?" Andy asked before lunging forward in a mock attack.

Slyn flinched, but then grabbed the crossbow, his low voice gurgling with frustration. Andy didn't let go, instead, he leaned in and whispered to the beast, "Tell me the name of your Master, and I won't humiliate you again."

Just as Andy was doubting its ability to speak, the creature clicked in a low guttural voice.

Andy glanced up at the stands ringing the plaza. They were filled with pupils from the hall, and a handful of brutox, but the most alarming presence was the tentacled monster he had seen in the optometrist's office.

"Dr. Ropt?" Andy asked. "Is that his name?"

Slyn glanced at the stands. He gulped, before nodding and tugging at the weapon.

Andy released and watched Slyn raise the crossbow aloft, as if he hadn't accepted it in an apology. The brutox rattled their weapons, but the Caspians were silent.

"Don't you want these?" Andy asked, un-shouldering the quiver and holding up the winch.

Slyn snatched them and, after a moment of glory, his eyes bulged with realization. He shuffled off to Ropt, who was sitting on a raised platform next to Pythia. Both Pythia and Ropt were surrounded by their guards. Andy sensed that Slyn was telling on him. The human audience grumbled confusedly.

Andy expected one of the Masters to rise and give a speech on peace and cooperation, but both were distracted by Slyn.

Tell the teacher—go on.

The Ropt creature stood and leaned forward. Andy felt him staring.

Annoyed at the rude, unbroken stare, Andy felt glib. "Don't be confused, Doctor, we've spoken before," he said.

Ropt's tentacles twisted for a moment. He raised a clawed arm, and the brutox surrounding the plaza leveled their weapons.

My mouth will get me killed.

Andy crouched and looked for an unguarded exit to the plaza.

Pythia called out, "Stay, you monsters! The boy is safe here!"

Her guards faced off against the brutox. It looked like fighting might break out.

If Letty wasn't in the booth with Pythia and Ropt, Andy thought they might try to escape in the chaos of a skirmish.

If I had only waited till now—there's no way the

guards will let me near her, not after our escape attempt.

Andy bent, his limbs surged with the need to make a move. Pythia and the Ropt creature were arguing. He couldn't make out what they were saying, but they were in a heated debate.

Andy flinched towards the booth, but the guards turned on him in a flash. He reached for the marble but saw that Pythia and Ropt had come to an agreement.

The guards noticed as well, and both sides put up their arms.

Pythia gave a silent command, and the crowd dispersed.

"That's it? Tell us, what you've decided!" Andy cried.

Pythia waved at him with a bright smile. Letty wouldn't meet his eye, and neither would the others.

After a few minutes, the plaza was almost deserted. He noticed two armored Caspian guards and two brutox standing about thirty feet to his right and left respectively.

Andy followed the crowd, and noticed that the guards trailed him, keeping a set distance.

"Really? Come on," Andy snapped, marching up to Pythia's armored lobster guards. They reeled backwards as he approached. "Hey—you there! Don't ignore me!" They kept moving. "What are your orders?"

Andy cornered them against a wall and stared them down until one began talking, "We're to keep an eye on you. You can't leave Caspia, and you can't bother Solstaci."

Not surprising.

"But what about them?" He pointed to the Brutox.

The guard shrugged. "The Mistress has made some arrangement with the ryle. You are free to wander the grounds, under watch, until your chambers are prepared."

"And then?"

The guards shared a look. "And then you will go to bed, like a good lad, and not cause any further diplomatic incidents. Aye?"

Andy didn't like the sound of that. "What about tomorrow—what happens then?"

The guards shrugged. "Just don't try anything; they have orders to kill if you run." He pointed at the Brutox, one of which was armed with a crossbow, while the other carried a glaive.

They stood in awkward silence before one of the guards cleared his throat.

"Say, that was something else, what you did with the silver blade, I mean."

"I can't explain it. I can't really explain anything," Andy said, producing the marble for them to see. "Why do you work with them? The brutox and the ryle, I mean. I know what they do— they took Letty from her family."

"It's poor company. The poorest. But believe me, Caspia is the best place for a human, particularly a Sensate."

The other guard nodded. "Those violet eyes are worse than a death sentence in most places, even the surface. I'd be more worried for yourself, come morning, than Solstaci; they've already made a deal for her."

Andy rounded on them. "Be clear! Are you saying Pythia bought Letty from the ryle?"

They looked uncomfortable under their helmets.

"Are the people here bought and sold?" Andy asked again.

"Not as such," the guard stammered, "deals are struck, but we're free here. As free as free gets."

The other guard shook his head as he leaned on his spear. "It's best to make peace. Get the Mistress to like you, if it's not too late yet. I heard them talking. They say you came in here on your own, not captured. That changes things in their eyes; no one else has done that. And you've got Sensate blood, which makes you valuable to them both. The ryle is claiming you and so is she. They almost came to blows, but now we're waiting to see who gets—er, who you go with."

They are trying to enslave me—like they did with Letty. Andy looked around at his armed guards. He felt thoroughly captured and then remembered the marble in his pocket. It was his only recourse, but could he bring himself to kill his four guards? He looked through the slits of the lobster helmets and saw clear, violet eyes.

Andy shook his head, knowing he couldn't murder these two. He sighed and let his mind wander.

"Could I ask you guys a few questions?"

The guards tilted in their armor and shared a

glance.

"What does the word Sensate mean?" Andy asked, before they could object.

"That's us. We with the odd eyes, who can see the ryle for what they are."

"Right, but I thought we were called Seers," Andy replied.

They shuffled nervously at that.

"Around here, we use the word Sensate. It keeps everyone happy."

It must have something to do with Pythia.

"Say, Lysander, there's a good spot to watch the sea, not too far from here," the guard spoke nervously, and rearranged his helmet straps. "Might be a nice sight before being—well, you know."

Andy nodded and let them lead the way. He looked over his shoulder and saw the brutox following along, not far behind. The one with the crossbow had his weapon aimed at Andy's back. If he ran or became violent, he expected a bolt, and wondered how true a shot the brutox was.

"I don't get it. Why are you being friendly?" Andy asked.

They were silent, but he sensed pity behind their apprehension.

Maybe they're talking because they don't know what else to do.

This side of Caspia was more ramshackle and cobbled together, and the buildings didn't look like Arke's designs. Fish bones and piles of clam shells filled alleys and empty lots. They passed the occasional Caspian, but these streets were mostly bare.

Hoping to draw them out again Andy said, "I prefer to go by Andy, I hate it when people call me Lysander."

One of the guards grunted.

"How about you guys?"

The one who grunted grabbed Andy's wrist for an awkward handshake. "Poll, they call me. Can't rightly remember what I like to be called." He slapped the other guard on the shoulder plate. "Caston here bet me ten shifts of watch duty that you would try something before the morning. Of course, you tried something at dinner."

A tinny laugh echoed from inside Caston's helmet. He turned and shook Andy's hand. "I can smell trouble, and whew, when I saw you at the stairs, what with that stolen crossbow."

Poll interrupted, "Right, right, but I didn't know that he'd taken the thing off that brute. If I'd known—"

"You aren't getting out of this." Caston clapped his friend heavily on the back. "Make it five shifts and we're square."

"Five!"

The bickering was disarming; Andy let his hand slip out of his pocket.

"Did you choose your names?" Andy interjected.

There was a pause.

"Not as such," Poll answered, "We're named at birth. And, if our Mistress has her way—you staying with us—she'll give you a name too. Realistically, you see, the name comes from one's character. So, in a way, we do choose our own names."

Caston spoke, "Listen to that drivel. What must be, will be. Though I say you gave us quite the licking earlier. I'm almost inclined to trip on a loose flagstone and give you a chance to visit our friends back there, with a few slices of that blade."

These two aren't slavishly loyal to Pythia. How does she control them? Do they really believe there is nowhere better than here? Is it actually true?

They walked in friendly silence up a set of well-worn stairs. At the top, Andy realized that they had mounted a wall that surrounded three sides of Caspia, the fourth being backed by the cliff. He could see a port on the other side of this wall and looked out onto a ketch tying off at the pier. Its crew was hauling in nets full of colorful fish.

Great view up here.

As if reading his mind, Poll said, "Best post in town, this wall." He disappeared into a tower and returned with a pair of rickety chairs. He went back for a third chair and a clay jug. "Get the cups will you, Cas?"

"Right, right." Caston followed and found a few worn, tin cups. He paused at the stairwell, looking down on the brutox, who were standing awkwardly at the base of the stairs. "No worries, friends, we're just having a few drinks. No need to come up."

Poll grunted as he took off his helmet and sat heavily onto the chair. Andy expected it to bend or break under his bulk; both Caston and Poll were far larger than he, but the chair was better made than the rickety driftwood implied.

Andy took an offered cup and joined them in the third chair. The drink was syrupy and blue. He cringed at the consistency but saw that they liked it.

He took a sip and was surprised to find it cool and only slightly sweet. The aftertaste reminded him of roses. "Not bad. Why are you—" he held out the drink questioningly. "Is this how you treat prisoners?"

"I can't say," Caston answered. "It's like she said, the ferocity. I like to see another fighter. It's just Poll and me. Well, Staza could handle either one of us, and Quill is a fair enough fighter. Most of the others drudge through militia practice." He shook his head.

"Sensitive types," Poll answered. "Always wailing about projects and seating assignments. No community here."

"It's true, but shut your mouth," Caston whispered.

Poll nodded.

"I heard you have your own project, Caston," Andy said.

"Well—" he fidgeted. "For defense—not a project in the strict sense. Just some chimes I strung up in a few ribs here and there, hardly worth mentioning."

Poll chuckled.

"It's defensive—it kills the slithers and maddens the brutes, but we haven't tested it on a proper ryle yet." He looked over his shoulder. "Have the urge though, now that we've got one in town."

"What do you mean it kills slithers and maddens the brutes?"

"Just that," Caston said. "Slithers raced up from the shore, not too far back. They mounted the walls and the chimes went off. They melted at the sound. Brutes came another time, by way of the stairs. The chimes went off, and they threw down their arms and ran off. Who could have expected it? I built them with communication in mind—sound the bell for dinner, for alarms, that kind of thing."

"Hmm." *Maybe there's something I can do with this.*

"Don't do it!" Poll knocked Andy's hand away from his chin. "Don't you try it—I can see him thinking, Cas. He'll try anything. Look at him!"

Andy raised his hands in surrender, "All right, I'll be good." He looked at Caston. "I think it might work though—could we get their Master, the ryle—"

"No!" Poll interrupted loudly. "We're not having this talk."

Caston looked at Andy with knowing but sad eyes.

Caston wants the glory, but Poll is more loyal.

"Tell me about the ryle. I want to know more, in case it comes down to it. I don't expect you guys to fight, but if he tries to take me prisoner."

Caston coughed and then spoke, "Yes, the ryle, or a red eye, depending on who you ask. This one is called Zyzqe Ziesqe. It looked like he knew you."

"Yeah, I've seen him before. He pretends to be something else above," Andy said.

"But how's that for a name," Poll interjected. "Just don't call him Zeezee; that nearly started the last war."

Andy chuckled. "Willing to kill over a

nickname? He is proud."

"He and our Mistress have deals going way back, back to before either of us were born." Caston tapped his fingers against his chest piece as he spoke. "She does buy us off him. It's like you said."

Andy stared at Caston's hard, yet downcast face. His violet eyes were misty. Andy felt his stomach clench.

"Buys us off him. But she keeps us well. We're free to do as we will—mostly. We're encouraged to find a trade, something artistic, and give our gifts to Caspia. We must share with the creators in the world around—or so it goes—" Caston trailed off and took a long drink from his cup. "Fine view though."

Andy gawked, "Wait, to be absolutely clear, no mistakes. Pythia—" Caston and Poll tensed at hearing her name, "—she purchases you from Zesq—Zy—Zeezee, the ryle?"

Poll nodded.

"What does she pay?"

There was a long silence. Andy wondered if they knew.

"She sees. She knows," Poll said.

"What, like prophecy?"

They both gave him a serious look.

Poll continued, "This ryle in particular has made arrangements with her, and he has profited. His banners sprout in the lands beyond our borders, overtaking many others. The ryle have no loyalty to each other, you see. Each warlord fights the others. Only rarely do they come together," Poll finished, looking to Caston for agreement.

Caston nodded, "Right, it's as he says. Those were tough times, Caspia surrounded by dozens of them. They would strike with their brutox—sometimes war against each other on our land. We got good at telling their warriors apart; it's the fine markings on their carapaces, you see."

Poll interrupted, "But Ziesqe, he was smarter than the rest; he allied with our Mistress. Somehow, he found us above—or so we're told—and she secured our freedom for the knowledge he'd use to defeat the others."

Caston sighed. "It's been quiet, quieter anyway. Hardly any chance for a fighter to earn favor recently."

So, you do want to earn favor? Perhaps that's why you built the chimes. Andy wanted to ask, but felt it was too personal.

"I know Ziesqe, but above he goes by a different name. He pretends to be an eye doctor. I was just on the other side of this." Andy shivered, remembering the red eyes, the burning symbols, and Letty disappearing. "Did Ziesqe bring Letty here?" Andy asked, knowing he had.

Caston nodded. "He sends the pre-born, tied up, and carried by the brutes. He leaves us with her for some time, before they discuss prices—tries to get her attached to the new ones—to up the price, you see. She just has to have them. He'd left Sol—your friend—and that trouble at the border caused him to return early. Of course, he wants to take payment." Caston filled Andy's cup. "Problem is, you've arrived."

Andy nodded, staring down into his cup. "I'm walking out of here, free, with Letty." He remembered talking to her at dinner. "She doesn't want to be here. I hope it won't come to blows again."

Caston and Poll were quiet for a while, before Poll spoke, "Never say never; another fight could be a laugh, just don't take any heads off and I'll leave you your teeth." He held out his heavy armored hand.

Andy grasped it, with a relieved smile, realizing Poll could deprive him of his teeth in a single strike.

"You shouldn't though," Poll said. "Our Mistress kills like nothing else. I've only seen it once, and I don't care to see it again."

As Caston was preparing to pour another round, four swift reports sounded from the chimes. The Brutox at the base of the wall groaned at the noise.

Andy looked over the edge and saw them drop their weapons and disappear around the corner.

"Ha! Look at them go," he laughed, holding the wall for balance.

"I wish I could, but that's the signal," Poll said as he stood and folded the chair. "We've got to take you to your room."

Andy helped them clear up. It was only a five-minute walk to what they called the palace.

"Titasticus," Poll said grandly, as he gestured.

Even in Caspia, an unceasing wonder to Andy's eyes, Titasticus was a stand-out. He remembered seeing it from the stairs, and, from above, it looked like the shell of a giant lobster. Approaching the building convinced Andy that this was what a lobster might look like to an ant. They neared the left claw, and the flagstones beneath and nearby were crushed and almost lost beneath moist ground.

Its plated shell was glossy black, mixed with red, and covered in patches of vines and mosses of bright colors. Andy saw evidence that people had been growing the plants in patterns on the massive shell. He saw bands of purple and white lichens striping across the thick plates, though in other areas the plants grew wild.

"Got to get around the claws. The mouth is behind them, in the gardens," Caston said, almost proud of the monstrosity.

"Right," Andy answered. His neck craned upwards as they rounded the left claw and came upon the right. Andy felt the ground under his feet change texture. The flagstones here were thoroughly crushed and ground into the loamy earth that now cushioned his steps.

"Guys?" Andy felt an uncertain anxiety, staring up at the massive limbs.

"He's a little closed up today—" Poll said, nearly tripping in a puddle.

"He hates the brutes, and the ryle most of all," Caston answered.

"The giant lobster doesn't like the ryle. Well, it's in good company," Andy said, intending to sound humorous, but coming off nervous.

They walked over a wide, churned path. The trunks of green and orange trees were rent and split apart, clearly crushed under the colossal arms.

"How quickly do these arms move?"

Caston and Poll both looked back at him.

"Just don't fall in the bog and nothing will go wrong. You'd have to be a tree to get crushed," Caston said.

Andy glanced at the dozens of upturned trees that littered their path. "Like those."

"Right, but they'll be fresh regrown in a few weeks," Caston said plainly.

They rounded the right claw and saw the face of the palace. Andy felt his feet stop.

It really is a giant lobster.

Silver and pink vines fell down the side of the dark shell in elaborate foliate patterns. It looked to Andy as if someone had painted the vines on the shell.

Falling water splashed into lily filled ponds in the few acres hidden behind the claws. Giant gemstones festooned the carapace between the brush strokes of the vines. The eyes above the doorway glittered like diamonds and looked to be the size of the largest beach-ball Andy had ever seen.

"I don't think Arke or Musi did any of this."

"No, of course not," Caston said. He had politely stopped when Andy did, "Not their style, is it? No. There are no names on the works here; people say Titasticus is older than anything in Caspia."

Poll inclined his head. "I believe it." And then in a lighter tone, "Most of us just assume that it crawled out of the sea and became entranced by our Mistress's loveliness."

"She made a house out of it," Caston laughed.

The curving stairs, leading to the toothed doorway, were guarded by Staza and a white plated brutox, which flexed its giant mandibles as Andy approached. It held a fantastic weapon, which appeared an amalgam of two swords tied together, handle to handle. The weapon stood at least six feet tall, but to Andy's eyes it looked fitting in the clawed grasp of the towering brutox that bore it.

Staza looks like a child standing next to a giant. What kind of insect is it?

Caston and Poll shouldered their way past the brutox and offered friendly nods to Staza, who reached out and grabbed Andy's shoulder as he passed. "Behave."

Andy gave her a sad smile. Looking back, he saw his personal pair of brutox trailing a dozen paces behind.

The foyer was an alarming amalgam of razor-sharp teeth that hummed, as if ready to crash down. An ornate coat check desk sat around a row of teeth. The brutox were asked by the guards inside to check their weapons, which they did, reluctantly. Caston and Poll were allowed theirs. Andy endured the inspection, but palmed the marble from pocket to pocket, avoiding any questions.

It would just jolt them anyway, he thought, as they passed into the entrance hall.

Stairwells to the left, right, and ahead filled the entryway, along with a few fine tables, chairs, and a well-trimmed, red grass carpet. The entrance reminded Andy of a hotel lobby.

"You're in the abdomen, top tier," Caston said, as they mounted the central set of stairs.

Andy tried not to grimace as he saw clear, fluid filled, veins that traveled the length of the hall. Giant crystalline shrimps and crabs swam this way and that through the veins, some laden with cutlery and dishes, while others walked along the hall in teams, carrying bedding. He noticed that each sported distinct coloration and markings.

Andy had just started to feel a bare sense of familiarity with the Netherscape, only to be confronted with crystalline arthropods. He forced himself to laugh at the sight, if only to keep from screaming.

The hallway down the abdomen was long and it curved into a small hill every dozen rooms. Andy found this even more disconcerting, as hills were universally an outdoor feature.

"We are under the plates of the lobster. The halls conform to the shape of the body," Caston said, noting Andy's distraction.

Andy felt the floor and walls moving slightly, reminding him that Titasticus was alive.

"Here we are," Poll said, reading the plaque on a door, "Malachite." He opened the door.

Andy realized his time was up. He'd have to sleep in a giant lobster, full of smaller, but still massively oversized crustaceans. "Guys—stay for a drink, maybe?"

A large crystalline crab interrupted Andy. It was the size of a St. Bernard, and had skittered into the hall from his room. Malachite toned, as advertised, it gestured him in with a wave of its claw.

"Guys—" Andy pleaded.

"I would, but I've got to be on the wall. One of mine will be on your door, Niclo, I think. Just drop my name and he'll get you anything you want— except out of here." Poll looked to Caston for a laugh.

"S'not funny, Poll."

"Hmm—well, enjoy the sleep anyway. Maybe we can get some sparring in sometime." Poll made an awkward goodbye.

Caston gave Andy a reluctant clap on the shoulder before turning to leave.

Damn.

Andy followed the crab into the room.

He looked up at the emerald grass, growing downward from the ceiling.

Sure.

He sat on the plush, yet oddly ovular bed, and looked down at his feet. His tennis shoes were filthy and torn. They stood out against the pristine orange and black swirls of smooth stone on the floor.

The crab started tugging at his shoelaces.

A *crab butler—what could make more sense?* Andy kicked off his shoes, and lay back on the bed. It was comfort itself. He felt himself falling asleep almost immediately, but a strange clicking noise picked up a few feet away.

Do I care anymore?

The clicking went faster.

Drowsily, Andy sat up and saw the crab. It was busy at work, pulling burrs and pebbles out of his shoes with its left claw, as its right clicked up a storm, carefully tweezing the small orange foxtails from his shoelaces.

"Thanks, Crabby!"

Andy's head hit the pillow, and he slept.

Chapter 12: Deals in the Darkness

"Andy! Wake up!" A sharp pinch forced Andy's eyes open. He sat up in bed.

"It's—weekend." He mumbled at Titus, who grabbed him by the ear.

"The week has certainly not come to an end! We are at an impasse! You need to be on your feet, now!"

"Not in my ear, please." Andy batted the mouse away and slumped back onto the pillow.

Titus waved to Taptalles, who was busy hogtying the malachite crab. "He's not waking up!"

Taptalles heaved as he tied off the last knot. "Stab the slugabed!"

Titus took a deep breath and drew his rapier. "This hurts me more than you know, lad." He poked Andy's nose.

"Ahh!" Andy shot up, forcing Titus to slide down the tumbling blankets to the floor.

Andy realized, with a fright, that he was sleeping in his boxers. "Where are my clothes? I didn't take them off, did I?" Andy recalled drowsily removing his dirty clothes sometime in the night. Burrs embedded in his pants and shirt had been prodding him as he rolled over. Though they should have been on the floor nearby.

"Listen, Andy! It is imperative!" Titus called up to him.

Impervious to Titus's begging, Andy raced around the room, accidentally kicking the crab in the process and causing it to spin wildly on its back.

"There!" Andy spotted his shirt and pants. But they were significantly altered. "My clothes!"

The shirt had been patched in many places with green cloth and the entirety was crisscrossed with applied red sea-shells. His pants had fared far worse, with barely any denim visible behind white and moss colored plaid patches. Hanging chainmail covered everything, barring the knees, which were armored with shining chitin plates, molded to fit above the kneecap.

"I can't wear that! It'll look like I crawled out of a post-apocalyptic cartoon."

"Imagine the noise of all that chain," Taptalles scoffed, pulling his cloak tight around his face.

Andy looked further and found his socks on the floor. One had been unraveled and the other was being mended with a mesh of seaweed. The finished sock would be more like a stocking, at nearly three feet long.

Andy looked over at the crab, who was still spinning softly on the floor. "Did you do this?" Andy asked, ignoring Titus's pleas to pay attention.

The crab only spun, its tiny glowing eyes fixed on him as it finally tipped over and halted.

Titus climbed up onto Andy's shoulder and tugged on his ear. "We have a plan."

"Why are you here? Isn't this against your orders?" Andy chided.

"It is, but my good sense caught up with me on the road." Taptalles nodded. "Now, we're going to save that girl!"

Andy sighed. "I tried. There are brutox

everywhere, and half the time she doesn't remember me. If the brutox left, that would be one thing, but I don't want to fight the Caspian guards, we know each other now."

Andy's brow tightened as he wondered if Pythia might have ordered the guards to be friendly, to earn his cooperation. They knew about his weapon and never tried to confiscate it.

Titus leaned in and spoke directly into his ear, breaking his train of thought, "I'm going to get Letty out of here, with or without your cooperation." Andy balked. "We distract the guards and the viper, you extract Letty. We believe she is with Pythia. Altogether, we'll meet at the wooden circle with the portals—you remember the one, we heard you tore down the watchtower there." Titus leaped off Andy and onto the bed before heading to the door. "Be quick extracting Letty from Pythia's chambers, or she'll swallow me up."

Andy stared mutely as Titus and Taptalles bounded out into the hall. *What did he just say—eat him up?*

"Really!" Andy fell backward onto the bed as he pulled the jangling, patchwork jeans on. "I'm not rescuing anyone in my boxers." He put on the shirt, and then the shoes, which the crab hadn't had time to alter. Everything had a snug, tailored fit, everything but the shoes. He had to leave the socks out of the equation; they were just bundles of string and seaweed on the floor.

"I hate shoes without socks," He complained, and leaped to his feet after popping the second shoe on.

Andy burst into the hall. "Pythia's chambers—Pythia's chambers?" He looked left, then right, down the long abdominal hall. "They didn't tell me how to find her chambers! He's off to get devoured, and I don't know which way to go!"

Cursing the mice, Andy stepped back into the room and looked around wildly. "She hates the mice, maybe she *would* eat them!"

Andy grabbed a carving knife from the end table and cut the crab free. "No funny stuff, now. I didn't tie you up."

Once loose, the crab righted itself and continued working on Andy's sock.

Andy gave it a soft tap. "I need to find Pythia's chambers, right now."

The crab gazed up and raised its claws in a gesture rather like confusion.

"Thanks," Andy said, rolling his eyes.

He was about to head to the hall again, but he felt a pinch at his shin. Looking down he saw the crab signaling with its claws. It looked to be miming an action.

"Hockey?" The crab waved its claws in negation. "Golf?" Again, no. "Sweeping?" The crab nodded.

Sweeping?

"Should I find somebody who's sweeping?"

The crab nodded again.

Filled with pain born from absurdity, Andy nodded. "Thanks buddy, and thanks for these," he gestured at his modified clothing. He wasn't sure, but he felt the crab had just waved him off dismissively, almost bashfully.

Andy stepped out into the hall for the second time.

Sweeping.

He turned left and jogged toward the foyer. This is the way to the entrance. *Maybe I can find someone and ask questions. Sweeping? At least I don't have to hide from the guards, I'm still allowed to be out—I think.*

He found the stairwell and took the stairs two at a time down to the foyer, where he stopped, confused.

He found it deserted. He approached the large doorway which led out to the garden between the claws. He expected Staza and the giant Brutox. Neither were there.

Wasn't there supposed to be a guard at my door? Niclo? Caston said Niclo would be on guard, but no one was there. Andy stepped outside and heard the distant sounds of chimes ringing and, a moment later, scores of angry shouts.

"Titus is making trouble," Andy said with a grin. "But I still don't know where to go."

Andy sighed, looking down onto the lily pads. He heard a clatter from behind and peeked back inside.

An annoyed, scraggly looking fellow, bearing a broom, complained loudly, "These crabs will be the end of me—people tracking chainmail all over my grass carpet." He swept up a few rings and held them out in Andy's direction, "A league beneath ridicule, this is!"

Andy looked down at his pants. *I didn't realize I*

was shedding. Wait! That's the guy!

Andy tried to restrain himself as he walked inside, though he wanted to grab the man by the shoulders and throttle him until he gave up the directions.

I can't do that. I need to play it cool.

Andy stepped forward and plucked a few more rings from the carpet. "Sorry about that—I'm new—"

"Of course you're new!" The gruff janitor interrupted. "*IF* you had any sense you'd realize the crabs need a few days to get anything done properly—and *IF* you had more sense than that you'd never let those clothes out of your sight—'cause the damn crabs will make anyone look a fool!"

"Right," Andy said, slightly paralyzed by the unexpected rant. "They're the only clothes I have; I'm not about to run around naked."

The man harrumphed and bent to his work, picking more rings from the grass. He seemed older than any of the students he had seen in Caspia, though still no older than thirty.

Andy made to help, but the man swatted him with his broom. "I'm not letting anyone else get the credit for my job. The favor goes to me."

Andy nodded and got back to his feet. *He wants favor? But do I deal with him, or try a trick?*

"You know who I am?" Andy asked.

The man grunted an affirmative.

"I'm on the run." Andy looked around. "No guards to stop me—I've lost my weapon."

The man eyed him. "Don't play me for a fool, boy."

"Fair enough," Andy sighed. "I need to find Pythia's chambers. You want favor." Andy paused and gave him a significant look. "I was running, and only you were there to stop me. You cracked me over the head with your broom, tied me up, and took me to your Mistress."

Andy held his hands out, but he palmed the marble out from his pocket before he did so.

The man gestured for Andy's shoe. Andy raised a brow before kicking it off and tossing it to him. "What do you want with my shoe?"

Ignoring him, the janitor unlaced it. He tossed the shoe, minus the lace, back to Andy. "Put it on."

Andy slid it on. *That's bad—I can't run with a loose shoe.*

The man bound Andy's hands with his own shoelace and then pushed him forward.

"Where do we go?" Andy asked, but the only answer was a sharp blow to the back of his head.

Andy stumbled, his face slammed into the floor; his tied hands were nearly useless in breaking the fall. His vision blurred, and he was sure that he had a chunk of red grass and soil in his mouth. He coughed and spat it out.

"Don't eat the grass, please."

"What the hell?" Andy growled, stumbling to his feet.

"Believability," the man said. Staring at his busted broom he spoke, as if to himself: "Thick noggin on this one."

Andy wanted to head-butt the man with his thick noggin, but was startled by sudden movement.

A stairwell made of glowing vines had descended from the roof. He noticed that a chandelier was missing. Andy felt dazed, but tried to work out what he was seeing. *The chandelier is made of these vines—with glowing tips for fake candles—it unties itself and descends to form this stairwell?* His head throbbed, and he nearly stumbled, but his mind kept working. *But what signaled it? I was on the floor—did he call it? Damn—he didn't have to break the broom over my head.*

The man pushed Andy toward the stairwell, which swayed, as if caught in a light wind.

"Neat trick." Andy said, trying not to slur. He felt dizzy, but still hoped to coax something out of the man with a little flattery.

"Shut up and walk," he said, jabbing the broken end of the broom into Andy's back.

Andy felt like he might vomit. He mounted the vines with some difficulty, but managed to climb. The man prodded him all the way to the top.

This can't be how she gets into her rooms. This is ridiculous.

When they finally came out at the top, Andy's eyes widened to take in the marvel of Pythia's antechamber. Its ceiling curved like the inside of a globe, with the glowing lines of the cavern drawn in vivid detail. Andy's eyes pulsed as the lines washed over him. *There are roads and borders, cities marked and nations too. There's the black sea; I saw it yesterday. But everything else is a chaos of veins of color, the same as on*

247

the cavern ceiling. He saw script here and there beside landmarks and what he assumed were settlements. *Degoskirke is huge, and there's Vychy, not far from Sentinel's Watch, and a central city called Yyonvere.*

The man struck him on the back and shoved him onto the polished hardwood floor.

Blood welled up in Andy's mouth. He had fallen on his face again, but this time his teeth tore a gash in his lip.

"You better hope I never get loose," Andy said to the man's thoughtless face as he stood.

"Do you want this to be believable?" he asked gruffly, pushing Andy forward.

Clenching his teeth, Andy kept quiet as they advanced to a large set of ivory double doors. The man rapped on the door three times in quick succession, then glanced heavily his way.

"Don't muck this up now," he said in a whisper.

A moment later a latch clicked, and the door opened slowly. Andy was startled to see Letty's serious face. The man was just as surprised.

Letty looked back and forth between the two before shaking her head in disapproval.

"He tried running, and he's wanted—for violence against your very person—now would you please go and get our Mistress? She'll be wanting to reward—"

Letty interrupted, "You idiot! Our Mistress is out killing mice, and you will be punished for harming this boy so grievously. I will see to it."

The man stood there, dumbfounded. "I was only—"

"Move!" Letty commanded, and he nearly fell over himself as he stumbled away.

Andy cracked a smile as he watched the man crash into the stairway and fall out of sight.

"Well done—you've still got that sharp tongue," Andy said with a smile. "What has she got you up here for?"

"Hiding me from you," Letty raised a brow, "though that hasn't worked, has it?"

She gave him a sly grin as she grabbed his arm and pulled him into the bedroom. Andy's head spun with pain as she pushed him to a large ornamental seat in front of an array of mirrors.

"Look what happens to you," she said reaching for a knife on the table by the mirrors.

"Yeah—I can't tie my own shoe—wait! Don't cut that."

But it was too late, she had sliced the shoelace restraints to get him loose.

"What?" She said, suddenly alarmed.

"Those were—hell, I can't run without shoelaces." Andy looked around for a replacement, but felt suddenly dizzy.

"What's wrong?" Andy heard Letty's voice, it sounded fuzzy and far off. He reached for the chair, needing to sit down, but wasn't sure if he had or not.

That's better, Andy thought as he felt his face suddenly flush with warmth.

He laughed as the sensation of tumbling worked through his mind and limbs. It was like sinking through warm water.

"Andy!" A voice pushed through the water and

almost caught his attention, but he was distracted by a vivid image of the barbarian named Thrag sitting on a pier next to a dapper man with long fingernails. Coming down the pier to meet them was a younger Pythia, hand in hand with—

After a slap across his face and a sudden burst of cold, Andy forced his eyes open.

"Letty!" he gasped, realizing he was splayed over a collapsed chair, lying mostly on his back.

She grabbed his hand and pulled him from the toppled furniture. She put her hands around his waist and helped him over to a bed so large that Andy didn't have the time to get a good account of it before he was sat down. Letty bent to stare into his eyes. "Follow my hand," she motioned, and he tracked the movement without trouble. "Thank goodness, I thought I might have lost you. A concussion and a split lip—" she complained.

"I was—somewhere else for a second." Andy mumbled, alarmed at the vanishing pain. He spotted a small blue vial in Letty's hand. "Did you heal me with that?"

Letty nodded. "They call it minoe, an extract of etherium—or so I'm told. I've seen her use it on wounds—and it looks like you've let your poor skull take a beating."

She's so friendly.

Andy wiped a thin sheet of sweat off his brow with a wide grin. "Whatever it is, I feel great." He leaped to his feet. "Like a full night's sleep and an energy drink. And no more pain."

She smiled. "That comes from using too much."

Andy grabbed her hands and pulled her to her feet. "Take some yourself, it's a long way back to—" Andy thought back. He traced his steps back to before Caspia. "—Sentinel's watch. We have friends in the city, and there's a portal there, I can get us back home."

Letty listened carefully; her face was at first hurt, and then wide eyed, and finally sad as she looked down.

"What?" Andy asked, confused by her behavior. "Let's get you out of that ridiculous dress—" her face shot up, cheeks red and mouth askew. Andy stumbled over his words in a rush to continue, "—and into something you can run in—we have to get across the city—dark colors are best." Andy tried to hide his embarrassed face in a wardrobe. He tore through dress after dress. "Jeans, maybe? Something camouflaged?"

She laughed and he pulled his head out of the wardrobe. He felt euphoric and saw refracted light shining at the edges of his vision. He knew he was forgetting something, but he wasn't sure what it was.

"Nothing suitable in there." He tried to scowl in her direction, but could only grin. "Do what you did earlier—rip the bottom half off that dress, and let's go!" Andy grabbed her hand and moved to the door.

"Careful—" she nearly stumbled to keep up with him, before kicking off her heels. "Don't need these!"

Andy bent down to grab one of the discarded shoes and held it like a weapon. "Makes a flimsy dagger."

She rolled her eyes and knocked the shoe out of his hands. "Don't hurt yourself."

They stumbled out into the foyer laughing. Andy lost his laceless shoe and nearly slipped on the polished floor as he stared up at the ceiling. "Shocking," he said softly as he held onto her shoulder, only half for balance.

"Isn't it amazing?" Letty asked, pulling Andy towards her. They both stared up.

"I wish we could stay—what was in that vial? I've never felt like this before!"

Letty laughed as she took Andy's hand and waist. She tried to dance with him.

Uhh? We need to go? But I—I'd like to stay—for a while at least, maybe learn to dance.

They laughed and tripped over each other's feet for a moment. Andy wanted to stay, but the urge to run still lingered.

Pythia will be back—and Titus—Titus! He's out there distracting them for us.

"We can't, Letty—we need to escape. This isn't forever." He wasn't sure what he was saying, the words just seemed to appear.

Letty shook her head as he tried to pull her away, and towards the stairs. "What's so bad if we stay, Cas?"

Cas?

"So what if we stay? I like it here." She dragged him back into the bedroom. Somehow, her feet had traction on the smooth floor, and it was all he could do to stay upright as he slid.

"Letty—Letty please," Andy pleaded with her.

"I have a new name," she said as they passed the threshold.

Andy's eyes went wide as he struggled from her grip.

"What did she do to you?"

Letty cried out in annoyance and sat angrily down on the bed. "Just go! You don't have to stay. You can rescue yourself! You always want to go!"

What does she mean by that?

"What did Pythia do to you, Letty? You chose your own name—why would you—what happened?"

She shrieked in anger and leaped from the bed. For just an instant Andy saw yellow, viper's eyes. He instinctively shied backwards and, thanks to his bare feet, slipped on the floor. "You're—you're not Letty."

She gave a disapproving look, and then his mind realized that he had been looking at Pythia the whole time.

The whole time!

Andy felt his spine crawl, thinking back to what happened between them just moments ago.

"Where's Letty? No more tricks!" Andy tried to sound intimidating as he pulled his shoes back on and stood.

She walked towards him with an angry hand outstretched. "You'll learn who asks questions here, boy!"

Andy rushed to pull the marble from his pocket, but found it absent. *I took it out earlier! I must have dropped it when she cut my bonds, when I fell over!*

Andy leaped aside and towards the chair he had knocked over, his eyes scanning wildly. There!

He lunged for the marble but Pythia held out a palm and something tripped him. His flailing sent the marble flying. It bounced off a mirror and rolled past him, towards Pythia. "Damn!"

Andy reached out, but it was far beyond his grasp. It rolled closer and closer to Pythia, who only stared down curiously.

Andy spotted barely discernible fright in her posture as she stepped slowly away.

He crawled on all fours to reach it. Pythia gestured softly and he was suddenly pinned to the floor. It was as if an elephant was holding him down with one leg. Andy felt that much more force could come down in an instant if he so much as struggled.

Pythia held out another hand and the marble lifted, to float and spin slowly up to her height. "So, this is how you caused so much mischief."

Andy thought she feared it.

She reached out to grasp the marble, but pulled her hand away at the last instant. She gestured and Andy felt the weight shift direction and pull him to his feet.

He pushed slightly against the force with his arms. *Maybe I can grab it.*

"Don't try to fight, dear boy. I can feel when you do," Pythia said, looking up at him, "and I don't like it."

Andy let himself be held upright for a moment as she stared, silently considering.

"Where's—" Before Andy could finish, he felt a clamp over his mouth.

Pythia motioned sweepingly with her right hand, and a flash drew his attention to the far side of the room.

Letty!

She stared at him with terrified eyes. Letty was standing straight and motionless, as if held in place as he was. Andy wasn't sure from this distance, but it looked like her face was red, as if crying. Andy paused. *Should I be crying? What can I do now?*

"How is it that I didn't see her there a moment ago?" Andy asked. He felt the clamp shut down on his mouth again.

Pythia didn't look at him, but spoke, "I have quite a bit of power, here in my palace." Before he could respond, Pythia continued, "You can touch this? You can even wield it?" Andy couldn't answer. "Well, from what I hear, you wield it about as well as a child wields a violin."

Andy tried to speak, but felt the clamp still holding his jaw closed.

"Hmm?" She said, the clamp dissipating.

"The marble explodes into a blade. The blade is like light, it shines through my fist—I don't know how it works." Andy wasn't sure why he was cooperating.

"Well, I think we have our work cut out for us, my boy." She paused, in thought, before a vicious grin split her face. "A little adventure will do you good, maybe jog your mind. A trip to a Juncture certainly would. You'll come away better in the end."

Andy dropped like a ragdoll as the force holding him suddenly vanished. He caught himself and stood. *How many times can I fall over in one day? This is ridiculous—wait, what's this about an adventure, and work?*

"What kind of work?" He glanced at Letty who trembled.

Pythia glided over the floor in her bare feet and grabbed Andy by the chin. "You're lucky I like your face—I'd have anyone else thrown into the sea for so many insulting questions. Now hurry, we're going to the disc. We'll have to teach you as we go."

Andy pretended to acquiesce and turned to obey, but in an instant reached out and swiped the marble from the air. The blade shot from his hand.

Pythia rushed towards him, a look of fury, but also betrayal flared across her face. She nearly lunged, but froze, an instant away from impaling herself on the blade. She raised a hand in anger, but then lowered it with a look of frustration.

I felt nothing. Does clasping the marble neutralize her power over me?

"Don't your powers work anymore?" Andy asked.

He saw her eye twitch.

Pythia exhaled heavily and composed herself. "Let's make a deal."

Andy tried to keep his jaw from dropping at the unexpected change in circumstance.

Pythia seemed close to tears. "You want my new child that badly—you want to return her, and yourself, to a life of slavery." Pythia was silent for a moment. "I will offer her alleged freedom, in exchange for your service."

Andy nearly leaped to agree, but managed to choke the words back. He had a sudden vision of Dean in his mind. Dean complained, *"Service? Ask for the complete definition of the term before you agree!"*

"How will I serve you?"

Pythia rolled her eyes and laughed. "In many ways, you little fool. You will obey every command without question, and you will be grateful for the new purpose that obedience creates."

"That sounds like a bad deal, Andy. You'd better try to negotiate—it's not like she has a gun to your head," Dean's imaginary voice chuckled nervously.

Andy grimaced and raised the weapon.

She huffed, her face full of consideration. Suddenly Letty fell over.

"Letty! Are you all right?" Andy wanted to rush to her side, but kept his weapon leveled.

"Of course I'm not all right!" She leaped to her feet and rushed to attack Pythia before hitting a wall of force.

"Don't push your luck, girl," Pythia scoffed and Letty skidded backwards, eventually stopping at Andy's side. "There she is—free and unharmed. Ready to be rescued."

Letty stared her usual harsh daggers: first at Pythia, and then at Andy. "I won't let you sell yourself into slavery for me. I'd rather die." She lunged towards Pythia. "Throw me into the sea— you said you would! You sad old cow!"

There was a loud slap and Letty recoiled.

"Enough, please!" Andy waved the blade for silence. "I need to think."

"Just agree!" Pythia demanded.

In the same instant Letty cried, "No you don't!"

Andy stood there silently. *I need to rearrange the deal.*

"Letty goes free, to do as she wishes, you offer us your protection against Ziesqe and his creatures. If you do this, I will agree to serve you for this one night only."

Pythia's face contorted in rage.

"Listen—before you explode. I see that you want me to wield this," he waved the blade. "I do not own the marble—it's borrowed—and I need to return it."

Pythia laughed. "It's an Argument, not a marble, silly boy, and you own it now. You'd be an even bigger fool if you simply returned it—who else can even use the cursed thing?"

Well, Letty for one.

Andy scowled. "A community has built up around the protection it provides." Andy said, recalling what Quill had told him. "Lives are in the balance. I will need to return it, or whatever happens to them will be on my hands."

Pythia tried to scowl, but ended up with a look of surprising softness on her face. "That isn't satisfactory."

Letty grabbed Andy's arm and leaned in to whisper in his ear. "Kill her, Andy! We can free everyone in Caspia!"

Pythia cast an angry glance, but Andy saw that her eyes were fixed on Letty's hands, specifically where Letty had grabbed him.

Andy whispered, "Some of her people want to live here; I've spoken to them."

"Well! What is it then?" Pythia snapped.

What would Dean do?

Andy bit his lip before finally speaking. "I will serve you one full day a year for the rest of my life, and I will find a way to secure this or another Argument, as you call it, for that service."

Pythia's brows rose as he spoke.

"In return, any person in Caspia is free to leave on the days of my service. I will escort them wherever they wish."

Pythia scoffed, "None of mine would follow you."

"Then you don't mind that being part of the agreement?"

She narrowed her eyes and stared expectantly. "That's all?"

Andy stuttered, "No—not all, you must give me a week's notice before my day of service, so I can make arrangements. You also provide protection from the ryle."

Pythia shook her head. "A day's notice, protection only available in Caspia, and you serve tonight for free." She held out her hand.

Dean's voice screamed in his head. *"She's going along too easily; there's a problem, Andy! Check the fine print!"*

Instead of heeding the advice, Andy raised a hand and took Pythia's. "It's agreed."

"Brilliant!" Pythia snapped a finger and paper

and quills floated over from a desk. The floating quills drew up two copies of the contract. "Go ahead and sign, please," Pythia said, handing Andy a quill.

Letty snatched the paper away from him and scanned it. Andy read and was surprised to find no fine print. Everything was as they agreed. He wondered if this was a bad sign, and wished Dean was on hand to advise.

Letty handed him the contract. "I can't find anything wrong with it," she said.

Andy signed the first contract and then the second, hoping this was the right course.

"Fantastic!" Pythia beamed. She reached out and grabbed Andy by the wrist. "We're off! The Nicomedian Ossuary awaits! Ah! I'm not dressed for archaeology." She released Andy, snapped her fingers and her flowing gown morphed into khaki pants and a loose white blouse. The pins in her hair grew and sewed themselves into a white meshed pith helmet.

Pythia looked in the mirror. "This is more for safari, but it'll do for tomb raiding."

Letty gave Andy a wide-eyed look and whispered. "Can you believe this woman? She's like a little girl."

Pythia spun and flourished, a silver riding crop suddenly appearing in her hand. She tapped Letty on the brow with it. "You can stay here and polish that sad face with a few more tears."

Andy released his grip on the marble; the blade fluttered away. His thoughts still stuck on the contract. *There wasn't any fine print, it was all as we agreed—but I know I missed something.* Looking back at Letty he could see it in her face. She thought the same.

"Come now. You're on my time tonight, Lysander."

Andy followed Pythia to the back of her huge, master bedroom, while staring sadly back at Letty. Letty held onto his copy of the contract.

She called out to him, "I'll wait for you in the room with all the spinning tables and chairs. Come find me when you get back!"

"I'll be there! But go out and make sure that nothing happened to the mice, please. If you find them, tell them I'll be late—" Andy stuttered as Pythia smacked him with her riding crop.

"I'm in too good a mood to be hearing about rats, now, please be silent." She gestured and a fine mosaic portrait began to open.

The mosaic featured a joyous Pythia impaling a sea serpent with a harpoon. The mosaic was splitting open at a seam between the waves.

She would have personalized art in her own bedroom.

After a moment, the mosaic was split, leaving Pythia on one side, and the bleeding sea serpent on the other. With a grin, she led the way up the stairs that appeared beyond.

"Come, come, we have a magnificent voyage of self-discovery ahead of us."

Andy cringed, the comment reminding him of overly-enthusiastic teachers. He looked back one last time at Letty's torn face before the wall sealed shut.

He followed along in the dark, taking the stairs carefully as he went. There was a click and a hatch opened at the top. Pythia almost floated through the hatch. Andy tried to follow, but his shoe fell off and he tripped on the last step.

"Oh, you are useless!" Pythia snapped, her demeanor reminiscent of a child whose fun had been ruined. "But you can't go into danger dressed like that. Hmm, I'm glad I noticed before we left."

She leaned her chin on the riding crop and furrowed her brow.

"Your crab did this to my clothes, and the shoelace—"

"Shh!" She called for silence before gesturing with her crop.

Andy looked down and saw his clothes morph into an elaborate blackened cuirass over a white tunic, topped by a billowing burgundy cloak. Bronze arm guards ran from his wrists to his elbows, and shining greaves protected his shins. His shoes were now heavy sandals that wrapped beneath the armor up to his knees.

"Charming! Just like a young praetorian."

He sighed, ignoring Pythia's grin. *Better not say anything. She could make hell for me if she wanted. Ridiculous cloaks might be the least of my worries—she mentioned going into danger.*

"What did you mean by—" Pythia frowned, cutting him short.

"Come now. We have to draw open the gate. Where is that Juncture again? Disputabat? Yes! That's the one; I still have creatures sieging the place." She turned, with a hop in her stride as she walked.

Looking around, Andy realized that he was on top of the giant lobster, somewhere close to the head; she was leading towards the tail.

He turned and couldn't help a quick glance down into the garden between the claws. *Some of the trees are growing back already.* He looked out into the city and saw that Caspia glowed. Its buildings stretched out in every direction. The towers that Arke built cut streaks across the glowing ceiling. Andy felt a tap on his head. "Come now, no time to dawdle. You do cut a fine figure in those clothes. Don't fret, I could have dressed you up like an Elizabethan, hose and all. Now don't push your luck with me and keep up."

Andy followed along. There were bridges, grown of a familiar red grass, at junctions between the huge armored plates of the lobster palace.

After a dozen segments, they came upon a field of chalk drawings surrounding a large bone doorframe, which stood out among the geometric patterns on the floor.

Andy felt his skin crawl and his eyes began to hurt as the symbols on the floor blurred. He shielded his face.

Pythia raised her crop and drew long sweeping arcs in the air before her. There appeared more unfamiliar markings, shimmering and fluttering. She drew five such symbols, and as she finished the last, they exploded in a flash of light. The five symbols burned in the air. Suddenly, the empty doorway burst like a bubble. An image of a mountain fortress that reached from the cavernous floor all the way up to the ceiling appeared beyond the door.

A portal.

"This is a rare treat for you. There aren't many who can call a gate like this."

Wind poured out from the portal and pulled at Andy's new cloak, while the view from beyond the portal flew across a side of the fortress. It felt like looking through an airplane window. He saw spurting gouts of blue flame licking across stones and dark inky shapes racing over turrets in droves. They dashed between the flames, sticking to the jagged walls, even at right angles. *Slithers.* The image finally panned to the ground. There was a shore near stairs leading up to the fortress gates.

Andy saw short, lanky, green-skinned figures littering an encampment at the base of the stairs. "What are they?"

Pythia huffed a sound of soft annoyance at the figures milling about. "Goblins. Unsavory, yes, but loyal. Don't be alarmed, and don't raise a weapon to them, they're of a nervous disposition."

Andy nodded.

Pythia stepped through the flashing portal. Andy followed close behind, his armor chafing and his cloak billowing as he went.

Chapter 13: The Broken Teeth

Andy stepped through the portal and stared down
at a few dozen creatures, all surprised at the sudden
entrance of a pair of tall humans. Pythia wasn't
lying, and though he had never seen such a thing, he
looked at these shabby wretches and saw goblins.

Pointy ears and sharp faces poked out from
tents, shacks, and from behind rocks. They dressed
in an assortment of tattered rags with a scant few
pieces of armor here and there, and what armor
there was didn't fit or was mangled to the point of
absurdity.

Pythia was instantly set upon by the tallest and
best equipped goblins. The older of the two had a
shiny badge stapled to his breastplate. The badge
proclaimed: Senior Marshal Squeeg. A badge on the
younger read: Junior Marshal Lojjy.

"Mist-i-ress! I beg you—if you'd please?"
Lojjy implored, falling to the ground and clutching
the hem of Pythia's dress. "The starvation—
destitutions! We're a pack of implorable,
incorrigibles without your beneficence! Please—"

"No begging tonight, it spoils my temperament."
Pythia kicked him away. The collected goblins took
this as a bad sign and many fell to their knees and
pulled at their ears or grasped at the ground in
desperation.

The Senior Marshal stepped forward, his
hand shying the Junior away. "No begging, Lojjy, 's
why you're only the Junior Marshal. Any upright
officer knows his lady can't rightly stand a'sight of

beggardom. Now, m'lady hhrm," he doffed his helm awkwardly, cleared his throat, and continued, "the camp suffers." He paused to gesture at the pile of groaning goblins all around, "Slithers, the inky kind, and even brutoxeys attack at all hours. We holds em, for now, but we've no gainings to speak of—"

"Before you bore me to tears, Squeeg, be quiet and listen." She paused to let the mass of groaning goblins perk their ears. "Listen well, gobbies—I've good news."

That got their attention. Dozens more spontaneously appeared from inside the rickety shacks and tents blanketing the shore. They were starving and scared but rushed to hear the good news.

The ground all around, for as far as Andy could see, was full of rushing goblins passing the word and muttering between themselves.

There must be hundreds, maybe a thousand. What are they doing here? He stared at the fortress. She wants them, to capture that?

Pythia bent low and held a finger to her lips. She looked all around, from face to filthy face. Their ruckus quieted. All Andy could hear was the nearby shore. Thousands of green, pointy ears were tense.

This is how she does it. They just love her.

"Tonight, you conquer!" Pythia cried.

An immediate wave of shrill cheers had Andy plugging his ears.

He couldn't hear her, but Andy watched Pythia laugh as she waved to the mob. After a moment, she held her hand out for silence. "And you will be led by one of my own." She gestured to Andy. "I have rarely seen ferocity such as his!"

Andy nearly collapsed.

"My own Lysander, may the spirit of Caspian guide your arm tonight!" There were a few scattered cheers but, mostly, the goblins stared.

"He's not our lady!" "No one kills em like she does..." He heard their muttering go back and forth. "But, m'lady, we want you!"

"Now, now, gobbies, let him prove himself."

They all, Pythia included, stared at Andy, as if in expectation.

Andy heard Dean's voice in his head, "Better give the people what they want."

Do I have to?

Andy palmed the marble and focused, he raised his fist to the air, and the blade crackled. It flickered in and out of existence. Somehow, it wasn't working.

The goblins took this as a good sign however and cheered a cautious huzzah for the show of mystical strength. Pythia, however, raised a doubtful brow. Andy recalled the Argument failing once before. Its inconsistency made him even more nervous.

"Say something!" Andy heard Pythia's voice. It sounded like she was yelling into his ear, but she stood at least two dozen goblins away.

Though willing, Andy wasn't sure what to say. "Uhm—Gobbies! We attack the—" he studied the high path that switched back and forth past gatehouse after gatehouse to the many fortified barricades and finally to the large portcullis of the mountain fortress. "We attack the fortress—shortly!" He raised his fist and the blade crackled again.

That was met with a few forced cheers, feet shuffling, and eyes rolling to the ground. He heard one goblin mutter, "At least he's a big target."

Andy flushed; even Pythia smirked.

Well, what do you expect? I had no idea you wanted me to lead an army of sad—unequipped—half-starved goblins!

Andy's glowering was interrupted by a tug at his sleeve. Squeeg and Lojjy were there. The Junior Marshal put his helmet on so he could raise the visor in salute. Andy saluted back.

"What is your plan of attack, Supersenior?" Squeeg asked.

Before Andy could think of an answer, Lojjy spoke up. "A Supersenior trained by Herself, o'course, would know dat a plan to attack mustest be based on basic precepts of strategical excellence. And had he hours to accumulate such specisic knowledge o' the situation, as such it stands, he'd conclude conclusively—"

"Spit out that pigs-water you rotten fool!" Squeeg blustered.

"I say! He'd conclude, conclusively, that my plan would mirrory match 'is very own plan, all thingses being equal!" Lojjy gestured with a flourish that knocked the helmet visor back down over his eyes.

Squeeg barged past Lojjy and implored, "A fool's plan, sir! A wrong waste of time. My plan—"

Andy saw a muscled, well-equipped goblin not

far behind the proceedings. This goblin was leering cockeyed at the marshals. He had several stripes on his shoulder plates. The goblin waved Andy over.

Squeeg had launched into recounting maxims that represented the axiom behind his plan. "Yes, yes," Andy interrupted, "but we need to see everything mapped out—our position, eh—the enemy's position, and uh, the plan itself, of course, if it's to be in accordance with supreme excellence." Andy coughed to stifle a laugh.

"Sir!" Both Squeeg and Lojjy protested.

"Supreme excellence!" Andy retorted, "Get that map going—work together. You don't want to see your Mistress in a bad mood." He said that last part plainly.

It had the desired effect. "Right, sir—we'd best get to th' command pavilions." Squeeg called to him as they bumped into each other in their rush to the largest tent on the shore.

Sad stuff, those two, but this one?

Andy approached the striped goblin. "Good work, getting marshals off your back. Come now. We're attacking tonight; we need to high-talk with our ychorite: the real brains behind the Broken Teeth." The goblin held out a bony hand, "Name's Mastery Surgeon Clang."

Andy took his hand. "Lysander—" he tried to think of a rank or code-name, but nothing came to mind.

Clang gestured that they head into camp. "Just a moment Clang—" Andy pointed to Pythia, "I need a quick word."

Clang folded his arms and nodded.

Andy rushed to Pythia, who was busy accepting colorful seashells from a thick crowd of eager goblins. Andy pushed past the line. "Hey! No cuts!"

Andy continued past them, but felt a flurry of sharp kicks to his shins.

I'm glad she put armor on me.

"Mistress!" Andy called over the buzz.

"It isn't polite to push ahead, Lysander," Pythia said, accepting another shell. "And shouldn't you be planning?"

"I—we need to talk about the attack."

"There is something in there I want very much. I expect that you will find it."

Andy paused, annoyed that she wouldn't even look at him. He yelled, "I can't do it—I," He stuttered as the green faces stared, all shocked that he would raise his voice to their Mistress. "I'm not able to lead an attack," he whispered to her.

Irritated, Pythia looked up from her offerings. "You have no idea what you can accomplish—and tonight you will capture that ossuary for me. The creatures that occupy it are more pitiful than this assemblage. Your blade can tear through the gates, now don't disgust me any further and attack!"

Andy wanted to yell at her. "It's a fortress, a mountain fortress—what the hell is an ossuary?"

The goblins started backing away.

"They keep bones in an ossuary, dear boy—among other things. Now get up that hill or tomorrow morning you will watch me feed that sad-faced girl to an abomination—I haven't decided which one, maybe you'll pick for me." Pythia snapped her fingers at the goblins, who cautiously came closer. She returned to accepting shells and administering pats to pointy heads.

I don't doubt she would.

Andy turned away and scowled at the fortress. *I'm sure this is my fault; maybe if I did something differently. Maybe—* He felt a tug on his sleeve, it was Clang.

"We've got to be off."

Andy nodded, grateful that this goblin looked competent.

Clang grunted. "I've trouble with bosses too. But listen clear, my bosses are small teeth to yours."

Andy thought he got the gist of that. "Yeah, you're probably right."

Clang snorted as he nodded his head. "Damn fool color to bare in a battle," he smacked at the billowing burgundy cloak, "everything with eyes sees it."

Andy grimaced. "I'd better keep it though, she put it on me."

Clang laughed at that. "Stay to the rear when we charge, and care that shiny sharp of yours is full actual, afore the fighting."

Andy considered the marble in his palm. *It hasn't failed me in a fight—has it?* He thought back, and remembered the first time it fluttered out on him. It was during his struggle with the Brutox for the crossbow. It stopped working halfway through, and he had no idea why.

Can I depend on it? The Argument it's called—I

need to depend on an Argument. He grinned, and paused to consider his condition, the people, the new clothes, and the looming fortress above. It all felt absurd and he wanted to burst out laughing. "Am I dead already—or maybe in a coma? I hear you have long dreams in comas."

"No time for pointless questions." Clang pulled on his cloak and got him going again.

"Who are you taking me to?" Andy asked as they negotiated a way through the ramshackle encampment.

"We go to the Martin, our smartest, our ychorite."

Hmm, an oddly normal name, followed by a few strange ones.

"You said Martin is the brain here?"

Clang grunted. "The Marshals pretend smartness, but the Broken Teeth don't move until the Martin nods."

"That's good; the Marshals aren't very inspiring."

Clang's cackle was as rough as his leathery skin.

The Mastery Surgeon led him through the camp, closer to the steep, rocky stairs. In a hollow beneath the stairs they came upon a cave, which reached into the mountain. As they passed inside Andy coughed from the acrid smoke coming from the goblin's lopsided torches and braziers. He had to crouch to avoid the low ceiling.

"How deep does the cave go?" Andy asked, between coughs.

"Not deep, but there is a big room, and then a

geary gate—all shut that is, though."

"A gate? There's a gate at the end of the cave? Does it lead into the fortress?"

Clang looked at Andy like he was a child, "Din't you hear? It's shut up tight. The Mistress been down here plenty to bang away and play with the gears. It never opens."

Andy ducked under a low hanging rock and stepped into the chamber that Clang had mentioned. Large and tattered black banners, emblazoned with crude images of broken teeth and fangs, hung on the ceiling and walls. Ropes crisscrossed the chamber, suspending hammocks and holding sacks and pieces of equipment off the ground. Andy found this curious.

The assembled goblins were of another sort altogether. They quieted their chatter when Andy stepped into view. Where the goblins outside had been cowering, these were attentive. Andy spotted a goblin with a missing ear nudging his sleeping comrades, alerting them to his presence.

Andy saw piles of equipment being repaired and blades being sharpened. A hunched goblin was busily fletching arrows on an overturned barrel.

A whisper had gone up and Clang raised a hand to quiet it. "The sharpest are a bit skittery," he said to Andy, before addressing a goblin ogling at them, "get the smartest—"

Clang was interrupted by a voice that came from above. "Please stop calling me that, Clang."

Andy jumped as a fox face poked out at them from behind one of the black banners. The face was

273

colored like the cave ceiling, but had a decidedly different texture. The Fox's eyes were hidden behind narrow lids, but what eye there was, was solid black, lacking pupil or iris. The air around the face shimmered, but as Andy looked closer, he realized that it was the creature's body blending into the background, like a chameleon.

Andy could make out a smile on the face. "I'm being rude to our guest, please excuse me." The shimmering air solidified into a reddish mass. Andy saw the creature's body.

It's like a—a—hmm. Well, I recognize pieces, but added up, this creature doesn't make sense.

Its body was almost completely feathered, save for the face, hands, and feet. The hands and feet were slightly clawed, but otherwise human. Andy's eyes widened at the tail. Its fox face put on a wry look and the feathers changed color. The feathers were at first a dull red, but they brightened slightly at the base, and further up, they sharpened to a blood red. At the tips of each feather a shock of yellow-orange burst out, giving the impression that his whole body had just ignited. As the fox face straightened, Andy saw that he was lithe and trim.

Amazing.

Andy sensed the fox face was becoming annoyed with him.

Clang coughed and nudged him. "Don't stare."

"No, it's all right Clang, let him look. But the staring stops after our introduction—just tell me when you're done." He spoke as if chastising a child.

Andy grinned at the remark. His face is so

expressive, and he's a quick wit too.

Andy held out his hand. "Lysander—Andy is better."

The creature took his hand with a gentle claw and shook it. "Martin, and not The Martin, please."

"Sure."

There was a pause as Andy wondered what to say next; it was hard not to stare.

"I hear that good and bad news follows your coming. The bad?" Martin looked around the room questioningly.

"The baddest news!" A few goblin voices echoed, desperation clear in their voices, "Attack! We must attack tonight!"

They are calmer than the other goblins, but they are still nervous. Of course they are, anything with half a brain would be. How much brain do I have left? When Andy realized that he wasn't about to run away, he had his answer.

"Yes!" Martin replied. "This is terrible news, on the face of it at least." He motioned at Andy. "But the good news?" He stared at the assembled faces, waiting for an answer.

"His flashy bladey." A voice called out from a bedroll.

Martin held his hand out to Andy.

Andy fumbled in his pocket for the marble. He readied it in a tight grip and summoned the blade. It flickered.

A few shrill cries bounced off the walls at the sight of the flashing blade. Andy saw Clang smack one of the scared goblins.

Martin stared at Andy's hand. "Twist your wrist; that should help you find the hone," he said.

Andy did so and found that the blade solidified. For a moment it almost had distinct definition, to the point of looking like a real, if crude, sword.

"It will take practice," Martin said.

Andy loosened his grasp and held the marble up for Martin to see. "You know what this is."

Martin stared, his fox brow furrowed up in thought. "To a degree." His feathers darkened to mottled gray-black. He shivered, and the feathers lightened. Andy wondered what he was thinking.

"Everyone calls it an Argument, and I hardly know any more than that."

Martin however, was distracted and lost in thought. "A Seer's sight isn't like a ryle's, but it's worth a try," Martin said, half to himself, before turning and walking deeper into the chamber. "Come on," he called to Andy, "You too, Clang."

Andy looked at Clang, who shrugged and followed.

At the far end of the chamber, a smaller passageway led further into the cave. Clang grabbed a torch, though Martin plunged ahead into the darkness.

Andy avoided cracking his head on the many low points in the passage, but he heard his armor scrape against the rocks along the way.

"There it is," Clang said.

Andy saw another light ahead. He realized, with a start, that the floor had suddenly become even, and he didn't have to hunch. He reached up and couldn't touch the ceiling. The cave ended; we're in a hallway now.

Clang grunted. "Don't touch the geary pieces."

Andy focused. There were indeed levers and motionless gears scattered in an insane pattern on the walls, throughout the hall. Andy wanted to stop and inspect them, but the smoke from Clang's torch made it hard to see.

"—no, the third horizontal axle on the lantic wall breaks off in the cave mouth." Andy heard an unfamiliar, high pitched voice talking with Martin.

A small lantern hung at the end of the hall, and miniature tables, covered with tiny charts and diagrams, sat in a few places. Past the lantern stood a barred door. The door, composed of thick, twisted gears and metal work, was almost impossible to see through.

"Who's the gawking surfacer?" an annoyed voice asked.

Martin stepped aside and held a hand out in introduction. "Blue, this is Andy, recently appointed commander of the invasion."

Blue, a mouse reminiscent of Titus and his people, only colored like an evening sky, sneered at hearing the news. "We already have two worthless commanders, three if you count the hag—she's the reason we're down here breaking our—"

Martin coughed, "Careful now, Blue; she could be listening." He tried to put a good face on Blue's querulousness. "Andy, this is Blue, exiled builder, expert tinkerer, and," he paused to scowl, "clearly the sharpest tongue for leagues."

Blue huffed at the last. "So—are we done wasting my time, or can I get back to this mess?" He gestured to the confusing machinery covering the walls.

"If you not figured it by now—" Clang started and was silenced by sharp stares.

Martin spoke, "I have bad news. We must attack, tonight. And with this door locked, our strike will likely be a suicidal one—up the races, to the gatehouses," Martin finished, shrinking back from an increasingly angry Blue.

Blue took a heavy breath before kicking over his little table, sending the charts flying. "Fine! Get yourselves killed!"

Martin raised a claw to calm the mouse. "I said likely—there's still a chance."

Blue paused, and Martin gestured to Andy, who smiled awkwardly.

Blue kicked over the second table.

This one's nothing like the other builders. Maybe that's why he's been exiled.

Blue looked to Clang. "It was a joke on day one, Martin! Enlisting with the Viper, who barely feeds or clothes us—her idiot marshals wasting everyone's time—and now a child commander!"

Clang nodded, and Blue threatened to hurl a chair into a wall. He took a breath, lowered the chair, and stormed off anyway.

"Wait! Just wait a minute!" Martin called.

Blue turned back to them and crossed his arms in false expectation. His brow furrowed so hard that his left ear furrowed along with it, giving him a fearsome look of cynicism.

Martin turned to Andy. "The Argument, please?"

Andy produced the marble for all to see, and then gripped it.

"No no—not like that—we don't need a blade, it won't cut through these bars. We need the sight. Do it properly." Martin gestured to his eyes.

Andy stood there, confused. "What do you mean, properly?"

Martin scratched his chin. "When I was aide for Master Boqreq he trained heavily with the Counter-Argument; all powerful ryle do. I saw him—" Martin reached out for the marble, Andy tensed, and nearly pulled it away, but Martin stopped short, "I'd better not touch it—I tried once. Somehow, the Master would take it into his sight before he began his experiments for the day. It always gave him the meanest purple eyes, but yours should go silver." Martin narrowed his gaze. "Try holding it up, like you want to look into it."

Andy sighed and held the marble up to his eye. At first, he saw only the sparkle of countless flecks across its surface. Looking closer, he saw the flecks were moving ever so slightly around one another. He saw a few purple and gray flecks converge, then scatter.

The surface is like liquid—well, like churning pieces of cereal—wait, are those letters?

He looked closer still and saw the lines between the flecks were actually letters and words. The darker flecks were bordered by the script he had come to associate with the ryle. However, the headache inducing letters didn't make him sick. He considered this odd, but wondered if he wasn't growing used to it.

Distracted by the occasionally legible text on the light flecks Andy looked closer still, but saw something like a wireframe face.

Martin?

Burning lights and dark letters were enmeshed and sewn into the wireframe that was Martin's face. Martin's eyes were a confluence of spinning pools full of broken letters, both light and dark. It was like nothing he had ever seen.

Martin's mouth moved, as if in speech, but he only heard a dull buzz.

Andy tried to tighten his grasp around the marble, but found it was gone. He pulled his hand away from his eye. What? What's happening to me?

The hallway wasn't exactly gone, as much as it was replaced, with a maelstrom of letters and words sewn into the shapes of what should have been there. The words of a gear on the wall sounded off in his head as his eyes passed over them, "Gear twenty eight thousand, link gear—" Trails of letters flashing across surfaces tangled and untangled as his eyes violently twitched away, looking for something sane. Andy felt certain he was screaming, but all he could hear was the dull roar of millions of words sounding off, all at once, in his mind.

He stumbled backwards and felt hands catching him, while voices shot through his head. He looked down at a black and white mesh lattice-work that resembled Clang's bony hand and arm.

"GOBLINOID-LITHE-Median axiom// 93% weighted-potency & physio-social-traitiality:(For details: see-Spleen)(__SELF?NAMED...,"

The speech wasn't cut off, but as his eyes strayed over other letters, the words were overcome by another language reading just as loudly. The two droned on indistinguishably.

Andy felt his heart beating out of his chest as he looked away from the hand that supported him. He closed his eyes tight, but he still saw everything, only under a slight misting of alpha-numerics. He covered his eyes with his hands but only saw the writing on his limbs.

There was a difference in his own arm. Deep inside the mesh of letters and shapes that made up his right arm, there was a painfully silver cord that ran down the limb and terminated at the end of his fingers. It was so bright that he couldn't bear to look for long.

"Andy!" the word was soft, barely audible. He saw Martin's nightmare face, though concern pulled at the lines of his features, despite his wireframe form.

"Andy—focus—"

Andy could barely make out every other word, though he tried. He tried to focus on the sound of Martin's voice.

Andy reached out and grabbed Martin's arm, he felt the feathers, both spiny and soft at once. Help! Andy felt like he was speaking, but he couldn't hear his own voice.

"I know how—back to normal." Martin said, slowly enunciating every word.

"How! How do I get this thing out of me?!"

Martin seemed able to hear his voice, but he shook his head. "First you need to—the door—now or never."

Andy tried to pull away, but he felt claws and bony hands hold him fast. "The door!" This time it was Clang's voice reaching through the roar.

They pulled him to his feet. He nearly stumbled, trying to find a place where his eyes could rest, but there was nothing.

They led him to the door. Andy felt dizzy as he stared at the mess of arcing shapes and twisting letters.

I can't do this.

Andy saw a hand come into his field of view. It was Martin. He reached forward and pointed to what might have been the locking mechanism.

Andy's eyes focused on what looked like a six-toothed clamp holding the door in place. It feels like I'm sorting through a pile of papers—with my eyes.

Pieces of door, wall, and mechanism seemed to filter away and the clamp came to the forefront. Each tooth of the clamp was connected to a lever or gear that fitted into an axle in the long hallway.

Wait—

Andy realized that all but one of the teeth were disengaged.

The door is almost open.

Andy focused on the last tooth and followed the connection of mechanisms. He stepped backward and felt hands keeping him upright. His legs trembled, but he kept track of the axle. It traveled a long way, back down the hall.

Andy pointed, and felt Clang and Martin help him along. He reached out and grabbed for the axle on the wall, using it as a guide. He looked down for a moment and saw Blue, still incredulous, even as a wireframe mouse.

Finally, the axle disappeared behind a boulder. Andy felt words passing between his supporters, and saw Clang rush off into the caves.

Andy leaned against the wall. I just need to take a break—I'll be ready when he gets back.

Splayed out on the floor, Andy saw Martin motioning, his hand above his eyes.

That's what got me into this mess.

Martin forced Andy's hand up. Andy resisted for a moment.

Martin was right about at least one thing—I have been using the marble incorrectly. Andy relented, and copied the hand gesture.

With a sudden pop, the roaring noise silenced. He felt the marble resting in his grasp. Everything was back to normal.

"A little warning next time," Andy said, letting out a heavy breath and pressing his head against the wall.

Martin stepped back as Clang and several other goblins arrived with pickaxes.

A spray of rock shards struck Andy's face as they tore the boulder to pieces. A moment later, Martin pulled Andy to his feet. "Your eyes went hollow and silver."

"But they're back to normal now?"

Martin looked closely. "Yes, back to normal. Normal being violet?"

"Yes, I think," Andy recalled Dean telling him about his violet eyes. "They are only this color sometimes; I don't understand it."

Martin nodded. "Adolescence. The ryle have studied it in the Seers for centuries."

"I get dizzy spells when I see these strange bright colors. Almost nobody else sees them. I thought I was going crazy," Andy paused and looked around at members of species he had either never heard of or suspected to be a fantasy. He wished it had stopped at crazy colors and dizzy spells.

Martin grinned, as if sensing Andy's self-doubt. "They call the colors you are seeing ultra-violet. Encountering these colors prompts your eyes to work harder to see them. The pain and imbalance should go away as you develop. Eventually, you won't feel a thing. If you ever have to use the Argument like that again, it should be easier; so don't be afraid."

Andy was about to ask another question, but Martin pointed towards the work.

The goblins were pulling pieces of rock away from the wall. Behind the debris sat a simple lever, as plain as any of the others, though, so far from the door that it was ridiculous.

Andy reached down and flipped it. A crack echoed in the hall. They watched the door swing open on its own.

Everyone stood in silence. Disbelief rang through the air.

They've been staring at this door for who knows how long?

The first person to speak was Blue. "Anyone could have done that!"

Martin ignored the complaint and looked to Clang. "We're going in, but only the sharpest. Someone wears a chime harness—make sure it's the repaired one. Leave a few guards at the gate, we don't want any incompetents following," Martin spoke seriously, as if certain of imminent danger.

Clang nodded and relayed the orders to his underlings, who rushed off with gleeful glints in their eyes. "If we're quick, there's no needing suicide assault on gates."

Andy nodded and saw Blue climb up on Martin.

"Not now, Blue, I need to focus."

Blue jumped down and looked over at Andy. They both stared awkwardly at each other. Andy shrugged and pointed to his shoulder.

Blue climbed up, slipping momentarily on Andy's greave, before coming to rest on his shoulder. "I don't like it any more than you do, surfacer."

"I'm used to it." Andy said, watching Martin, who, once all the orders were given, started stretching and focusing his breathing. Andy hadn't expected yoga either.

A few seconds later, it was difficult to pinpoint where Martin ended and the wall behind him began.

"What do you mean? How are you used to it?"

Blue asked, almost angrily.

Distracted by Martin, Andy answered with little thought, "My friends, Titus—and Taptalles—they like to ride up there too."

After a moment, Andy realized that Blue hadn't responded. He strained his neck to get a look at the mouse, who wouldn't meet his eye. Andy worried that he might have insulted him somehow.

"I—" Andy was cut short by a sudden bustle from all around. Dozens of armed and armored goblins moved forward and past him. They all came up to about his waist. Andy saw Clang pushing here and there, looking at their equipment and armament and making the occasional critique.

"Blade's dull," he said to one, "strap on helmet," to another, and "get outside, you incompetent!" to a third, who stumbled in a rush to leave.

After his inspection, the goblins with shields took the front positions and those behind chose short spears from the collection of weapons that each kept strapped to their bodies.

"What's the plan, Clang?" The silent and businesslike demeanor of the goblins had an effect, because Andy realized that he was whispering.

Clang pointed ahead. "That way—then we looks about."

Andy felt a tugging at his shoulder, and at first thought it was Blue, but after turning, he realized it was his cloak. It was snagged. Andy bent to loosen it, but found it wasn't stuck to anything. A thick string was trailing off behind him. Andy pulled on it, but found it taught, possibly stuck under someone's foot.

"Clang—" Andy gestured to his problem. Clang pulled a knife from his hip and cut the string, it took him a few heavy cuts to get through. "Thanks."

Clang grunted softly and unhooked the scabbard that went with the knife, before handing them to Andy.

"Won't you need it?" Andy asked, running the scabbard loop through his belt.

"I got plenty," Clang said. Andy had a quick look and saw it wasn't a boast. Clang had at least four knives that Andy could see. Boot, ankle, wrist, and an extra at the hip.

Andy inspected his new knife. It was clean and even looked sharp, and if it weren't for a few pits in the blade, he would have thought it was brand new. When he sheathed it, Andy realized the blade had been sharpened so often in its life that it was noticeably thinner than the scabbard, which was lined with cotton to keep it fitting snugly.

There was a slight tinkling. He turned and saw a goblin wearing a large harness covered in chimes, much like the ones he had seen in Caspia.

Clang made an angry face at this goblin. "Takka—silence the bones!" He said in a harsh whisper.

Takka carefully checked the network of threads he had wrapped around his wrist. Andy inspected the design and saw that each thread ran through a series of metal eyelets on the harness to its rank of chimes. A thick cord, of maybe fifty separate threads, converged at the waist, and was tied off at his wrist. Takka hunted for a cord that wasn't completely taut.

If even one thread is loose, the connected chimes are free to make noise. Keeping them taut is like a mute button—a really bad mute button. Takka followed a thread to a chime on his shoulder and found slack. He carefully tightened the offending thread and gave a signal to Clang. Clang nodded, but looked to Andy, concerned. Clang wasn't pleased, but, barring Takka, the rest looked dauntless.

A soft click came from Martin, and the whole procession moved forward.

It was dark on the other side of the gate, but Andy saw that gears and levers lined the wall here as well. He hoped there weren't any switches on this side, and imagined a goblin accidentally tripping one and locking them in.

The goblins further ahead called back in nearly silent clicks and chirps. Clang often replied with gestures. Andy thought they must have been able to see in the darkness, as he struggled to take a single step.

Small detachments broke off from the group to search side passages and chambers. Andy stepped into one room and nearly slammed into a giant rack of bottles before realizing he had found a wine cellar. Thousands of bottles were so covered in dust that it looked like a gray snowstorm had hit the place.

Further ahead, the party came upon a stairwell.

Andy paused when he felt a claw on his shoulder. He nearly jumped, but realized it was

Martin. The fox face appeared before him. "I suspect this is the only way up." He looked to Clang. "Wait five minutes, then follow silently. If you can clear this floor in that time, do so, if not, advance."

Clang nodded. "What if there are many floors?"

"I will do this," Martin raked a claw on a cornerstone at the stairwell. Three diagonal lines stood out clearly on the rock. "If you see this, the floor is safe to inspect—but only for five minutes, then advance. If there are no markings, expect enemies. If I have time, I'll leave you a message."

Martin's face shifted into nothingness. Andy strained to hear his silent steps up the stairs, but all he heard was the slow, regular breathing of the goblins.

He's going to scout out every floor. The mountain fortress was well above the cave we started in. Who knows how many floors there are?

They waited in silence for the agonizing five minutes. Clang tapped two of his teeth together, making a slight click. The party moved up the stairs. Andy stayed back until they passed. Afraid that his relative blindness would upset their advance, he fell back to the rear. One goblin stayed behind to keep an eye on him.

Maybe I can use the marble.

Andy readied the marble and gripped it. A glow appeared but then the blade flickered, lighting the space around. The goblin jumped in fright, shielding his eyes. He gestured wildly for Andy to stop.

A little less pressure.

Andy loosened his grip, and the blade

disappeared, but a softer glow still filled the hall.

Perfect.

Andy looked at the goblin questioningly. The goblin still seemed annoyed, but noticeably less so.

"That's better." A voice said in his ear.

Andy nearly jumped out of his shoes. The blade exploded from his hand and blinding light filled the hall. Andy realized that it was only Blue, who was sitting so quietly on his shoulder that Andy had forgotten he was there. He relaxed and dulled the light.

"Blinded me!" The goblin whispered angrily, reaching out to find the wall.

"Damned foolish thing to do," Blue complained in his ear.

"I didn't mean—you've been so quiet that— forget it."

Andy grabbed the goblin and put him on his free shoulder and took the stairs two at a time to catch up with the others.

At the next floor Andy found Clang listening to reports from his scouts. Clang glared at Andy's glowing fist, and the goblin draped over his shoulder, but said nothing.

Andy leaned in and whispered. "I'll turn it off on a dangerous floor—until there's a fight, then I'll need it to see."

Clang rolled his eyes. "No light if I say so." Clang gestured at him with two fingers pointed down. "If you see that, make dark."

"Sure." Andy considered the new floor. "Dusty."

Clang nodded. "No tracks anywhere—dead

spaces these—many years." Clang ran a finger across the floor and pulled up a thick layer of dust.

"Can I," Andy pointed to a doorway, "look around?"

"Fast peek—we move soon."

Andy strained his neck to get a look at Blue, who made no protest.

Blue's an odd one; I don't know when he's going to be mad, or when he'll be fine. I wonder what he did to get exiled.

Andy took a quick left and entered a barracks. He saw bunk-beds stacked three high. Chests sat at the foot of each bed, and some stuck out from underneath the bottom bunks. A few bunks still had sheets tucked in beneath the topmost mattress, to provide privacy for those below. It reminded him of fun times at home, building forts out of the couch pillows and bedsheets. Sadly, these were moth-eaten and tattered.

He touched one of the sheets and felt it crumble in his fingers.

Behind the crumbled sheet, on the central mattress, lay a tunic, trousers, and leather armor elements. A curious sea creature, like an ornamental bottlenose dolphin, was emblazoned on the chest piece. A helmet completely covered in thin, green rust sat nearby, the many white hairs of its plume lay a few inches beneath where they belonged on the comb. They looked like leaves long since fallen, but never blown away.

Andy reached out for the helmet, but heard a click.

That's Clang.

He turned and nearly tripped. His cloak had been unraveling again, and his foot was caught in a taught thread that led back to the doorway.

"This useless cloak!" Andy growled, struggling to stay quiet.

"I'll get it—" Blue said, sliding down what remained of his cloak. It looked a bit shorter than it was when he started. "Humans—" Blue muttered as he chewed through the thread, "can't do a thing right—and we're the lesser civilization."

"I didn't ask you—" Blue stared at him with a furrowed brow and angry eyes, "but thanks."

The thread snapped, and Andy hurried back to the stairs, with Blue mumbling the whole way.

The last few goblins were mounting the stairs. Andy took his place behind Takka, who was sweating in his harness. Andy watched him take each stair carefully, mindful of his potentially catastrophic clothing. His hands ran across the threads, softly plucking and checking for tautness.

What are we going to find in here anyway? Slithers, more brutox? Maybe a ryle?

On each of the next dozen floors they found Martin's mark. Every time they spotted it, Andy felt relieved, though he sensed the goblins were eager for a fight.

Andy explored when he could. He walked through libraries, armories, more barracks, alchemical laboratories, and even storage rooms full of food that had long since rotted to dust.

Who built this place? It must be centuries old,

at least, and what does Pythia want here?

At the thirteenth floor, Andy paused and spotted Martin's marking. Clang had seen it and had sent the scouts to explore. Reflecting, Andy was glad he didn't have to lead the goblins. Martin and Clang were qualified and held their loyalty. He would have been treated like another marshal. Andy shuddered at the thought of being that useless.

Better a third wheel than a hated incompetent.

Andy peeked into a high-ceilinged room. It was filled with symbols written in arcane sequences. They covered the floor and walls, though the room was otherwise bare of furnishing.

Andy looked at Blue questioningly. Blue shrugged, "Ancient mysticism involved symbology—a few quacks still practice it."

Andy nodded, noting these symbols weren't like the painful script he associated with the ryle. "Does it work? I mean, when they try to cast spells—does anything happen?"

Blue ruffled. "I don't care to talk about religion."

Andy had heard this answer once too often. "What does it have to do with religion? I already know that magic—of a kind at least," he looked at his glowing fist, "magic exists, it's a fact now. But, do symbols like these," he gestured around the large room, "actually affect the real world?"

"There's no such thing as magic—oh great leader—that Argument you found only allows you to wield it because you're committed. Worse yet, you're committed to the failed side—if you didn't already know." Blue laughed. "You see a blade no one else can wield, a glow that comes at will, and you can even take the Argument to eye and see beyond. All of this assures you that it is good. You have no idea what kind of enemies you make by doing so. You think the Viper needs you? I assume she made some deal with you—" Andy stared blankly. "Thought so. Don't believe for a moment that she couldn't wield the Argument if she cared to. She knows better."

Andy was speechless.

"It's rude to go flaunting your commitment publicly. People don't want to see that—it's an embarrassment from a painful past," He huffed, stuttering on his words. "Flash-in-the-pan upstarts like you descend every few decades—and you've no idea of anything, and then the Usurper finds you and—" Blue clenched his paws around Andy's collar and squeezed. "We're trying to move on!"

Did I make a terrible choice when I picked up the marble? Wait—every few decades?

Andy let Blue calm down, before asking, "How old are you, Blue?"

Blue suddenly loosened his grip, surprised by the question. "I stopped counting—what's it to you?"

Hmmm.

Andy hazarded a cautious guess. "You aren't over one hundred, are you?"

Blue shuffled on his shoulder awkwardly, "Well it's my fur—everyone always thinks I'm young."

He's bashful about looking younger, meaning he's a lot older than one hundred!

Andy shook his head as tried to understand. The

marble is a religious tool. Religious—something? That's all they'll say. But religion is looked down on? Maybe that's why no one ever gave me a straight answer. And things that look like magic aren't called magic, but are actually religious. And I should be ashamed of wielding the Argument-marble.

Andy chuckled.

This is what it's come to: the Argument-marble.

"What are you grinning at?"

Andy looked at Blue, who didn't seem angry at him, as much as he was angry in general.

"Nothing."

Does he speak for everyone in this? Have the people I've met been polite about my rudeness until now? Quill, Staza, Caston and Poll, Pythia? Maybe? But Titus and Taptalles didn't act like this about the Argument-marble. They just wanted me to bring it back.

Andy opened his mouth, a million questions nearly poured out, but instead, they heard Clang click his teeth.

And just when someone was starting to talk.

Andy stalked off towards Clang and the stairwell, shaking his head as he went. Now thoroughly confused, he started to feel dizzy.

His head swam as they mounted the stairs again. But this time, instead of another floor of basement, the last step opened into a massive dining hall. Andy knelt for a moment and closed his eyes until the spinning stopped.

Clang motioned for darkness. Andy loosened his grip and realized that he could still see.

There's light in here.

The goblins moved like silent rushing water, up from the stairs and out across the room. Andy watched them break off and slink between tables and overturned chairs. Bowstrings were tensed, and javelins readied. Andy saw Takka try to deal with his fistful of cords and a hatchet. After nearly getting the strings jumbled with the weapon, he jammed the hatchet back into a belt-loop and accepted being unarmed.

Andy spotted a light coming from the far left of the hall. Clang took a central position in the room and waved him over.

"Close," He whispered. "Brutoxies, the beetle kind—slitheries, the inky kind—red eye, likely young and weak." Clang pointed over to the left, where the light was coming from.

Red eye—he means a ryle.

"How do you know?" Andy whispered.

Clang pointed at a dusty tabletop. There were lines in the dust. Shapes and tally marks beneath them, and an arrow to the left above it all. He saw a large letter S with three Cs beneath it, then a large B with three X's beneath, and then a drawing of an eye with a jagged iris. There was just one mark beneath the eye.

"Martin is waiting." Clang checked a pouch on his belt, Andy peeked and saw vials filled with a silvery liquid. Clang tapped on the stoppers, before pulling one out. He wrapped it in a ragged tablecloth and handed it to Andy. "Cleanse ink with this."

"Ink?"

Clang glared at him before leaning in and whispering, "The slitheries here are weaker, inky kind. If many get to your skin," he shook his head, "they, like ink, stick to flesh. Too much can kill."

I see.

Andy's mind shot back to the inky mist he saw at Dr. Ropt's office, and the museum.

Clang motioned, and the dozens of goblins moved in sync with their leader.

Andy kept up, but noticed that more than a few fighters looked at Takka with various expressions, the most common was something like angry desperation.

At the far end of the hall there had been a collapse, probably decades ago. Where Andy imagined a door, there was a huge pile of rubble reaching up almost to the ceiling, where it looked like the roof had given way to the rock of the cavern outside. But, just above the pile of debris were a few holes through the walls leading into the next room. Light was spilling into the dining hall from these holes.

They came to a halt and considered the pile.

Andy heard a drum beat. He listened closely and heard rhythmic clicks and hums coming through the debris.

They won't be expecting us, but how are we—

Goblins loosened straps and removed their packs and extra equipment. They were preparing to climb.

He saw several agonizing over which weapons to carry. Most had to lighten their load if they were to climb the wall of debris, stay silent, and then surprise whoever was on the other side.

Clang walked from goblin to goblin making their choices for them. An axe here, a bow there. He whispered to Takka. "You stay behind until the fighting; eyes on the slitheries, nothing else."

Takka began to object.

Clang waved his hand before he had a chance. "Climb slow—if we hear you before fight—our Mistress will have Takka-ear necklace for tribute."

Takka nodded, wiping sweat from his brow. It looked like he would rip the threads right off the chimes, he held them so tightly.

"Lose the cloak." Blue said, as Andy moved to climb.

He's probably right.

Andy unclasped the cloak and placed it on a table, but not before noticing that it had snagged on something again, and he had been leaving a trail of thread for the third time.

It's either badly made, or suspicious.

Andy didn't have time to come up with a better explanation, and carefully began his climb up the pile of debris. He could feel Blue's paws holding tight to the hair on the back of his head.

"Do you mind?" Andy winced in pain, as he pulled himself up a cracked column.

"Well, I was holding onto the cloak before, and I can't get a grip on the armor. You'll just have to deal with it, surfacer."

Andy grabbed Blue with his free hand and set the mouse down on a chunk of rock. The mouse leered at him, before bounding up the wreckage, far faster than Andy could have climbed.

Why do they always insist on a ride if they can do that?

Having lost sight of Blue, Andy reached for the last handhold and peeked over the top. Blue wasn't around, but he could see through the cracks into the next chamber. It was a massive entryway.

He spotted the reinforced double doors, guarded by half a dozen brutox.

That must be the way outside.

The rest of the room was filled with equipment and what looked like nests full of sleeping brutox. He had seen creatures like this at Cair Fromage and then again in Caspia. He watched the flames reflect across their heavy, segmented bodies. A few sat around their fire and looked to be playing a game with small toy pieces, humming and clicking as they did so. Another tapped his axe haft on the ground to keep a beat.

Signs flashed back and forth between Clang and his squad leaders. They looked eager for the fight.

Clang noticed Andy staring and climbed over a few other goblins to get within earshot.

"Martin is waiting to strike—his count was right."

Andy thought back to the markings, "B XXX." That's thirty brutox, but what about the one eye, and the—C? What does C stand for again?

"Where are the rest?"

Clang pointed to the roof above the fire. There was something strange about the way the light hit the ceiling.

What are those shapes—oh.

Andy could just make out the ethereal bodies of hundreds of slithers, hung upside down from the ceiling.

C stands for hundreds. There are hundreds of them, and they do look like the ink.

"Many slitheries—easy fight, even for Takka—but red eye," he shrugged, "could be anywhere—will come at first sound of fight—we must be fast to kill his children."

"When do we attack?" Andy paused at the sound of rubble falling.

Clang's hand tensed and rent claw marks into the stone he was leaning on.

They both suspected Takka, who was motionless a few feet behind.

A sudden crash sounded in the entry way.

A massive, metal chandelier had collapsed into the far side of the room. Chunks of ceiling were crumbling away and falling.

That must have been Martin!

The Brutox were up and rushing to the aid of those who had been caught beneath.

Clang gestured and Andy was amazed as the goblins moved in an instant.

They climbed down and spread out. Andy heard their bowstrings tense, and saw javelins raise.

The brutox have no idea.

Takka's hands worked like lightning to loosen the strings, but his eyes were stuck to the ceiling, where swarms of slithers churned mindlessly. The slithers were roused by the noise, but confused by the lack of an enemy to swarm.

Clang clicked his tongue and a volley of arrows and javelins went flying.

The struck brutox clicked painfully but the others were still distracted, thinking the cries were coming from those beneath the chandelier.

Volley after silent volley whirled through the air before they finally realized what was happening. A roar went up and the dozens of brutox still standing charged towards the pile of debris.

Andy saw the slither swarms rushing his way. He nearly recoiled backward, to a painful tumble back down the debris.

"Takka! Now!" Andy cried.

Takka was ready and rang his chimes wildly right as a wave of inky bodies came close enough to touch. Andy saw the noise of the chimes rippling across their forms as they exploded into a foul-smelling mist.

He clenched his teeth as they kept charging, heedless of the destruction.

But suddenly the swarms shifted and split away from Takka. They climbed down the walls and onto the debris pile.

"They're attacking from behind!"

Takka jumped up and followed one half of the swarm, a few of his chimes ripping free of the harness and flying off into the air.

Andy saw mobs of slithers slam into unsuspecting goblins from behind. The slithers melded into their victims, changing the goblin's color to a darker and grayer shade with every successive slam. One goblin was hit by five and turned completely gray before falling to the floor, motionless.

Andy stared at the small knife Clang gave him, confused about why he had drawn it. He nearly threw it away to ready the marble, but forced himself to sheathe it first. The blade crackled and he climbed down. He bent low, so as not to fall, and swiped at the slithers who were surrounding the goblins.

As he struck they evaporated, well before his blade made contact. He swung and swung, the foul vapor filled his nostrils and made his eyes water. He fought until his arm was sore.

When he looked for more to swing at, he found none. Brutox lay broken in heaps of chitinous plates. He hadn't fought any of these brutox, distracted by the slithers. Though he realized that they hadn't decayed into dust, like his first brutox foe.

Martin was suddenly among them.

"Well done, lads. We caught most of them by surprise, but we can't celebrate." Martin pointed to a wide stairway that led to closed doors opposite the front entrance. "Clang, cure the gray and the wounded, but keep a watch on that door!"

Clang nodded, passing vials out to goblins who rushed to splash a few drops of the silvery minoe on their smitten friends.

Andy saw a goblin brushing thick black ink off another.

That looks familiar. Titus! Titus did the same for

me back home. It feels like forever ago.

"Over here, human!" Blue called out to Andy. "This one's gray."

Andy rushed over, fumbling for the vial in his pocket. "How do I—"

"Just a few drops, you fool—and hurry!"

Andy unstoppered the vial and tapped it gently over the gray goblin.

A few drops hit, and the gray drained from where the drops struck. Andy bent down and tried to scrape the ink off the goblin's arms. It came off in viscous sheets. The goblin twitched and coughed. Andy was surprised to see a sudden smile on his face. He spat out black ink and got to his feet.

"Thankses!" He smacked Andy on the leg. "Third time for me with the ink. I can't get the hang of slitheries."

"Are you feeling better?" Andy asked, taken aback by the goblin's good mood.

"Hah! Are you kidding? I feels like I've a full belly and a week's sleep."

Andy chuckled, remembering when he had been healed with this liquid.

It made me feel like nothing else.

"Name's Jygg! What kind-a surface-folk name you got?" Jygg held out a small clawed hand.

"Andy," he said wryly, as they shook hands.

"Simple name, isn't it—Andy—usually the taller they are, the taller the name. Cept our Mistress and all, though I 'spect she's gots other names, if you see my meaning." Jygg looked around at all the healing going on. "How did we do? Hopefully none stay gray."

"Pretty good, I think." Andy saw Takka splayed out on the floor, his limbs tied up in dozens of threads. The handful of surrounding goblins were vexed in their attempts to untie him. "Well, most of us came out all right."

Clang walked by, trailed by a dozen goblins, and flashed quick gestures at Jygg, who nodded and joined them in a rush.

They headed towards two stairwells, one on each side of the main set of doors. On an impulse, Andy followed. The stairs opened into a chamber that looked down onto the space just outside the front doors.

This is a gatehouse, on the walls of the fortress.

The goblins rushed forward to a pair of heavily rusted cranks. A few lowered the iron gate and raised the drawbridge, while the rest stood guard at the crenellations and kept watch on the mountain below.

Andy looked out over the wall and saw further down on the mountainside the many smaller gatehouses that guarded that path.

We bypassed all of that. I only had to plug the marble into my face.

A few dozen slithers and a handful of brutox saw what was happening and sounded an alarm. They tried to rush the gate, but it was too late. The frustrated brutox fired their crossbows up at them, but to little effect. The slithers climbed straight up the wall and over the crenellations into the gatehouse only to be struck down by the goblin sentries.

With the gates sealed shut, Andy took a breath and looked around at the smiling faces.

"Good lot, these goblins," Blue said, suddenly at his feet.

Andy was about to chastise the mouse for surprising him again, but heard a crash. It had come from the entry way.

Andy rushed back down the stairs, but halfway down he spotted Martin coming up. Martin was a toxic looking neon green. "Superlative violence, young slave. Commendation will be forthcoming."

"What?" Andy paused, surprised by Martin's flat tone.

Martin kept coming. Andy backed into the gatehouse.

"Who is least of the least?" Martin asked looking around at the goblins. "Open the gates, we must restate our aggression while the foe is in chaos."

"But Mr. The Martin, sir! We just now seal't the gates—many still out there!" a nearby goblin said, pulling drastically at an ear.

Martin passed Andy and, without warning, a wave of silver and purple arcs lit through the air accompanied by a noise akin to electricity sparking.

Startled, Andy stepped back and readied the marble.

Before he tightened his grip, the blade exploded into the air, bending and crackling towards the space behind Martin.

Andy saw a red eye shine in mid-air.

Martin flew forward into the confused looking goblins, his feathers flashing and cycling through hundreds of colors as he stumbled.

The ryle had been behind Martin, somehow making him speak. Andy was surprised and failed to raise his guard, allowing the ryle to grasp his arm. Andy struggled as the ryle lifted him from the ground with one arm. The ryle was surprised to see the silver blade. Andy took the initiative and stuck.

His blade met the body of the ryle, but didn't cut through. Instead, blindingly purple armor, which enfolded his foe's body, flashed at the strike and deflected the thrust. Andy felt his legs leaving the ground and in an act of desperation reached out with his empty hand and grabbed wildly for something to hold on to. He grasped a tentacle and felt his foe convulse and stumble.

He was falling, and the ryle was falling with him.

Gratefully, the lower level of the gatehouse was mostly mud, and not far down.

Andy hit the floor and groaned. It didn't sound like the ryle was doing much better.

You need to move! Get up—now!

Andy rolled onto his hands and knees, his eyes locked on his foe, who had yet to stir.

"Kill him, Andy!" Blue yelled in a piercing tone.

Andy leaped to his feet and rushed to the ryle. He struck with his blade. The ryle was up on his knees in a flash, and a purple blade burst from his fist.

The Counter-Argument!

"Stop!" The ryle ordered.

Surprised, Andy stopped.

"You can't fight like this, Seer!" The ryle hissed. "Your blade is without hone!"

Andy felt certain it was a trick and lunged forward. Surprisingly, the ryle stumbled backwards to get away. He held his blade at a distance.

What the hell is he doing?

Andy pressed his attack to the cheers of his friends above. Finally, the ryle deflected a chop that would have come too close.

Andy saw disappointment on the ryle's face, and then a crack, like thunder, filled his ears as he went flying backwards into the stone wall.

Fighting to stay conscious, Andy looked with wide eyes down into his hand. The blade and the marble were both gone.

"What happened?"

The light dissipated and he saw his Argument rolling in the mud. He almost didn't believe it when the Argument rolled to a stop on the floor next to his foot. He snatched it with a trembling arm.

Andy saw the ryle shaking his head.

"I'll never see another one of you for as long as I live, and this is what you give me?" he spat.

Andy pulled himself painfully to his hands and knees.

"Twist your wrist, when you call the blade!" Martin yelled.

The ryle nodded. "That ychoron of yours is also quite the find. You should listen to him."

Ychoron? I thought he was an ychorite.

Andy ignored the word and rolled to his feet before summoning the blade again. He twisted his wrist and saw the blade trying to solidify, but it wasn't constant.

The ryle scoffed and stepped forward. "Like this!" he twisted his own wrist in an awkward way. The purple blade fluttered and lost definition. "This is where you're at; you need to find the hone. Without it you might as well be committing suicide," The ryle said derisively.

Andy's eyes nearly bulged out of his head. The ryle's blade was unhoned.

Hit him! Now! His blade will fly away, like mine did!

The ryle saw his mistake too late. Andy swung his own unhoned blade at his foe's. Another burst rang out, and, this time, they both went flying.

"His armor's down!" Martin called from above. "Clang! Throw everything!"

Andy groaned, and rolled away in the mud as a volley of projectiles rained down. After a moment, the ryle looked like a pincushion. He struggled to his feet and stood there, silent, waiting for his foe to rouse, but he never did. The purple orb lay a few feet away from his. They had both lost their weapons in the blast. The ryle's armor had vanished with the blade. He wondered if they were connected.

Unable to figure it out, Andy let himself fall backwards into the mud. He shut his eyes and tried to get comfortable.

"Martin!" Andy called out, "Leave me down here for a few hours, maybe throw me something to eat.

Take a break, and then we'll tell her Mistressness about the victory."

"You most certainly will not!"

Andy's eyes shot open. A furious Pythia was standing on the battlements, looking down at him and shaking his abandoned cloak.

"Look what you did to your cloak—are you lying in the mud?"

Chapter 14: The Ossuary

Andy rolled his eyes as a dozen grubby hands pushed and pulled in an effort to brush all the mud and gunk from his clothes. He winced as a goblin, who was standing on his shoulders, yanked on his hair.

"Rollin' in the mud? Poor choice, Master," a goblin muttered in his ear as he worked a muddy pebble out of Andy's hair.

"Being climbed on will only make me dirtier," Andy muttered.

A goblin from behind called out, "Turn 'im round!"

Andy turned and barely had his hands up before he was hit with a bucket's worth of water.

Gratefully, and after a few more volleys, the cleaning wound down.

We took the fortress. Why does she care if I got muddy in the process?

Pythia fretted and paced, a foul bent to her mouth. Martin and Clang eyed the walls nervously, neither keen on being noticed. Andy endured the cleaning as Pythia stomped around the massive foyer, staring for long stretches of time at plain walls. Finally, her gaze fell on him and his dripping clothes. With her raised brow pointed his way, he felt unsure of her intentions.

She has what she wanted, but she's still looking at me like I'm a problem.

He knew that he had to say something, anything to get her talking. "We captured the fortress—that's good news," Andy said, stifling a wince as another hand pulled at his hair.

Pythia gave a noncommittal, "Hmm," before stepping forward to reattach his cloak. "Off! Off him, you beasts!" The goblins rushed away. "We may have taken the fortress, but that was just the beginning. Now your real work begins. It won't be force of arms—" she looked over to Clang and Martin, "—or low cunning, that wins this time."

Andy mulled over her words but stopped at the appearance of a specific cloak. It looked freshly repaired.

"How? That cloak has been unraveling and tripping me up all night."

Pythia attached the clasp at his neck. "Just a little trick. To help me keep track," she intoned with a grin.

So, the cloak snagging was deliberate. Andy sighed. *Tracking me is bad enough, but why yell at me about the damn thing, if it was made to fall apart in the first place?*

Andy scowled, but kept his mouth shut.

Sensing his annoyance, she chuckled and rolled her eyes dramatically. "Well, I wasn't about to let you run off without a lead, was I? It was dangerous—it still is. Hmm," she trailed off, suddenly distracted. "Mirror!" she snapped.

Andy heard grunts of exertion. A team of Goblins had been standing nearby with a large round mirror and its frame draped in sheets. They seemed ready for the command, and quickly assembled the mirror.

Pythia dusted off her shoulders, removed the

pith helmet, and tapped it against her wrist. It morphed into a tiara, which she carefully positioned on her up-swept hair. "I suppose we can stand some celebration," she whispered as her clothes lengthened and transformed into a series of gowns. One gown morphed into the next, colors and patterns changing every second.

The show went on and on, and everyone present allowed themselves a collective sigh of relief as Pythia was too busy finding an outfit, to be angry at them. But as the moments wore on, that relief disappeared as she became visibly frustrated.

"Is something wrong?" Andy asked.

Before she could answer, he noticed the assorted goblins grimace at his question.

"This bloody fortress! The lighting is absolutely wrong—never mind the color!" Pythia snapped without looking away from the mirror.

Andy hazarded a recommendation, "Maybe a dress that glows?"

"Please keep your bloody foolish—" she paused, and her morphing clothes ceased their shifting with her. "A glowing dress?"

"Maybe, dark red?"

"Hmm." Her gown was suddenly blood-red. Then dark silver trim snaked along the collar before coiling itself in bands around her wrists and hem. Letters of deepest violet blazed here and there, illuminating the room more than seemed possible as they burned their slowly-vanishing trails across the fabric. The effect was eerie, as smoldering letters carved one way, then the other.

She pondered her appearance quietly, before muttering, "One more detail." Her tiara grew into a tall onyx crown. Barely visible black flames ran up the jagged spikes, before lapping carelessly down her fall of hair. The aggressive look on her face softened as she ran a hand over a course of the burning letters at her waist.

Is she blushing?

She looked over at Andy suspiciously.

Why is she looking at me like that?

Before Andy could ponder an answer, she snapped her fingers and the two useless marshals, who moments ago were cowering in a corner, rushed forward.

"Yes, your Mistressness?" they both stammered over each other.

The new appearance made her more ferocious than she had been moments ago, and they couldn't bring themselves to look her way. Even the harder and more veteran Goblins under Clang were preoccupied with imperfections in their blades.

"Have every goblin on the beachhead moved inside the walls. Spread out and settle down—keep the looting to a minimum, and clear that pile of trash from the hall. Consider plugging up the cave with it. We don't want anyone using our own tricks against us."

"Of course! Right away!" The two marshals saluted and bowed nervously as they backed away.

Andy heard them rush off, yelling orders at the top of their lungs. The goblins in Clang's group ignored them, and they, despite their supposed superiority, weren't surprised.

Pythia snapped her fingers and pointed towards a blocked door in the foyer. She motioned for the debris, including the chandelier that Martin collapsed, to be moved out of the way.

Andy approached Martin and Clang. Before he could speak, Martin rushed forward and clasped his arm. "You saved me back there—with the ryle—he had me."

Andy shook his head. "No, you saved us. You brought the chandelier down."

"Distraction doubled our strength," Clang agreed, "but there is no victory without strong arms."

Martin nodded and spoke, "Or keeping a level head in the thick of it. For these reasons, today, the laurel is yours." Martin gestured for something to be brought forward.

Andy felt confused as Clang took a bundle from a nearby Goblin. Something in the bundle glinted, betraying a metallic surface.

"We all owe one another. This is how it should be in war," Martin said, his color mellowing from blood red to scarlet, "but without you, there would have been a sorry end for us, almost certainly. That ryle was skilled with the Counter. His armor was impervious to anything in our arsenal. If not for that trick, he would have slaughtered us."

Andy felt a little ashamed and stepped back as Clang handed Martin a roughshod laurel circlet. The leaves were perplexing. Most of the circlet's surface was covered in a rich, non-reflective green, but minute scratches revealed a deep orange gleam underneath.

Clang cleared his throat for attention. "We had the lads hammer one together while you suffered cleaning. It's rough working, even for the Teeth."

Andy stood awkwardly, not knowing what to do or say.

Clang coughed and gestured for him to take a knee. Andy did so.

Martin placed the laurel over his hair, and it rested on his brow.

"They found metal leaves at beachhead," Clang said.

Martin had a fey look in his eyes as he spoke, and Andy felt himself listening closely. "The metal reminds me of you. Dull on the surface, but when scratched, it reveals something different."

Clang grunted, slapping a hand on Martin's midsection, which nearly knocked the breath out of him. "Give it here," Clang said as Martin stepped aside.

Andy carefully took the circlet off and held it out to Clang.

"Look—" Clang gestured to writing inside the band. "The gobmarks speak of your victory and armaraderie to our clan. They who know Broken Teeth 'right and friendlike will see with different eyes if you show them these gobmarks."

"Armaraderie?" Andy asked, confused.

"You have been born in combat," Martin interjected. "The more heroic a birth, the higher they will value you. Sadly, we don't have the time right now—" Martin gestured to an impatient Pythia, who was waiting for wreckage to be cleared.

"Lysander!" Pythia called to him. The path was almost clear.

"Quick—do either of you know what she means when she said I still have work to do? Apparently, I haven't started yet."

Andy grimaced at the horde of goblins clearing the last boulder from the doorway. Pythia was tapping her foot anxiously.

Clang and Martin looked back and forth between themselves before Martin spoke. "We've been on that beach for ages, but no one's ever told us what's so important about this place."

Clang grunted. "Our Mistress is powerful, like sea, but is not power she hunts."

They stood in silence, considering Clang's words.

"If not power, then what? What could be worth all this?" Andy asked.

Before Martin could answer, he was interrupted by Pythia herself, "Lysander, the way is clear."

Martin and Clang shared a look of concern as Andy turned to go.

"Don't forget the laurels, boy!" Blue's high-pitched voice nearly made Andy jump out of his shoes. He had only been a few feet away, on a pile of fallen stone. "Who do you think swam through the wreckage to find those damned heavy leaves?"

Andy took the circlet and gave a quick nod to his friends before leaving.

It took a mob of goblins to open the double

doors. Pythia waved Andy forward, and a few dozen armed goblins took this as a sign and moved to catch up.

"We won't be requiring your company," Pythia said, looking down the vaulted hall. "Enjoy yourselves, but don't make this place any more of a mess while you do. Any cooking must be done under chimneys—I don't care if you cook in the kitchen or in the dining halls, but I will not suffer smoke stains on the ceilings!"

The goblins nodded their small heads as they tripped over one another in a collective attempt to escape her wrath.

After a while, the light from the Goblin's torches became too distant to see by, and only Pythia's magnificent gown lit the way. It wasn't enough and Andy's shoulder smacked into a door frame.

Pythia made an amused sound before speaking, "Do you know how to make light with that Argument of yours?"

Andy grasped the marble gently and a clear light filled the hall to about the same degree a lantern might have.

"Very good," she said. "You know, you would make an above average pupil in Caspia."

Andy was silent.

"You have already made friends and I'm considering you for a leadership position." She pondered for a moment before continuing, "What do the rats call their war leaders?"

Andy thought back to his short time with Titus and the Dextra. "They are called expeditious, or

317

expeditious extraordinary, I think."

"Expeditious extraordinary? Hmm—I don't like it. A mouthful of pointless assonance. How about strategos? Or maybe legate? The Greeks were fond of archon."

Andy made to speak, but she continued right over him.

"No, there's a better way. I'll let you structure the military. You can use whatever nomenclature you like, but no attempts at coup d'état please," she laughed, but Andy sensed that she was serious about the offer.

I'm not going to stay in Caspia, even if I get to play general. I have a family and school to get back to. But maybe if I—

Andy took a long while, to affect serious deliberation, before answering. "If I stayed, would I forget about the rest of my life? Would I forget my friends and family?" he asked.

Pythia was taken aback by the question. "No—not at first—and not if you don't want to."

"It's just that when I found Letty, she didn't remember me."

"Ah—she was still under the effect of Ziesqe's serums." Pythia answered.

Serum?

Andy struggled to understand. "But once it wore off, she would regain her memory, and return to normal? The serum doesn't do anything permanent?"

Pythia nodded. "You spoke with her a few hours ago. I assume she has always been a shrew?"

318

Andy cracked a smile. "A bit. But don't the others want to go back home too? How is it that Ropt brings you all these children and they just choose to stay in Caspia?"

Pythia struggled with a sour expression.

She doesn't like all these questions, but she wants to keep me happy.

"Well, if you stayed in Caspia for enrollment and birth, you would learn a little more about their perspectives. Here is a quick taste of reality for you: One day, those eyes of yours will finish developing and, unless you do something to hide it, they will take you. You might avoid it for months or years even. You will begin to see them up there, and the extent of their power would terrify you. Eventually they would capture you. In hours, you would find yourself living a nightmare you can't begin to imagine. Only then would you realize your immense good luck in finding me. All of my pupils come to understand this. I can count on one hand those who have left and not returned."

She's trying to scare me.

Andy changed the subject, "When I met Quill, he didn't know how to shake hands."

Pythia was silent.

"At first, I wasn't suspicious of this, but then I learned how you find your students. This means that Quill is from the surface, like me."

Pythia narrowed her eyes.

"How is it that he didn't know how to shake my hand?"

Silence.

"Would he know his parent's names if I asked him? Would he remember where he went to school?"

Finally, Pythia laughed, though it was sad. "This is a tragedy, Lysander. You are loyal to a reality so abusive that it surprises you to learn that, those who have escaped, learn to forget."

Quill did say how grateful he was to live in Caspia. He seemed normal otherwise; he talked about girls, was annoyed by Somni, and he helped me at dinner too.

Andy struggled with his doubts until Pythia suddenly stopped. They had arrived at a wide set of stairs. Pythia stared for a moment before raising an eyebrow at Andy.

She wants me to guess.

Andy shrugged. "What are we looking for?"

"Inside the Ossuary is a special space, well-hidden and unopened for some time. When we finally find it, it might try and trick us by looking particularly unimportant, but there is something different there."

"What's so special about this place?" Andy asked, nearly biting his tongue. He had grown too comfortable asking questions.

But she didn't seem all that bothered as she spoke. "I expect we will find a little piece of history, tucked away safe from the conflict, though I am hoping for much more."

Andy felt uncomfortable at hearing that.

"Well, since it's in the Ossuary, which is where they keep bones, I'd guess down." Andy pointed at the downstairs.

"That's fair logic, boy—but no. We are already down, very down, at least to common sense, but we can save my theories on interspaciality for another time. All you need to know is that we are heading to a place where your world and mine overlap."

"So—up?"

Pythia laughed as she approached the upward stairs.

Andy was huffing and puffing after a few dozen flights. "This doesn't make sense, I don't remember seeing a tower like this from the outside."

The climb didn't bother Pythia, who almost floated up the stairs. Andy saw her feet take soft, yet precise, steps. She was tireless, and spoke with a clear, calm voice, "Of course there was no tower to see from the outside. The keep itself is embedded in the cavern ceiling. It might make more sense for you to think of where we are as down a deep well, and now we're climbing up and out."

I'm dying here, and she's not even breathing heavily.

Andy's face scrunched with confusion and fatigue. He was torn between falling to his knees to take a breath and keeping up to continue the discussion. In the end, he chased after Pythia, breathing heavily between every few words, "So—my world—is above this world—the Nether—Netherscape?"

"You can think of it that way. The people who built this place certainly did, but no. At least I'm fairly certain that the two realms only appear to join in this fashion. Of course the name Netherscape implies that it lies beneath the realm-without-a-ceiling, or your surface world, as you call it. I dislike going myself, the ryle have the place firmly under control. I suppose that's something I regret."

Andy nearly stumbled on the stairs. She saw this and stopped, allowing him a moment to breathe.

"You regret the ryle being in control of my world?"

Pythia sighed. "Yes. I regret not doing more, when I had the chance. I was just..."

"It's true then. The ryle, the creatures like Dr. Ropt, Zeezee—" Andy was cut off as Pythia laughed and smacked him on the brow.

"None of that now. Don't even whisper that nickname or it could mean war. Probably not—he needs me—but still, he'd make it impossible to be diplomatic."

Andy looked annoyed. "Whatever the hell he likes to be called; his species conquered the surface—my world?"

"Centuries before you were born." Pythia's face saddened, and she had difficulty meeting his eyes for a moment. When she did finally look his way, Andy didn't like it. He didn't know why, but he almost felt like a zoo animal, behind glass.

They continued up the stairs in silence.

My whole world—everything—is run by them. Even down here they hold so much power. That sign outside Ropt's office—something about wards, and it had his ryle name. I saw it. But how could this be true? We would know—if they ran everything—we would know by now.

They reached the last step and walked out into

322

a colossal gallery. Andy forgot the crumbling ruin of his life and gazed up at the towering columns. Each was thoroughly embellished with detailed sculptures carved from something strange.

"Is that antler? Maybe ivory?" Andy asked, not wanting to know the answer.

"The sculptures are bone," Pythia said, reaching out and touching a column.

Andy's mouth dropped as he looked down the length of the hall. Tens of thousands of worked bones covered every surface in the hall.

"Human?" Andy asked, shuddering.

Pythia ignored him, bent down, and ran a nail over the floor. Andy hadn't noticed until now, but the floor shone in a strange way. He bent over for a closer look and saw what reminded him of overlapping fish scales. The scales were pale gray. Many were cracked, but they all bent ever so slightly, giving the floor an uneven feel underfoot.

Andy felt his stomach clench as he shot back up to his feet.

"This way," Pythia said, an odd tone in her voice, before stepping resolutely forward.

Andy followed, trying to keep steady as he walked. He felt sick and sensed that his eyes were straining, but he couldn't see what was causing it. He forced himself to look at the endless scenes of sculpture twisting up and down the columns. They were carved in high relief, and depicted acts of war, moments of argument, and ranks of heroes arrayed in ancient arms and armor. The work was frenzied and strained, the bones bent, but none had splintered.

Andy felt a shiver running up his spine. His eyes jumped from column to ceiling and even to the floor, but everywhere he looked there was something terrible. He felt the marble in his pocket rumble, but he couldn't look away. There were symbols carved next to life-sized figures on the walls and columns. He recognized the Infiniteye.

He thought the other symbols might have been the noble crests or heraldry associated with nearby figures.

"Who made this place?" Andy whispered, slowing down. He was overwhelmed by a battle circling one column. Exaggeratedly vicious brutox and ryle, with serrated claws the size of swords and barbed tentacles, fought outnumbered humans.

"Your ancestors." She reached out and grabbed his arm, before urging him on. "Keep moving."

Somehow, the work reminded him of what he had seen at Caspia. He felt his spine run with shivers, but he shook his head to relieve the feeling, and wrenched his arm from Pythia's grip. She didn't even look back when he did so. She was walking, but she moved at such a pace that Andy was quickly left behind. He jogged to keep up.

Andy tried to catch a glance of her face, but she looked away. "Oh, stop running!" She reached out to smack him.

"I can't keep up," he said, dodging the open palm.

"Don't be stupid!"

She slowed.

She's terrified. But how—I've seen what she can do. Andy's stomach turned and his feet wobbled. He realized that he had felt safe with her, despite her nature.

Andy didn't want to ask the question, but his anxiety insisted, "Is this what we wanted to find? Is this the history you wanted to see?"

She ignored him. She was trembling and her eyes were downcast. *What could she fear?*

Ahead, Andy saw an end to the hall. A pair of tall, narrow doors were crisscrossed with fine interlocking brass gears. The facade surrounding the doors was a riot of protruding bones. He could make out human shapes, but many were pierced by weapons or giant claws.

Pythia nearly walked into the wall. "Stop!" Andy called to her.

She stopped just short, her shoe pulling on the hem of her dress. She backed away, turned around and clasped her hands in frustration before looking at him. "Don't take long. I can't stand it."

"What?" Andy asked, frustrated and confused, "What am I supposed to do?"

She crossed her arms and angrily brushed away a tear, but in doing so she ripped a gash across her face.

Oh, God! Andy instinctively reached forward, but in an instant the wound was gone, as if it never existed.

Pythia took Andy's hand. "I'll be fine, just get to work." She gestured at the door without looking and then pushed his hand violently away.

Andy stepped back and felt his glance drift up to the door and wall. They towered above him, easily five floors high. He took a deep breath and felt a swirling mix of emotions clamor away in his head. He nearly stumbled before his thoughts cleared.

I must open the door.

"Use the Silversight—take the Argument into your vision. I was going to aid you, but it's all I can do to stand here. You must be committed, or else you wouldn't even be able to breathe."

Silversight, committed again, Andy thought, remembering the words.

I have to look into the marble. But I'll be alone. Last time I had Martin and Clang, they helped, but she might run away at any second.

Andy tried to make sense of the mechanism on the doors. His eyes picked a spot at random and followed lengths of gears and axles, but were soon lost amid the countless connecting parts.

It's like untying thousands of knots on one string, when you can't even see half of it. There is no way I can do this without the Argument. I can't even see how the door is sealed.

Andy stepped away from the doors and into the center of the hall. He turned in a slow circle, his eyes moving from macabre face to face until they rested on a figure holding thumb and forefinger out just above the hollowed eye.

Andy sighed and reached for the Argument. This is the only way. He pulled it free and felt it rumbling in his grip. He held tightly.

He looked into its silver surface and saw a man

high on the column holding a marble up to his eye. He looked closer and saw that the marble was both purple and silver. One color washed into the other, and it reminded him of a religious symbol he had seen once.

He tensed his fingers and realized that his marble was gone, and his arm was no longer solid, but wireframed.

Andy's eyes pulled back and he saw dozens, and then hundreds of people. The figures on the columns and walls were alive. His vision buzzed, and his eyes widened in shock.

Warriors locked in combat with juggernaut sized brutox, and others fought beasts that were massive jumbles of tentacles and bladed purple flesh.

All the bones, everything from before—it's all here— fleshed out and alive. But how?

Andy saw the wireframe world he remembered from before on the ceiling, but the columns and walls were vibrant with figures that seemed whole.

Andy felt his breath catch and he reached out to stop himself falling. A cold hand grasped his. He looked and saw a woman with silver eyes staring at him.

Andy gasped and pulled away, tripping and falling onto the floor, which shone bright with writing he couldn't understand.

He gazed up at the figure with the silver eyes. She resumed her pose and was still. Andy scrambled backwards, terrified and still feeling the cold grasp on his hand. His skin crawled as he realized the figures only seemed still.

They're moving, but it's faint.

He struggled to his feet. *This isn't how it looked before! When I was with Martin—it wasn't anything like this!*

Andy heard crying. He saw a swirling confluence of ocher colors forming the shape of a woman crawling on the floor. She appeared to exist only as a woman-shaped glow, interrupting his sight.

Pythia. She doesn't look like anything else. It's like she almost isn't there.

She reached out and grasped his ankle, before pointing up at the wall surrounding the door.

Heroes and their symbols adorned the wall. Tall and resplendent, armed and arrayed, some with the weapons and claws of their enemies still piercing their frames. Their haunted faces were slick with blood yet were no less noble. Andy felt his heart stop when he realized that the faces were looking at him. Scores of violet eyes glowered at him from under their stern brows. One raised an arm and he felt Pythia's nails dig into his leg as it did so.

Burning letters appeared in the air before him. He had the vague sense these letters were used in mathematics, but at a level far higher than he had ever learned.

"Pythia!" Andy bent over and grabbed her by her shoulders to pull her up.

She resisted. "No! Please!" her voice came to him as if through a fog, but he focused and found it clearer as he did so.

"Look!" Andy insisted, "I need you to try to read those letters."

He couldn't make out her features. There was just the vague form of a woman. He saw movement, and thought she was looking up. "There are no letters!" she moaned, "It's just pointing at us!"

Andy felt panic rising. *I'll never get another chance, I know it!* The letters burned, but the glow coming from them was softening.

"I see letters! They have math symbols in them, I don't know the language."

"It's probably Greek," she said hurriedly.

Andy's mind shot back and forth. *How do I explain the letters to her? What can I—my knife!*

Andy felt at his waist and found the knife Clang had given to him. He pulled it free and got onto his knees.

"What are you—" Pythia stared as he tried to carve letters into the floor. "No!" She knocked the knife out of his hand.

She ran her fingers over the floor and found it smooth.

"What? I have to do something! Should I carve it on my skin?"

"Nothing is surer to get us killed than vandalism. Why do you think the ryle closed off the way into this hall?"

The letters were growing duller by the second.

"Here!" Pythia pulled tight on her dress and made a taught surface out of a piece. Andy's eyes tensed and he struggled to see the dress, all he could make out was the glow coming off Pythia.

"Cut a piece off for me," he handed her the knife, "All I can see is you—I can't see the dress."

Andy wasn't sure if his eyes were seeing clearly, but he got the impression that Pythia tightened her limbs, as if shielding nakedness.

"Damn it—I can't see you naked—just an amber spot. Now cut a piece off that dress, please!"

Andy felt a sharp slap across his cheek.

Without a word, she set to work cutting out a piece. He heard the sounds of fabric shearing.

When the noise stopped, Andy reached out and grasped the cloth. He held it close and finally saw its shape. Laying it on the floor, he set about carving the letters into the fabric.

Pythia read as he carved: "Chi—Omega—"

Carving the letters calmed her. Andy scoffed at his shaking hands.

"Everything I see is different with the marble—the Argument."

"It's called Silversight," Pythia said, "It's been so long since I've seen it, I've forgotten what it does to the Seer. I never liked the eyes."

Andy wanted to stop and ask his hundred questions. *Silversight? And she's seen it before—that shouldn't surprise me. She's far older than even a hundred. What's worse is that she'd probably answer every question without a fight, right now. But I can't take the time, I have to carve this damn fabric.* He worked as swiftly as he dared, often making mistakes, and then running an X through them. The cloth felt like it was slowly ripping into pieces. He wanted to slow down, but the letters were now barely readable. Any undue haste, and the knife would tear the sheet to tatters.

"There!" Andy delicately held the cloth out to Pythia.

"Is it classical? No, it's Byzantine. Hmm." Pythia studied the cloth. "Quite a few mistakes here."

"Sorry, I was in a rush—and I've never written with a knife before."

She huffed at him, mumbling the words as she worked down the lines of script.

"A beloved traitor among us—in bone columns astride—born to see violet eyes."

"And?" Perplexed, Andy tried to get a gauge of her expression, but still could barely make out the vaguest features of her face.

"That's all," she said in a quiet voice.

"What?" Andy considered the ancients on the wall.

Their hardened and bloodied brows gave nothing away.

"I think they want us to find this traitor," Pythia said.

The room was covered in countless scenes. There were possibly thousands of events long lost to history. The faces and names, the deeds and glorious deaths all unknown to him.

"How can I possibly know the traitor?"

Andy got to his feet and picked a column. He cast his eyes as high as they would see, and started at the top. The scene featured men with slings and bronze swords hiding among rocks on a hillside. One was flanked by the Infiniteye, and the other featured a heraldic crest, a sea star among a field of upturned crescent moons. Andy turned to the wall surrounding the door, and among the dozens of faces and crests he found the sea star among crescents.

There he is.

The hero looked down on him with glowing violet eyes, his body pierced with half a dozen severed claws, the smallest of which was as long as Andy's arm.

He must have died in this fight.

Andy looked back to the column and saw the story of this man's fight against a caravan of ryle and their servants. These ryle didn't look like the one he had seen so far. Their brutox servants seemed far more cumbersome. They had spear-like claws and uncharacteristically slender frames.

The ryle were leading hundreds of chained people before an ambush by the heroes struck. One of the chained at next to a crest, a hand clasping daggers. Andy looked back and saw her, missing an eye, and bound by ropes.

Further down the column he saw the first hero succumb to his wounds and pass his Argument to the woman.

She had lost her eye to a rogue bolt, but went on to lead the warriors in another engagement that ultimately freed more Seers. Still further down, she was attended by a doctor who attempted to treat her eye. The column ended.

Andy found the next one, nearly tripping over Pythia in the process.

"There." He spotted the doctor from earlier,

bowing before a lord.

The lord had a jagged symbol carved next to him. Ryle script? The lord's eyes glowed with a purplish hue, and his symbol was not present on the wall. Further down, the hero without an eye was captured, bound, and thrown into a lake. The doctor watched, crying, from behind a tree.

It's the doctor, the doctor is the traitor. Even if he is repentant or was forced to speak by the ryle, he is the traitor.

Andy jumped ahead to the next column. There! He saw another hero fall prey to what seemed like dizziness, only to be treated by a different doctor.

"Fear physicians of the eye," Andy said, remembering a certain painting and walking ahead to another column.

"Yes—that is one of their schemes to capture your kind. The most successful," Pythia whispered, from not far behind.

"I know the answer—but what do I do with it?" Andy asked.

She was silent.

Andy returned to the tall set of double doors that stood beneath the heroes. He looked for the traitor on the wall, but found nothing.

Is there a switch? Maybe something leads to the locking mechanism from inside the hall? He focused on the mechanism, hoping to see what he saw before at the gate in the cave. What he saw was hundreds of times more complex.

Andy found a random array of mechanisms and followed it through the walls and floors onto a column. It terminated in a lever that was dangerously close to the face of an ancient brutox fighter.

"There are levers hidden among the scenes," He whispered.

He focused his vision at the same height behind the characters on another column and quickly spotted another lever, this one was right next to a hero's crest.

Each is next to an answer. They are all choices. But I must find the lever next to the optometrist.

Andy rushed from column to column, hunting for the traitor.

"Are you on to something? You know what to do?" Pythia asked, an excited tremor in her voice.

"I think so."

After a few more minutes they were back down the hall. He couldn't make out the wall and tall doors from this far away, but he knew what he was looking for.

"Is this the one?" Pythia asked.

Andy could discern her features more clearly than before. He was almost sure that she had a smile on her face.

"Well?"

"Oh—sorry." He approached and saw a curious looking character inspecting a prisoner's eyes. He bent over the prisoner, one hand holding a glass lens, the other behind his back, grasping a concealed dagger.

"There it is," Andy said, spotting the lever.

He reached out.

"Wait!" Pythia hissed, before laying a hand on

his shoulder. "We can't be wrong."

He felt his stomach sink, and the hair on his neck stood up straight.

"We need to think," Pythia said, more calmly. "Is the optometrist a traitor?"

"He betrays the Seers to the ryle."

Pythia nodded, "Yes, but what were the exact words?" She unfolded the haggard piece of cloth and read, "A beloved traitor among us—in bone columns astride—born to see violet eyes."

"'A beloved traitor,' it says. That must be him," Andy pointed to the figure holding the lens.

"Yes, but accusing him of being a traitor." She shook her head. "That is a very definite crime. To betray implies there was once loyalty."

They stood in silence for a long moment.

She's right. The eye physician was a stranger, not a Seer. How could they expect him to be loyal? He thought back to Ropt. There's no way the optometrists are beloved these days.

"Were the optometrists always enemies?" Andy asked, "Even if they regretted what they had done later, were they ever loyal to the Seers?"

Pythia took a moment before speaking, "They betrayed their own species certainly, but had they ever declared loyalty to the Seers? I think not."

"Did they?" Andy paused, thinking back to the quote from Rembrandt's painting. "Were the optometrists ryle from the start? If so, they never betrayed us, they simply served their own side."

They stood, quietly considering.

"Take your hand off that lever." Pythia said

cautiously.

"Yes." Andy did so. He shivered, thinking about what might have happened, and regretted rushing.

He looked to the ground in frustration. "I—"

There on the floor was a violet eye. It looked straight through him.

Andy stepped back. "Do you see anything there?" He pointed to the floor.

"Nothing."

Andy saw another eye far above, on the ceiling. It was looking off at an angle. Andy followed the glance, he rounded a column and looked closely. *There! Another eye hidden among a feast.*

"I think the key is in the word beloved," Pythia mused.

"The eye. The violet eye itself."

Pythia looked at him questioningly. "Do you see the eye?"

"Yes, it's here," he pointed. "It's hidden throughout the hall."

"But is it the answer? Is it the beloved traitor?"

"Read the last line again."

"'Born to see violet eyes.'"

That's it!

"There's a stop missing! Born to see, violet eyes. The violet eye must be the traitor! It unveils itself when it opens." Andy was ecstatic.

"Are you sure?" Pythia sounded excited, though still cautious.

"The violet eye is loyal to its owner. It can't help being loyal, but, by its nature, its color, it also betrays."

Pythia was quiet for a while. "Astute."

Andy understood the puzzle and followed the eyes. Each looked to the next, leaving a trail to follow. They led him on a chaotic path through the hall.

He found them carefully hidden behind foliage, or among a flurry of blades and shields. More than once he was sure that he had it wrong, but, despite his doubt, it was clear that they were being led out of the hall.

"Are you sure you went the right way? Maybe you are working backwards—Lysander?"

Andy pointed to the door they had come in from, what seemed like many agonizing hours ago.

"Lysander! This is ridiculous, you're going the wrong way."

Andy followed the eye's glance and ignored Pythia's complaints.

"This has to be it."

They exited the hall. Not twenty steps ahead Andy saw an Infiniteye staring squarely at him.

"What? I would have seen that on the way in."

Pythia scoffed, taking Andy's surprise for a confirmation of their heading in the wrong direction. "You see! As I said!"

Andy turned around to look in the direction the eye faced: back into the hall.

His eyes widened in shock. Pythia saw this, turned, and stifled a scream.

The massive hall they had just come from was gone, and what beckoned in its place was stark, empty space.

Chapter 15: The Juncture

"Nothing's there," Andy said, unbelieving.

"So it seems," Pythia whispered, stepping closer to the void. Grinning, she said, "That giant door was a trick. Can you imagine the ryle, choking to death in a room so aligned to the Argument, flailing about for centuries while trying to find the right lever?" She chuckled and slipped her hand through the doorway. It disappeared, as if submerged, and reappeared just as easily.

"Be on your guard, there may be something unfriendly on the other side," She said.

"Do you know that—or is this just another guess?" Andy asked.

Pythia avoided his stare. "I knew the people who built this place," she said, her arms crossed. "A century old rumor implied that bloody treason was the last thing seen in this Juncture."

Pythia ran a hand up her neck and looked away.

"Well, since you knew the people who built the place, why didn't you know about the eyes in the hall, or the riddle about the traitor? You even tried to stop me from going the right way."

She was silent and ponderous. Andy doubted he could trust what she might say.

"I expect a different riddle appears to every person who walks that hall. Therefore, the path is different every time." She clasped her hands together. "How could I know them all?"

That might be true.

Andy crossed his arms. "Okay, fine. But look, as

far as I'm concerned, I've done my job. Here is your opened door. I'm leaving now. I'm going to find Letty and go back home."

Pythia stood quietly.

No argument? Maybe she won't try to stop me.

Andy turned and headed towards the stairs.

"Your service isn't complete!" she snapped.

Andy continued, ignoring her.

She followed. He heard a clatter of rapid footsteps.

"I—I need your help."

Andy nearly tripped, trying to get away from her.

"Look!" she growled, grabbing Andy by his hair and stopping him dead in his tracks.

Andy tugged, but it was like pulling against a brick wall.

He stopped resisting, but she held on tight.

"Do you mind?" he asked.

"Will you listen?" she retorted. It was more of a command, but her usual tone of complete certainty had given way.

Andy sighed. "Yes."

She released her grip.

He turned to face her, and suddenly realized he was still looking through silver eyes. He held out a hand and felt the Silversight leave his vision. His palm glowed. On a whim he tightened his grip, and the blade appeared. The sudden shift back to regular sight was alarming, but not as alarming as how comfortable the Silversight had felt by the end.

With his vision normalized, he could see her

face again. Her steely contempt from the day before was miles away.

Something about the change made Andy feel a combination of anxiety and revulsion.

She's scared—she's actually scared to go in there without me. So what? I don't have to go along. I owe her nothing more.

She took a breath and looked at the blade. Her brow rose in annoyance.

Andy rolled his eyes and loosened his grip. The blade disappeared and the Argument rested in his palm.

Finally satisfied, Pythia addressed him seriously, "Of course you can leave—take your sad girl back home. I won't even void our agreement for your failure to live up to its terms. Recall that the service is complete when I say it is."

Andy narrowed his gaze, confused.

"Yes, you should be perplexed, and far more than you are now. What if you have your way? What if you leave the Netherscape this hour?"

"So far, this all sounds great," Andy said.

"Ziesqe, you idiot! You've insulted him, face to face. You humiliated his warriors, killed them even. He knows you—he's spoken to your family. He can find you, and worse yet: You live in his jurisdiction. He can do anything he likes, to you or them."

"How do you know all this? Is it just more educated guessing, like back in the hall?" Andy blustered.

"Yes, I was wrong, yes, you have me at a disadvantage, yes, I need you, and yes, you'll get your damned way! But please, be dignified about it. Your pettiness disgusts me." She looked away, biting at her clenched palm, as if unsure about whether she should go on.

Andy felt his face redden.

She took his silence as a cue to continue. "I know this because Ziesqe told me himself." She let that sink in. "Do you remember the moment you returned the crossbow to that spider of his? That was when he told me the names of your parents. He even shared what he'd do to you, should you lose my protection."

"And what is that?" Andy asked, resigned.

Here comes a lie, she'll say anything to keep me here.

Pythia's eyes glazed over. A moment later they were solid amber. She stared at Andy and, with every passing moment, her face contorted further and further into agony.

Is she having a vision?

"There are two paths before you. One is with me, and the other—if you go now you will be captured. His servants will feed you, clothe you, and even calm your suspicions, but, and despite this warning, you will fall asleep, and when you do, it will begin. You will be given a certain drug to keep you asleep, and another to make you dream. Finally, through the use of arcane machinery, he will control what you see in those dreams."

Andy blinked, astonished.

"So far, this is standard practice for them. But let me repeat that for you: You will be chained down and locked into a nightmare machine. This he would do for any captured Seer he didn't plan to give to me, but here is where he becomes particular. Here is where he gives you more attention."

Pythia paused. Andy felt that his throat had tightened and even if he could speak, he wouldn't know what to say.

She continued, "He will sit at your side for hours at a time, testing your character, seeing what you love and hate, what makes you proud and ashamed. He will grow close to you, he will come to know and even admire you. But that which is best in you will become a point of unease for him. He will make you fight monsters. When you die bravely, he will scoff. When he has run out of ways to kill you, he will modify the punishment. He will foolishly make you suffer his own worst fears. Equally foolishly, you will find them laughable. This will make him hate you and he will become certain that you are something else."

Pythia's eyes flashed, and he nearly gasped at the sight.

She cast her glance down and spoke in a whisper, "He will make of your next coming another vainglorious cataclysm. That is as far as I can see."

Andy's breath stopped, a tightness in his throat.

Her eyes cleared, and her face took on a look of overwhelming pity. She continued, "His ego will never be satisfied, and though you will lose your ability to understand, your suffering will not end."

"How is that possible!" Andy yelled. "Do you think I'm stupid?" He wiped tears from his eyes before they could fall.

"I'm sorry!" she snapped, crossing her arms and hiding her face. She choked back a sob.

Andy stared at her in a fury, she met his eyes and he searched her face. For a terrible moment he saw she had meant every word.

His legs trembled. He reached out for the wall, but fell to his knees.

She reached down and grabbed his arm, but he kept crumbling as his strength left.

He felt his throat burning and his eyes watering. He opened his mouth to curse her, but found that nothing would come out.

She bent down and wrapped her arms around him. Her fall of hair encircled his face, and he felt her breath, as shaky as his own, down the back of his neck.

He wanted to struggle, but felt that if he moved at all, he might burst out in tears. Biting down on his cheeks, he tried to convince himself that she was lying.

"Why?" he asked, choking back the urge to cry. "Why would he do it?"

"I can't tell you why, but only that it has happened before, many times," Pythia concluded, as if it were consolation.

"This will happen if I turn around and leave right now," Andy said to himself.

"There is another way," she responded.

"That was a prophecy," Andy said flatly, as if he hadn't heard her.

She was silent.

"That's what you do for him? That is what he

traded Letty for?"

She stood and wiped her face.

Andy pulled himself to his feet and waited for an answer.

None came.

"What do I do?" he asked.

"There might be something we can use in the Juncture, just a few steps away." She held out her hand for him to take. "Some of your future will not change, but much of it can."

His head was spinning. He didn't know what else to do, so he took her hand.

She walked him to the empty space and nearly stepped through before pausing. "The Argument can't go in here."

Andy's hand instinctively went for his pocket, but he saw nothing duplicitous in Pythia's face, and let himself relax.

"Why can't the Argument go in?"

"The Juncture is a place of neutrality. Neither one power nor the other can exist there. Though those who have become committed may travel the Juncture, any bound artifact will simply refuse to pass. You're going to have to leave it here, on the steps. If you don't believe me, go ahead and try to push it through."

Andy felt nervous at the prospect of leaving his only defense behind.

This little marble has saved my life. It's my only defense in this place, but after all that she said...

Andy held the Argument between two fingers and slowly moved it towards the doorway. It stopped, as if pressed against a solid wall. Andy tried his empty hand, and it slipped through without resistance.

"It's cold on the other side," he said, half to himself, as goosebumps ran up his arm.

He tried the Argument again, with more force. Eventually it slipped and a shearing sound made him jump back.

"Please, be careful!" Pythia said, stepping forward.

The Argument had rent what looked like a claw mark across the surface of the blank space. The mark slowly faded. Pythia had been honest; the Argument wouldn't pass.

Andy took off his cloak and wrapped the little orb within. Though he hated to do this, he doubted anyone would find it.

He left it on the first step and turned back. Pythia took his hand, and they stepped through.

Andy saw nothing, but felt a strong chill creep up his limbs.

"What now?" he asked, hearing her bated breath.

"This." She snapped her fingers.

Nothing happened.

"That's odd." She tried again.

Nothing.

Andy's eyes slowly focused, and he saw small specks of shimmering light all around.

"Look—I think they're stars. We're outside."

In that instant, a burst of light appeared.

"Sunrise," Andy said, astonished.

They were floating in space.

Pythia advanced. Her footsteps tapped, as if walking on a hard, smooth surface.

"Wait—this isn't possible," Andy said imploringly.

"It is a fiction, certainly, but why do you say it is impossible?"

Andy looked at her, his mouth nearly agape. "We're out in space. We should be dead," he paused, considering her uniqueness, "well, I should be. But besides that, there would be less gravity this high up, we might just float off this platform. It should be far, far colder, and—" he paused, distracted by what Pythia was approaching.

"Hmm. I've seen this surfacer fiction before, yet never heard it described as so lethal." She swept her hand over a nearly translucent crystalline table.

Andy hadn't spotted it, distracted by the immensity of space. His eyes traveled the surface of the table and he realized it was enormous. It was surrounded by equally translucent, high-backed crystal chairs. The table likely seated one hundred, or more.

"I am also galled by this place," Pythia said, feeling at a speck on the table. "It isn't responding to my push, and—" She wiped away a dark spot.

"What is it?" Andy asked.

She held up her finger. "Blood stains this table. Ryle blood."

Andy walked along the table, with a hand outstretched to keep from smacking into the almost invisible furniture. He felt his feet crunch, and

346

noticed a chair was missing. "Someone shattered a chair—and there's another."

Further along, the table had been fire-stained, and almost every chair lay toppled or shattered.

"What was this place?" Andy asked, a tremor running up his spine as he nearly slipped on still wet blood and broken glass.

"They met here. Emissaries from both sides of the conflict. Though there are no bodies, the meeting clearly didn't succeed. It might also explain—" She held her palm up and focused.

"It might explain what?"

She ignored him, and a spark jolted above her palm.

"The Juncture is nearly impossible to fold."

Andy stepped back, annoyed. "I'm just guessing, but this isn't what you were hoping to find, is it?"

Pythia lowered her palm.

"What should we have found?" Andy asked.

She sighed. "So much changed when I looked away. This place was marvelous. If you had the knack, and few did, you could conjure up anything imaginable, and then some." Much to Andy's amazement, she smiled. "I might have gotten carried away once or twice and stayed for a few years." She waved her hand and a few dozen pieces of broken glass rustled away. "Now I can barely raise the wind."

"You wanted to come here to play?" He paused and felt that thought settle. "Really? Goblins died— they sat there on that beach for who knows how long—so you could play make-believe."

Pythia turned and nearly struck Andy, who recoiled, not wanting to discover her true strength.

"Why do you hate me so?" She picked up and flung a crystal chair like it was nothing, a frustrated scream leaving her mouth as she did so. The chair exploded into a rain of shards; Andy felt one nick his arm. "This is more for you than it is for me," she said, giving up.

Andy realized this place held no solution for him, though he wasn't surprised.

Pythia turned away and looked down on the slowly rising sun. "This wasn't what we were supposed to find."

"What was?" Andy snapped.

She huffed at his tone, and responded sharply, "Artworks, you impatient child! Hundreds of lost masterpieces made by your people and belonging to the greatest Seer heroes. They should be here."

Artworks? How would art help—oh. The pieces might contain messages like the ones in Rembrandt's paintings. Those saved me at least once. If hundreds of important artworks were here—yes, one of them might have a key, some way to stop Ziesqe and make my friends and family safe again.

"I thought the struggle to find this place and seeing the old masterpieces would help you—" Pythia was silenced by a sudden screech.

The sound was like nails scraping against glass. She winced and Andy stepped back, reaching for the Argument, before realizing he had left it outside.

"What was that?" Andy asked, trying to spot the source of the sound.

There was another screech, and Pythia shrunk away. The sound made Andy shiver.

"There!" He pointed at a chair.

"What was it?"

"The chair moved," Andy said, stepping further back with her.

They both held their breath.

Andy heard a heavy footstep.

"Something's there," he whispered.

"Can't you see it? Your eyes should still work here!"

"Shh!" Andy hushed her and stared. He tried to focus his eyes, but there was nothing.

Step.

They backed up nearly to the edge of the platform. Andy felt his foot slip off the side, but Pythia grabbed and righted him.

"This way," she said, moving around the table and away from the sound.

The steps increased in speed.

"I don't know how to fight it!" Pythia cried, her fists clenched, "I can't fold this space."

Andy stopped, and struggled to pick up a chair with both hands. With a grunt of effort, he threw it towards the noise. The chair shattered in mid-air. A moment later, the fragments crunched, as if under the foot of something substantial.

"Yes!" Pythia cried, "I have it!" She leaped over the table.

The steps stopped and Andy saw a chair move.

"Keep it distracted," Pythia said, moving towards the stained section of the table.

349

"How?" Andy cried, picking up another chair and hurling it towards the invisible figure.

The crystal shattered, and Andy watched the fragments crunch again under an invisible heel. It was coming for him.

Andy stepped back, pulling chairs out to block the path. Every time a chair scraped across the floor he winced. When he reached the end of the table, he saw the chairs jerking aside as it advanced.

"Hurry! I'm out of chairs!" Andy called to Pythia, who was slowly waving her hands over the table. Andy could just see the blood moving across the translucent surface.

"Go around to the other side and keep blocking the path. I need a little longer," Pythia said, strain in her voice.

"Sure!" Andy yelled, sarcastically.

He rounded the end of the table and noticed the footsteps getting faster. He nearly tripped over a chair, before running to get away. In his haste, he only knocked over a single chair.

"We're coming up on you!" Andy yelled to Pythia. He nearly froze when a chair lifted from the floor.

He raised his forearms as it slammed into him and then shattered on the floor.

Andy stumbled backwards and felt the footsteps through the crystalline floor. It was right on him.

Andy rolled over the broken crystal and passed underneath the table. He scrambled to his feet and his eyes tracked the movement in the broken shards. He absentmindedly brushed the fragments off his arms, barely feeling the sting of a dozen cuts.

"Watch out! It's coming your way!" He called out.

Pythia held her hands out, one above the other, and, floating between, was something Andy didn't recognize.

What is that? It looks like a dark-red blob.

Pythia was ready for its approach. Andy moved closer and realized that the floating blob was blood from the table.

Pythia growled as she threw the dark mass at the figure.

It stopped still, as if shocked.

Pythia hopped across the table and rushed towards Andy, who met her half way.

"Good trick, is that what you meant when you said you could fold this place?" Andy asked.

"Not at all," Pythia said, her breath only slightly elevated, where he was heaving, "under normal circumstances, I could have drowned that thing under an ocean of blood."

Andy was startled by her choice of words.

"That would have worked, but what do we do now?" he asked.

Pythia opened her mouth, but stayed silent. The figure was moving again.

It faced them, and Andy got a clearer sense of what they were dealing with. It was man shaped, huge, and covered in blades.

The blood had stuck to it in some places, but had not reached others. The half-solid, half-empty effect nearly made Andy panic.

"We can't fight it," he said, fear in voice.

"I would make it writhe! If I could only—" Pythia held her hands out, and they tensed with strain.

Chunks of broken crystal floated up from the ground.

Pythia shook her head and spoke through gritted teeth, "I'd crush it under shards until the pressure liquified the glass and then I'd call up a frost to freeze it in place!"

"That sounds like a great plan—why can't we do that?" Andy felt helpless without the Argument.

The bloody figure moved again.

Pythia exhaled. Her arms fell to her sides, as if weighed down, and the few hundred broken shards tumbled to the floor.

The figure stared at them from the far side of the table, as if sick of the chase. It brought its bladed fist down onto the table and split it in half with a deafening crack.

"What do we do?" Andy yelled.

The figure reached out and grasped half of the table in each hand, and, with no apparent strain, lifted them high into the air.

Andy's legs were shaking.

Why the hell did I agree to come in here?

He prepared to dodge the split pieces of table. Instead of striking out with them, the figure lowered them, effectively creating impromptu walls that blocked their path of escape. The only choices left were, straight ahead towards the bloody figure, or behind and off the platform into empty space.

But it isn't really space.

It came closer. Shards crunched under the figure's steps as it raked its blades over the broken table.

Andy reached for Pythia and pulled her towards the edge.

"It's our only chance!"

Andy leaped off, but felt his grip on Pythia's hand slip away. He looked to see if she had made it, but he was tumbling and could see nothing, save the swirling stars and the dark planet below.

He felt his breath grow heavy and his eyes shut, as if pressed down by great pressure. He struggled to open them, but only saw clouds. He felt mist blowing across his skin at such speed it almost hurt. The space around was now more like sky, and beneath, green and blue surface. He spun so violently that all he could take in was color before his eyes shut again.

After a long moment he took a deep breath and forced his eyes open. The pressure changed direction and he felt a great force pushing him upwards and away from the land. Though he was still coming down, his descent had slowed.

Colossal trees reached up to brush against a blue-green sky. Between spans of lush forest were lakes as smooth as glass, and bluer than anything he had ever seen.

A moment later his feet touched down on soft grass.

I can't pretend this is all a dream anymore.

He shook his head and looked up to the sky.

Did Pythia escape? If she fell, she might be anywhere in this forest.

Andy turned about and considered his surroundings. The trees were huge, larger than redwoods, and the canopy was towering, it made him feel like he was in a cathedral. There was almost no sound, save for the slightest hint of flowing water. He took in a deep breath and felt the moisture.

The air is incredible. It's fresh and clean.

He saw flocks of colorful birds flying so high it made them difficult to spot, yet they were still somehow beneath the canopy.

Not knowing what to do, Andy picked a direction at random and started walking. The thick grass underfoot made it feel like he was walking on a rubber floor, with a slight spring.

Andy shook his head in astonishment.

This place is too perfect. Nothing in nature was ever like this.

He stared with defiant eyes, but still felt himself to be immeasurably small compared to the space around him. It made him feel relaxed and serene, despite his fear for Pythia.

I shouldn't feel this calm. Forget the surroundings; I was nearly killed.

Andy paused for a moment.

Was I nearly killed? If this place isn't real—

He inspected the small cuts on his arms from rolling through the glass. They didn't even sting. He remembered the blood on the table and the chair that hit him.

I did throw the first chair.

Thinking back, he felt certain that the bladed figure could have killed him.

But Pythia—she must have made it. She'll be down here somewhere.

Andy felt like calling out for her, but couldn't bring himself to do it, realizing that thing might be nearby as well.

He picked up his pace and noticed how easily his body moved. It felt like he weighed half what he should.

Is there less gravity here? Wait—

Far off through the trees he saw a speck of quicksilver sparkle with a violet afterglow. Light bounced off it like the sun's reflection on water, but only for a moment, and then it was gone.

I have to get over there.

Andy broke out into a jog and arced around a calm lake. The air whipped as he ran. It felt like he had never moved faster in his life. The grass rushed by at such a clip that it blurred, but he kept his focus on the spot where he had seen the shine.

He couldn't see the strange speck of violet, but there was something off about the trunk of the tree ahead. It looked to have a square shape on its surface.

It's a painting.

Andy approached and stopped. He noticed that his breath was even and calm, despite the run. He would have given that more thought, but the painting took his complete attention. It looked like a portrait, though there was something more.

The painting was large, four feet wide and twice as tall. It was a portrait of a lady in robes; she was holding a set of unbalanced scales in one hand, while the other held a golden arrow, pointing at her right eye.

Andy felt his eyes tense. He feared becoming dizzy, like he had at the museum. If that monster was nearby, he had to be ready to run.

His head buzzed, but it wasn't disorienting enough to make him look away.

There, on the lintel of the building behind her, appeared glowing Latin characters. They shimmered like quicksilver with the glassy violet sheen he had seen from across the lake.

This must be what Pythia was looking for.

Andy stopped. He heard a brushing sound somewhere in the distance. It sounded like someone scraping against a tree.

He held his breath and looked around. He spotted one, then two, and then several other canvases hanging from the trunks of the surrounding trees.

There's a whole museum down here.

Andy listened for a moment longer, but there was nothing.

He looked back to the woman in her robes. Her face was tranquil, save for a hint of mischief around the eyes.

I wish I had my sketch pad.

Andy nearly jumped out of his shoes when a sketch pad appeared on the ground before him.

In disbelief, he reached down and picked it up.

Flipping through the pages he realized that it was his sketch pad, the one he had at the museum. He even found his rough drawings of the Infiniteye.

He paused.

How about a pen?

Nothing.

Andy held his hand out, and remembered Pythia trying to fold reality.

There is a pen in my hand.

There was a pen in his hand.

Hmm. I wonder how over the top I should go with this.

Andy felt a grin growing across his face. He gazed over to the lake and imagined a hundred-floor skyscraper exploding from the water. Then he considered a dozen tanks rolling out of the water onto the shore, and then he imagined commanding them to blow holes in a newly summoned school building.

I don't hate school, but you've got to take advantage of something like this.

Andy raised his hand, the stupid smile on his face began to hurt his cheeks. He wanted so badly to make a tank appear. He took a heavy breath, gritted his teeth, and finally sighed.

He let his hand drop.

If I start, I might not be able to stop. Pythia said she spent years at a time in here; this is why. I will only change the Juncture if I need to.

Andy looked back to the painting and opened his sketchpad. He began a sketch of the figure, and then carefully added the characters. After a few minutes, he felt his legs straining.

Maybe I can have a little fun.

He paused and considered what would serve his needs best.

There is a chair—a comfortable chair, that rolls, and has a cup holder—right here.

A plush chair on wheels appeared. Andy hopped onto it and continued sketching.

There is a can of my favorite drink in the cup holder.

The can appeared. It featured a charging animal. Andy popped the tab and took a sip. His face pinched at the sharpness of the drink.

He laughed to himself. *I hope my parents don't find out; I'm not allowed to have these.* He leaned back in the chair and gave it a slow spin.

He thought back to where it all started. *Jumping out of the car that day was the first thing I shouldn't have done.* He tried to consider the staggering numbers of choices he probably shouldn't have made since then. *I don't know why I'm in such a rush to get back. Even if I don't tell them a single thing about any of this, they will still kill me.*

Laughing, Andy gave the chair another spin and looked at his notes.

La révolution n'a jamais pris fin. Le Lyceum se bat sur.

Andy read the message as well as he could. He was glad for the Latin characters, though it was still beyond his comprehension.

Something about a revolution? I think it's French. That's progress, at least.

Andy wanted to stay at this painting and take time filling in his sketch with the smaller details. There were newspaper clippings on the floor and angry looking people following the lead figure, but he needed to move on.

Andy narrowed his brow.

Camera!

An old, throw-away camera appeared.

I can't use that! I need a digital camera. Several dozen mega-pixels or more—charged, with a memory card.

The camera changed into a contemporary design. Andy powered it on and took a few snaps of the painting. He looked at the images on the camera's screen and noticed that they weren't right. The writing was missing from the digital image. It reminded him of when he looked for Rembrandt's work online. Realizing he couldn't depend on the camera, he tapped his sketch pad.

Maybe I can find that art girl when I get back, I have her email address. She might have something to say about these paintings.

Andy tried to scoot his chair towards the next painting, a good hundred paces away, and hanging from the trunk of another tree, but his chair refused to roll on the turf. Andy nearly stood to walk, but that grin returned instead.

Engine! Joystick! Paved sidewalk!

All three appeared. The engine connected to the chair's wheels, the joystick on the chair's arm, and a pleasant sidewalk led the way forward, to the next canvas. Andy laughed like a maniac as he leaned back and drove his chair to the next canvas.

The second painting shone so brightly of quicksilver, he had to cover his eyes.

Andy peeked at the painting, bit by bit, to let his

eyes adjust to the color.

The whole canvas undulated with waves of soft color appearing over the quicksilver. It glittered as if touched by some unseen light.

Andy stood, his hand still half-covering his eyes, and stepped closer. He leaned in and inspected a small section. There was something familiar there.

It's writing. The painting is covered in tiny writing. Wait—it's English!

Andy thought for a stepladder, and it appeared. He climbed up to the top and started at the left.

'*To those with the sight, stare not too long at this canvas—*'

Andy shook his head at the contradiction. *What do you mean, 'stare not too long'? You wrote a novel here.* Andy felt like complaining, but he had a sudden fear of tempting fate, and continued reading.

'*—even if you have the stomach for the violence of the color. My name is Vincent Denofre, and I fear that, despite my efforts, this work might be hanging in a public gallery. BE WARNED! If this is so, you must be on guard against our enemy. Museums are dangerous for us. I have learned to frequent salons and small galleries instead. Thusly I have chosen to compose in the revolutionary fashion to avoid popularity—*'

Andy climbed off the stepladder.

Revolutionary fashion?

Confused, he grabbed his camera and snapped a photo.

Oh, he means modern art.

The image showed none of the writing and was so different that Andy had to look twice. *His writing really does cover the whole canvas. This painting would stand out to anyone with eyes like mine.* What he saw in the snapshot was concentric shapes: large and small circles and squares. The colors of the mundane composition shifted between the layers of overlapping shapes. Any one shape was one color, but when two shapes overlapped, the space they shared would be filled with a third, complimentary color. The effect was engaging, though Andy couldn't say why.

Andy laughed at himself for a moment. His skepticism satisfied, he climbed the stepladder again and continued reading. He opened his sketch pad to a blank page and transcribed the message. After a few minutes, he felt his focus slipping, but he kept on.

'*I was deployed by the SSB in Anatolia before the war broke out. My mission took me to the mountains of the Caucuses and the lands of the Armenian peoples. During my travels I endeavored to appear as a native, but wherever I went the locals found me out. Though, to my surprise, I was never turned in to the Ottoman garrisons. Far from it, I was often spirited away and fed dark leaved plants and vegetables. On this point they wouldn't relent. I was eventually told by a child that I matched the description of a local legend. Specifically, it had something to do with my eyes. In another town, I was told that my eyes were a special color. At this I am still perplexed, as I recall my eyes to have been green and nothing else my whole life, but then I was given a mirror, and lo, my eyes were indeed violet. Though, after heavy consumption of the prescribed foods, I was shocked to see them returned to their original state—*'

This sounds familiar.

'Please, reader, you will doubt my story, and indeed, it is worth the greatest doubt, but step aside from my canvas. Take a moment and observe. Does anyone else notice the immense oddity of this work like you did? No, they will walk right past it. If, on the off chance someone does notice it, endeavor cautiously to make friends with this person, it may be a trick, but finding a companion might be worth the risk.'

Andy skipped ahead.

'I was escorted by the mice to a city called Degoskirke, an absolute madhouse that gave me a migraine the moment we passed through the gates, before even. After some time there, I suspected the population to be in the many hundred thousands, though my faculties were not about me. On reflection, however, I must add that if one considers the number of fantastic races, the population inflates to a few million residents, at least.'

Degoskirke? I've heard of it. I wonder why the mice took him there.

'I learned quickly that the multitude of factions there saw me as more of a political prop than anything else. Yes, the rather arcane Order Occidentalis did indeed train me, and the Argument is handier than an automatic pistol, but I barely escaped the opposition party, the so-called Vychy. They ambushed us, treacherously disguised as friendly mice.'

Andy stopped reading for a moment. *I know about the Vychy too, they are mice who want their people to stop helping seers. The bit about being a political tool—this might have happened to me. They threatened execution too.*

'A friendly face told me to avoid artifacts owned by one, Usurper. My attempt to learn more was dashed by a pair of guards noticing us.'

A rush of wind whipped through the trees, causing Andy to grab hold of the tree for a moment, in fear of the ladder tipping.

The wind abated and Andy continued.

'Luckily, I was helped out of the city by a type of abomination they term an ychorite. I spent who knows how long on an exceptionally unseaworthy corvette. I recall us sailing through a peculiar portal in the sea, and, once on the other side, the spectacular colored ceiling was gone. No sky, that you or I would recognize, appeared to replace it. We were somewhere else; another part of the scape was all I could glean before we tied to a port as rickety as our vessel. At the ychorite's prompting, I went ashore and found my own people in a wild encampment called Delta's Drift. More about the city will appear on my next work, as I seem short of canvas. Indulge me in one final word of warning please: If you do follow the symbols, I implore you to take major cautions in the underworlds, or so-called Netherscapes. Even our supposed allies are not to be completely trusted—'

Andy shook his head, struck by unnervingly suspicious feelings of the mice.

I also met a helpful ychorite, Martin, but I've never heard of Delta's Drift. What does he mean when he says he found his 'own people' there?

Andy paused to catch up his transcription, but he nearly tipped over the stepladder when he heard his wheeled chair move.

There was an indentation in the grass next to his sidewalk.

Andy leaped from the ladder and rolled on the ground, still clutching his sketchpad. He saw the invisible figure leave heavy footprints as it came for him.

"I need to finish reading that!"

Andy threw his sketchpad away and stepped back.

Paint!

A torrent of orange paint splashed through the air, covering the figure, sidewalk, and chair, though gratefully missing the painting. The same bladed body stood there facing him.

Andy raised his hand.

Sharpened log.

A massive, pointed log appeared and floated in the air above.

Andy moved his hand slightly and saw that the log twitched, as if in tune with him.

Like Pythia was trying to do on the platform.

Andy reared back with his arm and let it fly.

The figure shot into the air, and even stood on the log for a split-second, before it rolled to the ground and lashed out with its bladed fists.

Andy leaned back, but its reach was too great, and he felt the claws rake his cheek. He screamed with the shock.

His hands and feet struggled for purchase, but Andy managed to roll to his feet and run.

My sketchpad! I can't leave it!

Andy stopped, and saw the figure likewise pause to consider his sketchpad.

"No you don't!"

Andy motioned with his hands, and the floor beneath the figure pulled away. It fell into the pit and Andy covered the hole by motioning for the land nearby to slump over and collapse into the space.

He ran and grabbed his sketchpad, all the while, his eyes stuck to the upturned earth.

As he ran, he saw the bladed hand reach up from beneath the ground. Shaking, Andy looked away. He passed a painting and then another. Both were covered in writing.

He tried to force himself to stop, and finally at the third painting he did.

Is this German or Dutch writing again? German has the two little dots above vowels, right?

He barely had a second to consider the work, a naval scene, before he copied the quicksilver letters. They were written over the sails of the ships. He tried to focus, but found himself looking around and listening every few seconds. He knew it was still out there.

His hands shook and he erased several mistakes. Ready to leave, he realized that he had lost his camera in his tussle to escape.

Damn! I'm going to miss so much!

He created another camera, smaller this time, and snapped a photo before rushing off. Looking for his next target, he saw there were canvases hanging from trees in every direction. There were dozens, possibly hundreds. He could never see them all.

That thing will climb out of the hole and kill me.

Andy looked over his shoulder for signs of the figure.

It's out there somewhere; it won't stop. Andy struggled with the urge to run. *I need to keep trying.*

He picked a painting at random and charged towards it.

"There you are!" A female voice spoke to him from behind.

He stopped dead and turned around. The trees and all the world blurred. The borders between all he saw stretched out indefinitely as his body took ages to finish turning. When it finally did, everything was different, but somehow it all made sense.

His sense of urgency confused him for a moment. He felt his heart beating like he was being chased.

"We're going to be late," Pythia snapped, taking his hand and leading him down the platform.

A loud whistle shocked him and he turned to see the locomotive start rolling away.

Oh, right—wait.

"Late for what?" He asked.

"Lord, you can't go ten seconds reading that paper or you'll forget everything," she laughed and snatched the newspaper from his other hand, before tossing it into a bin. "Here," she said, passing him a pair of tickets. "I still can't believe you obliged my terrible caprice and actually bought us tickets," her smile wilted, "yet, it is the third showing; there won't even be a red carpet—"

He ignored the nagging, as his head buzzed. He looked at the tickets, they were for a performance of the latest Puccini.

I hate the opera.

Walking through the station, he spotted a

curious canvas hanging in the lobby. He stopped and stared. The painting featured a man on his knees tearing at his hair. Mice emerged from piles of clothes strewn around the floor of what looked to be a common tavern.

"Just a moment," he said, fumbling around in his coat pocket.

Pythia put her hands on her hips and waited impatiently.

He found his little notebook and a pencil.

"I need to write this out—just a moment, please."

He focused on the glowing letters painted on the floorboards at the bottom right of the composition.

'They were once us.'

He wrote down the short message and looked at the characters in the composition. The mice were all unique. The artist took care to capture each face, and though, despite their surface inhumanity, their reactions underscored their individuality.

I think I knew a mouse like them. Titus. And another, Tap—Tap tails.

He paused, startled by shattering glass from behind. Somewhere in the station a scuffle was breaking out.

Pythia grasped his arm with notable strength and tugged him along. "We have to go now," she said.

He looked over his shoulder and saw figures fighting on the platform.

"Is that blood?"

"Whatever has gotten into you?" She laughed and smacked his hand away. "It's just a little wine."

He looked, and felt the world stretch again, the burning smell and rumbling of the trains gave way to the soft rush of water, and the tart smell of freshly corked wine. He was sitting in a boat.

Startled, he got to his feet, and immediately felt the boat begin to tip.

"Get back down, you idiot! You'll ruin my hair," she yelped, "and you've spilled another one!"

"Sorry—sorry." He sat back down and looked for a cloth to clean up the mess.

"It's fine, let me," she said, pulling a napkin from her basket.

He sat there, his face red, while she cleaned up the mess.

"At least it's a pleasant day," he remarked, looking around the riverside.

"It is absolutely glorious out," she said with some effort, as she scrubbed away at the small puddle of wine.

"Weren't we supposed to go to the opera sometime soon?" He asked, as an odd memory rose in his mind.

"You despise the opera, and you just took me a few weeks ago. I wouldn't dream of putting you through it again, at least not until next season."

He cracked a smile at that, and let his concern slip away.

"Dearest?" she asked.

"Yes?"

"Does something seem familiar about all this? Anything... about me?"

He smiled at the bobbing reeds and then at her.

"I suppose it does seem rather familiar."

Up ahead at the river's bend he saw an intriguing sparkle coming off a piece of statuary.

"Look at that," he pointed, leaning forward.

She rolled her eyes and sighed.

"What do you suppose it is?" he asked.

Wringing out the spilled wine into the river, she paused for a moment and looked. "A statue. It probably belongs to the Yeolends. This is their wood after all."

"Really?" He said, still intrigued by the shimmering colors. "What makes it shine like that?"

She paused again, clearly annoyed, and gave the statue a considering glance. A moment later her brow rose and she whispered, "You don't need any more wine."

"What? Don't you see it?"

"Well, I suppose it is somewhat shiny," she said, not wanting to press the issue.

What's wrong with her? Somewhat shiny? It's like sunset on water, or mercury under a spotlight.

He readied the oars and rowed closer.

"Oh, you are such a romantic, always mad about some piece of art or another. I suppose I should be grateful that it isn't other women," she said, spreading cuts of meat and vegetables onto a pair of plates.

"Yes, yes," he said noncommittally as he tied the boat to a small dock not far from the statue, "I'll just be a moment."

"Our charming lunch is almost ready, so please rush back."

369

He stepped off the boat and onto the creaky dock, poking about in his pockets as he went.

There it is.

He pulled free his notepad and flipped past all the pages full of mystifying sketches, and one long, written entry, to an empty page.

Wonderful.

The statue featured a brazen man caught in a struggle with a tentacled beast of the sea. The man held the beast by its throat, though he was draped in the constricting fleshy tentacles, which looked like they would subdue him by force of weight alone.

As his eyes focused, he saw changing color. There was a hint of silver over the man, and purple over the beast. Every scale had a figure drawn on it, and they hurt his eyes to see. The man was likewise ringed in the tightest bands of script, the letters so small, he could barely recognize that they were letters.

I'd need a magnifying glass to read it.

He stepped back and saw a brass plaque on the stone plinth beneath the statue, the artist's name was there.

"Come now, the food will go bad if you don't hurry," Pythia complained.

"Start without me, it'll just be a moment."

He made a quick sketch of the statue and wrote down the artist's name.

I must look into Lord Leighton, maybe he's still alive. Either way, I must come back.

"Who owns this land again?" he asked.

"I'll not answer until you get back in the boat,"

she whined, waving a full glass of wine.

"Fine," he put his notebook down and untied the boat before stepping on.

"Here darling, eat these," She said, holding up a bunch of grapes, "they should improve your mood."

He took a few and popped them into his mouth, his knuckle brushed against his mustache as he did so. The feeling was so alien that he put the last grape down and investigated his face.

Mustache? And a beard! When did that happen?

Pythia saw the look on his face.

He felt his ears pop and the back of his head hit soft ground. The world around him swirled as he blinked. The tinkling of water mixed and then gave way to bursts of schoolyard laughter.

"Hahahah! You got him in the face!"

He felt a hand slap his cheek a few times. "Hey buddy, you okay?"

Several other voices laughed and conversed light-heartedly. One said, "A soccer ball can't knock someone out—can it?"

"Sure it can. Just last week—"

Andy stopped paying attention and opened his eyes. He saw Dean.

"Hey man, are you with us?" Dean asked.

His head was spinning, but he wasn't in any pain. "I'm fine, just help me up," he said.

Dean offered a hand and helped him to his feet.

"That hit really took it out of me. I'd swear I was just in a boat, or maybe at a train station," Andy's face twisted with apprehension.

"Just walk it off, Andy. I'm sure you'll be fine in a

minute," Dean said.

"Stop talking, there's only a minute left!" Letty yelled.

A whistle blew and the ball was in play again.

He tried to keep track of what was going on, but before he could figure out what position he was supposed to be playing, the whistle blew again and the game was over.

"What's going on with you today?" Letty asked, as Andy walked with Dean towards the locker rooms.

"Come on," Dean complained, "he got hit in the face. You saw that kick."

She laughed dismissively and headed towards the girl's side with her friends.

"How have you been, Dean? It feels like I haven't seen you in ages."

"Jeez man, you might want to see the nurse." Dean stopped him before continuing, "Here, follow this finger," Dean tried to test his vision, "how many fingers do you see?"

Andy pushed past and continued to the locker room. "I'm fine; I just need lunch."

In the locker room he stood and stared at the combination lock on his locker.

Spin twice to the right—then stop at nine. But what next?

He fiddled with it, sure of failure, but was surprised when it popped open.

Muscle memory, I guess.

He changed into a trim, black button-down and crisp blue jeans, he instinctively tucked the shirt in and then tied his shoe laces.

Stepping outside, he found Dean pretending not to stare at the cheer squad, who were having lunch practice on the field outside the gym.

"They let the new girl onto second string," Dean said.

"What?"

"Don't tell me you haven't seen her." Dean grinned.

He looked over at the girls. They were waving their pom-poms in various patterns.

"She's the one with, um, what do you call that color? Auburn? Yeah, that's it, auburn hair."

It only took a moment to spot her.

There she is. Tall and trim, even more so than the rest of the squad.

"Have you ever seen hair like that?" Dean asked dreamily.

He struggled to not burst out laughing. "What happened to you? The hormones finally take over?"

"Tell me that she doesn't have the best hair out there," Dean challenged him.

Sure, why not?

Gawking wryly, he looked from girl to girl. None had bad hair, as far as he could judge, but the new girl's hair was radiant. Her light curls bounced around one another in a way that was almost hypnotizing in the sunlight.

Well, he's right. She has the best hair.

Taking the silence as a sign, Dean nudged him. "That's right, buddy."

A sudden explosion rang out in the distance. A

fireball rose over the trees.

Everyone on the field ran for the gate that separated the exercise area from the rest of the school. The only holdout was the new girl, who stared at the rising smoke.

Dean also seemed oddly at ease.

"Shouldn't we run too?"

"Nah, it's just lunch. You in a rush for cardboard pizza?" Dean replied, most of his attention still on the new girl.

"But the explosion."

A score of armored police cars sporting mounted machine guns drove past. They were escorting a bulldozer to the site of the blast.

"Quick response," Andy said.

Dean ignored him, and suddenly turned away from the field. "She's looking over here."

He glanced and saw the new girl was gazing their way. He felt his cheeks flush, and then immediately was angry.

Why do I care if the new girl looks at me?

He pushed Dean towards the gate. "Let's go. I'm starving."

Dean peeked over his shoulder as they went. "She's coming this way."

"I don't care."

They shuffled with the mass of people at the narrow gates. Dean was clearly annoyed, but he went with Andy despite that.

"Hey, Dean!" a female voice called to them from somewhere in the crowd.

Andy stepped back just in time to dodge a plush

ball that smacked Dean in the face.

It was Letty and Emma. They were whispering between themselves.

Dean picked up the ball. "They've got another thing coming, if they think they're getting this back."

The crowd cleared and Letty, with Emma in tow, approached the two boys. "Did you see the new girl at cheer practice?"

"What do you care? You aren't even in cheer," Dean fired back.

What grade am I in? I thought we didn't have cheer.

Ignoring the girls, Andy spoke, "Hey Dean. What year are we?"

Letty laughed, patting his forehead carefully. "That hit took it out of you. Maybe sit out the next game."

"Yeah, maybe you should, Andy. I'm starting to worry," Dean replied.

Andy was about to angrily repeat his question, but someone else spoke first.

"Hello, may I join your party?"

They all turned and saw the new girl. She had caught up with them and was looking shy but brave.

Wow, she's stunning. Better not let Dean know I think so, it might upset him. Wait—did she say, 'May I join your party?' Who talks like that?

"Uh, sure—" Dean answered.

"No way, new girl," Letty said, standing off against her.

Emma scoffed. "Go beg for attention somewhere else."

The new girl smirked at Emma. "Maybe skip the vomitorium. You look like you might die, just standing there, and you'll clear up that awful breath in the process," she finished by rolling her eyes, and then looked at Letty. "You on the other hand, might want to tone it down at lunchtime. Maybe stick to greens for a few months."

Dean was smirking, and the girls shared a horrified look.

Andy looked at the girls and felt confused by what he saw.

They don't look right. Letty is too large and Emma is too small.

Instead of arguing, or hurling another string of insults, Letty and Emma wore defeated looks.

"Would you gentlemen care to escort me to the cafeteria?" the new girl asked.

Dean leaped to it and took her arm. She looked at Andy questioningly.

"Don't mess this up for me," Dean leaned in and whispered.

"Sure," he said, following along. "What's your name?"

She paused for just a second before answering, "Thea."

Andy felt himself walking to the cafeteria under a fog of tedious compliments and pointless questions from Dean to Thea. Letty and Emma followed along, but were silent.

They found all the tables full, but Thea walked up to one and, in an instant, everyone sitting there stood, took their trays, and left.

Andy sat and prepared himself to stomach the pizza and tater-tots served by the cafeteria. He looked away as he took a bite, and was shocked when the pizza was delicious. Though he hadn't seen how the pizza had arrived on a plate before him, its flavor was enough to forgive that.

"So, Thea, what classes are you taking?" Dean asked, nearly simpering.

Andy ignored them as he noticed something strange about the table.

He moved his tray to the bench and got a closer look at the table top.

Someone has drawn something here. It looks like a map.

He instinctively reached for a breast pocket, but found he didn't have one.

That's odd. I know I have a sketch pad somewhere though.

He was surprised to find a small notepad in his pants pocket.

"Hey—put that down and join us," Thea said.

Glancing over, he saw that everyone was annoyed with him, Dean especially.

"Just a second," he said, equally annoyed.

In his attempt to copy the image he realized that he would need a far larger piece of paper. After pushing aside a few three-ringed folders, and frustrating his peers in the process, he had a fuller grasp of the image.

It's the globe. And the writing, the writing is in English. That's important. But the glowing, they aren't glowing letters, but numbers.

He started writing the numbers down.

I think these are coordinates.

"You make me so happy," Thea said to him, her voice full and overpowering.

He blinked and the map twisted. The curved lines bent into the contours of a concrete sidewalk.

He looked up and saw his hand holding a corsage. He was holding it out to her.

Smiling, she took it and pinned it to a ribbon at her wrist.

Things are changing.

Dancing music poured out of the assembly hall, and with it came a constant stream of couples. Looking flushed from dancing. The students were dressed in ill-fitting tuxedos and colorful dresses.

This isn't right, I was just eating lunch.

"Look at them, Cas. Everything is either too big, disastrously small, or stupidly colored," she hinted at a neon green, strapless pencil dress.

I was writing something down.

His hand went for his pocket, but Thea caught it midair and grasped tightly.

"Here, take one," Thea said, pulling out two pieces of chewing gum. She put one in her mouth and held the other one out for him.

He rolled his eyes but took it between his teeth and chewed.

If it will shut her up.

It tasted like honey and then cinnamon, as he chewed.

"Let's go in," she whispered in his ear.

"Sure," he said, feeling a pain behind his eyes.

"You look brilliant." She smirked and ran a hand over his shoulder.

Feeling a twinge of self-consciousness, Caspian checked that his coat was laying correctly and then ran a finger over his cuff-links. He looked at his shoes as he walked and saw a remarkable polish shine back. By some long-lost habit he twisted his neck, forcing it to crack. He took in a deep breath of the cool evening air. It was invigorating. He felt the cords in his arms and chest ripple as he stretched in his suit. Thea smiled at him and he gazed into the sky at the chilly moon.

Thea slipped her arm into his and gave him a slight jab. "Let's not keep everyone waiting," she said.

They turned and walked past the groups still waiting to get in. He raised a sneering brow at a pair of couples too slow in getting out of their way.

"She looks amazing," whispered one girl. "She had surgery," scoffed another.

"Careful now," Caspian said to the group, his sharp eye moving from male to male. They balked.

At the door, the ticket taker stepped aside to let them in.

I've never seen a disco ball before.

He felt a wave of despair and wonder as countless refracting beams of light sped around the room, simultaneously illuminating and then concealing the couples. The feeling clashed with his burgeoning sense of strength.

Something's not right, but I feel so—

She took his hand and put an arm around his

shoulder. He put his hands around her waist and felt his feet move, as if they knew the steps all on their own.

Thea sighed and laid her head on his chest as they danced. They danced through a dozen songs. It was a dreamlike blur. At one point, as he came up for air, he opened his eyes and realized the floor had emptied, and the hundreds of others stood clear of their dance.

The songs ended again and again, before Thea finally looked up at him. He blinked and saw that the hall was back to normal. Everyone was dancing.

"I propose a challenge, something you should enjoy, love," she said mischievously, putting a finger on his chin and pulling his attention back from the lively company. For a moment he saw something like fear flash in her eyes.

"Oh?" He said.

She took a long heavy needle from her hair, causing it to tumble down. "See this?" She waved the pin.

"Yes. What are you getting at?"

She twisted at the top. "It's a flask. There's something special inside."

He nearly missed a step.

"Careful now, it's not that bad. But we're going to play—and the loser has to drink first."

"The drink is a punishment?" he asked.

"No. Whoever loses, loosens up."

There couldn't possibly be enough alcohol in that needle, even if it is the size of a chopstick.

Before he could ask what she meant, Thea left

his side and worked her way off the dance floor. She went up to a rather dour looking fellow standing by himself against the wall. He couldn't hear what she was saying over the music, but at one point she gestured across the hall to a sad girl, also standing alone.

The dour fellow seemed baffled as Thea left. A huge grin worked its way across her face. She ran up to Caspian, causing another couple to stumble as she pushed past. She wrapped her arms around him before breaking out in laughter.

"Is he going?" She peeked up from his shoulder and looked, "Oh no, he's going to do it!"

"Did you tell him to ask that girl to dance?"

"Don't be stupid," she slapped him playfully across the cheek, "of course I didn't—oh look, they're going to dance."

"Well done," he said, unsure of whether this was cruel.

"Now it's your turn," she said pushing him away.

He stumbled backwards into another couple, mumbled a curt apology, and looked around the room for an easy target.

He saw the odd couple that Thea had just put together. It looked like they were making awkward conversation. The male pointed over to him and Thea.

That girl. I think I know her.

He moved through the crowd to get closer.

The girl had a sudden look of recognition on her face and he heard Thea laugh again. "Not them, Cas, find someone else," she said, loud enough for everyone to hear.

The girl had a wounded look on her face and ran for the back door.

Her name is Letty.

The back door opened and he saw two specks of brilliant light coming from the next room.

"She really ran for it, what did you say?" Thea was all smiles and instantly at his side.

He ignored her and pushed his way through the crowd and was confronted by the dour kid.

"That was very rude, what you pulled!" He gestured to the door.

Astonished, he felt an indignant and aggressive impulse to attack, but that urge was mixed with remorse and disgust. He stared into the dour face, his mouth agape, before finally saying, "I'm sorry."

The dour face softened, despite itself.

"What?" Thea grabbed his arm as he walked towards the door. "You're just going to let him speak that way to you?"

He was surprised by her strength, but refused to relent, and she slid across the smooth wooden floor in her high heels.

He pushed open the door and saw what he suspected was a painting, incongruously existing as part of the wall in the storage room. Though it was dark, and piles of furniture blocked the image, he saw the two points of light. He pushed aside a stack of chairs to get a closer look.

"You lose," she spoke angrily, gesturing with the needle, "and now it's time to have a drink."

"In a minute," he said, flipping on a light switch.

A calm, weather-worn face stared at him from the wall. Two shimmering eyes looked into his.

I know this man.

He wore a blackened helmet, which reminded him of those worn by the conquistadors. Paired with the helm was a heavy breastplate. His hand lay above his heart, and on his wrist was a symbol which glowed much like the eyes.

I know that symbol too.

He went for his breast pocket but felt a hand wrap around his wrist.

He looked and saw Thea lean in. "I'm far more interesting, Cas."

Cas?

She leaned in to kiss him, but her lips landed on his cheek. He was still and refused to meet her waiting lips. She burrowed her face into his shoulder and breathed heavily.

"I thought I'd find something in here to bring you back. I feel it—you're so close."

Behind her stood a prop mirror, and when he looked into the reflection, he saw a stranger staring back.

His head hurt.

He pulled away and gave her a calm smile. "What's my name?"

She brushed her fingers across his cheek, "Always a stupid game with you, Caspian." She lifted the opened flask to his lips.

He tore away from her.

"What's wrong?" she cried.

The door to the hall burst open, but instead of

the hundreds of dancers, there was a rain drenched field, littered with smoking wreckage.

She dropped the needle and her eyes widened.

He heard slow and heavy footsteps entering the room.

Thea grabbed his wrist and spoke plainly, "We are not here."

But before she finished speaking, he had wrenched himself free. There was a small puff of wind, and she was gone. Eyes wide, he stared at the empty space.

The footsteps were faster, and he backed against the wall.

Panicking, he said the first thing that came to mind, "I am not here!"

Chapter 16: The Escape

He tumbled down stairs as a piece of dark, heavy cloth tangled in his legs. On his hands and knees, his mind raced.

Thea! She's—where is she?

Looking around, he thought the stairwell was familiar. He felt something resting on his brow and swatted at it, thinking it was a bug, but to his surprise he nicked his hand on something dense and sharp.

He removed the headgear and gave it a close look. It was a bronze wreath. It too was familiar.

He returned it to his brow and freed his tangled legs from the cloth. He picked it up, but was startled when a small silver orb appeared from beneath the folds.

Certain it was important, he lunged down the stairs, and caught the orb.

Splayed out, he stared at it for a long moment.

This is an Argument. It doesn't belong to me. I borrowed it, and I must return it.

He couldn't remember who it belonged to.

His head was foggy. What should have been basic knowledge was past fleeting. Bare images of faces jogged through his mind, yet not a single name rose with any of them. He felt himself panic, and his hand tightened around the Argument as if the action were a reflex. Its closeness was comforting and that fact made him further doubt his sanity.

Pushing away the sense of madness, he looked closely at the marble. *What is it about this thing? I know, it—guards me.* But that thought felt unbalanced. He wondered if he was dreaming.

Getting nowhere, he forced himself to forget the Argument by putting it in his pocket. *I need to be practical.* He looked for more clues. He picked up the cloth, and realized that it was a cloak. He put it on, grinned at the absurdity of it, and the pieces of armor he wore, before finally turning around. His jaw dropped when he saw a massive hall lined with pillars the size of sequoias.

He took a few steps into the hall and looked the pillars up and down.

The carving and all the bones, even this weird fish-scale floor, I know it. I know this room; I've been here before.

He walked up the hall, passing between the pillars and forcing his memory to abandon its opacity and show what he had done here. The grandeur of the hall implied that, whatever it was must have been important.

His memory refused to jar.

He sighed and returned to the stairs, before leaning against a wall. *I can't remember—wait.* He felt something poking him in the side. He reached in his pants pocket and found a notebook stuffed tightly within. He struggled for a moment, before finally pulling it free.

Recognition and ignorance don't belong together, Andy thought to himself, knowing he had written in this notebook, but not remembering the words.

Feeling petulant and hopeless he flipped open the notebook.

He saw sketches. It was his own drawing and

writing. Every image seemed familiar, and only familiar, until he reached the last drawing.

Rembrandt. He's wearing armor here.

He looked closely and remembered the original.

His eyes glowed. He was on a wall. Wait—Thea?

He remembered the dance.

We were at school, in the assembly hall.

He flipped the notebook back a page and saw his sketch of the man fighting against the sea monster.

I know this! I saw this—from a boat? No...

His eyes widened.

I saw it with Letty and Dean—I'm sure!

He turned the notebook back another page and then another. Slowly the course of events sewed itself back into coherency.

The bladed monster. It chased me, and that's when I found—no, that's when Pythia found me.

His eyes narrowing, he felt the Argument humming in his pocket.

The blade. Yes, and it belongs to the mice.

He remembered Titus waking him up, once at home in his own bed, and then again inside a giant lobster.

We had a plan. Letty! I need to get back to Letty!

He saw the stairwell and was grateful there was only one way to go.

I'm in the fortress. I fought here with Martin and Clang. They gave me this.

He had to hold the wreath as he took the stairs in a rush; it nearly flew off his head in the first bound.

Pythia told them to occupy this place—it's called—the

Ossuary? Nico-something Ossuary.

Minutes later, and covered in a thick layer of sweat, he hit the last stair and stepped out onto an empty floor. There were more stairs in another stairwell going down, or he could travel across this floor into darkness. He pondered for a moment, remembering that he traveled up many flights.

It's this way. I came this way with Pythia.

Andy shivered at the scattered images that came back to him from minutes ago. He resolved to never enter that Juncture again.

A faint light glittered in a chamber far ahead, and he heard the sounds of labor. Shovels scraping, high-pitched disagreements, and grunts of toil filled the hall, sharpening as he approached the light.

He felt something snag his feet.

What—ahh!

Ropes tightened around his legs and his feet were pulled out from under him. He slammed into the ground, but the rope kept pulling until he was suspended, upside-down in the air.

Shocked and gasping, he felt the circlet fall off his brow, but it didn't clatter on the ground. Ignoring that, he reached for his ankles and tried to pull at the rope.

He felt a bony hand cover his mouth. "Quiet— no noise."

"Clang?" Andy whispered.

It was shadowy, but he recognized Clang's gnarled silhouette.

"Aye," he grumbled back. "Wait, quiet like."

Andy nodded.

Clang skulked off into the darkness. Andy heard a rope tear, and braced himself to hit the floor. But to his surprise, he slowly descended.

"Andy must not see others," Clang whispered, loosening the snare.

Getting to his feet, Andy asked, "Why?"

Clang led him towards a side door, and after a few turns Andy was lost.

"Pythia ordered Goblins to catch you," Clang finally answered.

"Why? I did what she wanted."

I think I did.

"While we were fighting, she said, if we see you not with her, to catches you. Martin says to Broken Teeth that we do not obey. I agree." Clang stopped at a doorway and peeked through, gesturing for Andy to keep back.

"But—"

Clang lifted a finger for silence, before slinking around the corner and leaving Andy alone in the dark.

She went back on her word. That's what it sounds like. We had a deal.

A moment later, he heard whispering coming from the other room.

A fox face appeared out of nowhere.

Andy recoiled in fright.

Wait, I know this face. It's Martin.

"What's wrong? Don't recognize me?" Martin's feathers went blue.

"No," Andy whispered angrily, "you appeared out of thin air, inches from my face."

Martin shrugged off the complaint and clapped Andy on the shoulder, "I was excited to see you again, though it's a little dangerous for you right now."

"Right now," Andy repeated, sarcastically.

Martin waved for silence. "She's ordered you captured, but we've come up with a plan." Martin paused, "I assume you want to get back to that portal?"

Andy nodded. "I need to get back to Caspia to find Letty—she's a friend of mine," Andy explained.

"I think we can get you there," Martin said, gesturing for Andy to come into the next room.

He recognized the dining hall, once filled with a pile of debris.

Martin left a count of the enemy for us on that table, Andy recalled.

Clang clicked his tongue and his goblins appeared from under tables and behind piles of wreckage. Takka was in the group, lacking his chime harness.

"Where is that harness of yours?" Andy whispered.

Takka pulled on an ear before complaining a little too loudly, "Suspended—I've been suspended from special weapons!"

A score of angry glares shot their way.

"Sorry, sorry," he whispered.

"Just be good, and I'm sure they'll un-suspend you. Wait, didn't you hate that thing?"

Takka nodded. "But nobody else has the qualified fingers, see?" He wagged his fingers spryly.

"Only I, but now I can't, 'til I practices more."

Clang approached and shoved Takka toward the work he'd been avoiding.

Clang leaned in and whispered, "He found mandolin on beach once; played mandolin. Martin make mandolin into Takka hat." Clang grunted an abrupt guttural laugh.

Poor guy, can't catch a break. I wonder why they keep him around.

The Goblins had assembled a few crates, which were mostly filled with debris. The crates bore long poles on opposite sides for hauling. Andy rolled his eyes in realization.

Martin approached with an apologetic smile.

"You don't have to say anything," Andy preempted, "which crate is mine?"

Martin chuckled, leading Andy to his empty crate.

Andy stepped inside and shrunk down as much as he could. He had his knees up by his ears, and there still wasn't much room.

They put the lid on and hammered in four nails. Andy felt an instant pang of fear.

He heard the sounds of exertion and felt gravity shift.

The ride was jarring, and he wished that he had taken off the armor before stepping in. He felt his skin catch and pinch between metal and crate; his head smacked the lid every other step, and before long he felt a cramp running up his side, likely from being compressed for so long.

A thin voice complained, "Look at the crates!"

"Oh! The sharpest can loot, but the rests of us can't?" a goblin whined acerbically.

Andy heard a slap, followed by general grumbling.

We must be in the Foyer. Are they going to take me down the fortified road to the beach?

Andy cursed himself as the ride became bumpier. There was a sudden dip and a corner of the crate smacked into the ground.

"I slipped 's all—no, no! No needs to help me up!" a goblin complained.

A moment later, Andy heard Clang yell, "Open the gate!"

And then a few fainter voices called out, "Not till we gets ours!"

"Yea!"

"We never gets nothin'!"

"Open the bleedin' gate or I go fishing with your toes!" Clang replied angrily.

Only a few seconds passed before Andy heard gears working.

There was a tap on the side of the box. It was Martin, who whispered, "That's the hard part done. We'll have you at the shore in no time."

Andy knew he had come here with Pythia, through a portal. He wondered if the way back was still open.

He endured the down-hill slog, but wished that they had let him out after the gatehouse. The trip was agonizing, but, shortly, he heard the sweet sound of water lapping.

The crate lowered with a thud, and he heard

someone working away at the lid. He winced at the creak of nails being pulled from wood. At the cry of the fourth nail he pushed up against the lid and heard a yelp.

Takka hit the floor, "Ow! You couldn't waits a second?"

"Sorry!" Andy stumbled out of the crate and bent to help Takka.

"S'lright, I've had worse," he said getting to his feet.

Andy looked around and saw the crowded beachhead camp had been dismantled. All that remained were broken bits of pottery, cracked planks, and ragged pieces of discarded clothing.

On a stone promontory that jutted out into the sea stood the glowing portal and the bulk of the Broken Teeth. It looked like they were arrayed against the portal. Crouched, with shields up and arrows knocked, they were ready for a fight.

"What's going on here?" Andy asked.

"Your kind block the way," Clang answered.

My kind?

"Who exactly is in the way, Clang?" Andy asked.

Clang gestured for his fighters to pull back from the portal before answering, "Pythia's other children. Eyes like you; their fighters wear sea monsters."

Takka leaned in. "I'll get the harness, Mastery Surgeon; we'll chime them away."

Clang reeled back to throw a slap, but Takka, dancing like an experienced dodger of angry fists, was well out of reach.

"They don't suffer by chime! Different fighting against humans," Clang insisted.

Martin had a hand on his chin in consideration. "It's true, the human fighters are more dangerous than most brutox. I estimate the worth of one of her children at about five of our own."

Andy was surprised by that estimate. "It can't be that much, Martin. I saw these goblins in action," Andy said.

Clang grunted approvingly.

"Look, I'll talk with them," Andy said.

Clang and Martin glanced at each other before Martin answered, "They might listen to you. For some reason they think we are attacking. We were only keeping an eye on the portal, in case servants of the Ryle try to sneak through..." He shook his head. "I don't know why we care if she is attacked in her own home—it might knock some sense into her."

They think she's incompetent for leaving the portal open! Ha! It was my only chance for escape, too.

Takka pulled on his ear nervously.

Clang spoke, "Careful with these words, Martin. She hears much."

Martin crossed his arms and turned a lighter shade of red.

"Fine," Andy said, readying the Argument. He tightened his fist and observed the blade, "I'm going for it."

Andy walked closer to the portal. The goblins cleared a path for him, but they never lowered their weapons. Andy saw the armored lobster guards standing behind tall shields on the other side. They were also alert and ready to strike.

Andy turned around, he felt there was more he needed to say. "Don't be afraid to speak your mind, Martin. She doesn't deserve blind obedience. And—I want the rest of you to know that she broke her word with me. She betrayed my trust when I put my life on the line for her. Right now, she's in a play world, imagining up dances and bullies. I barely escaped, but she might not be back for years. Leave while you have the chance. You deserve better."

Turning his back to the fortress, ossuary, and Juncture, Andy raised his weapon and stepped through the portal.

"Halt!" "Lower that blade!" "Get back on the other side!" A score of angry voices yelled contradictory instructions as he stepped through.

Andy saw at least thirty armed fighters. Crossbows, toothed axes, spears, and spiked shields glittered in the sparkling amber light coming off the portal. So far above, he saw the colors arcing across the ceiling.

Right, they don't have that back at the ossuary, just dark ceiling.

"Put down your weapon or we will shoot!" a female voice called out to him.

Andy recognized Staza's wild red hair shooting out from underneath a helmet. She looked like a fearsome lobster with a red mane.

"It's me—Andy! I'm back from my service."

Another female pushed past the fighters and took her helmet off. It was Somni.

"Where is our Mistress?" She was furious, with a frenzied expression across her previously mischievous face.

"She's back at the Juncture," Andy answered, stepping forward.

"Halt!" Somni screamed.

"Oh, be quiet, we know him," Quill retorted angrily, pushing through the crowd.

Yes! Quill is here. He'll talk them down.

Somni wasn't satisfied. "Do not obey him; I'm regent of Caspia, not him." She cast her glance from face to armored face, glowering down any dissent. "Tell us again, in exact detail, precisely where our Mistress is."

Andy sighed, and spoke plainly, "We left Caspia for the Nicomedian Ossuary."

The collected pupils looked at each other questioningly. They were clearly unaware of the name. Andy wondered how little Pythia told them. They also seemed ignorant of the goblins, and their service to Pythia.

"We made a deal, which is between her, Letty, and myself. I won't talk about the details, but the terms have been satisfied. Letty and I are free to go."

That did nothing to please them.

"So, she remains behind, while you are here." Somni said, sounding less furious. "Why?"

"I helped find her treasure, and now she's enjoying it."

Maybe I shouldn't tell them that she might be gone for years.

And to his chagrin, her next question came,

396

"When will she return?"

Before Andy could answer, another fighter ran up and jostled through the group to whisper a message to Somni. Somni held a palm up at Andy for silence as she spoke secretly with a few of her allies.

"Poll? Caston? Are you here?" Andy asked the group.

"Be quiet and listen!" Somni yelled. "When will she return to us? What did she tell you?"

"Look, why would she tell me any more than she tells you? I'm not even a pupil here. I was basically a mercenary, and now I've finished my job."

Andy stepped forward and the fighters backed away, lowering their weapons.

"No!" Somni screamed, reaching out and pushing Andy back towards the portal. "This is not satisfactory! Go back and return with her!"

Andy recognized her desperation and realized that she might do anything. He raised his blade before speaking, "You might try stepping through the portal and talking to the goblins there, they also serve your Mistress. They might know more. Failing that, just find her yourself."

Andy pushed by, but Somni followed, fast on his heels. He recalled the portal was high on the roof of the giant lobster, Titasticus, in the heart of Caspia. He tried to remember how he got up here. His thoughts were interrupted again by Somni.

"We are going to accept your explanation—the news of goblin servants is strange, but any who serve our Mistress are as good as kin." There were both nods and grumbles at that. Andy imagined the posturing around the spinning tables with hundreds of goblins in the mix.

The collected pupils, unsure of what to do, followed.

Andy ignored them and saw another runner coming to the group, she had climbed up a rope-ladder which was bolted onto the palace roof.

I remember a hidden passage Pythia used to get up here, but I'd have no idea how to open it. They'd just arrest me for breaking into her private chambers anyway. I'd better take that rope-ladder.

Andy veered off course and had to watch his step as the armored shell of Titasticus curved more sharply. He loosened his grip on the Argument, pocketed it, and then took the rope-ladder down. The mass of pupils, jabbering heatedly between themselves, followed.

Once at the base of the lobster, Andy realized that he didn't know which way to go.

I remember Letty telling me to meet her—somewhere in Caspia. I wonder if she found Titus. I'd ask, but these people aren't happy with me.

Angry that he had to do so, he waited for the others to climb down. It was a sad display as they were all armed. Carrying weapons down a ladder, in full armor, didn't look simple.

What were they doing up there in the first place? Probably looking for Pythia. Then they saw the goblins on the other side.

Somni approached him with an affected grin. "This way, please," she said, forcing a coy smile.

Andy could see tears welling up in her eyes. Scowling, he followed.

He swallowed his frustration and finally asked, "Where are we going?"

Somni laughed, "It's not 'to where' that's pertinent, but 'to whom.'"

Andy glowered and she smirked in response.

"Quill? Where are you?" Andy called out to the crowd.

Quill jostled through the pupils before answering, "Right here."

"No collaboration!" Somni yelled, and pointed at Quill, "Restrain him."

"Oh, shut up!" Andy yelled pushing past her.

A few pupils tried to restrain Quill. They stood between him and Andy.

"Step aside," Andy said, tired of the pettiness.

They hesitated, and he brandished the Argument, which convinced them to back off, despite Somni's repeated orders.

"Where are we going, Quill?"

"Letty's barricaded herself in the dining hall. She's been yelling about a deal you two made with Pythia. She claims that she is no longer a pupil, but refuses to come out until you return." He leaned in and whispered, "She has a pair of rats with her."

Titus and Taptalles. They made it.

Staza elbowed one of Somni's men in the face. He stumbled and hit the ground, his hands clutching at his helmet, which was dented.

Staza slipped between Andy and Quill with a smile on her face, and said, "Glad you made it back in one piece, but you need to do something about your friend."

"Why, did she—" Andy paused mid-sentence, "Is Ziesqe still in Caspia?"

"No, but his brutox are. They're waiting for an answer from Pythia," Musi said.

Somni butted between them. "You, Staza—I'm going to have you expelled for sharing Caspian secrets."

Andy expected Staza to smack Somni silly, but she appeared cowed by the threat.

And another person will suffer because of me.

Andy tried to think of something that would take the attention off Staza.

"Listen, Somni, I'm your enemy here, just focus on me, okay?"

"I am," she said calmly, "and no disloyalty will be forgotten."

Andy scoffed and the group awkwardly moved forward.

They approached the dining hall. The doors were split in places, as if by hacking, and a few armored pupils stood guard outside.

"Go on then," Somni commanded.

The group stayed clear of the doors as Andy approached.

"Letty?"

Andy heard a twang and ducked as something whistled past his ears.

"Letty! I'm back."

He heard a mechanism working on the other side of the door.

"Hold your fire! It's me, Andy. I'm back from—well, forget where I'm back from, but my service is complete and we can leave!"

He heard her voice through the door. "Andy?" There was a pause. "How do I know it's you?" she asked.

"Uhm…" he paused, considering, "you are friends with Emma, and I've been hanging out with Dean recently."

"Anyone could know that!" She yelled.

Andy ducked, anticipating another shot, moments before it whizzed past and smacked into a building across the way. "Whoa! Hold on! Why don't you ask me a question then?"

"Okay—just give me a second. It hasn't been easy since you left."

He heard the mechanism working again, and then there were whispers.

"No, no, that's not secret enough," she said to someone on the other side.

"Any question," Andy said.

"What happened in Pythia's chambers? When she was pretending to be me—what happened."

Andy bit his tongue and heard uncomfortable grumbling coming from the crowd of armed pupils.

"She healed my wounds," Andy said reservedly.

"No! What else happened?"

Andy knew what she wanted to hear.

"We—that is she, well… We might have danced—just for a second though."

"It was disgusting!" Letty yelled.

"What? Obviously! I didn't know it was her!"

401

Andy looked at the crowd. The faces ranged in expression from shock, to complete disbelief, to outrage. One person laughed.

"Letty, we can't talk about this now. We've got to get going!"

Andy heard arguing coming from the other side, and then the heavy scraping of dense furniture, followed by cursing and a loud crash.

The door opened and Letty stormed out. Her outfit was torn and her face bloodied. She reared back and punched Andy in the mouth. "You left me here!"

Andy stepped back and shielded himself from another blow. He felt his lip burn and tasted blood.

"This was the plan!" he retorted, dizzy with pain.

This should have been a happy moment.

She was livid and her eyes sparkled, wild and aflame, as she yelled, "I've been here for hours! Days even! I don't know how long—We've been fighting the whole time. There were giant insects and these stupid cult people!" She nearly spat at the mob of pupils.

"I didn't have it any better!" Andy was baffled at her outrage. "You can't even imagine how sick I feel after what happened out there, and I can't even remember half of it!"

"Excuses!" Letty paused in her retribution and leveled her hate at the crowd of gawking pupils. "What the hell are you looking at?" She raised her crossbow and the crowd scattered.

An armored guard appeared from around the

corner. He ran towards the large group, heaving in exhaustion. He took a few heavy breaths and removed his helmet before speaking, "I need to see our Mistress!"

Somni spoke up, "She's still not in the city!"

Disheartened, the guard spoke, "I've come from the cliff watch, ryle beasts have massed and are rushing past the border into Caspian lands. They'll be at the stairs in minutes."

Andy gawked, wondering what prompted the attack.

Somni could only stare vacantly at the news. Someone nudged her imploringly, and she finally spoke, "I—we need to send a runner through the portal and find her."

Feeling the urge to leave them to their fate, Andy almost took the chance to slip away.

I can't condemn them. I know these people now; I even like them. Andy remembered Quill, Staza, Arke, Musi, and even the guards, Caston and Poll. They had been good to him, even when he was their prisoner.

They might die if I don't help.

"Look," Andy interrupted, "Pythia is inside something called the Juncture. A test controls passage inside. You do not have the time to pass that test, and even if you did, the Juncture is not a normal place. It's a nightmare. You have to accept that she can't help you."

Quill stepped forward in the quiet that followed and spoke, "He's right. We have to respond to their aggression immediately. We cannot be divided in this. I say we defend the stair from its base. We'll have cover in the buildings, and they'll be exposed if they try to climb down the cliffs." Quill paused, and looked to the guard who delivered the report, "Whose banner did you see?"

Still shaken, the guard answered, "No banner— but I recognized the pattern on the brutox; it's Ziesqe's forces."

An anxious wave of whispering rose at that.

"How many?" Quill asked.

"More than I could count."

Quill looked at the ground and then over at Andy and Letty.

"Ziesqe sent them here to capture Letty and I," Andy said plainly. "If we leave, they'll have no reason to stay."

"We need to get them out of Caspia, for their sake and ours," Quill insisted.

"No—we'll just hand them over," Somni said decisively, "It's the only way to ensure peace."

"Is this what Pythia would want?" Quill raised his trident and yelled.

"Capture them unharmed!" Somni commanded.

Weapons raised, the pupils split into three groups. On one side stood Somni and her group of about twenty guards. In the center stood the largest group, the undecided. They stepped back as violence threatened to erupt. The smallest group contained Letty, Andy, Quill, and Staza.

With weapons raised all around, Andy held the Argument tightly in his grip. Somni's guards were spreading out to surround them when the chimes roared to life.

A burst of flames shot into the air from the other side of the city.

Somni was livid; she yelled out in frustration, "The brutox can capture them! To the stairs, now! We need to negotiate a peace!"

Her followers and the bystanders rushed off towards the column of flame.

Andy followed, but felt Letty's hand grasp his shoulder. She was holding him back. He tried to pull away, but she latched on with both arms.

"No! What's wrong with you? They'll kill us or worse!" She screamed.

"What if they don't accept the negotiations? We can't just let them fight alone!" Andy insisted.

"Listen Andy, they're in the city already, Titus has seen them." Letty said.

Quill interrupted, "What do you mean? There are more brutox in the city? They all left hours ago."

Andy was surprised to see Titus and Taptalles scurry out from under Letty's hair and stand on her shoulders.

"They are in the bowels of your city, in force," Titus said. "We have evaded them so far, but if more are coming, then it is likely that they mean to take Caspia."

"Perhaps not. Quill, had a point; he said that they are after these two," Taptalles gestured at Andy and Letty, "the city might not be the target. They might have waited for Andy to return."

Staza looked surprised and Quill paled, as they listened to the mice.

"Even if we run, the attackers will still destroy Caspia looking for us," Andy argued, still struggling.

"You shouldn't be concerned with that," Staza said plainly, "Somni will tell them that we've escaped. She'll tell them we aided you too."

That statement struck Quill, who was devastated as he spoke, "I hate it, but Staza's right. With Pythia gone, there's nothing stopping them from capturing and torturing us to find out where you've gone."

Andy was silent.

"There! Are you satisfied? We need to escape, not fight," Letty pleaded, her eyes locked onto his.

Pythia said that Ziesqe wanted me. She thought he would find me on the surface, but it looks like he's in a rush.

Andy stopped resisting. "How do we get out of here?"

"Up the coast—ugh," Quill sputtered as Staza elbowed him aside.

"I know the trails best. You stick to fine words, Quill. We'll slip through the sally gate and travel inland; there will be more cover," Staza said, leading the way.

As they moved, Andy spotted an abalone manhole cover lift up. Staza speared the ascending brutox through the skull as she ran past. "Hurry! They could come from anywhere."

Andy hoped that speared brutox corpse wouldn't give their enemies a clue as to their direction.

They rushed through the back-streets, occasionally passing another confused or terrified pupil, but luckily, they didn't see another brutox. The chimes continued to sound in prolonged bursts. But, right as they passed through the unguarded sally gate, the chimes went silent.

"That's them agreeing to a truce," Quill said.

"Perhaps they've surrendered?" Titus asked.

Both Staza and Quill turned unpleasant looks on the mouse.

"It's a fair assumption," Titus said, defensively.

Past the sally gate, they traveled a cobbled path for a while. Minutes later, they turned off the main path and were now traveling down a narrow side trail, flanked on both sides by tall grass.

"Is the ryle leading the attack personally?" Taptalles asked.

"I expect that he is," Quill answered.

"Good. At least we know he's behind us," Taptalles concluded.

"Yes," Staza interjected, "but a few people saw us heading to the gate. They'll be on our trail soon."

"Then we can't stop," Letty said, "but where are we going?"

"I don't know," Staza said, frustrated. "I can get you out of our territory. I can even hide us in the hills, at least for a few days."

"We need to get to the circle," Titus said. "There are portals there we can use to return to the surface. None of Ziesqe's servants would dare to follow us there."

"Yes," Taptalles agreed, "and then we'll be on their turf," he motioned at Andy and Letty. "Food and shelter are much more common on the surface."

"What, brother, are you afraid to return home?" Titus asked, confused.

"No, I mean for the Caspians," he said, pointing at Quill and Staza. "They can't mean to come back here—can they?"

He's right, what are they going to do? Since they helped us, they won't be safe back in Caspia.

At hearing that, the group slowed and finally stopped.

Letty was the first to speak, "Okay, so we're headed for the portals. Once we're on the other side, Andy and I will find a place for you two. I can get the key to my aunt's apartment, she's out of town."

Staza slammed her spear into the ground, and Quill looked distraught.

"We can't just leave our people like this," Staza said, her voice cracking, "Quill is a leader. Even if Somni thinks she is in charge, people will listen to him."

"But that's not what happened," Andy said firmly, remembering the argument with Somni and the pupils, who were mostly undecided. "You can't go back," Andy said. "We know what will happen if you do."

Staza grimaced and tightened her grip on the spear until the wood creaked.

"But our eyes," Quill said, "how will we hide them? How do you do it?"

Letty and Andy shared a look.

"We don't hide them," Letty replied, confused.

"That's how they find us, Letty," Andy said. "They set up traps for us, and we fell into one at the gallery and then at the optometrist's office."

Andy suddenly remembered reading about a man who had been fed certain foods which masked his violet eyes. He felt his pockets and found a notebook.

"Andy, what's that thing you're wearing?" Letty asked.

Distracted, he glanced up. "Oh, the laurel. Martin and Clang made it for me—"

That answer begged further questions, but Letty saw he was distracted.

"Here it is," Andy said, stopping on a page, "when I was in the Juncture, I found a painting, but it was covered in words, like from someone's journal." Andy's audience appeared skeptical. "He mentioned a way to hide our eye's true color," Andy said, handing his notebook to Letty.

Titus interrupted, "We don't have time for this. Listen, Caspians and surfacers, there are ways to veil your eyes. We can help you with that, but now we must be decisive. Caspians, are you coming to the surface?"

Quill and Staza shared a hopeless glance.

"You've only heard terrible things about where we live. It isn't that bad," Andy said.

Quill coughed and raised a hand to his mouth, his eyes tightened, and he stared at the ground. Staza bit her lip so hard that a thin line of blood ran down her chin.

Andy clasped Quill on the shoulder. "You won't be alone."

They stood in sad silence.

Finally, Quill nodded. He looked to Staza and asked, "Can you stand it?"

She spat a mouthful of blood into the grass. "What would they say about me if I couldn't?" she replied quietly, before hefting her spear and leading the way.

They were quiet. Bent low, they moved through the tall grass, turning at Staza's lead, down ever shrinking trails.

Finally, they came to a point in the trail where they would pass a cliff that flanked the city.

Quill stopped and looked back.

This is the point of no return.

The city was silent, and obscured by the thickening foliage, but the walls were still just in sight, lit from above by the amber glow.

Staza turned and stared.

"It's like a bandage," Letty said, "best to get it over with quickly."

"You can return when things quiet down," Titus pointed out.

Quill sighed and turned back to the path. The group continued.

The trail, ever shrinking, had in the past few minutes ceased to exist. It was now solid grass and low hanging branches. Staza handed her spear to Letty and used her short sword to cut a path through. Quill gave his trident to Andy and waited to help.

"Maybe another hour of this before we arrive at the circle," Staza said, slicing at another thin branch.

"Is there a faster way? Maybe something with

fewer bushes," Letty asked.

"There is—" Staza grunted, swinging again, "but we're in their territory now, and we can't risk being on the roads."

Hearing this, Andy readied the Argument and drew the blade. "Let me help," he said moving to relieve Staza and Quill. The branches fell to the Argument without resistance.

Titus interrupted, "Perhaps the Argument isn't the subtlest means to clear the path."

Taptalles had leaped from Letty's shoulder, and climbed on Andy, without the latter noticing. "Put the blade out, boy! The light will give us away!"

Andy's eyes widened as he loosened his grip and the blade fluttered out.

"Sorry—I didn't realize," Andy cringed, and stepped aside.

Quill borrowed the short sword and took his turn clearing the way.

Staza leaned in and whispered to Andy, "Don't worry, we're so far out. I don't think anyone saw. But they're right; you shouldn't do that again."

Letty made a strange face when she saw Staza whispering to Andy.

"Right—" Quill swung, "it was too bright, but it ripped through these branches without a sound."

No one cared to disagree.

Quill eventually handed the blade to Andy for a turn. Finally, Staza tapped Andy on the shoulder. She motioned for him to be quiet and pointed through the foliage.

"Down," she whispered.

They got to their hands and knees and crawled under the branches where they could.

Silently, they passed the last of the bushes and reached the grassy perimeter that ringed the circle of portals. Andy was surprised to see the tower had been rebuilt.

Two brutox guards stood watch in the tower, though fallen tents and broken carriages now littered the once clear circle.

Andy whispered, "Do we make a run for the portal? How do we know which one to take, Titus?"

Titus tugged at his whiskers.

"And where will it take us exactly?" Letty asked, readying her crossbow.

"Hey Letty, where did you get that?" Andy asked quietly.

She grinned. "I borrowed it from one of the bugs before I took over the dining hall. It might have been the same one you had."

Andy didn't recognize the weapon, but he gave Letty an approving smile.

Titus's whiskers looked frayed as he waved a paw for silence. "There once was a portal in this circle that led to a tunnel beneath your city. It must still be here."

"Great," Andy said, enthused. "Which one is it? What does it look like?"

There might have been fifty doorways, implying fifty potential portals. Andy hoped Titus had a strong memory.

Titus coughed before speaking, "I can't see the portals from here—but I can probably point it out when we get down there." He didn't sound confident.

Andy saw the problem; the circle was recessed about a floor deep, hiding many of the potential portals.

"Shouldn't we be able to see them from here? The portals ring the whole circle, don't they?" Andy asked.

Staza and Quill shared grim looks.

"There's something wrong down there. We should be able to see half of the portals from here, but they look blank, like it's just a dirt wall there," Staza said.

"I'm often here on patrol," Quill started, "Ziesqe's creatures have blocked these portals with wooden frames. I don't know why."

Andy felt his stomach sink. "How will we know which one to take?" he asked.

They were all silent. Titus and Taptalles's ears dipped.

The crackle of a brazier at the base of the tower mixed with the nearby sound of shore and, for a moment, Andy felt himself go lightheaded.

The feeling of defeat almost made him forget where he was.

"Is there another way?" Letty asked, breaking the silence.

"Maybe we could go to Sentinel's Watch," Andy whispered excitedly.

Titus grimaced at this.

"What is it?" Andy asked.

Taptalles shook his head. "Sentinel's Watch is under siege," he said plainly, "that's how Titus came to be here. He was on his way back home when he learned of the attack. There is no way into the city through the besieging army."

"What?" Andy asked, shocked.

Taptalles tugged at the whiskers on the right side of his face. "It isn't unprecedented," he said, careful of his friend, "they've withstood worse, but it could be ages before the attackers give up and leave."

Titus raised his teary face to the group. "The ryle and brutox would have no way of closing the portals. The one we want must be down there, behind a barrier."

"We need a plan," Quill said deferentially to the mouse.

Andy realized how few of them would be going home.

Titus nodded. "Letty is a fine shot with that crossbow. She'll take out the guards, allowing us to sneak down into the circle. Once there, we learn how to uncover the portals. If we meet an enemy, we must dispatch them quickly and quietly, or they will bring reinforcements. Remember that a large force is nearby, and it's only a matter of time before they realize we are here."

They all agreed, but Andy felt hesitation.

He grasped the Argument, but was careful not to activate it. Letty crawled forward through the undergrowth for a better shot.

"How is she supposed to hit both of them? One will still be standing after the first shot, and he'll raise the alarm," Andy whispered to the group in general.

"You haven't seen her shoot," Taptalles muttered.

Looking at her crossbow Andy realized that it was more compact than the one he had used before, and there was no winch.

How does she pull back the cord?

She fired her first shot and a Brutox fell from the tower.

"Good shot!" Titus whispered excitedly.

In a flash, Letty grabbed a lever on the crossbow and pulled, arcing the cord to its nock. She lay a second bolt in place and aimed.

The second Brutox turned to look, but was confused when it saw nothing. Andy heard the soft twang, and the remaining Brutox slumped over the guard rail.

"Wow," Andy whispered.

"It's not all me," Letty said, brushing off the praise, "it's mostly the bolts." She held one up.

Andy saw the tip sparkle with a slight trace of silver.

"A little etherium goes a long way," Titus said. "We might have borrowed some from the city's stores."

They advanced beyond the shrub line, still moving softly and listening for any sign of more brutox. They hopped over the verge of the circle.

"I'll keep an eye out," Andy said, looking down the road. He remembered it from his time with Quill. Andy felt a strange sense of dysphoria as memories of all that had happened since flashed through his mind.

It's like a different person walked down that road, what was it, just a few days ago?

"Look, they've painted planks and leaned them up against the portals," Staza said, removing one of the planks.

Andy saw a small string that was recessed in the earth pull away. It was tied to the plank.

"Wait!" He clenched his fist and swiped at the string with his blade, but it was too late.

A loud shriek pierced the silence, the noise was reminiscent of a tinny fire engine.

"The planks were rigged!" Titus yelled.

The noise was almost deafening, and the shock of it froze them all with fright.

"What now?" Quill cried, readying his trident.

"Quick, pull them all down and find the right portal!" Letty yelled, reaching for one and tearing it down.

They ran to the planks and pulled them away. As they did so, the siren blared.

Andy rushed to the source of the sound. A strange looking speaker was secreted in a barrel near the base of the rebuilt tower. He summoned the blade and sliced the barrel in two, silencing the noise, and revealing the mechanisms and canisters within.

"Good! There are only a few more," Taptalles said, grasping tightly to Letty's shoulder.

A sudden glow of torches sprung up from the grass.

Brutox marched towards the circle. Andy saw

one that was quite tall and pale.

"I'll hold them off, keep searching!" Andy turned to the encroaching mass.

The brutox were wary of his blade, but, after a brave few hunched and made to attack, the rest readied themselves for the fight. Andy wasn't sure which would attack first when a beetle charged.

He struck it down, and then raced to cleave a second that had followed. They collapsed into heaps of purple sand. The brutox clicked in frustration and pulled back. The pale brutox watched passively.

I must keep them out of the circle.

Andy heard a whistle past his ear and a third brutox fell.

The light from the now exposed portals glinted off the many glossy surfaces. Carapace and weapon alike shimmered as the mass of warriors spread out, each looking for an opening.

"Still alive?" A voice whispered, just inches away from Andy's ears.

Andy swung wide at the voice, but there was nothing there.

"I'm here."

Andy swung again.

Nothing.

Then Andy saw. The crowd of brutox parted. His lithe frame was sheathed in glowing armor and floating above his open palm was a purple orb, far denser than Andy's Argument.

Ziesqe.

Andy glanced over his shoulder and saw there were only a few panels left standing. He hoped Titus remembered which one to take.

Wait. Ziesqe is here—he can follow us through!

"I have never experienced a Seer in the wild before," Ziesqe said in a curious tone.

A sudden certainty creeped upon Andy. *I'm not going home.*

He resigned himself to delaying the enemy to allow his friends time for escape.

Taking a breath, Andy finally spoke, "Do you always hide behind your slaves?"

The brutox jutted forward at his question, but a quick hiss from Ziesqe pulled them back.

"When you rule as much as I do, you begin to see many things as mere extensions of oneself." He flexed his clawed fingers and gestured widely to his brutox. "They, through force, make even my speech a hundred-fold more potent than you."

"Andy!" Letty yelled, "We've got it!"

He saw them gathered around a portal. Titus and Taptalles waved for him to pull back and rout with them.

Almost involuntarily, Andy stepped back at the call.

The brutox, sensing his retreat, lunged.

Andy struck one's axe from its hands before slicing it in two. A second leaped, its sword high and slicing downward. Andy raised his blade a moment too late. The blade grazed across his unarmored shoulder. Pain shot through his body.

"Andy, run!" The voices yelled. He felt like they were still a mile away.

Ziesqe snapped his claws, and again his

warriors pulled back. He pointed to the giant pale brutox who happily leveled its double sword.

Seeing the weapon held aloft, Andy remembered its height, taller than himself.

I can't fight that.

He turned to run.

"I will come for your family," Ziesqe said, his voice almost sad.

Andy stopped, recalling Pythia's words.

He turned his back to the outraged screams of his friends.

"Kill my champion now, and I will leave them be."

The pale brutox rushed. Andy rolled to dodge the blow.

"How can I trust you?" Andy yelled, barely parrying a strike.

The colossal weapon deflected his blade. It was nightsteel.

As he backed away, Andy heard a low rumbling. At first, he wasn't sure what it was.

The brutox pressed against Andy's guard, knocking him backwards. As Andy stumbled, the brutox lunged, elbowing him sharply across the face.

Andy hit the ground. The brutox grabbed him by the throat and lifted him high into the air. The silver blade fluttered out.

Andy clutched at the armored fist, but it held fast. The rumble sharpened and increased in intensity.

He's laughing.

Andy saw the other brutox had surrounded him and were fighting Quill and Staza at the portal.

A sharp whistle cracked and thudded into the brutox's shoulder. An etherium-tipped bolt jutted out.

The pale brutox growled in pain. Its grip loosened enough for Andy to pull his head free. He fell to the ground, somehow standing, and within the brutox's guard. He tightened his fist against his foe's chest.

The blade exploded through its armored flesh. It collapsed into a pile of powder, its massive sword clattering to the ground.

Andy saw through the crowd of warriors. Ziesqe stood a dozen feet away.

I have to kill him. It's my only chance.

"Tell me! How can I trust you?" Andy yelled.

"Trust? Demanding trust is proof of your worth."

Andy spotted an opening in the mob and rushed towards Ziesqe.

A tiger-striped Brutox responded with lightning speed. It lunged to stop Andy, who impaled it and ducked beneath the blow of another. Ziesqe was within reach.

Mid-stride, Andy raised his blade to strike. The pain in his wounded shoulder jolted, tearing through his limbs. He almost stumbled.

Ziesqe had grasped the Counter-Argument and, with his blade, tapped Andy's unhoned blade away.

The crackling explosion pushed him backwards. Andy felt the immediate absence of the Argument.

Sudden pain and fatigue overwhelmed him. He had felt it all along, but the Argument had held it at bay. Now, he was helpless. The slice in his shoulder seared through his mind. The wound burned and everything lost focus.

"No! I won't defeat you like this!" Ziesqe snapped. "Pick up your weapon!"

Andy bit down and groaned through the pain as he crawled to the Argument. He grasped it and felt the pain subside.

"Don't just clamp down on the Argument. Articulate your grip and focus on the blade. Watch my hand." Ziesqe released his grasp, and then bent his fingers carefully around the purple orb. He twisted his wrist as he tightened it and his blade appeared.

Andy waited for Ziesqe to present an unhoned blade, but the chance never came.

"If you fight with an unhoned blade, you will find it shooting out of your hand the first time you come upon the Counter."

It's already happened twice now.

"Do it," Ziesqe ordered.

Andy focused and tried to imitate the motion. The blade appeared, more solidly than it had before, but still not like Ziesqe's.

If I had only practiced.

Andy twisted his wrist and focused. The fluttering blade sharpened.

"Not perfect, but enough," Ziesqe said, approaching with his own blade. "You have a quick mind."

Ziesqe feinted and swiped at Andy, who parried then lunged. His blade bounced off Ziesqe's armor. Ziesqe used the opening to strike Andy across the face with his free hand.

Andy crumpled to his hands and knees before suffering another strike, this one to his brow. He heaved and fell to his hands and knees, the blade flickering out. One swift kick to the chin knocked him backward, and he felt the Argument fly from his grasp.

Ziesqe clicked.

In an instant, the mob of brutox rushed forward and piled onto him. Though a dozen hard plated hands held each of his limbs still, he knew that even one hand could have held him down. A brutox retrieved Andy's laurel, which must have fallen away in the struggle. Ziesqe accepted the laurel and inspected it.

Andy bent against the clutching hands for a sight of his friends. He heard their voices. "Go!" He yelled, hoping they could still hear him.

The mass of grasping limbs carried him away, but through it, he saw Letty wielding the blade, his blade, and trying to cut a way through to him.

"You have to go! Letty, just leave!" his voice was hoarse and feeble.

Ziesqe snapped his claws and the brutox held him aloft for his friends to see. He heard another clipped command and suddenly the claws wrenched and dug into his flesh, forcing him to cry out in agony.

He kept his eyes open for long enough to see

Quill and Staza pull Letty, struggling and screaming, through the portal.

She was gone, safe on the other side.

It wasn't the end he'd hoped for, but as Letty slipped beyond his sight, something within Andy gave way. His heart fluttered, and he gasped. The sound, a soft declaration, gave the brutox pause. Several turned their glances to Ziesqe, wose red eyes narrowed in a moment of hesitation.

Blood dripped from Andy's torn flesh and fell on the dry earth, like warm rain twisting down his arms and hands. The heavy breath of the creatures might have been the rumble of engines on the street, on his way to the bus during a breathy, misty morning. His head rolled back, and he saw the riotous vinlight. There, in the swirls, dancing colors and shapes coalesced to bear wonders. As his eyes dimmed, pain lost its hold, and there shone sparkling, blue eyes. Hair, cresting like waves, black as the night sky, glittered with diamonds. Soft lips and cheeks, the color of rose and ancient marble smiled, and he knew she smiled for him.

To the reader:

Thank you for sticking with Andy on his hazardous journey through the Netherscape. He may be in dire straits, but Letty, the Caspians, and the mice won't abandon him to Ziesqe. I hope you'll return for the next installment, and join Letty as she begins her quest: to rescue the boy who rescued her. He may be Ziesqe's prisoner, but Andy might be more trouble than he's worth.

If you were moved by Andy's adventure and want to share the experience with your peers, I invite you to leave a written review and tell your friends. There are countless likely readers ready for adventure; please help them on their way.

I would like to recognize my editors and those who read the first drafts. Some insisted that I leave the mice in, others wanted more goblins, and a few tore out whole pages in their hunt for rogue misspellings and comma splices. It's been a few years in arriving, but the work is far stronger than it would have been without their efforts. In no particular order, thanks go to: Noa Zilberman, Oliver Pinchot, Jon Addley, Thomas and Rie Kreuzberger, Owen Croak, Jon Lin, Oxana Antonova, Chereese Graves, and especially Alexey Rudikov, for his exceeding talent and endless patience—his handiwork graces this book's cover.

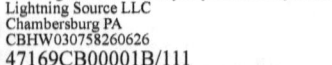
www.ingramcontent.com/pod-product-compliance
Lightning Source LLC
Chambersburg PA
CBHW030758260626
47169CB00001B/111